Mr. Perfect

Books by Linda Howard

A LADY OF THE WEST

ANGEL CREEK

THE TOUCH OF FIRE

HEART OF FIRE

DREAM MAN

AFTER THE NIGHT

SHADES OF TWILIGHT

SON OF THE MORNING

KILL AND TELL

NOW YOU SEE HER

ALL THE QUEEN'S MEN

Published by POCKET BOOKS

Mr. Perfect

LINDA HOWARD

POCKET BOOKS

New York London Toronto Sydney Singapore

 POCKET BOOKS, a division of Simon & Schuster, Inc.
1230 Avenue of the Americas, New York, NY 10020

ISBN: 0-671-03406-5

First Pocket Books hardcover printing August 2000

10   9   8   7   6   5   4   3   2   1

POCKET and colophon are registered trademarks of
Simon & Schuster, Inc.

Printed in the U.S.A.

Many thanks to Sgt. Henry Piechowski of the Warren, Michigan, Police Department, for patiently and cheerfully answering all of my questions. He took my phone calls, gave me his time, and did his best to make sure I got it right. Any errors are strictly mine. Thanks, Sergeant.

Mr. Perfect

Prologue

T his is ridiculous!" Clutching her purse so tightly her knuckles were white, the woman glared across the desk at the school principal. "He said he didn't touch the hamster, and my child doesn't lie. The very idea!"

J. Clarence Cosgrove had been principal of Ellington Middle School for six years, and a teacher for twenty years before that. He was accustomed to dealing with irate parents, but the tall, thin woman seated before him and the child sitting so sedately beside her, unnerved him. He hated to use the vernacular, but they were *weird*. Though he knew it was a wasted effort, he tried to reason with her. "There was a witness—"

"Mrs. Whitcomb put him up to saying that. Corin would never, *never* have hurt that hamster, would you, darling?"

"No, Mother." The voice was almost unearthly sweet, but

the child's eyes were cold and unblinking as they stared at Mr. Cosgrove, as if weighing the denial's effect on him.

"See, I told you so!" the woman cried triumphantly.

Mr. Cosgrove tried again. "Mrs. Whitcomb—"

"—has disliked Corin from the first day of school. *She's* the one you need to be interrogating, not my child." The woman's lips were thin with fury. "I spoke with her two weeks ago about the filth she was putting in the children's heads, and told her that while I couldn't control what she told the other children, I absolutely would not have her speaking about"— she darted a glance at Corin— "s-e-x to *my* child. That's why she's done this."

"Mrs. Whitcomb has an excellent record as a teacher. She wouldn't—"

"She *has!* Don't tell me what that woman won't do when she obviously has! Why, I wouldn't put it beyond her to have killed the hamster herself!"

"The hamster was her personal pet, which she brought to school to teach the children about—"

"She could still have killed it. Good God, it was just a big rat," the woman said dismissively. "I don't understand what all the fuss is about even if Corin *had* killed it, which he didn't. He's being persecuted—*persecuted*—and I won't stand for it. Either you take care of that woman or I'll do it for you."

Mr. Cosgrove removed his glasses and wearily polished the lenses, just to give himself something to do while he tried to think of a way to neutralize this woman's poison before she ruined a good teacher's career. Reasoning with her was out; so far she hadn't let him complete a single sentence. He glanced at Corin; the child was still watching him, wearing an angelic expression totally at odds with those cold eyes.

"May I speak with you privately?" he asked the woman.

She looked taken aback. "Why? If you think you can convince me my darling Corin—"

"Just for a moment," he interrupted, hiding his tiny spurt of relish at being the one doing the interrupting this time. From her expression, she didn't like it at all. "Please." He tacked that on, though he was almost beyond being polite.

"Well, all right," she said reluctantly. "Corin, darling, go stand outside. Stay right by the door, where Mother can see you."

"Yes, Mother."

Mr. Cosgrove got up and firmly closed the door behind the child. She looked alarmed at this turn of events, at not being able to see her child, and half rose out of her chair.

"Please," he said again. "Sit down."

"But Corin—"

"—will be all right." Another interruption scored on his side, he thought. He resumed his seat and picked up a pen, tapping it against his desk blotter as he tried to come up with a diplomatic way to broach his subject. There was no way diplomatic enough for this woman, he realized, and decided to jump right in. "Have you ever considered getting help for Corin? A good child psychologist—"

"Are you crazy?" she hissed, her face twisted with instant rage as she surged to her feet. "Corin doesn't need a psychologist! There's nothing wrong with him. The problem is with that bitch, not with my child. I should have known this meeting was a waste of time, that you'd take her side."

"I want what's best for Corin," he said, managing to keep his voice calm. "The hamster is just the latest incident, not the first one. There's been a pattern of disturbing behavior that goes beyond mischief—"

"The other children are jealous of him," she charged. "I know how the little bastards pick on him, and that bitch does nothing to stop it or protect him. He tells me everything. If you think I'll let him stay in this school and be hounded—"

"You're right," he said smoothly. On the scoreboard her interruptions outnumbered his, but this was the important one. "Another school would probably be best, at this stage. Corin doesn't fit in here. I can recommend some good private schools—"

"Don't bother," she snapped as she strode to the door. "I can't imagine why you think I'd trust *your* recommendation." With that parting shot, she jerked open the door and grabbed Corin by the arm. "Come along, darling. You won't ever have to come back here again."

"Yes, Mother."

Mr. Cosgrove moved to his window and watched as the pair got into an old two-door Pontiac, yellow with brown rust spots pocking the left front fender. He had solved his immediate problem, that of protecting Mrs. Whitcomb, but he was well aware that the bigger problem had just walked out of his office. God help the faculty at whatever school Corin landed in next. Maybe, somewhere down the line, someone would step in and get Corin into counseling before too much damage was done . . . unless it was already too late.

Out in the car, the woman drove in stiff, furious silence until they were out of sight of the school. She stopped at a stop sign and, without warning, slapped Corin so hard his head banged against the window. "You little bastard," she said through gritted teeth. "How dare you humiliate me that way! To be called into the principal's office and talked to as if I were some *idiot.* You know what you're going to get when we get home, don't you? *Don't you?*" She screamed the last two words at him.

"Yes, Mother." The child's face was expressionless, but his eyes gleamed with something that could almost be anticipation.

She gripped the steering wheel with both hands, as if trying to throttle it. "You'll be perfect if I have to beat it into you. Do you hear me? *My* child will be *perfect.*"

"Yes, Mother," Corin said.

one

Warren, Michigan, 2000

Jaine Bright woke up in a bad mood.

Her neighbor, the blight of the neighborhood, had just roared home at three A.M. If his car had a muffler, it had long since ceased functioning. Unfortunately, her bedroom was on the same side of the house as his driveway; not even pulling the pillow over her head could block out the sound of that eight-cylinder Pontiac. He slammed the car door, turned on his kitchen porch light—which by some evil design was positioned to shine directly into her eyes if she was lying facing the window, which she was—let his screen door slam three times as he went in, came back out a few minutes later, then went back in, and evidently forgot about the porch light, because a few minutes later the light in the kitchen blinked out but that damn porch light stayed on.

If she had known about her neighbor before she bought this house, she never, never would have closed on the sale. In the two weeks she had lived here, he had single-handedly managed to destroy all the joy she'd felt on buying her first house.

He was a drunk. Why couldn't he be a happy drunk? she wondered sourly. No, he had to be a surly, nasty drunk, the kind who made her afraid to let the cat go outside when he was home. BooBoo wasn't much of a cat—he wasn't even hers—but her mom loved him, so Jaine didn't want anything to happen to him while she had temporary custody. She would never be able to face her mom again if her parents returned from their dream vacation, touring Europe for six weeks, to find BooBoo dead or missing.

Her neighbor already had it in for poor BooBoo anyway, because he'd found paw prints on the windshield and hood of his car. From the way he had reacted, you'd have thought he drove a new Rolls rather than a ten-year-old Pontiac with a bumper crop of dings down both sides.

Just her luck, she had been leaving for work at the same time he did; at least, she'd assumed at the time he'd been going to work. Now she thought he'd probably been going to buy more booze. If he worked at all, then he had really weird hours, because so far she hadn't been able to discern a pattern in his arrivals and departures.

Anyway, she had tried to be nice on the day he spotted the paw prints; she'd even smiled at him, which, considering how he had snapped at her because her housewarming party had woken him up—at two in the afternoon!—had been a real effort for her. But he hadn't paid any attention to the peace-offering smile, instead erupting out of his car almost as soon as his butt hit the seat. "How about keeping your damn cat off my car, lady!"

The smile froze on her face. Jaine hated wasting a smile, especially on an unshaven, bloodshot-eyed, foul-tempered jerk. Several blistering comments sprang to mind, but she bit them back. After all, she was new to the neighborhood, and she had already gotten off on the wrong foot with this guy. The last thing she wanted was a war between them. She decided to give diplomacy one more shot, though it obviously hadn't worked during the housewarming party.

"I'm sorry," she said, keeping her voice even. "I'll try to keep an eye on him. I'm baby-sitting him for my parents, so he won't be here much longer." Just five more weeks.

He had snarled some indistinct reply and slammed back into his car, then roared off, the powerful engine rumbling like thunder. Jaine cocked her head, listening. The Pontiac's body looked like hell, but that motor ran smooth as silk. There were a lot of horses under that hood.

Diplomacy evidently didn't work on this guy.

Now, here he was, waking up the entire neighborhood at three A.M. with that blasted car. The injustice of it, after he had snapped at her for waking him up in the middle of the afternoon, made her want to march over to his house and hold her finger against his doorbell until he was up and as wide awake as everyone else.

There was just one little problem. She was the teeniest bit afraid of him.

She didn't like it; Jaine wasn't accustomed to backing down from anyone, but this guy made her uneasy. She didn't even know his name, because the two times they'd met hadn't been the "hello, my name is so-and-so" type of encounters. All she knew was that he was a rough-looking character, and he didn't seem to hold down a regular job. At best, he was a drunk, and drunks could be mean and destructive. At worst, he was involved in illegal stuff, which added *dangerous* to the list.

He was a big, muscular guy, with dark hair cut so short he almost looked like a skinhead. Every time she had seen him, he looked as if he hadn't shaved in two or three days. Add that to the bloodshot eyes and bad temper, and she came up with *drunk*. The fact that he was big and muscular only added to her uneasiness. This had seemed like such a *safe* neighborhood, but she didn't feel safe with him as her next-door neighbor.

Grumbling to herself, she got out of bed and pulled down the window shade. She had learned over the years not to cover her windows, because an alarm clock might not wake her up, but sunlight always did. Dawn was better than any clanging noise at getting her out of bed. Since she had, several times, found her clock knocked onto the floor, she assumed it had roused her enough to attack it, but not enough to completely wake her.

Her system now was sheer curtains over a shade; the sheers kept anyone from seeing inside unless a light was on, and she raised the shade only after she'd turned out the light for the night. If she was late to work today, it would be her neighbor's fault, for forcing her to rely on the clock instead of the sun.

She stumbled over BooBoo on the way back to bed. The cat jumped up with a startled yowl, and Jaine damn near had a heart attack. "Jesus! BooBoo, you scared the hell out of me." She wasn't used to having a pet in the house, and she was always forgetting to watch where she stepped. Why on earth her mother had wanted *her* to baby-sit the cat, instead of Shelley or Dave, was beyond her. They both had kids who could play with Boo-Boo and keep him entertained. Since school was out for summer vacation, that meant someone was home at both their houses almost all day, every day.

But, *nooo.* Jaine had to keep BooBoo. Never mind that she was single, was at work five days a week, and wasn't used to having a pet. If she did have a pet, it wouldn't be one like BooBoo, anyway. He'd been in a feline pout ever since he'd been neutered, and he took out his frustration on the furniture. In just one week, he had frayed the sofa to the point that she would have to have it reupholstered.

And BooBoo didn't like her. He liked her well enough when he was in *his* home, coming around to be petted, but he didn't like being in her home at all. Every time she tried to pet him now, he arched his back and hissed at her.

To top it off, Shelley was mad at her because Mom had chosen Jaine to baby-sit her precious BooBoo. After all, Shelley was the oldest, and obviously more settled. It didn't make sense that Jaine had been chosen over her. Jaine agreed with her, but that didn't soothe the hurt feelings.

No, what really topped it off was that David, who was a year younger than Shelley, was mad at her too. Not because of Boo-Boo; David was allergic to cats. No, what had him steamed was that Dad had stored his precious car in her garage—which meant *she* couldn't park in her own garage, since it was a single, and it was damned inconvenient. She wished David had the blasted car. She wished Dad had left it in his own garage, but he'd been afraid to leave it unattended for six weeks. She understood that, but she didn't understand why she'd been chosen to baby-sit both cat and car. Shelley didn't understand the cat, David didn't understand the car, and Jaine didn't understand any of it.

So both her brother and sister were mad at her, BooBoo was systematically destroying her sofa, she was terrified something would happen to Dad's car while it was in her care, and her sot of a neighbor was making her life miserable.

God, why had she ever bought a house? If she had stayed in her apartment, none of this would be happening, because she hadn't had a garage and pets hadn't been allowed.

But she had fallen in love with the neighborhood, with its older, nineteen-forties-vintage houses and corresponding low prices. She had seen a good mix of people, from younger families with children to retired people whose families visited every Sunday. Some of the older folks actually sat on their porches during the cool of the evening, waving to passersby, and children played in their yards without worrying about drive-by shootings. She should have checked out all her neighbors, but at first blush this had seemed like a nice, safe area for a single woman to live, and she had been thrilled at finding a good, solid house at such a low price.

Because thinking about her neighbor was guaranteed to prevent her from going back to sleep, Jaine linked her hands behind her head and stared up at the dark ceiling as she thought about all the things she wanted to do with the house. The kitchen and bath both needed modernizing, which were big-ticket improvements and something she wasn't financially ready to tackle. But new paint and new shutters would go a long way toward improving the exterior, and she wanted to knock down the wall between the living and dining rooms, open it up so the dining room was more of an alcove than a separate room, with an arch that she could paint in one of those faux-stone paints so it looked like rock . . .

She woke to the annoying beep of the alarm clock. At least the damn thing had woken her up this time, she thought as she rolled over to silence the alarm. The red numbers shining at her in the dim room made her blink, and look again. "Ah, hell," she groaned in disgust as she leaped out of bed. Six-fifty-eight; the alarm had been going off for almost an hour, which meant she was late. Way late.

"Damn it, damn it, damn it," she muttered as she jumped into the shower and, a minute later, jumped out again. As she brushed her teeth, she dashed into the kitchen and opened a can of food for BooBoo, who was already sitting beside his bowl glaring at her.

She spat into the sink and turned on the water to wash the toothpaste down the drain. "Of all days, why couldn't you have jumped on the bed when you got hungry? No, today you decided to wait, and now *I* don't have time to eat."

BooBoo indicated that he didn't care whether she ate or not, so long as he had food.

She dashed back into the bathroom, did a hurried makeup job, slipped earrings into her earlobes and her watch onto her wrist, then grabbed the outfit she always grabbed when she was in a hurry because she didn't have to fuss with it: black trousers and a white silk shell, with a snazzy red jacket topping it off. She jammed her feet into her shoes, grabbed her purse, and was out the door.

The first thing she saw was the little gray-haired lady who lived across the street, putting out her trash.

It was trash-collection day.

"Hell, damn, shit, piss, and all those other words," Jaine muttered under her breath as she wheeled and rushed back into the house. "I'm trying to cut back on my swearing," she snapped at BooBoo as she pulled the trash bag out of the can and tied off the tapes, "but you and Mr. Congeniality are making it tough."

BooBoo turned his back on her.

She dashed out of the house again, remembered she hadn't locked the door, and dashed back, then dragged her big metal garbage can down to the curb and deposited the morning's offerings inside it, on top of the other two bags already in it. For once, she didn't try to be quiet; she *hoped* she woke up the inconsiderate jerk in the house next door.

She ran back to her car, a cherry red Dodge Viper that she loved, and just for good measure, when she started the engine, she revved it up a few times before putting it in reverse. The car shot backward and with an almighty clang collided with her garbage can. There was another clang as the can rolled into her next-door neighbor's can and knocked it over, sending the lid rolling down the street.

Jaine closed her eyes and tapped her head on the steering wheel—gently; she didn't want a concussion. Though maybe she *should* give herself a concussion; at least then she wouldn't have to worry about getting to work on time, which was now a physical impossibility. She didn't swear, though; the only words that came to mind were words she really didn't want to use.

She put the car in park and got out. What was needed now was control, not a temper tantrum. She righted her dented can and placed the spilled bags back inside it, then jammed the warped lid back on top. Next she returned her neighbor's can to its full and upright position, gathered the trash—he wasn't nearly as neat with his trash collection as she was, but what did you expect from a drunk—then walked down the street to collect the lid.

It lay tilted against the curb in front of the next house down. As she bent to pick it up, she heard a screen door slam behind her.

Well, she had gotten her wish: the inconsiderate jerk was awake.

"What in *hell* are you doing?" he barked. He looked scary, in his sweatpants and torn, dirty T-shirt, a black scowl on his unshaven face.

She turned and marched back to the worse-for-wear pair of cans and slammed the lid down on top of his can. "Picking up your garbage," she snapped.

His eyes were shooting fire. Actually they were just bloodshot, as usual, but the effect was the same. "Just what is it you have against letting me get some sleep? You're the noisiest damn woman I've ever seen—"

The injustice of that made her forget she was a little afraid of him. Jaine stalked up to him, glad she was wearing shoes with two-inch heels that lifted her up so she was level with his . . . chin. Almost.

So what if he was big? She was mad, and *mad* beat *big* any day of the week.

"I'm noisy?" she said through gritted teeth. It was tough to get much volume when her jaw was locked, but she tried. "*I'm* noisy?" She jabbed her finger at him. She didn't want to actually touch him, because his T-shirt was torn and stained with . . . something. "I'm not the one who woke the whole neighborhood at three o'clock this morning with that piece of junk you call a car. Buy a muffler, for God's sake! I'm not the one who slammed his car door once, the screen door three times—what, did you forget your bottle and have to go back for it?—and left his porch light on so it shone into my bedroom and kept *me* from sleeping."

He opened his mouth to blast her in return, but Jaine wasn't finished. "Furthermore, it's a hell of a lot more reasonable to expect people to be sleeping at three o'clock in the morning than it is at two in the afternoon, or"— she checked her watch—"seven-twenty-three in the morning." God, she was so late. "So back off, buddy! Go crawl back into your bottle. If you drink enough, you'll sleep through anything."

He opened his mouth again. Jaine forgot herself and actually poked him. Oh, yuk. Now she'd have to boil her finger. "I'll buy you a new can tomorrow, so just shut up. And if you do anything to hurt my mom's cat, I'll take you apart cell by cell. I'll mutilate your DNA so it can never reproduce, which would probably be a good thing for the world." She swept him with a blistering look that took in his ragged, dirty clothes and unshaven jaw. "Do you understand me?"

He nodded.

She took a deep breath, reaching for the rein on her temper. "Okay. All right, then. Damn it, you made me cuss; and I'm trying not to do that."

He gave her a strange look. "Yeah, you really need to watch that damn cussing."

She pushed her hair out of her face and tried to remember if she had brushed it this morning. "I'm late," she said. "I haven't had any sleep, any breakfast, or any coffee. I'd better leave before I hurt you."

He nodded. "That's a good idea. I'd hate to have to arrest you."

She stared at him, taken aback. "What?"

"I'm a cop," he said, then turned and walked back into his house.

Jaine stared after him, shocked. A *cop?*

"Well, fuck," she said.

two

very Friday, Jaine and three friends from Hammerstead Technology, where they all worked, met after work at Ernie's, a local bar and grill, for a glass of wine, a meal they didn't have to prepare, and girl talk. After working all week in a male-dominated atmosphere, they really, really needed the girl talk.

Hammerstead was a satellite company supplying computer technology to the General Motors plants there in the Detroit area, and computers were still largely a male domain. The company was also fairly large, which meant the general atmosphere was a little weird, with its sometimes uneasy blending of computer geeks who didn't know the meaning of the words "appropriate for the office" and the usual corporate management types. If Jaine had worked in any of the research-and-development offices with the weirdos, no one would have noticed she was late to work that morning. Unfortunately, she was in charge of the payroll department, and her immediate supervising manager was a real clock watcher.

Because she had to make up the time she was late that morning, she was almost fifteen minutes late getting to Ernie's, but the other three had already gotten a table, thank God. Ernie's was already filling up, the way it always did on a weekend night, and she didn't like waiting in the bar for a table even when she was in a good mood, which she wasn't.

"What a day," she said as she dropped into the empty fourth chair. While she was thanking God, she'd add to the list her thanks that today was Friday. It had been a bitch, but it was the last bitch—at least until Monday.

"Tell me about it," Marci muttered as she stubbed out a cigarette and promptly lit another one. "Brick's been on a tear lately. Is it possible for men to have PMS?"

"They don't need it," Jaine said, thinking of her jerk of a neighbor—a *cop* jerk. "They're born with testosterone poisoning."

"Oh, is that what's wrong?" Marci rolled her eyes. "I thought it was a full moon or something. You'll never guess—Kellman grabbed my ass today."

"Kellman?" the other three said in synchronized astonishment, their combined voices drawing the attention of everyone around them. They burst into laughter, because of all the possible offenders, he was the least likely.

Derek Kellman, age twenty-three, was the walking definition of *nerd* and *geek*. He was tall, gangly, and moved with all the grace of a drunken stork. His Adam's apple was so prominent in his thin neck that it looked as if he had swallowed a lemon that became permanently lodged in his throat. His red hair was a stranger to a brush; it would be matted flat in one place and standing out in spikes in another: a terminal case of bed head. But he was an absolute genius with computers, and in fact they

16

were all sort of fond of him, in a protective, big-sisterly way. He was shy, awkward, and absolutely clueless about everything except computers. The office buzz was that he'd heard there were two sexes, but wasn't certain the rumor was true. Kellman was the last person anyone would suspect of being an ass grabber.

"No way," Luna said.

"You're making that up," T.J. accused.

Marci laughed her husky smoker's laugh and took a deep drag off her cigarette. "Swear to God, it's true. All I did was walk past him in the hallway. The next thing I know, he grabs me with both hands and just stands there, holding my ass like it's a basketball and he's about to start dribbling."

The mental image had them all giggling again. "What did you do?" Jaine asked.

"Well, nothing," Marci admitted. "The problem is, Bennett was watching, the jerk."

They groaned. Bennett Trotter thrived on picking on those he considered his subordinates, and poor Kellman was his favorite target. "What could I do?" Marci asked, shaking her head. "No way was I going to give the asshole more ammunition to use against the poor kid. So I patted Kellman on the cheek and said something flirty, along the lines of 'I didn't know you cared.' Kellman turned as red as his hair and dodged into the men's room."

"What did Bennett do?" Luna asked.

"He got that nasty smirk on his face and said that if he'd known I was so hard up I'd settle for Kellman, in the interest of charity he'd have offered his services a long time ago."

That set off an epidemic of eye-rolling. "In other words, he was his usual jerk self," Jaine said in disgust.

There was political correctness, and then there was reality, and the reality was that people were people. Some of the guys they worked with at Hammerstead were nasty leches, and no amount of sensitivity training was going to change that. Most of the guys were okay, though, and it all evened out because some of the women were barbed-wire bitches. Jaine had stopped looking for perfection, in the workplace or anywhere else. Luna thought she was too cynical, but then Luna was the youngest of their group and her rose-tinted glasses were still intact—a bit faded now, but intact.

On the surface, the four friends had nothing in common other than their place of work. Marci Dean, the head of accounting, was forty-one, the oldest of the group. She had been married and divorced three times and, since the last trip through the courtroom, preferred less formal arrangements. Her hair was bleached platinum blond, her smoking was beginning to take its toll on her skin, and her clothes were always just a bit too tight. She liked beer, blue-collar men, rowdy sex, and admitted to a fondness for bowling. "I'm a man's dream," she'd say, laughing. "I have beer tastes on a champagne budget."

Marci's current live-in boyfriend was a guy named Brick, a big, muscle-bound oaf whom none of the other three liked. Privately, Jaine thought his name was appropriate, because he was as dense as a brick. He was ten years younger than Marci, worked only occasionally, and spent most of his time drinking her beer and watching her television. According to Marci, though, he liked sex just the way she did and that was reason enough to keep him around for a while.

Luna Scissum, the youngest, was twenty-four and the *wunderkind* of the sales division. She was tall, willowy, and had both the grace and dignity of a cat. Her perfect skin was the color of pale, creamy caramel, her voice was gentle and lyrical, and men dropped at her feet like flies. She was, in effect, the direct opposite of Marci. Marci was blatant; Luna was remote and ladylike. The only time anyone had ever seen Luna angry was when someone referred to her as "African-American."

"I'm an *American,*" she had snapped, whirling on the offender. "I've never even been to Africa. I was born in California, my father was a major in the Marine Corps, and I'm not a hyphenated anything. I have a black heritage, but I also have a white one." She had held out one slim arm and studied the color of it. "Looks to me like I'm brown. We're all just different shades of brown, so don't try to set me apart."

The guy had stammered an apology, and Luna, being Luna, had given him a gracious smile and forgave him so gently that he ended up asking her out on a date. She was currently dating a running back for the Detroit Lions football team; unfortunately, she had fallen hard for Shamal King, while he was known for his wild partying with other women in every city where there was an NFL team. All too often Luna's dark hazel eyes held an unhappy expression, but she refused to give up on him.

T.J. Yother worked in human resources, and she was the most traditional of the four. She was Jaine's age, thirty, and had been married to her high-school sweetheart for nine years. They lived in a nice suburban home with two cats, a parrot, and a cocker spaniel. The only obvious fly in T.J.'s ointment was that she wanted children and her husband, Galan, did not. Privately, Jaine thought T.J. could be a little more independent. Though Galan worked as a supervisor on the three-to-eleven shift at Chevrolet and wasn't at home anyway, T.J. was always checking her wristwatch, as though she had to be home at a certain time. From what Jaine gathered, Galan didn't approve of their Friday night get-together. All they did was meet at Ernie's and have dinner, and they were never out later than nine; it wasn't as if they were hitting all the bars and drinking until the wee hours.

Well, no one's life was perfect, Jaine thought. She hadn't done so great in the romance department herself. She'd been engaged three times but hadn't yet made it to the altar. After the third breakup, she had decided to give dating a rest for a while and concentrate on her career. Here she was, seven years later, still concentrating. She had a good credit record, a nice bank account, and had just bought her first very own house—not that she was enjoying the house as much as she had thought she would, what with that nasty-tempered, inconsiderate cretin next door. He might be a cop, but he still made her uneasy, because cop or not, he looked like the type who would burn down your house if you got on his bad side. She had been on his bad side from the day she moved in.

"I had another episode with my neighbor this morning," she said, sighing as she propped her elbows on the table and rested her chin on her entwined fingers.

"What did he do this time?" T.J. was sympathetic, because, as they all knew, Jaine was stuck, and bad neighbors could make your life a living hell.

"I was in a hurry and backed into my trash can. You know how when you're running late you always do things that would never happen if you took your time? Everything went wrong this morning. Anyway, my can knocked his down, and the lid bounced into the street. You can imagine the noise. He came charging out the front door like a bear, yelling that I was the noisiest person he'd ever seen."

"You should have kicked his can over," Marci said. She wasn't a believer in turning the other cheek.

"He'd have arrested me for disturbing the peace," Jaine said mournfully. "He's a cop."

"No way!" They all looked incredulous, but then, they had heard her describe him, and red eyes, beard stubble, and dirty clothes didn't sound very coplike.

"I guess cops are just as likely to be drunks as anyone else," T.J. said, a little hesitantly. "More so, I'd say."

Jaine frowned, thinking back to the morning's encounter. "Come to think of it, I didn't smell anything on him. He looked like he'd been on a three-day drunk, but he didn't smell like it. Damn, I hate to think he can be that grouchy when he *isn't* hungover."

"Pay up," Marci said.

"Damn it!" Jaine said, exasperated with herself. She had made a deal with them that she'd pay each a quarter every time she cursed, figuring that would give her the incentive to quit.

"Double it," T.J. chortled, holding out her hand.

Grumbling, but being careful not to swear, Jaine dug out fifty cents for each of them. She made certain she always had plenty of change these days.

"At least he's just a neighbor," Luna said soothingly. "You can avoid him."

"So far I'm not doing a very good job at it," Jaine admitted, scowling at the table. Then she straightened, determined to stop letting the jerk dominate her life and her thoughts the way he had for the past two weeks. "Enough about him. Anything interesting going on with you guys?"

Luna bit her lip, and misery chased across her face. "I called Shamal last night, and a woman answered."

"Oh, damn." Marci leaned across the table to pat Luna's hand, and Jaine had a moment of envy at her friend's verbal freedom.

The waiter chose that moment to distribute menus that they didn't need, because they knew all the selections by heart. They gave him their orders, he collected the unopened menus, and when he left, they all leaned closer to the table.

"What are you going to do?" Jaine asked. She was an expert at breaking up, as well as at being dumped. Her second fiancé, the bastard, had waited until the night before the wedding, the rehearsal night, to tell her he couldn't go through with it. Getting over that had taken a while—and she wasn't going to pay up for words she *thought,* but didn't say out loud. Was "bastard" a curse word, anyway? Was there an official list she could consult?

Luna shrugged. She was close to tears, and trying to be nonchalant. "We aren't engaged, or even seeing each other exclusively. I don't have any right to complain."

"No, but you can protect yourself and stop seeing him," T.J. said gently. "Is he worth this kind of pain?"

Marci snorted. "No man is."

"Amen," Jaine said, still thinking of her three broken engagements.

Luna picked at her napkin, her long, slender fingers restless. "But when we're together, he . . . he acts as if he really cares. He's sweet, and loving, and so considerate—"

"They all are, until they get what they want." Marci stubbed out her third cigarette. "That's personal experience speaking, you understand. Have your fun with him, but don't expect him to change."

"Isn't that the truth," T.J. said ruefully. "They never change. They may put on an act for a while, but when they think they have you sewed up and tied down, they relax and Mr. Hyde shows his hairy face again."

Jaine laughed. "That sounds like something *I* would say."

"Except there weren't any curse words," Marci pointed out.

T.J. waved a signal to cut the jokes. Luna looked even more miserable than before. "So I should either put up with being one of a herd, or stop seeing him?"

"Well . . . yeah."

"But it shouldn't be that way! If he cares for me, how can he be interested in all those other women?"

"Oh, that's easy," Jaine replied. "The one-eyed snake has no taste."

"Sweetheart," Marci said, her smoker's voice as kind as she could make it, "if you're looking for Mr. Perfect, you're going to spend your whole life being disappointed, because he doesn't exist. You have to get the best deal you can, but there will always be problems."

"I know he isn't perfect, but—"

"But you want him to be," T.J. finished.

Jaine shook her head. "Isn't going to happen," she announced. "The perfect man is pure science fiction. Not that we're perfect, either," she added, "but most women do at least *try*. Men don't try. That's why I gave up on them. Relationships just don't work out for me." She paused, then said thoughtfully, "I wouldn't mind having a sex slave, though."

The other three burst out laughing, even Luna.

"I could get into that," Marci said. "I wonder where I can get one?"

"Try Sexslaves-R-Us," T.J. suggested, and they dissolved into laughter again.

"There's probably a Web site," Luna said, choking a little.

"Of course there is." Jaine was totally deadpan. "It's on my Favorites list: www.sexslaves.com."

"Just type in your requirements and you can rent Mr. Perfect by the hour or the day." T.J. waved her glass of beer, carried away with enthusiasm.

"A day? Get real." Jaine hooted. "An hour is asking for a miracle."

"Besides, there is no Mr. Perfect, remember?" Marci said.

"Not a real one, no, but a sex slave would have to pretend to be exactly what you wanted, wouldn't he?"

Marci was never without her soft leather briefcase. She

opened it and dug out a pad of paper and a pen, slapping them down on the table. "He most certainly would. Let's see, what would Mr. Perfect be like?"

"He'd have to do the dishes half the time *without being asked*," T.J. said, slapping her hand down on the table and drawing curious looks their way.

When they managed to stop laughing long enough to be coherent, Marci scribbled on her pad. "Okay, number one: Do the dishes."

"No, hey, doing the dishes can't be number one," Jaine protested. "We have more serious issues to address first."

"Yeah," Luna said. "Seriously. What do we think a perfect man would be like? I've never thought about it in those terms. Maybe it would help if I had it clear in my mind what I like in a man."

They all paused. "The perfect man? Seriously?" Jaine wrinkled her nose.

"Seriously."

"This is going to take some thinking," Marci pronounced.

"Not for me," T.J. said, the laughter fading from her face. "The most important thing is that he wants the same things out of life that you do."

They lapsed into a little pond of silence. The attention their laughter had gotten from the diners at the surrounding tables moved on to more promising targets.

"Wants the same things out of life," Marci repeated as she wrote it down. "That's number one? Are we agreed?"

"That's important," Jaine said. "But I'm not sure it's number one."

"Then what's number one for you?"

"Faithfulness." She thought of her second fiancé, the bastard. "Life's too short to waste it on someone you can't trust. You should be able to depend on the man you love not to lie to you or cheat on you. If you have that as a base, you can work on the other stuff."

"That's number one for me," Luna said quietly.

T.J. thought about it. "Okay," she finally said. "If Galan wasn't faithful, I wouldn't *want* to have a baby with him."

"I'll go along with that," Marci said. "I can't stand a two-timer. Number one: He's faithful. Doesn't cheat or lie."

They all nodded.

"What else?" She sat with the pen poised over the pad.

"He should be nice," T.J. offered.

"Nice?" Marci looked incredulous.

"Yes, *nice.* Who wants to spend her life with a jerk?"

"Or next door to one?" Jaine muttered. She nodded in agreement. "Nice is good. It doesn't sound exciting, but think about it. I think Mr. Perfect would be kind to kids and animals, help old ladies across the street, not insult you when your opinion is different from his. Being nice is so important it's close to being number one."

Luna nodded.

"Okay," Marci said. "Hell, you've even convinced me. I don't guess I've ever known a nice guy. Number two: Nice." She wrote it down. "Number three? I have my own idea on this one. I want a guy who's dependable. If he says he's going to do something, he should do it. If he's supposed to meet me somewhere at seven, he should be there at seven, not come strolling in at nine-thirty or maybe not at all. Is there a vote on this one?"

They all four raised their hands in an aye vote, and "Dependable" went down in the number three slot.

"Number four?"

"The obvious," Jaine said. "A steady job."

Marci winced. "Ouch. That one hurt." Brick was currently sitting on his butt instead of working.

"A steady job is part of being dependable," T.J. pointed out. "And I agree, it's important. Holding down a steady job shows maturity and a sense of responsibility."

"Steady job," Marci said as she wrote.

"He should have a sense of humor," Luna said.

"Something more than an appreciation for The Three Stooges?" Jaine asked.

They began snickering. "What is it with men and The Three Stooges?" T.J. asked, rolling her eyes. "And bodily function jokes! Put that at number one, Marci—no toilet jokes!"

"Number five: Sense of humor." Marci chuckled as she wrote. "In the interest of fairness, I don't think we can dictate what form the humor takes."

"Sure we can," Jaine corrected. "He's going to be our sex slave, remember?"

"Number six." Marci called them to order by tapping her pen on the rim of her glass. "Let's get back to business, ladies. What's number six?"

They all looked at each other and shrugged. "Money's nice," T.J. finally offered. "It isn't a *requirement,* not in real life, but this is fantasy, right? The perfect man should have money."

"Filthy rich or comfortable?"

That called for more thought.

"I like filthy rich, myself," Marci said.

"But he would want to call all the shots if he was filthy rich. He'd be used to it."

"No way is that going to happen. Okay, money is nice, but not too much money. Comfortable. Mr. Perfect is financially comfortable."

Four hands went up, and "Money" was written in beside the number six.

"Since this is fantasy," Jaine said, "he should be good-looking. Not drop-dead gorgeous, because that could be a problem.

26

Luna's the only one of us pretty enough to hold her own with a handsome guy."

"I'm not doing so good at it, am I?" Luna replied with a tinge of bitterness. "But, yeah, for Mr. Perfect to be perfect, you should enjoy looking at him."

"Hear, hear. Number seven is: Good to look at." When she had finished writing, Marci looked up with a grin. "I'm going to be the one to say what we've all been thinking. He should be great in bed. Not just good; he should be great. He should be able to make my toes curl and my eyes roll back in my head. He should have the stamina of a Kentucky Derby winner and the enthusiasm of a sixteen-year-old."

They were still rolling with laughter when the waiter plunked their orders down on the table. "What's so funny?" he asked.

"You wouldn't understand," T.J. managed to gasp.

"I get it," he said wisely. "You're talking about men."

"Nope, we're talking science fiction," Jaine said, which sent them off again. The people at the other tables were staring at them again, trying to overhear what was so funny.

The waiter left. Marci leaned over the table. "And while I'm at it, I want my Mr. Perfect to have a ten-incher!"

"Oh, my!" T.J. pretended to swoon, fanning herself. "What I couldn't do with ten inches—or rather, what I *could* do with ten inches!"

Jaine was laughing so hard she had to hold her sides. Keeping her voice down was an effort, and her words shook with hilarity. "C'mon! Anything over eight inches is strictly for show-and-tell. It's there, but you can't use it. It might look good in a locker room, but let's face it—those extra two inches are leftovers."

"Leftovers," Luna gasped, holding her stomach and shrieking with laughter. "Let's hear it for l-leftovers!"

"Oh, boy." Marci wiped her eyes as she scribbled rapidly. "Now we're cooking. What else does Mr. Perfect have?"

T.J. weakly waved her hand. "Me," she offered between giggles. "He can have me."

"If we don't trample you getting to him," Jaine said, and raised her glass. The other three lifted theirs, and they touched rims with ringing clinks. "To Mr. Perfect, wherever he is!"

three

Saturday morning dawned bright and early—way too bright, and way the hell too early. BooBoo woke Jaine at six A.M. by yowling in her ear. "Go away," she mumbled, pulling the pillow over her head.

BooBoo yowled again, and batted the pillow. She got the message: either get up, or he was going to unsheathe his claws. She pushed the pillow aside and sat up, glaring at him. "You're evil, y'know that? You couldn't do this yesterday morning, could you? No, you have to wait until my day off, when I don't *have* to get up early."

He looked unimpressed with her outrage. That was the thing about cats; even the scruffiest one was convinced of its innate superiority. She scratched him behind his ears and a low rumble shivered through his entire body. His slanted yellow eyes closed in bliss. "You just wait," she told him. "I'm going to get you addicted to this scratching stuff, then I'm going to stop doing it. You're going to go cold turkey, pal."

He jumped down from the bed and padded to the open bedroom door, pausing to look back as if checking to make certain she was getting up. Jaine yawned and threw back the covers. At least she hadn't been disturbed by her neighbor's noisy car during the night, plus she had pulled down the window shade to keep out the morning light, so she had slept soundly until Boo-Boo's wake-up call. She raised the shade and peeked through the sheer curtains at the driveway running beside hers. The battered brown Pontiac was there. That meant she had either been exhausted and slept like the dead, or he'd gotten a new muffler on the thing. She thought the exhausted-and-dead part was more likely than him getting a new muffler.

BooBoo evidently thought she was wasting time, because he gave a warning meow. Sighing, she pushed her hair out of her face and stumbled to the kitchen—*stumbled* being the operative word, because BooBoo helped her along by winding around her ankles as she walked. She desperately needed coffee, but knew from experience that BooBoo wouldn't leave her alone until he was fed. She opened a can of food, dumped it on a saucer, and set it on the floor. While he was occupied, she put on a pot of coffee, then headed for the shower.

Stripping off her summer sleepwear of T-shirt and panties—during winter she added socks to the ensemble—she stepped into a nice warm shower and let it pummel her awake. Some people were larks; some were owls; Jaine was neither. She didn't function well until after a shower and a cup of coffee, and she liked to be in bed by ten at the latest. BooBoo was upsetting the natural order of things with his demands to be fed before anything else was done. How *could* her mom have done this to her?

"Just four weeks and six days more," she muttered to herself. Who would have thought that a cat that was normally so loving would turn into such a tyrant when he wasn't in his regular environment?

After a long shower and two cups of coffee, her synapses started connecting and she began remembering all the things she needed to do. Buy the jerk next door a new trash can—*check*. Buy groceries—*check*. Do laundry—*check*. Mow the lawn—*check*.

She felt a little excited at the last item. She had grass to cut, her very own grass! She had lived in apartments since leaving home, none of which had come with lawns. There were usually some tiny patches of grass between the sidewalk and the building, but maintenance always took care of mowing them. Hell—*heck*, they were so tiny the job could have been done with scissors.

But her new home came with its very own lawn. In anticipation of this moment, she had invested in a brand-new lawn mower, self-propelled, state-of-the-art, guaranteed to make her brother, David, turn green with envy. He'd have to buy a riding mower to one-up her on this, and since his lawn wasn't any bigger than hers, a riding mower would be an expensive sop to his ego. Jaine figured his wife, Valerie, would step in before he did anything that foolish.

Today, she would have her inaugural grass-cutting. She could barely wait to feel the power of that red monster pulsing under her hands as it decapitated all those blades of grass. She had always been a sucker for red machinery.

First things first, though. She had to make a run to Wal-Mart and buy a new trash can for the jerk. A promise was a promise, and Jaine always tried to keep her word.

A quick bowl of cereal later, she pulled on a pair of jeans and a T-shirt, stuck her feet in a pair of sandals, and was on her way.

Who knew a metal trash can would be so hard to find?

Wal-Mart had only the plastic kind in stock. She invested in one for herself, but didn't feel she had the right to change her neighbor's type of trash can. From there she drove to a home-and-garden supply store, but struck out there, too. If she had bought her own metal can she would have known where to find another one, but it had been a housewarming present from her mother—that was Mom, Queen of the Practical Gift.

By the time she finally located a large metal trash can, at a hardware store—well, *duh*—it was nine o'clock and the temperature was already edging out of warm into uncomfortable. If she didn't get the grass mowed soon, she would have to wait until sundown for the heat to abate. Deciding that grocery shopping could wait, she wedged the can into her minuscule backseat and headed south on Van Dyke until she reached Ten Mile Road, then turned right. Minutes later she turned onto her street and smiled at the neat, older houses nestled under their mature shade trees.

A few of the houses had tricycles and bicycles on the front lawns. These older neighborhoods were seeing an influx of younger couples as they discovered the reasonable price of the aging houses. Instead of disintegrating, the houses were receiving face-lifts and remodels; in a few years, the price of real estate would shoot up again, but for now this area was just right for people just starting out.

As she got out of the car, the neighbor on the other side of her house walked over to the waist-high white picket fence separating the properties and waved. "Good morning!" Mrs. Kulavich called.

"Good morning," Jaine replied. She had met the pleasant old couple the day she moved in, and Mrs. Kulavich had brought her a nice thick pot of stew the next day, with fragrant homemade rolls. If only the jerk on the other side could have been more like the Kulavichs, Jaine would have been in seventh heaven, though she couldn't even begin to picture him bringing her homemade rolls.

She walked over to the fence for a neighborly chat. "It's a beautiful day, isn't it?" Thank God for weather, because the world would be hard up for a conversational gambit without it.

"Oh, my, it's going to be a scorcher." Mrs. Kulavich beamed at her and brandished a trowel in one gloved hand. "I have to do my gardening early, before it gets too hot."

"I had the same idea about mowing my lawn this morning." Others were of the same mind, she noticed. Now that she was paying attention, she could hear the roar of a lawn mower three doors up from Mrs. Kulavich and another across the street.

"Smart girl. Take care not to get too hot; my George always wets a towel and puts it on the back of his neck when he mows, though our grandsons help him with the mowing and he doesn't do it as often as he used to." She winked. "I think he cranks up the old mower now just because he's in the mood to do something manly."

Jaine smiled and started to excuse herself, but something occurred to her and she turned back to the old lady. "Mrs. Kulavich, do you know the man who lives on the other side of me?" What if the jerk had lied to her? What if he wasn't really a cop? She could just see him having a good laugh at her expense, while she tiptoed around and tried to be nice to him.

"Sam? My, yes, I've known him all his life. His grandparents used to live there, you know. Lovely people. I was so glad when Sam moved in after his grandmother finally passed last year. I feel much safer having a policeman so close by, don't you?"

Well, that shot that theory in the ass. Jaine managed a smile. "Yes, of course." She started to say something about the strange hours he kept, but saw the gleam in Mrs. Kulavich's bright blue eyes and bit back the words. The last thing she needed was for her elderly neighbor to think she had any interest in the jerk and maybe *tell* him, since Mrs. Kulavich was obviously on good terms with him. She took care of that by adding, "I thought he might be a drug dealer or something."

Mrs. Kulavich looked scandalized. "Sam, a drug dealer? Oh, my. No, he would never do anything like that."

"That's a relief." Jaine smiled again. "I suppose I'd better start mowing before it gets much hotter."

"Be sure to drink plenty of water," Mrs. Kulavich called after her.

"I will."

Well, drat, Jane thought as she wrestled the trash can out of her backseat. The jerk was a cop; he hadn't lied. There went her dream of seeing him hauled away in handcuffs.

She deposited the can by his back porch, then released the plastic can she had bought for herself from the trunk. If the can hadn't been plastic, she never could have gotten it in there, but plastic compressed. When she opened the trunk, it sprang at her like something alive. She put the can behind her small kitchen stoop, neatly out of sight from the street, then went inside and quickly changed into shorts and a halter top. That was what suburban ladies wore to mow their lawns, wasn't it? Then she remembered her older neighbors, and changed the halter top for a T-shirt; she didn't want to give some old gent a heart attack.

She felt a thrill of anticipation as she unlocked the padlock on the garage doors and slipped inside, fumbling until she reached the switch that turned on the single overhead light. Her dad's pride and joy sat there, completely covered by a custom-made canvas tarp, lined with felt so it wouldn't scratch the paint. Damn, she wished he had left it at David's. The car wasn't as much trouble as BooBoo, but she worried about it a lot more.

The deciding factor in leaving it at her house, she thought, was that her garage still had the old-fashioned double doors rather than a modern garage door that slid up. Her dad worried about the car being seen from the street; she could get into her garage without opening the doors more than the twelve inches required for her to slip through, while everything in David's double garage was visible every time he raised his door. First chance she got, she was putting in an automatic garage door.

She had covered her new lawn mower with a sheet so it wouldn't get dusty. She removed the sheet and stroked her hand over the cool metal. Maybe her low-tech garage wasn't the deciding factor in her baby-sitting the car; maybe it was because she was the only one of her dad's children who shared his enthusiasm for cars. She was the one who had hung over the fender of their family sedan, staring into the mysterious mechanical bowels as her dad changed the oil and spark plugs. By the time she was ten, she had been helping him. By the time she was twelve, she had taken over the chore. For a while she had considered going into automotive mechanical engineering, but the training took years and she wasn't really that ambitious. All she wanted was a job that paid well and that she didn't hate, and she was as good with numbers as she was with motors. She enjoyed cars; she didn't want to turn them into a job.

She wheeled her lawn mower past her dad's car, taking care not to touch it. The canvas tarp protected it from the ground up, but she didn't take any chances where that car was concerned. Opening one of the garage doors only enough to let her get the lawn mower out, she ushered her new baby out into the sunlight. The red paint gleamed; the chrome handlebars glistened. Oh, it was pretty.

At the last minute, she remembered something about the mowing ritual, and moved her car to the street; one had to be careful about accidentally slinging a rock that could break a window or chip a paint job. She looked at the jerk's car and shrugged; he might notice BooBoo's paw prints, but he'd never notice another dent in that thing.

With a happy smile, she fired up the little motor.

The thing about cutting grass, she discovered, was that you had an instant sense of achievement. You could see exactly where you had been and what you had accomplished. Her dad and David had always taken care of that chore when she was growing up, much to her relief, because mowing the lawn had looked boring. Only as she had grown older had she seen the lure of having your own grass, and now she felt as if she had finally, at the age of thirty, stepped into full adulthood. She was a home owner. She mowed her lawn. Cool.

Something tapped her on the shoulder.

She shrieked and released the lawn mower handles, jumping to one side and whirling to face her attacker. The mower stopped in its tracks.

The jerk stood there, bloodshot eyes, snarl on his face, dirty clothes: his usual presentation. He reached over and slid the lever on the mower to the off position, and the efficient little engine growled to a stop.

Silence.

For about half a second.

"What in *hell* did you do that for?" she roared, her face turning red with temper as she stepped closer, unconsciously balling her right hand into a fist.

"I thought you were trying to quit cussing," he taunted.

"You'd drive a saint to cussing!"

"That let's you out, doesn't it?"

"You're damn right!"

He eyed her right hand. "Are you going to use that, or are you going to be reasonable?"

"What—?" She glanced down and saw that her arm was half-cocked, her fist already drawn back. With great effort she uncurled her fingers. They immediately assumed the fight position again. She really, *really* wanted to slug him, and she got even angrier because she couldn't. "Reasonable?" she yelled, stepping even closer. "You want *me* to be reasonable? You're the one who scared the hell out of me and turned off my mower!"

"I'm trying to sleep," he said, enunciating the words with clear pit stops between each one. "Is it asking too much for a little consideration?"

She gaped at him. "You act as if I'm out here mowing at dawn. It's almost ten o'clock! And I'm not the only one who's committing the high crime of *cutting grass*. Listen," she commanded, as the muted roar of neighborhood mowers hummed up and down the street.

"*They* aren't mowing right outside my bedroom window!"

"So get in bed at a decent hour. It isn't my fault you stay up most of the night!"

His face was getting as red as hers. "I'm on a task force, lady! Irregular hours are part of the job. I sleep when I can, which, since you moved in, hasn't been very damn often!"

She threw up her hands. "All right! Fine! I'll finish the job tonight, when it cools down." She made a shooing motion. "Just stagger on back to bed. I'll go inside and *sit* for the next eleven hours. Or will that disturb your beauty rest, too?" she inquired sweetly.

"Not unless you have firecrackers in your ass," he snapped, and stalked back into his house.

There was probably a law against throwing rocks at someone's house, she thought. Fuming, she wheeled her lawn mower back into the garage, carefully padlocked the doors, then retrieved her car from the curb. She'd like to show him what she could do with a few firecrackers, and she sure wouldn't be sitting on them.

She stomped inside and glared at BooBoo, who ignored her while he washed his paws. "A task force," she growled. "I'm not unreasonable. All he had to do was explain, in a calm voice, and

I'd have been glad to put off mowing until later. But *nooo,* he'd rather make an ass of himself."

BooBoo looked at her.

"Ass isn't a swear word," she said defensively. "Besides, it isn't my fault. I'll let you in on a secret about our neighbor, Boo-Boo: Mr. Perfect, he's not!"

four

Jaine managed to get through the weekend without another confrontation with her jerk neighbor and was at work fifteen minutes early in an effort to atone for her Friday lateness, even though she had worked overtime on Friday to make up for it. As she stopped at the gate, the watchman leaned out and eyed the Viper with disapproval. "When're you going to get rid of the piece of junk and buy a Chevrolet?"

She heard it almost every day. This was what happened when you worked in the Detroit area in anything remotely connected with the automotive industry. You had to show brand loyalty to whichever of the Big Three directly or indirectly employed you. "When I can afford it," she replied, as she always did. Never mind that the Viper had cost the earth, even though it was used and had over fifty thousand miles on it when she bought it. "I just bought a house, you know. If my dad hadn't given this to me, I wouldn't be driving it."

That last was a direct lie, but it tended to get people off her back for a while. Thank God no one here knew who her father was, or they would have known he was a Ford man through and through. He had been insulted when she bought the Viper and never failed to make a few derogatory remarks about it.

"Yeah, well, your dad should have known better."

"He doesn't know anything about cars." She tensed, expecting lightning to strike her dead for that whopper.

She parked the Viper at a back corner of the lot, where it was less likely to get dinged. People at Hammerstead joked that the car was being shunned. She had to admit it was inconvenient, especially during bad weather, but getting wet was better than letting the Viper get injured. Just driving on I-696 to get to work was enough to give her gray hair.

Hammerstead occupied a four-story red-brick building with a gray arched portico and six curving steps leading up to impressive double doors. That entrance, however, was used exclusively by visitors. All the employees entered by a metal side door with an electronic lock into a narrow, puke green hallway, on which were the offices of maintenance and electrical, and a dark, dank room labeled "Storage." Just what was stored there, Jaine didn't want to know.

At the end of the puke green hallway were three steps that led up to another metal door. This one opened onto a gray-carpeted hall that ran the length of the building, front to back, and off which offices and other hallways branched like veins. The two lower floors were reserved for the computer nerds, those strange and irreverent beings who talked in a foreign language about bytes and USB ports. Access to these floors was limited; one had to have an employee's access card to get into the puke green hallway, then another to enter any of the offices and rooms. There were two elevators, and at the far end of the building, for the more energetic, were the stairs.

As she entered the gray-carpeted hall, a large hand-lettered sign caught her attention. The sign was posted directly above the call buttons for the elevators. In green and purple crayon, outlined with black Magic Marker for emphasis, was a new company directive: EFFECTIVE IMMEDIATELY, ALL EMPLOYEES WILL BE REQUIRED TO TAKE A COMBINATION OF GINKGO AND VIAGRA, SO YOU CAN REMEMBER WHAT THE FUCK YOU'RE DOING.

She began giggling. The nerds were in fine form today. By nature they rebelled against authority and structure; such signs were commonplace, at least until someone in management arrived and took them down. She imagined eyes all up and down the hallway were plastered to tiny cracks as the culprits enjoyed others' reactions to their latest attack on corporate dignity.

The door behind her opened, and Jaine turned to see who the next arrival was. She barely refrained from wrinkling her nose.

Leah Street worked in human resources, and she could be counted on to not see the humor in anything. She was a tall woman whose ambition was to rise into management, though she didn't seem to know how to go about doing so. She wore rather girlish clothes instead of the more businesslike suits that would have complemented her willowy build. She was an attractive woman, with feathery blond hair and good skin, but clueless when it came to fashion. Her best feature was her hands, which were slim and elegant, and which she always kept perfectly manicured.

True to form, Leah gasped when she read the sign, and began turning red. "That's disgraceful," she snapped, reaching out to take it down.

"If you touch it, your fingerprints will be on it," Jaine said, totally deadpan.

Leah froze, her hand only a fraction of an inch from the paper.

"There's no telling how many people have already seen it," Jaine continued as she punched the up button. "Someone in management is bound to hear about it and investigate even if the sign isn't here any longer. Unless you plan on eating it—which I wouldn't, the germ count on that thing must be in the gazillions—how are you going to dispose of it without being seen?"

Leah flashed Jaine a look of dislike. "You probably think this disgusting trash is funny."

"As a matter of fact, I do."

"I wouldn't be surprised if you put it up yourself."

"Maybe you should tell on me," Jaine suggested as the elevator doors opened and she stepped inside. "Try calling 1-800-WHO-CARES."

The elevator doors closed, leaving Leah standing outside them glaring at her. That was the most acrimonious exchange they'd ever had, though Leah wasn't known for the ability to get along with others. How she had ever landed a job in HR was beyond Jaine. Most of the time, she simply felt sorry for the woman.

Today wasn't one of those times.

Mondays were always the busiest day of the week in the payroll department, because that was when all the time cards for the week before were turned in. Hammerstead worked at supplying computer technology to General Motors, not at putting its own payroll system on computer. They still did it the old-fashioned way, with time cards that were punched by a clock. It was a lot of paperwork, but so far payroll had not been stopped by a software glitch or a hard-drive crash. Maybe that was why Hammerstead hadn't upgraded: the payroll, like the mail, had to go through.

By ten o'clock, she was ready for a break. Each floor had a snack room, with the usual assortment of vending machines, cheap cafeteria tables and metal chairs, a refrigerator, a coffeemaker, and a microwave oven. There were several women and one man grouped around a single table when Jaine entered, all of the women laughing their heads off and the guy looking indignant.

Jaine poured herself a much-needed cup of coffee. "What's up?" she asked.

"A special edition of the newsletter," one of the women, Dominica Flores, answered. Her eyes were wet from laughing. "This one is going down in history."

"I don't see what's so funny," said the guy, scowling.

"*You* wouldn't," a woman said, snickering. She held out the newsletter to Jaine. "Take a look."

The company newsletter wasn't officially sanctioned, not by any stretch of the imagination. It originated from the first two floors; give that many imaginations access to desktop publishing, and it was bound to happen. The newsletter appeared at irregular intervals, and there was usually something in it that had management trying to round up all the copies.

Jaine took another sip of coffee as she took the newsletter. The guys actually did a pretty professional job of it, though with the equipment and software at their disposal, it would have been a disgrace if they hadn't. The newsletter was named *The Hammerhead* and a nasty-looking shark was the logo. It wasn't a hammerhead shark, but that didn't matter. The articles were set in columns, there were good graphics, and a fairly witty cartoonist who signed his work "Mako" usually poked fun at some aspect of corporate life.

Today the headline was set in huge boldface letters: DO YOU MEASURE UP? Below it read, "What Women Really Want," with a tape measure coiled like a cobra ready to strike.

"Forget about it, guys," the article began. "Most of us are nonstarters. For years we've been told it's not what we've got, it's how we use it, but now we know the truth. Our expert panel of four women, friends who work here at Hammerstead, have come up with a list of their requirements for the perfect man."

Uh-oh. Jaine almost groaned, but managed to bite back the sound and show nothing but interest in her expression. Damn it, what had Marci done with that list she had written down? They would all be teased unmercifully, and this was the kind of thing that stuck forever. She could just see tape measures by the dozen turning up on her desk every morning.

Hastily she skimmed down the article. Thank God; none of their names were mentioned. They were listed as A, B, C, and D. She was still going to wring Marci's neck, but now she wouldn't have to fold, spindle, and mutilate her.

The entire list was there, starting with "faithful" in the number one spot. The list wasn't bad until it hit number eight, "great in bed," but after that it deteriorated rapidly. Number nine was Marci's ten-inch requirement, complete with all their accompanying comments, including her own about the last two inches being leftovers.

Number ten had to do with how long Mr. Perfect should be able to last in bed. "Definitely longer than a television commercial," had been T.J.'s—Ms. D's—rather scathing indictment. They had settled on half an hour as the optimum length of lovemaking, not counting foreplay.

"Why not?" Ms. C—that was Jaine—was quoted as saying. "This is a fantasy, right? And a fantasy is supposed to be *exactly* what you want it to be. My Mr. Perfect could give me thirty minutes of thrusting time—unless you're having a quickie, in which case thirty minutes would kind of defeat the purpose."

The women were all howling with laughter, so Jaine figured some expression must be on her face. She just hoped it looked like astonishment rather than horror. The guy—she thought his name was Cary or Craig, something like that—was turning redder by the minute.

"You wouldn't think it was so funny if a bunch of men said that their ideal woman had to have big boobs," he snapped, getting to his feet.

"Oh, come off it," Dominica said, still grinning. "Like men haven't gone for big boobs since their knuckles still dragged the ground. It's nice to see a little payback."

Oh, great. A battle between the sexes. Jaine could just imagine the conversations going on around the building. She forced a smile as she handed back the newsletter. "I guess we're going to hear about this for a while."

"Are you kidding?" Dominica asked, grinning. "I'm going to frame my copy and hang it where my husband sees it first thing in the morning when he wakes up and last thing at night when he goes to bed!"

As soon as Jaine got back to her office, she dialed Marci's extension. "Guess what I just saw in the newsletter," she growled, keeping her voice low.

"Oh, damn." Marci groaned aloud. "How bad is it? I haven't seen a copy yet."

"From what I read, it's pretty much verbatim. Damn it, Marci, how could you?"

"That's a quarter," Marci said automatically. "And it was an accident. I don't want to say too much here in the office, but if you can meet me for lunch, I'll tell you what happened."

"Okay. Railroad Pizza at twelve. I'll call T.J. and Luna; they'll probably want to be there, too."

"This sounds like a lynch party," Marci said mournfully.

"Could be," Jaine said, and hung up.

Railroad Pizza was about half a mile from Hammerstead, which made it a popular place with the employees. They did a booming take-out business, but they also had half a dozen booths and about that many tables. Jaine got the back booth, where they would have the most privacy. Within minutes, the other three arrived and slid into the booth, T.J. next to Jaine, Marci and Luna across from them.

"God, I'm sorry," Marci said. She looked miserable.

"I can't believe you showed the list to someone!" T.J. was horrified. "If Galan ever finds out—"

"I don't see why you're so upset," Luna said, puzzled. "I mean, yeah, it'd be a little embarrassing if people found out we're the ones who made the list, but it's really kind of funny."

"Would you still think it's funny six months from now when guys are still coming up to you offering to show you that they measure up?" Jaine asked.

"Galan wouldn't think it's funny at all," T.J. said, shaking her head. "He'd *kill* me."

"Yeah," Marci said glumly. "Brick isn't what you'd call sensitive, but he'd get pissed that I said I wanted ten inches." She gave a weak smile. "Guess you can say he'd come up short."

"How did it happen?" T.J. asked, burying her face in her hands.

"I went shopping Saturday, and I ran into Dawna what's-her-name, you know, that Elvira look-alike on the first floor," Marci said. "We got to talking, went for a late lunch, had a couple of beers. I showed her the list, we had a good laugh, and she asked for a copy. I didn't see why not. After a few beers, I don't see why not about a lot of things. She asked a few questions, and somehow I wound up writing down everything we'd said."

Marci had an almost photographic memory. Unfortunately, a few beers didn't seem to affect her memory, just her judgment.

"At least you didn't give her our names," T.J. said.

"She knows who we are," Jaine pointed out. "Marci had the list, so any idiot can figure out she's one of the four friends. Take it from there."

T.J. covered her face with her hands again. "I'm dead. Or divorced."

"I don't think anything will come of it," Luna said soothingly. "If Dawna was going to spill the beans on us, she would already have told her pals on the first floor. We're safe. Galan will never know."

five

Jaine was on edge the rest of the day, waiting for the other shoe to drop. She couldn't imagine how nervous T.J. must have felt, because if this ever got out and Galan found out about it, he'd deal T.J. misery for the rest of her life. When it came down to the bottom line, T.J. was the one who had the most to lose. Marci was in a relationship, but at least she wasn't married to Brick. The thing Luna had going with Shamal King was on-again, off-again at best, without commitment.

Of the four, Jaine was the one who would have the least difficulty if their identities became known. She wasn't in a relationship, having given up on men, and she answered to no one but herself. She'd have to endure the teasing, but that was all.

Once she analyzed the situation and came to that conclusion, she stopped worrying so much. So what if some office clown tried to show off his wit? She could hold her own with any bozo.

Her improved mood lasted until she got home and found that BooBoo, in an attempt to impress on her how upset he was at having to stay in a strange house, had completely shredded one of the cushions on her sofa. Tufts of stuffing were scattered all over the living room. She closed her eyes and counted to ten, then to twenty. There was no point in getting angry at the cat; he probably wouldn't understand, and wouldn't care even if he did. He was as much a victim of circumstance as she was. He hissed at her when she reached for him. She usually left him alone when he did that, but in a moment of pity she scooped him up anyway and burrowed her fingers into his fur, kneading the limber muscles of his back. "Poor kitty," she crooned. "You don't know what's going on, do you?"

BooBoo snarled at her, then ruined the effect by lapsing into a rumbling purr.

"Just hold on for four weeks and five days. That's thirty-three days. You can put up with me that long, can't you?"

He didn't look as if he agreed, but didn't care as long as she continued kneading his back. She carried him into the kitchen and gave him a treat, then put him on the floor with a fuzzy toy mouse to battle.

Okay. The cat was trashing her house. She could cope. Her mom would be horrified at the damage and pay for it, of course, so all in all Jaine was just being a little inconvenienced.

She was impressed by her own mellowness.

She got a drink of water, and as she stood at the sink, her neighbor arrived home. At the sight of that brown Pontiac she could feel her mellowness begin to circle the drain. But the car *was* quiet, so evidently he had replaced the muffler. If he was trying, so could she. Mentally she put a stopper in the drain.

She watched out the window as he got out of the car and unlocked his kitchen door, which faced hers. He was wearing slacks and a white dress shirt, with a tie hanging loose around his neck and a jacket slung over his shoulder. He looked tired, and when he turned to enter the house, she saw the big black pistol in the holster on his belt. This was the first time she had seen him wearing anything except old, dirty clothes, and she felt a bit disoriented, as if the world had shifted off center. Knowing he was a cop and seeing him as a cop were two different things. The fact that he was wearing street clothes instead of a uniform meant he wasn't a patrol officer, but was at least a detective in rank.

He was still a jerk, but he was a jerk with heavy responsibilities, so maybe she could be more understanding. She had no way of knowing when he was asleep, short of knocking on his door to ask him, which kind of defeated the purpose if she didn't want to disturb him when he was sleeping. She just wouldn't mow her lawn when he was at home, period. That didn't mean she wouldn't tear a strip off his rhinoceros hide whenever he disturbed *her,* because fair was fair, but she would try to get along with him. After all, they would probably be neighbors for years and years.

God, that thought was depressing.

Her mellowness and charity toward all lasted . . . oh, a couple of hours.

At seven-thirty, she settled down in her big easy chair to watch some television and read for a while. She often did both simultaneously, figuring that if anything really interesting happened on the tube, it would get her attention. A cup of green tea steamed gently at her elbow, and she antioxidized herself with an occasional sip.

A loud crash destroyed the quietness of her little neighborhood.

She surged out of the chair, sliding her feet into her sandals as she ran for the front door. She knew that sound, having heard it hundreds, thousands of times in her childhood, when her dad would take her to the test sites where she watched them crash car after car.

Porch lights were coming on up and down the street; doors were opening and curious heads were popping out like turtles peeking out of their shells. Five doors down, illuminated by the corner streetlight, was a tangle of crumpled metal.

Jaine ran down the street, her heart thumping, her stomach tightening as she braced herself for whatever she might see and tried to remember the basic first aid steps.

Other people were pouring out of their houses now, mostly elderly people, the women wearing bedroom slippers and shapeless dresses or robes, the men in their sleeveless undershirts. There were a few high-pitched, excited children's voices, the sound of mothers trying to keep their kids corralled, fathers saying, "Keep back, keep back, it might explode."

Having seen a lot of crashes, Jaine knew an explosion wasn't likely, but fire was always a possibility. Just before she reached the car in the street, the driver's side door was thrust open and a belligerent young man erupted from behind the steering wheel.

"What the *fuck!*" he yelled, staring at the crumpled front end of his car. He had rear-ended one of the cars parked along the curb.

A young woman came running from the house directly beside them, her eyes wide with horror. "Omigod, omigod! My car!"

The belligerent young man rounded on her. "This your car, bitch? What the fuck you doin' parking it in the street?"

He was drunk. The fumes hit Jaine's nose, and she moved back a step. Around her, she could hear the collective neighborhood concern changing to disgust.

"Someone go get Sam," she heard an old man mutter.

"I will." Mrs. Kulavich headed back down the street, shuffling as fast as she could in her terry-cloth bedroom slippers.

Yeah, where was he? Jaine wondered. Everyone else who lived on the street was out here.

The young woman whose car had been smashed was crying, her hands over her mouth as she stared at the wreckage. Behind her, two young children, about five and seven, stood uncertainly on the sidewalk.

"Goddamned bitch," the drunk snarled, starting toward the young woman.

"Hey," one of the older men piped up. "Watch your language."

"Fuck you, pops." He reached the crying woman and clamped a heavy hand on her shoulder, spinning her around.

Jaine started forward, pure anger flaring in her chest. "Hey, buddy," she said sharply. "Leave her alone."

"Yeah," a quavering elderly voice said from behind her.

"Fuck you, too, bitch," he said. "This stupid bitch wrecked my car."

"You wrecked your own car. You're drunk and ran into a parked car."

She knew it was a losing effort; you couldn't reason with a drunk. The problem was, the guy was just drunk enough to be aggressive and not drunk enough to be staggering. He shoved the young woman, and she stumbled backward, caught her heel on a protruding root of one of the big trees that lined the street, and sprawled on the sidewalk. She cried out, and her children screamed and began crying.

Jaine charged him, bulldozing into him from the side. The impact sent him staggering. He tried to regain his balance but instead fell on his butt, his feet in the air. He struggled up and with another lurid curse lunged for Jaine.

She dodged to the side and stuck out her foot. He stumbled, but this time managed to stay on his feet. This time when he turned, his chin was lowered, tucked close to his chest, and there was blood in his eyes. Oh, shit, she'd done it now.

She automatically fell into a boxing stance, learned from many fights with her brother. Those fights were years in the past, and she figured she was about to get stomped, but maybe she'd get in a few good punches.

She heard excited, alarmed voices around her, but they were oddly distant as she focused on staying alive.

"Somebody call nine-one-one."

"Sadie's getting Sam. He'll handle it."

"I've already called nine-one-one." That was a little girl's voice.

The drunk charged, and this time there was no evading him. She went down under his onslaught, kicking and punching and trying to block his punches all at the same time. One of his fists hit her in the rib cage, and the power behind it stunned her. Immediately they were surrounded by her neighbors, the few younger men trying to wrestle the drunk off her, the older guys helping by kicking him with their slippered feet. Jaine and the drunk rolled, and a few of the older guys were mowed down, collapsing on top of the heap.

Her head thudded against the ground, and a glancing blow stung her cheekbone. One arm was pinned by a fallen neighbor, but with her free hand she managed to grab a chunk of flesh at the guy's waist and twist it, pinching as hard as she could. He bellowed like a wounded water buffalo.

Then abruptly he was gone, lifted from her as if he weighed no more than a pillow. Dazed, she saw him slam to the ground beside her, his face mashed into the dirt as his arms were wrenched behind him and handcuffs snapped around his wrists.

She struggled to a sitting position and found herself practically nose to nose with her neighbor the jerk. "Damn it, I might have known it was you," he snarled. "I should arrest both of you on drunk and disorderly charges."

"I'm not drunk!" she said indignantly.

"No, *he's* drunk, and *you're* disorderly!"

The unfairness of his charge made her choke with rage, which was a good thing, because the words that hung in her throat probably would have gotten her arrested for real.

Around her, anxious wives were helping doddering husbands to their feet, fussing over them and checking for scrapes or broken bones. No one seemed much the worse for the fracas, and she figured the excitement would keep their hearts beating for several more years, at least.

Several women were clustered around the young woman who had been shoved down, clucking and fussing. The back of the woman's head was bleeding, and her kids were still crying. In sympathy, or maybe because they were feeling left out, a couple more kids began wailing. Sirens screeched in the distance, coming closer with every second.

Crouched beside the captive drunk, holding him down with one hand, Sam looked around in disbelief. "Jesus," he muttered, shaking his head.

The old lady from across the street, her gray hair in pin curls, leaned over Jaine. "Are you all right, dear? That was the bravest thing I ever saw! You should have been here, Sam. When that . . . that hoodlum shoved Amy down, this young lady knocked him flat on his butt. What's your name, dear?" she asked, turning back to Jaine. "I'm Eleanor Holland; I live across the street from you."

"Jaine," she supplied, and glared at her next-door neighbor. "Yeah, Sam, you should have been here."

"I was in the shower," he growled. He paused. "*Are* you all right?"

"I'm fine." She scrambled to her feet. She didn't know if she was fine or not, but she didn't seem to have any broken bones and she wasn't dizzy, so there couldn't be any major damage.

He was looking at her bare legs. "Your knee is bleeding."

She looked down and noticed that the left pocket of her

denim shorts was almost torn off. Blood trickled down her shin from a scrape on her right knee. She jerked the torn pocket the rest of the way off and pressed the cloth to her knee. "It's just a scrape."

The cavalry, in the form of two patrol cars and a fire medic truck, arrived with flashing lights. Uniformed officers began wading through the crowd, while neighbors directed the medics to the injured.

Thirty minutes later, it was all over. Wreckers had hauled the two damaged cars away, and the uniforms had hauled the drunk away. The injured young woman, kids in tow, had been taken to an emergency room to have the cut on the back of her head stitched. Minor scrapes had been cleaned and bandaged, and the elderly warriors shepherded home.

Jaine waited until the medics were gone, then peeled the huge wad of gauze and tape off her knee. Now that the excitement was over, she was exhausted; all she wanted was a hot shower, a chocolate chip cookie, and bed. She yawned as she began trudging down the street to her house.

Sam the jerk fell into step beside her. She glanced up at him, then focused straight ahead. She didn't like the look on his face or the way he loomed over her like a dark cloud. Damn, the man was big, a couple of inches, maybe three, over six feet, and with shoulders that looked a yard wide.

"Do you always jump feetfirst into dangerous situations?" he asked in a conversational tone.

She thought about it. "Yeah," she finally said.

"Figures."

She stopped in the middle of the street and turned to face him, her hands planted on her hips. "Look, what was I supposed to do, just stand there while he beat her to a pulp?"

"You might have let a couple of the men grab him."

"Yeah, well, no one *was* grabbing him, so I didn't wait around."

A car turned the corner, coming toward them. He took her arm and moved her out of the street. "You're, what, five-three?" he asked, assessing her.

She scowled at him. "Five-five."

He rolled his eyes, and his expression said, *Yeah, right.* She ground her teeth. She *was* five-five—almost. What did a tiny fraction of an inch matter?

"Amy, the woman he hurt, is a good three inches taller than you and probably outweighs you by almost thirty pounds. What made you think you could handle him?"

"I didn't," she admitted.

"Didn't what? Think? That was obvious."

I can't slug a cop, she thought. *I can't slug a cop.* She repeated that to herself several times. Finally she managed to say, in an admirably even tone, "I didn't think I could handle him."

"But you jumped him anyway."

She shrugged. "It was a moment of insanity."

"No argument there."

That did it. She stopped again. "Look, I've had it with your snide remarks. I stopped him from beating that woman to a pulp in front of her kids. Jumping him like that wasn't a smart thing to do, and I fully realize I could have been hurt. I'd do it again. Now carry your ass on down the street, because I don't want to walk with you."

"Tough," he said, and latched on to her arm again.

She had to walk, or be dragged. Since he wouldn't let her walk home by herself, she picked up her pace. The sooner they parted company, the better.

"You in a hurry?" he asked, his grip on her arm reeling her back in and forcing her to match his more leisurely stride.

"Yeah. I'm missing—" She tried to think what was on television, but drew a blank. "BooBoo's due to cough up a hair ball, and I want to be there."

"You like hair balls, huh?"

"They're more interesting than my present company," she said sweetly.

He grimaced. "Ouch."

They drew even with her house, and he had to release her. "Put ice on the knee so it won't bruise," he said.

She nodded, took a few steps, then turned back to find him still standing at the end of her walk, watching her. "Thanks for getting a new muffler."

He started to say something sarcastic, she could see it in his expression, but then he shrugged and merely said, "You're welcome." He paused. "Thank you for my new trash can."

"You're welcome." They stared at each other for a moment longer, as if waiting to see which one would start the battle anew, but Jaine put an end to the standoff by turning around and going inside. She locked the door behind her and stood for a moment, looking at the cozy, already-familiar, feels-like-home living room. BooBoo had been at the cushion again; more stuffing was strewn on the carpet.

She sighed. "Forget the chocolate chip cookie," she said aloud. "This calls for ice cream."

Six

Jaine woke up early the next morning, without benefit of clock or sun. The simple act of rolling over woke her, because every muscle in her body screamed in protest. Her ribs ached, her knee stung, her arms ached every time she moved them; even her butt was sore. She hadn't had this many aches and pains since the first time she went roller-skating.

Groaning, she eased into a sitting position and inched her legs over the side of the bed. If she felt this bad, she wondered how the old guys felt. They hadn't been punched, but the fall would have been rougher on them.

Cold was better for sore muscles than heat was, but she didn't think she was brave enough to face a cold shower. She'd rather tackle a belligerent drunk any time than stand naked under a freezing blast of water. She compromised by showering in tepid water, then gradually turned the hot water completely off. Gradually working up to the cold water didn't help; she stood it for about two seconds, then climbed out of the shower much faster than she had climbed in.

Shivering, she quickly dried off and stepped into her long, blue, front-zip robe. She seldom bothered with it during the summer, but today it felt good.

Getting up early had one advantage: she got to wake up Boo-Boo, rather than the other way around.

He didn't take kindly to having his beauty rest disturbed. The disgruntled cat hissed at her, then stalked off to find a more private place to sleep. Jaine smiled.

She didn't have to hurry that morning, since she had gotten up too early, which was good, because her sore muscles made it plain hurrying wasn't on the agenda today. She lingered over her coffee, a rare weekday treat, and instead of making do with cold cereal the way she usually did, she popped a frozen waffle into the toaster and sliced up some strawberries to go on top. After all, a woman who had been in a brawl deserved a little extra treat.

After finishing the waffle, she drank another cup of coffee and pulled up the robe to examine her scraped knee. She had put ice on it as directed, but there was still a nice large bruise, and her entire knee was stiff and sore. She couldn't loll around all day on a pile of ice packs, so she popped a couple of aspirin and resigned herself to discomfort for a couple of days.

Her first real surprise of the day came when she began dressing and put on a bra. As soon as she fastened the front hook, tightening the band around her sore rib cage, she knew the bra had to go. Standing in front of her closet, naked except for her panties, she faced another dilemma: what did a braless woman wear if she didn't want anyone to know she was braless?

Even in an air-conditioned office, the weather was too hot for her to keep a jacket on all day. She had some pretty dresses, but her nipples would be plainly outlined beneath the thin fabrics. Hadn't she read something once about Band-Aids over the nipples? Anything was worth a try. She got two Band-Aids, plastered them over her nipples, then pulled on one of the dresses and examined herself in the mirror. The Band-Aids were clearly outlined.

Okay, that didn't work. Plain surgical tape might do the trick, but she didn't have any. Besides, the dress revealed her scraped knee, and it looked gross. She peeled off the Band-Aids and went back to examining the contents of her closet.

In the end she settled on a long hunter green skirt and a white knit top that she covered with a cadet blue silk shirt. She knotted the shirttails at her waist, put on blue and green stretchy bead bracelets, and was rather impressed when she consulted her mirror.

"Not bad," she said, turning to examine the result. "Not bad at all."

Luckily her hair was no problem. It was thick and glossy, a nice dark reddish brown, and had plenty of body. Her current style was a sort of modified shag that required no more than brushing, which was good, because raising her arms made her ribs hurt. She made short work of the brushing.

But there was a bruise on her cheekbone. She scowled in the mirror and gingerly touched the small blue spot. It wasn't sore, but it was definitely blue. She seldom did a full makeup job— why waste it on work?—but today she would have to bring out the big guns.

By the time she sashayed out the door in her chic serendipitous outfit and with full battle paint in place, she thought she looked pretty damn good.

The jerk—Sam—was unlocking his car door when she stepped out. She turned and took her time locking the door behind her, hoping he would simply get into his car and leave, but no such luck.

"Are you okay?" he asked, his voice right behind her, and she nearly jumped out of her skin. Stifling a shriek, she whirled. Bad move. Her ribs protested; she gave an involuntary groan and dropped her keys.

"Damn it!" she shouted, when she could breathe again. "Stop sneaking up on me like that!"

"It's the only way I know," he said, his face expressionless. "If I waited until you turned around, I wouldn't be sneaking." He paused. "You cussed."

As if she needed him to point that out. Fuming, she dug in her purse for a quarter and slapped it in his hand.

He blinked as he looked down at the quarter. "What's this for?"

"Because I swore. I have to pay a quarter when I'm caught. That's how I'm motivating myself to stop."

"Then you owe me a hell of a lot more than a quarter. You said a couple of words last night."

She curled her lip at him. "You can't go back into the past and collect. I'd have to empty out my bank account. You have to catch me at the time."

"Yeah, well, I did. Saturday, when you were mowing your lawn. You didn't pay me then."

Silently, her teeth gritted together, she dug out another quarter.

He looked extremely smug as he pocketed his fifty cents.

Any other time she might have laughed, but she was still mad at him for scaring her. Her ribs hurt, and when she tried to stoop down to retrieve her keys, they hurt even more. Not only that, her knee refused to bend. She straightened and gave him a look of such frustrated fury that one corner of his mouth twitched. If he laughs, she thought, I'm going to kick him under the chin. Since she was still standing on her stoop, the angle was perfect.

He didn't laugh. Cops were probably taught to be cautious. He bent down to pick up her keys. "The knee won't bend, huh?"

"Neither will the ribs," she said grumpily, taking the keys and easing down the three steps.

His brows lowered. "What's wrong with your ribs?"

"He landed a punch."

He blew out an exasperated breath. "Why didn't you say something last night?"

"Why? They're not broken, just bruised."

"You know this for a fact, huh? You don't think maybe they could be cracked?"

"They don't feel cracked."

"And you have so much experience with cracked ribs you know how they feel."

She set her jaw. "They're *my* ribs, and I say they're not cracked. End of discussion."

"Tell me something," he said conversationally, strolling beside her as she stalked, as best as she was able, to her car. "Is there ever a day when you don't pick a fight?"

"The days when I don't see you," she shot back. "And you started it! I was prepared to be a nice neighbor, but you snarled at me every time you saw me, even though I apologized when BooBoo got on your car. Besides, I thought you were a drunk."

He stopped, surprise etched on his face. "A drunk?"

"Bloodshot eyes, dirty clothes, getting home in the wee hours of the morning, making a lot of noise, grouchy all the time as if you had a hangover . . . what else was I to think?"

He rubbed his face. "Sorry, I wasn't thinking. I should have showered, shaved, and dressed in a suit before I came out to tell you that you were making enough noise to raise the dead."

"Just grabbing a clean pair of jeans would have sufficed." She unlocked the Viper and began to consider another problem: how was she going to get into the low-slung little rocket?

"I'm refinishing my kitchen cabinets," he offered after a short pause. "With the hours I've been working lately, I'm having to do it a little at a time, and sometimes I fall asleep with my dirty clothes on."

"Did you ever think of leaving the cabinets until your off days and getting a little more sleep? It might help your disposition."

"There's nothing wrong with my disposition."

"No, not if it belongs to a rabid skunk." She opened the car door, stowed her purse inside, and tried to psych herself up for the effort of sliding behind the wheel.

"Hot set of wheels," he said, looking the Viper over.

"Thanks." She glanced at his Pontiac and didn't say anything. Sometimes silence was more charitable than words.

He saw the glance and grinned. She wished he hadn't done that; the grin made him look almost human. She wished they weren't standing out in the early morning sun, because she could see how dense his black eyelashes were and the rich brown striations in his dark eyes. Okay, so he wasn't a bad-looking man, when his eyes weren't red and he wasn't snarling.

Suddenly his eyes went cold. He reached out and gently rubbed his thumb along her cheekbone. "You have a bruise there."

"Da—" She caught herself before the word slipped out. "Darn it, I thought I had it covered."

"You did a good job. I didn't see it until you were standing in the sun." He crossed his arms and scowled down at her. "Any other injuries?"

"Just sore muscles." She looked ruefully at the car. "I've been dreading having to get in the car."

He looked at the car, then at her as she gripped the open door and slowly, painfully lifted her right leg and eased it inside. He blew out a breath, as if steeling himself to perform an unpleasant task, and held her arm to steady her as she inched her way under the wheel.

"Thanks," she said, relieved the task was over.

"Sure." He crouched down in the open door. "You want to file charges for assault?"

She pursed her lips. "I hit him first."

She thought he might be fighting another grin. God, she hoped he won; she didn't want to see another one so soon. She might start thinking he was human.

"There is that," he agreed. He stood up and started to close the car door for her. "A massage will help the soreness. And a steam bath."

She gave him an outraged look. "Steam? You mean I had a cold shower this morning for *nothing?*"

He began laughing, and she really, really wished he hadn't done that. He had a nice deep laugh and very white teeth.

"Cold is good, too. Try alternating heat and cold to loosen up. And get a massage if you can."

She didn't think Hammerstead had a spa hidden anywhere on the premises, but she might call around and book one for this afternoon when she got off work. She nodded. "Good idea. Thanks."

He nodded and closed the door, stepping back. Lifting one hand in a wave, he walked to his car. Before he even got the door open, Jaine had the Viper purring down the street.

So maybe she could get along with him, she thought, smiling a little. He and his handcuffs had certainly come in handy the night before.

Despite lingering to talk to him, she was still early to work, which gave her time to ease out of the car. Today the sign above the elevator buttons said: FAILURE IS NOT AN OPTION; IT'S BUNDLED WITH YOUR SOFTWARE. Somehow she thought management would frown more on that than on the sign from the day before, but all the geeks and nerds on the first two floors probably thought it was hilarious.

The office gradually filled. The conversation that morning was exclusively about the article in the newsletter, split fifty-fifty between the contents and speculation about the identity of the four women. Most were of the opinion the entire article was the brainchild of the author, that the four friends were fictitious, which suited Jaine just fine. She kept her mouth shut and her fingers crossed.

"I scanned the article and sent it to my cousin in Chicago," she overheard someone say as he walked past in the hallway. She was fairly certain he wasn't talking about an article in the *Detroit News.*

Great. It was spreading.

Because she winced at just the thought of having to get into and out of the car several times to go to lunch, she made do with peanut butter crackers and a soft drink in the snack room. She could have asked T.J. or one of the others to bring her back something for lunch, but didn't feel like going into explanations of why she had problems getting into her car. Saying she tackled a drunk would sound like bragging, when in truth she had simply been too angry to think about what she was doing.

Leah Street entered and took her neatly packed lunch out of the refrigerator. She had a sandwich (turkey breast and lettuce on whole wheat), a cup of vegetable soup (which she heated in the microwave), and an orange. Jaine sighed, torn between hate and envy. How could you like someone who was so organized? People like Leah, she thought, were put on earth to make everyone else look inefficient. If she had thought, she could have packed her own lunch instead of having to make do with peanut butter crackers and a diet soda.

"May I join you?" Leah asked, and Jaine felt a twinge of guilt. Since they were the only two people in the snack room, she should have asked Leah to sit down. Most people at Hammerstead would simply have sat down, but maybe Leah had been made to feel unwelcome often enough that she felt she had to ask.

"Sure," Jaine said, trying to infuse some warmth into her voice. "I'd like the company." If she were Catholic, she'd definitely have to confess that one; it was an even bigger whopper than saying her father didn't know anything about cars.

Leah got her nutritious, attractive meal arranged and sat down at the table. She took a small bite of the sandwich and chewed daintily, blotted her mouth, then ate an equally small spoonful of soup, after which she blotted her mouth again. Jaine watched, mesmerized. She imagined the Victorians must have had the same table manners. Her own manners were good, but Leah made her feel like a barbarian.

After a moment Leah said, "I suppose you saw that disgusting newsletter yesterday."

Disgusting was one of Leah's favorite words, Jaine had noticed.

"I assume you mean that article," she said, because it seemed pointless to dance around. "I glanced at it. I didn't read the entire thing."

"People like that make me ashamed to be a woman."

Well, *that* was going a little too far. Jaine knew she should leave it alone, because Leah was Leah and nothing was going to change her. But some little demon inside—okay, the same demon that always prompted her to open her mouth when she should keep it shut—made her say, "Why is that? I thought they were honest."

Leah put down her sandwich and gave Jaine an outraged look. "Honest? They sounded like whores. All they wanted in a man was money and a big . . . a big . . ."

"Penis," Jaine supplied, since Leah didn't seem to know the word. "And I don't think that was *all* they wanted. I seem to remember something about fidelity and dependability, sense of humor—"

Leah dismissed that with a wave of her hand. "Believe that if you want, but the entire point of the whole article was sex and money. It was obvious. It was also vicious and cruel, because just think how it made men who didn't have a lot of money and a big . . . thing—"

"Penis," Jaine interrupted. "It's called a penis."

Leah pressed her lips together. "Some things aren't meant to be discussed in public, but I've noticed before you have a potty mouth."

"I do not!" Jaine said heatedly. "I admit I swear sometimes, but I'm trying to stop, and *penis* isn't a dirty word; it's the correct word for a body part, just like saying 'leg.' Or do you have an objection to legs, too?"

Leah gripped the edge of the table with both hands, holding so tightly her knuckles turned white. She took a deep breath. "As I was saying, think how it made those men feel. They must think they aren't good enough, that they're somehow inferior."

"Some of them are," Jaine muttered. She should know. She had been engaged to three of the inferior ones, and she wasn't thinking about their genitals, either.

"No one should be made to feel that way," Leah said, her voice rising. She took another bite of sandwich, and Jaine saw, to her surprise, that the other woman's hands were shaking. She was genuinely upset.

"Look, I think most people who read the article thought it was funny," she said in a conciliatory tone. "It was obviously meant to be a humorous piece."

"I don't feel that way at all. It was filthy, ugly, and mean-spirited."

So much for conciliation. "I don't agree," Jaine said flatly, gathering up her trash and depositing it in a can. "I think people see what they expect to see. Someone who's mean expects others to be just as mean, the way people with dirty minds see smut everywhere."

Leah went white, then red. "Are you saying I'm dirty-minded?"

"Take it any way you like." Jaine went back to her office before their little disagreement escalated into open warfare. What was wrong with her lately? First her neighbor, and now Leah. She didn't seem able to get along with anyone, not even Boo-Boo. Of course, no one got along with Leah, so she didn't know if that should count, but she was definitely going to make a bigger effort to get along with Sam. So he rubbed her the wrong way; she had evidently been doing a good job of rubbing him the wrong way, too. The problem was, she was out of practice in getting along with men; since the breakup of her third engagement, she had been off men in a big way.

But what woman wouldn't be, with her history? Three engagements and three breakups by the time she was twenty-three wasn't a good track record. It wasn't that she was dog food; she had a mirror, and the mirror reflected a slim, pretty woman with almost-dimples in her cheeks and an almost-cleft in her chin. She had been popular in high school, so popular that she had gotten engaged to Brett, the star pitcher on the baseball team, in her senior year. But she had wanted to go to college and Brett had wanted to give baseball a shot, and somehow they had just drifted apart. Brett's baseball career had been a nonstarter, too.

Then there was Alan. She had been twenty-one, fresh out of college. Alan had waited until the night before the wedding, rehearsal night, to let her know he was in love with an ex-girlfriend and he had only gone with Jaine to prove he was really over the ex, but it hadn't worked, sorry, no hard feelings.

Sure. In your dreams, bastard.

After Alan she had eventually become engaged to Warren, but maybe she had been too gun-shy by then to truly commit herself. For whatever reason, after he asked and she said yes, they both seemed to pull back and the relationship had kind of died a slow death. They had both been grateful to finally bury the thing.

She supposed she could have gone ahead and married Warren, despite the lack of heat on both their parts, but she was glad she hadn't. What if they had had children, then split? If she ever did have children, Jaine wanted it to be in a solid marriage, the kind her parents had.

She had never thought the demise of her engagements was her fault; two had been mutual decisions, and one had definitely been Alan's fault, but . . . was something wrong with her? She didn't seem to inspire lust, much less devotion, in the men she had dated.

She was jerked out of her unhappy thoughts when T.J. stuck her head in the office door. T.J. looked pale.

"A reporter for the *News* is here talking to Dawna," she blurted. "God, you don't think—?"

T.J. looked at Jaine; Jaine looked at T.J.

"Ah, hell," Jaine said in disgust, and T.J. was so upset she didn't even demand her quarter.

That night, Corin stared at the newsletter, reading and rereading the article. It was filth, pure filth.

His hands were shaking, making the little words dance. Didn't they know how this hurt? How could they *laugh?*

He wanted to throw the newsletter away, but he couldn't. Anguish gnawed at him. He couldn't believe he actually worked with the people who had said all these hurtful things, who mocked and terrorized—

He took a deep breath. He had to control himself. That was what the doctors said. Just take the pills, and control yourself. And he did. He had been good, very good, for a long time now. Sometimes he even managed to forget himself.

But not now. He couldn't forget now. This was too important. *Who were they?*

He needed to know. He had to know.

seven

It was like having the Sword of Damocles hanging over her head, Jaine thought gloomily the next morning. It hadn't dropped yet, but she knew it would. The "when" depended on how long it took Dawna to spill the beans that she had gotten the list from Marci. Once Marci's identity was known, they might as well all start wearing signs that said, "I'm guilty."

Poor T.J. was worried sick, and if Jaine had been married to Galan Yother, she would probably have been worried sick, too. How could something that had been innocent fun between four friends have turned into something that might break up a marriage?

She hadn't slept well, again. She had taken more aspirin for her sore muscles, soaked in a hot tub, and by the time she went to bed, she was feeling much more comfortable. Fretting about that darn article kept her awake long past her usual bedtime, and woke her before dawn. She positively dreaded getting the morning paper, and as for going to work—she would rather wrestle another drunk. On loose gravel.

She drank coffee and watched the sky lighten. BooBoo had evidently forgiven her for waking him again, because he sat beside her washing his paws and purring whenever she absently scratched behind his ears.

What then happened wasn't her fault. She was standing at the sink rinsing out her cup when the kitchen light in the house across the way flicked on and Sam walked into view.

She stopped breathing. Her lungs seized, and she stopped breathing.

"Sweet baby Jesus," she croaked, and managed to inhale.

She was seeing more of Sam than she had ever thought she would; everything, in fact. He stood in front of the refrigerator, stark naked. She barely had time to admire his buns before he took a bottle of orange juice from the fridge, twisting off the top and tilting it to his mouth as he turned around.

She forgot all about his buns. He was more impressive coming—no pun intended—than he was going, and that was saying something, because his butt was severely cute. The man was hung.

"My God, BooBoo," she gasped. "Take a look at that!" The fact was, Sam looked pretty damn good all over. He was tall, lean in the waist, hard-muscled. She wrenched her gaze north just a little and saw that he had a nice, hairy chest. She already knew he had a good face, if a bit battered. Sexy dark eyes, white teeth, and a good laugh. And he was hung.

She pressed a hand to her chest. Her heart was doing more than pitter-pattering; it was trying to sledgehammer its way through her sternum. Other parts of her body were joining in the excitement. In a moment of insanity, she thought about running right over to audition as his mattress.

Oblivious of the tumult going on inside her, as well as the heart-stopping view across the way, BooBoo continued licking his feet. His priorities were obviously a real mess.

Jaine gripped the sink to keep from folding in a limp heap on the floor. It was a good thing she was off men, or she really might have charged across the two driveways and right up to his kitchen door. But off men or not, she still appreciated art, and her neighbor was a work of art, hovering somewhere between classic Grecian statue and porn star.

She hated to do it, but she had to tell him to close his curtains; it was the neighborly thing to do, right? Blindly, not wanting to miss a moment of the show, she reached for the phone, then paused. Not only did she not know his number, she didn't even know his last name. Some neighbor she was; she had lived here two and a half weeks and still hadn't introduced herself to him, though if he was any kind of a cop, he had found out her name. Of course, *he* hadn't rushed over to introduce himself, either. If it hadn't been for Mrs. Kulavich, she wouldn't have known his first name was Sam.

She wasn't stymied, though. She had written down the Kulavich's phone number on the pad by the phone, and she managed to tear her gaze from the spectacle next door long enough to read it. She punched in their number, and belatedly worried that they might not be awake yet.

Mrs. Kulavich answered on the first ring. "Hello!" she chirped so enthusiastically Jaine knew she hadn't woken them.

"Hi, Mrs. Kulavich, it's Jaine Bright, next door. How are you?" Social niceties had to be observed, after all, and with the older generation that could take a while. She was hoping for ten or fifteen minutes. She watched as Sam killed the bottle of orange juice and tossed the empty.

"Oh, Jaine! It's so nice to hear from you!" Mrs. Kulavich said, as if she had been out of the country or something. Mrs. Kulavich was evidently one of those people who talked in exclamation points when she was on the phone. "We're fine, just fine! And you?"

"Fine," she answered automatically, not missing a minute of the action. Now he was getting out the milk. *Eewwh!* Surely he wasn't going to mix orange juice and milk. He opened the milk and sniffed it. His biceps bulged as his arm lifted. "My, oh, my," she whispered. Evidently the milk didn't pass muster, because he jerked his head back and set the carton aside.

"What was that?" Mrs. Kulavich said.

"Uh—I said fine, just fine." Jaine wrenched her attention from its wayward path. "Mrs. Kulavich, what is Sam's last name? I need to call him about something." That was an understatement.

"Donovan, dear. Sam Donovan. But I have his number here. It's the same number his grandparents had. I'm so glad, because that way I can remember it. It's easier to get older than it is to get wiser, you know." She laughed at her own wit.

Jaine laughed, too, though she didn't know at what. She groped for a pencil. Mrs. Kulavich slowly recited the number, and Jaine jotted it down, which wasn't easy to do without looking at what she was writing. Her neck muscles were locked in the upright position, so she had no choice but to look through the kitchen window next door.

She thanked Mrs. Kulavich and said good-bye, then took a deep breath. She had to do this. No matter how it hurt, how it would deprive her, she had to call him. She took another deep breath and dialed his number. She saw him cross the kitchen and pick up a cordless. He was standing in profile to her. Oh, wow. Double wow.

Saliva gathered in her mouth. The damn man had her all but slobbering.

"Donovan."

His deep voice was rusty, as if he wasn't truly awake yet, and the single word clipped with irritation.

"Um . . . Sam?"

"Yeah?"

Not the most welcoming of responses. She tried to swallow and found it was difficult to do when her tongue was hanging out. She reeled it in and sighed with regret. "This is Jaine, next door. I hate to tell you this, but you might want to . . . close your curtains."

He wheeled to face the window, and they stared at each other across the two driveways. He didn't dart to the side, or squat out of sight, or do anything else that might indicate embarrassment. Instead, he grinned. Damn, she wished he wouldn't do that.

"Got an eyeful, did you?" he asked as he walked to the window and reached for the curtains.

"Yes, I did." She hadn't blinked in five minutes, at least. "Thank you." He pulled the curtains together, and her whole body went into mourning.

"My pleasure." He chuckled. "Maybe you can return the favor sometime."

He hung up before she could reply, which was a good thing, because she was speechless as she closed her blinds. Mentally she smacked her forehead. *Duh!* All she would have had to do at any time was close her own blinds.

"Yeah, like I'm stupid or something," she said to BooBoo.

The image of taking her clothes off for him shook her—and excited her. What was she, an exhibitionist? She never had been in the past, but now . . . Her nipples were hard, standing out like raspberries, and as for the rest of her . . . Well. She had never gone in for casual sex, but this sudden lust for Sam the jerk, of all people, floored her. How could he go from jerk to tempting just by taking off his clothes?

"Am I so shallow?" she asked BooBoo, and considered the idea for a moment, then nodded. "You betcha."

BooBoo meowed, evidently in agreement.

Oh, dear. How could she look at Sam again without remembering how he looked naked? How could she meet him without blushing or letting him see that she had a major case of the hots for his body? She was much more comfortable having him as an adversary than she was seeing him as an object of lust. She preferred her lust objects at a safer distance . . . say, on a movie screen.

He hadn't been embarrassed, though, so why should she? They were both adults, right? She had seen naked men before. She just had never seen *Sam* naked before. Why couldn't he have had a beer belly and a shriveled wiener, instead of rock-hard abs and an impressive morning erection?

She began drooling again.

"This is disgusting," she said aloud. "I'm thirty years old, not a teenager screaming over . . . whoever it is they scream over now. I should at least be able to control my saliva glands."

Her saliva glands thought differently. Every time an image of Sam popped into her head, which was about every ten seconds—she had to enjoy the image for about nine seconds before she banished it—she would have to swallow. Repeatedly.

She had left for work early yesterday morning, when Sam had been leaving at the same time. If she left at her regular time today, he should already be gone, right?

But he'd said he was on a task force and kept irregular hours, therefore he might leave at any time. She couldn't time her departure so it didn't coincide with his; she would have to carry on as usual and keep her fingers crossed. Maybe tomorrow she would be able to face him with more composure, but not today, not with her body revved and her saliva glands working overtime. She should just forget about it and get ready for work.

She stood in front of her open closet door and found herself in a dilemma. What did one wear when she might meet her neighbor whom she had just seen naked?

Thank God for the scrape on her knee, she finally decided. It was pants or long skirts until the knee healed, which prevented her from sashaying out in the black, above-the-knee sheath with spaghetti straps that she usually wore to parties when she wanted to look sleek and sophisticated. The black sheath made a statement, something along the lines of "Look at me, don't I look sexy," but was definitely inappropriate for work. The scraped knee saved her from a major faux pas.

Better to err on the side of caution, she finally decided, and chose the most severe man-tailored pants outfit she owned. Never mind that she had always liked the way the pants clung to her butt, or that it never failed to elicit a few admiring remarks from the male contingent at work; she wasn't going to see Sam today. He had to be even more uncomfortable about what had happened than she was. If anyone avoided anyone, *he* would avoid *her.*

Would a man who was embarrassed have flashed her that wicked grin? He knew he looked good; better than good, damn it.

In an effort to get her mind off exactly how good he looked, she turned on the television to catch the morning news while she dressed and did her makeup.

She was applying cover-up stick to the bruise on her cheek-bone when the female anchor of the local morning newscast said in a chirpy voice, "Freud never found out what it is that women want. If he had talked to four area women, however, he would have known the answer to his famous question. Find out if *your* husband or boyfriend is Mr. Perfect when we return, after these messages."

Jaine was so stunned she couldn't even think of a curse word to say. Her legs suddenly weak, she sank down on the closed toi-let seat. Dawna, the bitch, must have given them up immedi-ately. No—if she had named names, the phone would have been ringing nonstop. So far they were still anonymous, but that was bound to change today.

She hurried into the bedroom and dialed T.J.'s number, silently praying that her friend hadn't yet left for work. T.J. lived farther out than Jaine did, so she left home a little earlier.

"Hello." T.J. sounded rushed, and a little irritable.

"It's Jaine. Have you seen the news yet this morning?"

"No, why?"

"Mr. Perfect made the news."

"Oh. My. God." T.J. sounded as if she might faint, or vomit, or both.

"They don't have our names yet, I don't think, since no one has called. Someone at Hammerstead will figure it out today, though, so that means by afternoon it'll be common knowledge."

"But it won't be on TV, will it? Galan always watches the news."

"Who knows?" Jaine rubbed her forehead. "I guess it depends on how slow news is today. But if I were you, I'd turn off all the phones and unplug the one that's hooked to the answering machine."

"Done," T.J. said. She paused and said bleakly, "I guess I'll find out if Galan and I have anything worth holding on to, won't I? I can't expect him to be happy about this, but I *do* expect him to be understanding. After we talked about our Mr. Perfect last week, I did some thinking, and, well . . ."

And Galan hadn't compared very favorably, Jaine thought.

"On second thought," T.J. said very quietly, "I'm not going to turn off the phones. If it's going to happen, I'd rather just get it over with."

After she hung up, Jaine hurried to finish getting ready. The quick phone call hadn't taken long, and the television commercials were just ending. The newscaster's perky voice made her flinch.

"Four area women have gone public with their list of requirements for the perfect man . . ."

Three minutes later, Jaine closed her eyes and sagged weakly against the vanity. *Three minutes!* Three minutes was an eternity of airtime. Of all the days for there to be no shootings or accidents blocking the freeways or a war, a famine—*anything* to keep such an insignificant story off the air!

The news story had stopped short of the raunchy requirements, but made sure the viewers knew they could get the List, as it was being called, and the accompanying article, in their entirety, on the station's Web site. Women and men had been interviewed for their reaction to items on the List. Everyone seemed to agree with the first five requirements, but after that opinions began to vary widely—usually with women taking one view and men the other.

Maybe if she took a week's vacation, starting immediately, this would all have blown over by the time she got back from Outer Mongolia.

But that would be the coward's way out. If T.J. needed supporting, Jaine knew she had to be there for her. Marci could also be facing the end of a relationship, but in Jaine's opinion, losing Brickhead wouldn't be much of a loss, and besides, Marci deserved some flack for spilling this whole thing to Dawna in the first place.

With dread weighting down her every step, she forced herself out to the car. As she unlocked it, she heard a door open behind her and automatically glanced over her shoulder. For a moment she stared blankly at Sam as he turned to lock his kitchen door; then memory came roaring back, and in panic she fumbled with the door handle.

Nothing like a little notoriety to make a woman forget she wanted to avoid a certain man, she thought savagely. Had he been *watching* for her?

"Are you feeling better today?" he asked as he strolled up.

"Fine." She half-tossed her purse into the passenger seat and slid under the wheel.

"Don't put it there," he advised. "When you stop at traffic lights, anyone can come up, pop the window, grab the purse, and be gone before you know what's happening."

She grabbed her sunglasses and slid them on, pathetically grateful for the protection they gave her as she dared to glance at him. "Where should I put it, then?"

"In the trunk is the safest place."

"That isn't very convenient."

He shrugged. The movement made her notice how broad his shoulders were, and that reminded her of other parts of his body. Heat began to build in her cheeks. Why couldn't he have been a drunk? Why wasn't he still wearing sweatpants and a stained, torn T-shirt, instead of oatmeal slacks and a midnight blue silk shirt? A cream-and-blue-and-crimson tie was knotted loosely at his strong throat, and he carried a jacket in one hand. That big black pistol rested in a holster against his right kidney. He looked tough and competent, and way too good for her peace of mind.

"I'm sorry if I embarrassed you this morning," he said. "I was still half-asleep and wasn't paying attention to the windows."

She managed a nonchalant shrug. "I wasn't embarrassed. Accidents happen." She wanted to leave, but he was standing so close she couldn't shut the door.

He hunkered down in the V formed by the car and the open door. "Are you sure you're okay? You haven't insulted me yet, and we've been talking"—he glanced at his watch—"about thirty seconds already."

"I'm in a mellow mood," she said flatly. "I'm saving my energy in case something important comes along."

He grinned. "That's my girl. I feel better now." He reached out and lightly touched her cheekbone. "The bruise is gone."

"No, it isn't. Makeup is a wonderful thing."

"So it is." His finger trailed down to the dent in her chin and lightly tapped it before withdrawing. Jaine sat frozen, ambushed by the abrupt realization that he was *flirting* with her, for God's sake, and her heart was doing that sledgehammer thing again.

Oh, boy.

"Don't kiss me," she said warningly, because he seemed somehow closer, though she hadn't seen him move, and his gaze was centered on her face in that intent look men get before they make their move.

"I don't intend to," he replied, smiling a little. "I don't have my whip and chair with me." He stood up and stepped back, his hand on the car door to close it. He paused, looking down at her. "Besides, I don't have time right now. We both have to get to work, and I don't like rush jobs. I'll need a couple of hours, at least."

She knew she should keep her mouth shut. She knew she should just close the car door and drive away. Instead she said blankly, "A couple of *hours?*"

"Yeah." He gave her another of those slow, dangerous smiles. "Three hours would be even better, because I figure that when I *do* kiss you, we'll both end up naked."

eight

"Oh," Jaine muttered to herself as she drove to work on autopilot, which in Detroit traffic was more than a little hazardous. "*Oh?*" What kind of snappy comeback was that? Why hadn't she said something like "In your dreams, buddy," or "My goodness, did hell freeze over while I wasn't looking?" Why hadn't she said *anything* except *oh*, for cripes sake. She could do better than that in her sleep.

She hadn't said it nonchalantly, as if she had been asking for information and the answer wasn't very interesting. No, that damn syllable had been so weak it didn't even register on the Wuss-O-Meter. Now he'd think all he had to do was waltz over to her house and she'd fall on her back for him.

The worst part of it was, he might be right.

No. No, no, no, no, *no.* She didn't do casual, and she wasn't good at serious, so that pretty much took care of the romance department. No way was she going to have a fling with the next-door neighbor, whom only yesterday—or was it the day before?—she had thought of as "the jerk."

She didn't even like him. Well, not much. She definitely admired the way he had slammed that drunk facedown on the ground. There were times when brute force was the only satisfying response; she had felt extremely satisfied, seeing the drunk smashed into the dirt and handled as easily as if he'd been a child.

Was there anything else she liked about Sam, other than his body—that was a given—and his ability to manhandle drunks? She thought for a moment. There was also something appealing about a man who refinished his cabinets, though she couldn't put her finger on exactly what it was; a touch of domestication, maybe? He definitely needed something to offset all that macho swagger. Except he didn't swagger; he strolled. He didn't have to swagger when he wore a pistol as big as a hair dryer on his belt. As far as phallic symbols went, he pretty much had that aced—not that he needed a symbol with the real deal he had right there in his pants . . .

She clenched her hands on the steering wheel, trying to control her breathing. She turned on the air-conditioning and adjusted the vents so the cold air blew on her face. Her nipples felt tight, and she knew if she checked, she'd find they were standing up like little soldiers.

Okay. What she was dealing with here was a major case of the hots. The fact was there, and she had to face it, which meant she had to be a sane, intelligent adult about this and get on birth control pills as fast as possible. Her period was due any day, which was good; she could get the pills and get started on them almost immediately. Not that she would tell *him.* The pills were just a precaution, in case her hormones overruled her gray matter. Such a silly thing had never happened before, but then she had never before practically had a meltdown at the sight of a man's sticky-out part, either.

What in hell was wrong with her? she wondered wrathfully. She'd seen sticky-out parts before. Granted, Sam's was impressive, but as an intensely curious young woman in college she'd seen a couple of porn films, flipped through the occasional *Playgirl*, so she'd seen bigger. Besides, for all the fun they'd had talking about their Mr. Perfect and how big his penis had to be, the penis wasn't nearly as important as the man to whom it was attached.

Mr. Perfect. Memory returned like a slap in the face. Damn, how could she have forgotten?

The same way she had earlier forgotten about Sam and his Mr. Happy because she'd been preoccupied with the silly newscast, that was how. As distractions, both subjects ranked right up there with, say, her house burning down.

Today should be fairly quiet, she thought. Out of the eight hundred and forty-three people who worked at Hammerstead, the odds were several of the people who knew them had seen the newscast and would guess their identities. Someone would directly ask Dawna, she would spill the rest of the beans, and the information would flash over the entire building with the speed of E-mail. But as long as that information was contained to Hammerstead, T.J. had at least a chance of keeping Galan from finding out. He didn't socialize much with his wife's coworkers, except for his obligatory attendance at the company Christmas party, where he stood around looking bored.

Surely there would be something more important that would happen today, locally if not nationally. These were the dreaded dog days of summer, when Congress wasn't in session and all the senators and representatives either had gone home or were junketing around the world, so there wasn't much national news unless there was some sort of catastrophe. She didn't want a plane to crash or anything like that, but maybe something that didn't involve loss of life could happen.

She began praying for a stomach-churning stock market dip— so long as the market began recovering by the end of the day, of course. Another roller-coaster ride before the market suddenly surged to an all-time high would be nice. That should keep the newscasters occupied long enough for Mr. Perfect to be forgotten.

As soon as she pulled up to the gate at Hammerstead, though, she saw that her expectation of a quiet day had been optimistic. Three television news vans were parked off to the side. Three scruffy-looking men with Minicams were each filming one of three individuals, a man and two women, who stood in front of the fence with Hammerstead in the background. The three reporters were spaced far enough apart that they didn't intrude on each other's shots, and they were talking earnestly into their microphones.

Jaine's stomach made a dive. She still had hope, though; the stock market hadn't opened yet.

"What's going on?" were the first words she heard when she entered the building. Two men were walking down the hall ahead of her. "What's with the TV crews? Have we been bought out or closed down, or something?"

"Didn't you watch the news this morning?"

"Didn't have time."

"Seems some of the women who work here have come up with their own definition of Mr. Perfect. All of the television stations are running it as a human-interest feature, I guess."

"So what's their definition of Mr. Perfect? Someone who always puts the lid down on the john?"

Whoops, Jaine thought. They had forgotten that one.

"No, from what I heard it was the usual Boy Scout junk: faithful and honest and helps old ladies across the street, shit like that."

"Hey, I can do that," the first man said in a tone of discovery.

"Then why don't you?"

"I didn't say I wanted to."

They laughed together. Jaine entertained herself with a wonderful fantasy of punting both of them through the door ahead, but was content with asking, "Are you saying you're unfaithful? What a winner!"

They both looked around as if startled to see her there, but they had to have heard the door opening and someone walking behind them, so she didn't fall for the innocent act. She knew their faces but not their names; they were junior management types, late twenties or early thirties, spiffed up in their French blue dress shirts and conservative ties.

"Sorry," the first man said in insincere apology. "We didn't see you."

"Right," she said, rolling her eyes. Then she caught herself; she didn't need to get involved in these conversations. Let this particular battle of the sexes be waged without her; the less attention she and the other three drew, the better for them.

In silence she and the two men strode to the elevators. There was no sign posted there today, making her feel deprived.

Marci, looking tense, was waiting for her in the office.

"I guess you saw the news," she said to Jaine.

Jaine nodded. "I called T.J. and gave her a heads-up."

"I can't tell you how sorry I am this has happened," Marci said, lowering her voice as someone walked by the open door.

"I know," Jaine said, sighing. There wasn't any point in staying pissed at Marci; what was done was done. And this wasn't the end of the world, not even for T.J. If Galan found out about it and went so ballistic that he and T.J. ended up divorced, then the marriage wasn't very strong anyway.

"Dawna gave them my name," Marci continued. "The phone drove me nuts all morning. All the stations want interviews, and so does the *News*." She paused. "Did you see the article this morning?"

Jaine had totally forgotten about the morning paper; the peep show next door had been too distracting. She shook her head. "I haven't read the paper yet."

"It was actually pretty cute. It was in the section where they always put recipes and things like that, so maybe not many people read it."

That was good to hear; it was being treated as human interest rather than news, and a lot of people never read what was still thought of as the "women's section." Unless an animal was involved, or a baby, human-interest stories tended to fade fast. This one had already lived past its natural life span.

"Are you going to talk to them? The news people, I mean."

Marci shook her head. "No way. If it was just me, yeah, I'd have a little fun—so what if Brick gets his drawers in a wad? But with you guys involved, it's different."

"T.J.'s the one with the big worry. I thought about it yesterday, and I don't have anything to lose if my name gets out there, so don't fret about me. Luna didn't seem worried, either. But T.J.—" Jaine shook her head. "That's a problem."

"Big time. Personally, I don't think it would be much of a loss if she and Galan split, but I'm not her, and she probably thinks the same about Brick." Marci grinned. "Shit, most of the time *I* think the same about him."

No argument there, Jaine thought.

Gina Landretti, who also worked in payroll, entered the office. Judging from the way her eyes lit when she saw Marci and Jaine talking, the penny had dropped. "Hey," she said, a big grin spreading across her face. "It's you! I mean, you're the four friends. I should have realized when I read Marci's name, but it just now clicked. The other two are that pretty girl in sales and the one in human resources, right? I've seen you go to lunch together."

There was no point in denying it. She and Marci looked at each other, and Jaine shrugged.

"This is so cool!" Gina enthused. "I showed the newsletter to my husband yesterday, and he got really pissed when he got to number eight on the list, like he isn't always turning around to look at women with big boobs, you know? I had to laugh. He still isn't speaking to me." She didn't look very worried.

"We were just having fun," Jaine said. "This has gotten out of hand."

"Oh, I don't think so. I think it's great. I told my sister in New York about it, and she wanted a copy of the whole article, not just the little bit that was in this morning's paper."

"Your sister?" Jaine's stomach got that sinking feeling again. "Your sister who works for one of the networks?"

"ABC. She's a staffer on *Good Morning America.*"

Marci began to look alarmed, too. "Uh—she just had a personal interest, right?"

"She thought it was hilarious. I wouldn't be surprised if you got a call from them, though. She mentioned what a great feature the List would make." Gina sailed to her desk, happy with her part in providing them with publicity.

Jaine dug a dollar out of her purse and gave it to Marci, then said four very pithy words.

"Wow." Marci looked impressed. "I've never heard you say that before."

"I save it for emergencies."

Her phone rang. Jaine eyed it. Since it wasn't yet eight o'clock, the phone had no business ringing. There could be nothing but bad news waiting if she answered.

On the third ring, Marci scooped it up. "Payroll," she said briskly. "Oh—T.J. This is Marci. We were talking—Oh, damn, honey, I'm sorry," she said, her tone changing to helpless concern.

Jaine snatched the receiver from Marci. "What's happened?" she demanded.

"I'm outed," T.J. said bleakly. "I just picked up my voice mail messages, and there are seven calls from reporters. I bet you have the same calls on your voice mail, too."

Jaine looked at the message light. It was blinking like it had a tic.

"Maybe if Marci and I talked to them, that would keep them off you and Luna," she suggested. "All they want is a story, right? They need a face to go with the story; then it's over with and they move on to something else."

"But they have all our names."

"That doesn't mean they need four interviews. *Any* comment should satisfy them."

Marci, having followed the conversation just by listening to Jaine's end of it, said, "I can do the interviews by myself, if you think it would work."

T.J. heard Marci's offer. "It's worth a shot, I suppose. But I'm not going to run from this. If they aren't satisfied after they talk to you and Marci, or just Marci, then we'll all four sit down and give them their interview, and whatever happens will happen. I refuse to feel guilty and worried because we were having fun and made up a silly list."

"Okay," Marci said when Jaine hung up. "I'll call Luna and fill her in, and then I'll call those reporters back and set up something for lunch. I'll take all the heat, downplay it as much as I can." She crossed her fingers. "This can work."

All morning long people stuck their heads in the door and made laughing comments to her; at least, the women did. Jaine also received a couple of measuring offers, as she had expected, from two of the guys and a few sarcastic remarks from others. Leah Street gave her a horrified look and stayed far away, which suited Jaine just fine, though she expected to see a "whore of Babylon" sign appear on her desk at any time. Leah was having more problems with this than T.J., and that was saying a lot.

All the messages on her voice mail were from reporters; she deleted them and didn't return any of the calls. Marci must have been busy doing her mop-up campaign, because there weren't any additional calls after about nine. The sharks, promised some chum, were now circling Marci.

Just in case the barbarians were still at the gate, Jaine chickened out and bought her lunch from the snack room vending machines again. If the diversion didn't work and this was only the quiet before the storm, she intended to make the most of it. As it turned out, there wasn't that much quiet, because the snack room was full of people who had brought their lunches that day, including Leah Street, who was sitting alone at a table even though the other tables were crowded.

The buzz of conversation transformed into a mixture of catcalls and applause when Jaine appeared. The applause, predictably, came only from women.

There was nothing she could do but take a bow, sweeping as low as her scraped knee and sore ribs would allow. "Thank you very much," she said in her best Elvis imitation.

She fed her money into the machines and escaped as fast as possible, trying to ignore the comments of "That was so funny!" and "Yeah, you women get bitchy if some guy makes a remark about—"

The snack room quickly became a battleground with the lines drawn between the sexes.

"Damn, damn, damn," Jaine muttered to herself as she went back to her office, diet soft drink and crackers in hand. Whom did she pay when she swore only to herself? she wondered. Should she put the money in a fund to pay for future transgressions?

Lunch had long been over and the time was closing in on two when Marci called. She sounded tired. "Interviews are over," she said. "Let's see if the heat dies down."

The reporters were no longer camped at the gate when Jaine left work. She raced home to catch the local news, skidding to a stop in her driveway and slinging small gravel. She was glad Sam wasn't home, or he'd be coming out to read her the riot act.

BooBoo had been at the cushion again. Jaine ignored the clumps of stuffing scattered over the carpet and grabbed the remote, clicking on the television and sitting on the edge of her easy chair. She waited through the stock market report—no crashes or dramatic dips, damn it—the weather, and the sports. Just when she was beginning to hope Marci's interview wouldn't air, the newscaster said in a dramatic tone, "Coming up next: the List. Four local women tell what they want in a man."

She groaned and flopped back in her chair. BooBoo jumped into her lap, the first time he had done so since coming to stay with her. Automatically she scratched his ears, and he began to vibrate.

The commercials ended and the newscast resumed. "Four local women, Marci Dean, Jaine Bright, T.J. Yother, and Luna Scissum, have put together a list of desirable qualities for the perfect man. The four friends work at Hammerstead Technology, and the List, as it has become known, was the result of a recent lunchtime brainstorming session."

Wrong, Jaine thought. They'd been at Ernie's, after work. Either the reporter hadn't asked and just assumed they'd been having lunch together, or "lunchtime" sounded better than "met at a bar after work." Come to think of it, lunchtime would probably work better for T.J., since Galan didn't like those Friday after-work get-togethers.

Marci's face flashed on the screen. She was smiling, relaxed, and at the reporter's question, threw back her head for a hearty laugh.

"Who doesn't want Mr. Perfect?" she asked. "Of course, each woman would have different requirements, so what we put on our list wouldn't necessarily be on someone else's list."

Okay, that was diplomatic, Jaine thought. This was good; nothing controversial so far.

Then Marci blew it. The reporter, politically correct down to her toenails, made a comment about the shallowness of the physical requirements on the List. Marci's eyebrows arched, and she got a beady look in her eyes. Watching, Jaine could only groan, because those were Marci's warning signs before she went on the attack.

"Shallow?" Marci drawled. "I think it's honest. I think every woman daydreams about a man with, shall we say, certain generous parts, don't you?"

"You didn't edit that out!" Jaine shrieked at the television, jumping to her feet and dumping poor BooBoo to the floor. He leaped to safety barely in time, turning to glare at her. She ignored him. "This is in family time! How could you put something like that on the air?"

Ratings, that was how. With news at a premium, television stations across the country were scrambling for viewers. Sex sells, and Marci had just sold it for them.

nine

The phone rang. Jaine hesitated, debating whether or not to answer it. No more reporters should be bothering to call, since Marci had given them their story, but considering the timing, the call was probably from someone who knew her and had just heard her name on television and wanted to talk to her, as if her fifteen minutes of dubious fame could somehow rub off on him/her by association. She didn't want to rehash anything about that damn list; she just wanted it to die.

On the other hand, it might be Luna or T.J. or Marci.

She finally answered on the seventh ring, prepared to lapse into an Italian accent and pretend to be someone else.

"How could you do this to me?" her brother, David, snapped.

Jaine blinked, trying to shift gears. God, would he never get over not being given temporary custody of their dad's car? "I didn't do anything to you. It isn't my fault Dad wanted to leave the car here. I'd rather you have it, believe me, because now I have to park my car in the driveway instead of the garage."

"This isn't about the car!" he half-yelled. "That thing on television! How could you do that? How do you think it'll make me look?"

This was getting weird. She thought rapidly, trying to come up with some way this would affect David, but the only thing she could think of was perhaps he didn't meet all the list's criteria and he didn't want Valerie to know there *were* criteria. Discussing her brother's physical attributes wasn't something she wanted to do.

"I'm sure Valerie won't make any comparisons," she said as diplomatically as possible. "Uh, I have a pot boiling on the stove, and I need to—"

"Valerie?" he demanded. "What's she got to do with this? Are you saying she was in on this . . . this *list* thing?"

Weirder and weirder. She scratched her head. "I don't think I know what you're talking about," she finally said.

"That thing on television!"

"What about it? How does it affect you?"

"You gave your name! If you'd ever gotten married, you wouldn't still have 'Bright' as your last name, but no, you have to stay single, so your name is the same as mine. It isn't a real common name, in case you've never noticed! Just think of the ribbing I'm going to take at work because of this!"

This was going a bit far, even for David. His paranoia was usually much less pronounced. She loved him, but he'd never quite gotten over his conviction that the universe revolved around him. His attitude had at least been understandable when he'd still been in high school, because he was tall and handsome and had been wildly popular with the girls, but he'd been out of high school for fifteen years.

"I don't think anyone will notice," she said as carefully as possible.

"That's your problem; you never *think* before you open your big mouth—"

She didn't think now; she just did what came naturally. "Kiss my ass," she said, and slammed down the phone.

Not the most mature reaction, she thought, but a satisfying one.

The phone rang again. No way was she answering it, she thought, and for the first time wished she had Caller ID. Maybe she needed it.

The ringing went on and on. After she counted twenty, she snatched up the receiver and yelled, "What!" If David thought he could harass her like this, see what he thought when she called him at two in the morning. Brothers!

It was Shelley. "Well, you've done it now," was her sisterly opening shot.

Jaine rubbed between her eyebrows; a definite headache was forming. After the exchange with David, she waited to see where this one was going.

"I won't be able to hold up my head in church."

"Really? Oh, Shelley, I'm so sorry," Jaine said sweetly. "I didn't realize you have the dreaded Limp Neck disease. When were you diagnosed?"

"You are such a show-off. You never think of anyone but yourself. Did it ever cross your mind, *just once,* how something like this would affect me, or the children? Stefanie is mortified. All her friends know you're her aunt—"

"How do they know? I've never met her friends."

Shelley paused. "I suppose Stefanie told them."

"She's so mortified she owned up to the relation? Strange."

"Strange or not," Shelley said, regrouping, "that's a disgusting thing for you to put out there in public."

Swiftly Jaine mentally reviewed Marci's television spot. It hadn't been *that* specific. "I didn't think Marci was that bad."

"Marci? What are you talking about?"

"The spot on television. Just now."

"Oh. You mean it's on television, too?" Shelley asked in rising horror. "Oh, no!"

"If you didn't see it on television, what are *you* talking about?"

"That thing on the Internet! Stefanie got it from there."

The *Internet?* Her headache exploded into full bloom. One of the geeks at work had probably posted the newsletter article, in its entirety. Fourteen-year-old Stefanie had indeed had an education.

"I didn't put it on the Internet," she said tiredly. "Someone at work must have."

"Regardless of who did it, you're behind that . . . that list even existing!"

Suddenly Jaine was fed up past the gills; she felt as if she had been walking a tightrope for several days now, she was stressed to the max, and the people who should be most concerned and supportive were giving her hell. She couldn't take any more, and she couldn't even think of anything scathing to say. "You know," she said quietly, interrupting Shelley's harangue, "I'm tired of the way you and David automatically assume I'm to blame without even asking me how this whole thing happened. He's mad at me about the car and you're mad at me about the cat, so you attack without asking if I'm okay with all this attention about the list, which if you thought for one second, you'd know I'm not okay with it at all. I just told David to kiss my ass, and you know what, Shelley? You can kiss my ass, too." With that, she hung up on yet another sibling. Thank God, there weren't any more.

"That was me at my peacemaking, mediating best," she said to BooBoo, then had to blink away an uncharacteristic dampness in the eyes.

The phone rang again. She turned it off. The numbers in the message window on the answering machine said she had way too many messages. She deleted them without listening to any of them and went to the bedroom to get out of her work clothes. BooBoo padded in her wake.

The prospect of getting any comfort from BooBoo was dubious, but she picked him up anyway and rubbed her chin against the top of his head. He tolerated the caress for a minute—after all, she wasn't doing the good stuff, scratching behind his ears—then wiggled free and jumped lightly to the floor.

She was too tense and depressed to sit down and relax, or even eat. Washing the car would burn off some energy, she thought, and quickly changed into shorts and a T-shirt. The Viper wasn't very dirty—they hadn't had any rain in over two weeks—but she liked it to gleam. All that washing and polishing, besides burning off stress, was satisfying to her soul. She definitely needed some soul-satisfying right now.

She fumed as she collected the things she would need to make the Viper beautiful. It would serve Shelley right if Jaine took BooBoo over there and left him to destroy *her* cushions; since Shelley had new furniture—it seemed she always had new furniture—she likely wouldn't be as sanguine as Jaine about losing cushion stuffing. The only thing that kept her from transferring BooBoo was the fact that their mom had entrusted her beloved cat to *her* custody, not Shelley's.

As for David—well, it was pretty much the same situation. She would have transfered Dad's car to David's garage except for the fact her dad had asked her to take care of it, and if anything happened to it while it was in David's custody, she would feel doubly responsible. Any way she looked at it, she was stuck.

After gathering her chamois cloths, pail, special car-washing soap that wouldn't make the paint job lose its luster, wax, and window cleaner, she let BooBoo out onto the kitchen porch so he could watch the proceedings. Since cats didn't like water, she didn't think he'd be very interested, but she wanted the company. He settled in a tiny patch of late afternoon sunshine and promptly took a kitty nap.

The driveway next door was bereft of dented brown Pontiac, so she didn't have to worry about accidentally spraying the thing and arousing Sam's ire, though in her opinion, a good wash job wouldn't hurt it. Probably wouldn't *help* much, either—it was too far gone for such surface beautifying to make much difference—but a dirty car offended her. Sam's car offended her a lot.

She settled down to industriously washing and rinsing, one section at a time, so the soap didn't have time to dry and cause spots. This particular soap wasn't supposed to spot, but she didn't trust it. Her dad had taught her to wash a car this way, and she had never found a better method.

"Hey."

"Shit!" she shrieked, jumping a foot in the air and dropping her soapy cloth. Her heart nearly exploded out of her chest. She whirled, water hose in hand.

Sam jumped back as water sprayed across his legs. "Watch what the hell you're doing," he snapped.

Jaine was instantly incensed. "Okay," she said agreeably, and let him have it full in the face.

He yelped and dodged to the side. She stood braced, water hose in hand, watching as he rubbed a hand across his dripping face. The first water attack, accidental as it had been, had wet his jeans from the knees down. The second one had pretty much taken care of his T-shirt. The front of it was soaking wet, sticking to his skin like plaster. She tried not to notice the hard planes of his chest.

They faced each other like gunfighters, separated by no more than ten feet. "Are you fucking crazy?" he half-shouted.

She let him have it again. She sprayed with a vengeance,

chasing him with the stream of water as he tried to dodge and dance out of its way.

"Don't tell me I'm crazy!" she shouted, putting her finger over the nozzle to narrow the opening and thus get more force, and distance. "I've *had* it with people blaming me for everything!" She got him in the face again. "I'm so damn sick of you, and Shelley, and David, and everyone at work, and all the stupid reporters, and BooBoo shredding my cushions! I'm fed up, do you hear?"

He abruptly switched tactics, from evade to attack. He came in low, like a linebacker, not trying to evade the blast of water she aimed at him. About half a second too late, she tried to dodge to the side. His shoulder crashed into her midriff, the impact driving her back against the Viper. Quick as a snake striking, he snatched the water hose from her grip. She lunged for the hose, and he wrestled her back into place, pinning her to the Viper with his weight.

They were both breathing hard. He was soaking wet from head to toe, water leaching out of his clothes into hers until she was almost as wet as he. She glared up at him, and he glared down at her, their noses only a few inches apart.

Water was clinging to his lashes. "You sprayed me," he accused, as if he couldn't believe she had done such a thing.

"You scared me," she accused in return. "It was an accident."

"That was when you sprayed me the first time. You did it on purpose the second time."

She nodded.

"And you said 'shit' and 'damn.' You owe me fifty cents."

"I'm putting in a new rule. You can't incite me to riot, then fine me for rioting."

"You're welshing on me?" he asked in disbelief.

"You bet. It's all your fault."

"How's that?"

"You deliberately scared me, and don't try to deny it. That makes the first word your fault." She gave an experimental wiggle, trying to slide out from under the pressure of his weight. Damn, he was heavy, and about as unyielding as the sheet metal behind her.

He squelched her escape attempt by settling even more heavily against her. Water from his clothes dripped down her legs.

"What about the second one?"

"You said f—" She caught herself. "My two words added together aren't nearly as bad as your one word."

"What, they have a points system now?"

She gave him a withering look. "The point is, I wouldn't have said either word if (*a*) you hadn't scared me and (*b*) you hadn't cussed at me first."

"If we're assigning blame here, I wouldn't have cussed if you hadn't sprayed me."

"And I wouldn't have sprayed you if you hadn't scared me. See, I told you it was all your fault," she said triumphantly, tilting her chin at him.

He took a deep breath. The movement of his chest flattened her breasts even more than they already were, making her abruptly aware of her nipples. Her nipples were acutely aware of *him*. Uh-oh. Her eyes widened in sudden alarm.

He was looking down at her with an unreadable expression. "Let me go," she said, more nervous than she cared to reveal.

"No."

"No!" she repeated. "You can't say no. It's against the law to hold me against my will."

"I'm not holding you against your will; I'm holding you against your car."

"By force!"

He shrugged an admission. He didn't seem very alarmed at the prospect of violating any laws against manhandling neighbors.

"Let me go," she said again.

"I can't."

She eyed him suspiciously. "Why not?" Actually, she was afraid she knew why not. "Why not" had been growing in his wet jeans for a few minutes now. She was doing her dead level best to ignore it, and from the waist up—except for her rebellious nipples—she was mostly succeeding. From the waist down, she was an abject failure.

"Because I'm going to do something I'll regret." He shook his head, as if he didn't understand it himself. "I still don't have a whip and chair, but what the hell, I'll risk it."

"Wait," she squeaked, but it was too late.

His dark head dipped.

The late afternoon spun away. From somewhere up the street she heard a child shriek with laughter. A car drove by. The faint sound of hedge clippers drifted to her ears. All of that seemed very far away and disconnected from reality. What was real was Sam's mouth on hers, his tongue tangling with hers, the warm male scent of his body in her nostrils and filling her lungs. And his taste—oh, his taste. He tasted like chocolate, as if he had just eaten a Hershey bar. She wanted to devour him.

She realized she was clutching fistfuls of wet cotton fabric. One at a time, without breaking the kiss, he peeled her hands off his shirt and tucked them around his neck, allowing him to settle more completely against her, from knee to shoulder.

How could just a kiss arouse her so totally? But it wasn't just a kiss; he used his entire body, rubbing his chest against her nipples until the friction made them stand out, hard and aching, moving the bulge of his erection against her stomach with a slow, subtle rhythm that was nevertheless as powerful as a sea surge.

Jaine heard the wild, smothered sound that erupted from her throat, and she tried to climb him, tried to get high enough to position that bulge where it would do the most good. She was burning hot, dying with heat, half-mad from the sudden on-slaught of sexual need and frustration.

He was still holding the water hose in one hand. He locked both arms around her and lifted her the few inches needed. The stream of water arced wildly, splattering BooBoo and making him jump up with an outraged hiss, then splashing against the car and wetting them even more. She didn't care. His tongue was in her mouth, and her legs were wrapped around his hips and that bulge was right where she wanted it.

He moved—another of those subtle, rolling thrusts—and she damn near climaxed right there. Her nails bit into his back, and she made a guttural sound, arching in his arms.

He tore his mouth free from hers. He was panting, the expression in his eyes hot and wild. "Let's go inside," he said, the words so low and rough they were almost unintelligible, not much more than a growl.

"No," she moaned. "Don't stop!" Oh, God, she was close, so close. She arched against him again.

"Jesus Christ!" He closed his eyes, his expression savage with lust barely restrained. "Jaine, I can't fuck you out here. We have to go inside."

Fuck? Inside?

Oh my God, she was about to do it with him and she wasn't on the pill yet!

"Wait!" she yelled in panic, pushing against his shoulders, uncoiling her legs from around his hips and kicking wildly. "Stop! Let me go!"

"*Stop?*" he said in outraged disbelief. "You said 'don't stop' just a second ago."

"I changed my mind." She was still pushing on his shoulders. She was still accomplishing exactly nothing.

"You can't change your mind!" He sounded desperate now.

"Yes, I can."

"Do you have herpes?"

"No."

"Syphilis?"

"No."

"Gonorrhea?"

"No."

"AIDS?"

"No!"

"Then you can't change your mind."

"What I have is a ripe egg." That was probably a lie. Almost positively a lie. She would probably start her period tomorrow, so the little ovum was long past viability, but she didn't take chances with potential offspring. If any life was left in the bundle of DNA, Sam's sperm would jump-start it. Some things were just a given.

The ripe-egg news gave him pause. He thought about it. Offered: "I can use a condom."

She gave him a withering look. At least, she hoped it withered him. So far, he was remarkably unwithered. "Condoms have only about a ninety to ninety-four percent success rate. That means, at best, their fail rate is six percent."

"Hey, those are good odds."

Another withering look. "Oh, yeah? Can you imagine what would happen if even *one* of your little marauders jumped my girl?"

"They'd tie up and fight like two wildcats in a sack."

"Yeah. Like we just did."

He looked horrified. He released her and stepped back. "They'd be in the sack before they even introduced themselves."

"We've never introduced *our*selves," she felt compelled to point out.

"Shit." He rubbed a hand over his face. "I'm Sam Donovan."

"I know who you are. Mrs. Kulavich told me. I'm Jaine Bright."

"I know. She told me. She even told me how you spell your name."

Now, how on earth had Mrs. Kulavich known that? "It was supposed to be Janine," she explained. "But the first *n* got left off the birth certificate form, and Mom decided she liked it that way." Jaine wished she had been a Janine. "Shelley," "David," "Janine"; the names all fit. Jaine was a wild card, the odd one out.

"I like 'Jaine' better," he said. "It suits you. You aren't a Janine."

Yeah, she thought morosely. That was the problem.

"So what's this problem you're having with . . . who was it? Oh, yeah. Shelley, David, everyone at work, the reporters, and BooBoo. Why are you having trouble with reporters?"

She was impressed by his memory. *She* couldn't have rattled off a list of names that had been shouted at her while she was being sprayed with cold water.

"Shelley is my older sister. She's mad at me because Mom asked me to baby-sit BooBoo and she wanted the honor herself. David's my brother. He's mad at me because Dad asked me instead of David to baby-sit his car. You know who BooBoo is."

He looked over her shoulder. "He's the cat on your car."

"On my—" She whirled in horror. BooBoo was pussyfooting across the Viper's hood. She snatched him off before he had time to evade, and indignantly returned him to the house. Then she rushed back to the Viper and bent down to inspect the hood for even the tiniest scratch.

"Don't guess you like a cat on your car either," Sam said smugly.

She tried out another withering look on him, though she had noticed the egg news had done a good job of withering him anyway. "There's no comparison between my car and yours," she growled, then gave the empty driveway a startled look. No brown Pontiac. But here was Sam. "Where *is* your car?"

"The Pontiac isn't mine. It belongs to the city."

She felt weak with relief. Thank God. It would have been a serious blow to her self-esteem if she'd slept with the owner of that wreck. On the other hand, maybe she needed the Pontiac as a mental brake on her sexual impulses. If it had been sitting there, the preceding episode probably wouldn't have gotten so out of hand.

"Then how did you get home?" she asked, looking around.

"I keep my truck parked in the garage. Keeps the dust and pollen and bird deposits off it."

"Truck? What kind of truck?"

"Chevy."

"Four-wheel drive?" He looked like a four-wheel-drive kind of guy.

He gave her a superior sneer. "Is there any other kind?"

"Oh, man," she sighed. "Can I see it?"

"Not until we finish our negotiations."

"Negotiations?"

"Yeah. About when we're going to finish what we just started."

Her mouth fell open. "You mean you aren't going to let me see your truck until I agree to have sex with you?"

"You got it."

"You're crazy if you think I want to see your truck that bad!" she shouted.

"It's red."

"Oh, man," she whined.

He crossed his arms. "Put up or shut up."

"Don't you mean 'put out'?"

"I said we'd negotiate a date. I didn't say we'd do it now. You couldn't pay me to go anywhere near your egg."

She gave him a speculative look. "I'll show you my power plant if you'll show me your truck."

He shook his head. "No deal."

She never told anyone about her dad's car. For all her friends knew, he was simply paranoid about the family sedan. But it was a bargaining chip to top all bargaining chips, the ace in the hole, the guaranteed result-getter. Besides, Sam was a cop; it probably wouldn't hurt to have him in the loop, so he would know that her garage needed protecting at all times. The car was insured for a fortune, but it was also irreplaceable.

"I'll let you see my dad's car if you let me see your truck," she said slyly.

Despite himself, he looked interested. Probably her expression told him that her dad's car was out of the ordinary.

"What kind is it?"

She shrugged. "I don't say the words out in public."

He leaned down and offered his ear to her. "Whisper them."

She put her mouth against his ear and felt faint from the warm male scent that wafted to her nostrils again. She whispered two words.

He straightened so abruptly he bumped her nose. "Ouch!" She rubbed the aching tip.

"Let me see it," he said hoarsely.

She crossed her arms, mimicking his earlier position. "Do we have a deal? You see my dad's car, and I see your truck?"

"Hell, you can *drive* my truck!" He turned and looked at her garage as if it were the Holy Grail. "It's in there?"

"Safe and secure."

"It's an original? Not a kit?"

"Original."

"Man," he breathed, already striding to the garage.

"I'll get the key." She dashed inside for the key to the padlock, and returned to find him waiting impatiently.

"Be careful and open the door just enough to slide through," she cautioned. "I don't want it seen from the street."

"Yeah, yeah." He took the key from her and inserted it in the padlock.

They entered the dark garage, and Jaine fumbled for the light switch. The overheads came on, illuminating the low-slung, tarp-covered hump.

"How did he get it?" Sam asked in a half whisper, as if he were in church. He reached for the edge of the tarp.

"He was on the development team."

He gave her a sharp look. "Your dad is Lyle Bright?"

She nodded an admission.

"Man," he sighed, and lifted the tarp.

A low moan broke from his throat.

She knew how he felt. She always felt a little breathless herself when she looked at the car, and she had grown up with it.

It wasn't particularly flashy. The automobile paints back then hadn't had the shine of today's paints. It was a kind of silvery gray, spare, without the luxuries so taken for granted by today's consumer. There wasn't a cup holder in sight.

"Man," he said again, bending to look at the instrumentation. He was careful not to touch the car. Most people, ninety-nine out of a hundred, couldn't have resisted. Some would have been brash enough to swing a leg over the low frame and slide into the driver's seat. Sam treated the car with the reverence it deserved, and an odd sensation squeezed her heart. She felt a little light-headed, and everything in the garage began to fade out of focus except for his face. She concentrated on breathing, blinking fast, and in a moment the world clicked back into place.

Wow. What was that all about?

He re-covered the car as tenderly as a mother covers a sleeping infant. Wordlessly he fished his keys out of his jeans pocket and held them out to her.

She took them, then looked down at her clothes. "I'm wet."

"I know," he replied. "I've been looking at your nipples."

Her mouth fell open, and she quickly clamped her hands over the pertinent portions of her wet T-shirt. "Why didn't you say something?" she demanded hotly.

He made a scoffing noise in the back of his throat. "What, you think I'm crazy?"

"It would serve you right if I drove your truck without changing clothes!"

He shrugged. "After you let me see this, plus your nipples, I guess I owe you."

She started to argue that she hadn't *let* him see her nipples, that he had looked without her permission; then she remembered that she had seen a lot more than his nipples that morning and decided not to bring up the subject.

Like he was going to give her the choice. "Besides," he pointed out, "you saw my cock. That has to be worth more points than nipples."

"Hah," she said. "Value is in the eye of the beholder. And I *did* tell you to cover up, if you'll remember."

"After you'd watched for how long?"

"Only long enough to call Mrs. Kulavich and get your number," she said self-righteously, because it was the truth. So what if she'd had to chat with Mrs. Kulavich for a minute? "And *you* didn't seem to think it was important enough to cover up. No, you waved it around like you were starting a race with it."

"I was enticing you."

"You were not! You didn't know I was looking."

He arched an eyebrow.

She threw the keys back at him. "I wouldn't drive your truck now if you begged me! It probably has cooties in it! You lech, you disgusting . . . disgusting *penis-waver*—"

He fielded the keys with one hand. "Are you saying you weren't enticed?"

She started to tell him she hadn't felt even a twinge of enticement, but her tongue refused to utter what would have been the biggest lie of her life.

He smirked. "Thought so."

There was only one way to recover the upper hand. Jaine put her hands on her hips, letting her nipples thrust against the thin wet layers of bra and T-shirt. Like a laser-guided missile, his gaze homed in on the front of her shirt. She saw him swallow.

"You don't play fair," he said thickly.

She smirked in retaliation for his smirk. "Remember that," she said, and turned to leave the garage.

He slipped past her. "I go first," he said. "I want to see you stepping into the sunlight."

Her hands clamped back in position over her breasts.

"Spoilsport," he muttered, and slid sideways through the narrow opening. He stepped back inside so abruptly she collided with him.

"You have two problems," he said.

"I do?"

"Yeah. First, you left the water on. You're going to have a hell of a water bill."

She sighed. The driveway must be awash by now. Sam had obviously driven her insane, or she would never have been so careless.

"What's the second problem?"

"Your yard is full of those reporters you mentioned."

"Oh, shit," she moaned.

ten

am handled the situation. He left the garage, locking the padlock behind him so no particularly nosy reporter could peek inside and see her—though she rather thought he was protecting the car more than he was her. She listened at the door as he walked over to the Viper and said, "Excuse me, but I need to get to that faucet to turn off the water. Would you move, please." He was extraordinarily polite. Jaine wondered why he was never that polite when he was talking to *her.* Of course, his tone was such that it was more of an order than a request, but still . . .

"What can I do for you guys?"

"We want to interview Jaine Bright about the List," a strange voice said.

"I don't know a Jaine Bright," Sam lied.

"She lives here. According to public records, she bought this house a few weeks ago."

"Wrong. I bought this house a few weeks ago. Damn, there must have been an error when the deed was registered. I'll have to get this straightened out."

"Jaine Bright doesn't live here?"

"I told you, I don't know a Jaine Bright. Now, if you guys don't mind, I need to get back to washing my car."

"But—"

"Maybe I should introduce myself," Sam said, his tone suddenly soft. "I'm Detective Donovan, and this is private property. You're trespassing. Do we need to continue this discussion?"

Evidently they didn't. Jaine stood motionless as engines started and cars departed. It was a miracle the reporters hadn't heard her and Sam talking in the garage; they must have been talking among themselves, or they would have. Certainly she and Sam had been so engrossed in their own conversation they hadn't heard the reporters arrive.

She waited for Sam to come unlock the garage. He didn't. She heard water splashing and tuneless whistling.

The jerk was washing her car.

"You had better be doing it right," she said between clenched teeth. "If you let the soap dry, I'll skin you alive."

Helplessly she waited, not daring to yell and bang on the door in case a reporter was still lurking. If any of them had half a brain, they'd know that while Sam *might* be able to squeeze into the Viper, no way would he spend that kind of money to buy a car he'd have to drive with his knees jammed up around his ears. Vipers weren't made for tall, linebacker types. He was better suited to a truck. She thought of the red Chevy four-wheel drive and began to pout. She had almost bought one, before the Viper won her over.

She wasn't wearing her wristwatch, but she estimated it was over an hour, closer to an hour and a half, before he unlocked the door. Twilight was deepening into night and her T-shirt was dry, that was how long she had stood impatiently waiting to be freed.

"You took your sweet time," she hissed as she stalked out of the garage.

"You're welcome," he said. "I finished washing your car, then I waxed and buffed it."

"Thank you. Did you do it right?" She rushed over to the car, but there wasn't enough light left to tell if there were any streaks.

He didn't take umbrage at her lack of faith. Instead he said, "Want to tell me about the reporters?"

"No. I want to forget the whole thing."

"I don't think that's going to happen. They'll be back as soon as they check the records and find out I own the house next door, which will be first thing in the morning."

"I'll be at work by then."

"Jaine," he said, and this time he used his cop tone of voice.

She sighed and sat down on the porch steps. "It's that stupid list."

He settled beside her and stretched out his long legs. "What stupid list?"

"About the perfect man."

He came to attention. "*That* list? The one that was in the paper?"

She nodded.

"You wrote it?"

"Not exactly. I'm one of the four friends who came up with the list. All this hullabaloo about it is an accident. No one was ever supposed to see the list, but it got into the newsletter at work and it's even on the Internet, and everything has snow-balled from there." She folded her arms on top of her drawn-up knees and rested her head on them. "It's a mess. There must be no other news at all for the list to be getting this kind of attention. I've been praying for a stock market crash."

"Bite your tongue."

"Just a temporary one."

"I don't get it," he said after a minute. "What's so interesting about the list? 'Faithful, nice, employed.' Big deal."

"There's more than what was in the newspaper," she said miserably.

"More? What kind of more?"

"You know. More."

He thought about it, then said cautiously, "*Physical* more?"

"Physical more," she agreed.

Another pause. "How much more?"

"I don't want to talk about it."

"I'll just look it up on the Web."

"Fine. You do that. I don't want to talk about it."

His big hand settled on the nape of her neck and squeezed. "It can't be that bad."

"Yes, it can. T.J. might end up divorced because of this. Shelley and David are both mad at me because I'm making them look bad."

"I thought they were mad about the cat and the car."

"They are. They're using the cat and the car as a springboard to get even angrier about the list."

"They sound like pains in the ass to me."

"But they're family, and I love them." She hunched her shoulders. "I'll go get your money."

"What money?"

"For the cuss words."

"You're gonna pay me?"

"It's the only honorable thing to do. But now that you know the new rule about making me swear, this is the only time I'll

pay you when it's your fault. Seventy-five cents, right? Two earlier, then one when you saw the reporters."

"Sounds about right."

She went inside and dug out seventy-five cents. She was out
of quarters; she had to pay him off in dimes and nickels. He was
still sitting on the step when she returned, but he stood up to
drop the change in his pocket. "Are you going to invite me in,
maybe cook dinner for me?"

She snorted. "Get real."

"Yeah, that's what I thought. Okay, then, do you want to go
grab a bite to eat?"

She thought about it. There were definite pros and cons to
accepting. The obvious benefit was not having to eat alone, if
she had felt like going to the trouble of preparing something,
which she didn't. The biggest con was spending more time with
him. Spending time with Sam could be dangerous. The only
thing that had saved her earlier was that they hadn't been in a
private place. If he got her alone in his truck, there's no telling
what would happen. On the other hand, she *would* get to ride in
the truck . . .

"I'm not asking you to solve the meaning of life," he said ir-
ritably. "Do you want to grab a burger or not?"

"If I go, you can't touch me," she warned.

He held up both hands. "I swear. I've already said you
couldn't pay me to go anywhere near that sperm-eating egg of
yours. So when are you going on the pill?"

"Who said I was?"

"I'm saying you'd better."

"You stay away from me and you won't have to worry about
it." No way would she tell him she'd already planned to go on
the pill. She had forgotten to call the clinic today, but that
would be her first call in the morning.

He grinned. "You talk a good game, babe, but it's the bottom of the ninth and I'm ahead ten to nothing. The only thing left for you to do is lie down."

If any other man had said that to her, she'd have handed him his ego in shreds. The best she could do now was delay him. "Am I still at bat?"

"Yeah, but it's two down and a three-oh count."

"I can still hit a home run."

"Not likely."

She growled at his disparagement of her resistance. "We'll see about that."

"Oh, hell. You're making this a contest, aren't you?"

"You're the one who started it. Bottom of the ninth and you're ahead ten to nothing, my ass."

"That's another quarter."

" 'Ass' isn't a cuss word."

"Says who—" He stopped himself and heaved a big sigh. "Never mind. You sidetracked me from the subject. *Do you want to go get something to eat or not?*"

"I'd rather have Chinese than a burger."

Another sigh. "Fine. We'll eat Chinese."

"I like that place on Twelve Mile Road."

"All right," he yelled.

She gave him a brilliant smile. "I'll go change."

"So will I. Five minutes."

Jaine hurried into the house, well aware that he was hurrying as well. He didn't think she could change in five minutes, did he? She'd show him.

She stripped to the skin as she raced to the bedroom. Boo-Boo trailed after her, meowing plaintively. It was long past his dinnertime. She pulled on a pair of dry panties, hooked herself into a dry bra, pulled a red short-sleeved knit top over her head, jerked on a pair of white jeans, and stepped into sandals. She ran back into the kitchen and opened a can of food for BooBoo, dumped it into his plate, grabbed her purse, and was out the door just as Sam jumped off his kitchen porch and headed to his garage.

"You're late," he said.

"I am not. Besides, you only had to change clothes. I changed clothes *and* fed the cat."

He had a modern garage door. He pressed the button on the control in his hand, and it slid up like oiled silk. She sighed, assailed by a bad case of garage-door envy. Then, in the light that came on automatically when the door opened, she saw the gleaming red monster. Chrome twin pipes. Chrome roll bar. Tires so big she would have had to vault into the seat if he hadn't also had chrome bars to aid those not blessed with his length of leg.

"Oh," she breathed, and clasped her hands. "This is just what I wanted until I saw the Viper."

"Bench seats," he said, and lifted a wicked eyebrow at her. "If you're really good, after you get on the pill and your eggs are under control, I'll let you seduce me in the truck."

She managed not to react. Thank God he didn't realize how tenuous her self-control really was, though it was the thought of seducing him rather than the location that revved her up again.

"Nothing to say?" he asked.

She shook her head.

"Oh, damn," he said as he put both hands around her waist and effortlessly lifted her into the cab. "Now I'm worried."

Marci's plan hadn't worked. T.J. faced the inevitable after the third reporter called. God, why didn't this thing just go away? What was so fascinating about a funny list? Not that Galan would think it was at all funny, she thought, depressed. He didn't seem to think anything was funny anymore, unless it was something that happened at work.

He had been so much fun when they were dating, full of laughter and jokes. Where had that cheerful boy gone?

They didn't even see each other much anymore. She worked eight to five, he worked three to eleven. By the time he got home, she was asleep. He didn't get up until after she had left for work. The most telling thing, she thought, was that he didn't *have* to work the three to eleven shift. He had chosen it. If his intention had been to get away from her, she thought, he had accomplished his aim.

Maybe their marriage was already over and she simply hadn't faced the fact. Maybe Galan didn't want to have children because he knew it was on the rocks.

The thought made her chest hurt, deep inside. She loved him. Rather, she loved the person she knew he was, inside the surly exterior that was all she had seen for the past few years. If she were sleepy or thinking of something else and he popped into mind, the face she saw was the young, laughing Galan, the one she had loved so desperately in high school. She loved the clumsy, fumbling, eager, loving Galan who had made love to her, the first time for both of them, in the back of his dad's Oldsmobile. She loved the man who had brought her a single red rose on their first anniversary because he couldn't afford a dozen.

She didn't love the man who hadn't said "I love you" in so long she couldn't remember the last time.

T.J. felt so helpless, compared to her friends. If anyone tried to give Marci guff, she blew him off and looked for someone to fill his shoes—or rather, her bed. Luna was upset over Shamal, but she didn't sit at home waiting for him; she carried on with her life. And as for Jaine—Jaine was complete in a way T.J. knew she herself wasn't. Whatever life handed her, Jaine faced with humor and guts. Not one of the three would take the grief from Galan that she had been silently enduring for over two years.

She hated her own weakness. What would happen if she and Galan split? They would have to sell the house, and she loved her house, but so what? She could live in an apartment. Jaine had lived in one for years. T.J. could live alone, though she never had. She would learn to handle everything herself. She would get a cat—no, a dog, for protection. And she would date again. What would it be like to spend time with a man who didn't insult her every time he opened his mouth?

When the phone rang, she knew it was Galan. Her hand was steady when she lifted the receiver.

"Have you lost your mind?" were his first words. He was breathing heavily, telling her he had worked himself into a rage.

"No, I don't believe so," she said calmly.

"You've made me a laughingstock here at the plant—"

"If anyone is laughing, it's because you let him," she interrupted. "I'm not going to talk to you about it on the phone. If you want to talk to me *in a civil tone* when you get home, I'll wait up for you. If you intend to rant and rave, I have better things to do than listen to you."

He hung up on her.

Her hand was shaking a little now as she replaced the receiver. Tears blurred her eyes. If he thought she would beg him for forgiveness, he was sadly mistaken. She had lived the last two years on Galan's terms and been miserable. Maybe it was time she lived her life on *her* terms. If she lost Galan, at least she could hold on to her self-respect.

The phone rang again half an hour later.

T.J. frowned as she went to answer it. She didn't think Galan was likely to call back, but maybe he'd thought about what she said and realized she wasn't going to roll over and play dead this time when he raised his voice.

"Hello," she said.

"Which one are you?"

She frowned at the ghostly whisper. "What? Who is this?"

"Are you Ms. A? B? Which one are you?"

"Get a life," snapped the new T.J., and she slammed down the phone.

eleven

J aine jumped out of bed early the next morning, determined to leave for work before Sam was stirring. While her heartbeat accelerated with excitement at the thought of sparring with him again, her head told her he had likely pulled up the list on the Web last night after they returned home from pigging out on small Chinese doughnuts. He was worse than a pit bull in not letting go of anything, and he had bugged her about the rest of the list the entire time they were eating. She did *not* want to know his thoughts on anything after number seven on the list.

She was on her way out the door at the ungodly time of seven A.M. when she saw that her answering machine was full of messages again. She started to hit the delete button, but hesitated. With her parents traveling, anything could happen: one of them could become ill, or there might be some other sort of

123

emergency. Who knows? Shelley or David might even have called to apologize.

"Fat chance," she muttered as she hit the play button.

There were messages from three reporters, one print and two television, requesting interviews. Two hang-ups, back-to-back. The sixth call was from Pamela Morris, who introduced herself as Gina Landretti's sister. Her voice had the mellow, modulated tones of a television announcer as she informed Jaine she would *love* to book her on *Good Morning America* to talk about the List, which was absolutely *sweeping* the country. The seventh message was from *People* magazine, requesting the same.

Jaine fought down rising hysteria as she listened to three more hang-ups. Whoever it was waited for a long time, silently, before hanging up. Idiot.

She cleared the calls; she had no intention of returning any of them. This whole situation had moved beyond silly into downright ridiculous.

She made it out of the driveway without sight of Sam, which meant her morning was off to an even-tempered start. She felt so good that she tuned the radio to a country station and listened to the Dixie Chicks singing that Earl had to die. She even sang along, and wondered if Sam the cop would think Earl's death was justifiable homicide. Maybe they could even argue about it.

She knew she had it bad when the thought of arguing with Sam was more exciting than, say, winning the lottery. She had never before met anyone who not only didn't blink an eye at anything she said but could go toe-to-toe with her—verbally, that is—and not break a sweat. It was a very freeing notion, that she could say anything and he wouldn't be shocked. Sometimes she had the feeling he enjoyed rousing her temper. He was cocky—in more ways than one—and irritating, macho, smart, and sexy as hell. And he had the proper reverence for her dad's car, plus he had done a pretty good job washing and waxing the Viper.

She had to get those birth control pills, fast.

There were more reporters at the Hammerstead gates. Someone must have tipped this bunch off about what she drove, because flashbulbs began exploding as she slowed for the guard to lift the barrier arm. He grinned down at her. "Wanna take me for a test drive and see if I meet the requirements?" he asked.

"Let me get back to you," she said. "I'm already booked for the next two and a half years."

"Figures," he said, and winked.

She was so early that the puke-green hallway was empty. She was not so early, however, that some of the nerds weren't ahead of her. She paused to read the new elevator sign: REMEMBER: FIRST YOU PILLAGE, THEN YOU BURN. THOSE WHO DO NOT COMPLY WILL BE SUSPENDED FROM THE RAIDING TEAM.

There, she felt better; a day without an elevator sign was a terrible thing to endure.

She was in her office before she realized the reporters and guard hadn't upset her. They weren't important. Her battle with Sam was far more interesting, especially since they both knew where it was heading. She had never had an affair before, but she figured the one she would have with Sam would singe the sheets. Not that she intended to be too easy for him; he was going to have to fight to get her, even after she was on birth control pills. It was the principle of the thing.

Besides, frustrating him would be fun.

Gina Landretti came into work early, too. "Oh, good," she said, her eyes lighting when she saw Jaine at her desk. "I need to talk to you, and I hoped you would be in early so we wouldn't have an audience."

Jaine gave an internal groan. She could see what was coming from a mile away.

"Pam called me last night," she began. "You know, my sister. Anyway, she's been trying to get in touch with you, and guess what? She wants to book you on the show! *Good Morning America*! Isn't that exciting? Well, all four of you, of course, but I told her you were probably the spokesperson."

"Ah . . . I don't think we have a spokesperson," Jaine said, a little nonplused by Gina's assumption.

"Oh. Well, if you did, you would be it. The spokesperson."

Gina seemed so proud that Jaine cast about for a diplomatic way of saying, "No way."

"I didn't know your sister was a program booker."

"Oh, she isn't, but she spoke to the booker and *she's* very interested, too. This would be a feather in Pam's cap," Gina confided. "The word is out the other networks will probably contact you today, so Pam wanted to get the jump on them. This could really help her career."

Meaning that if she, Jaine, didn't cooperate, any setbacks in Gina's sister's career would be laid directly on her doorstep.

"There might be a problem," Jaine said, looking as contrite as possible. "T.J.'s husband isn't happy with all this publicity—"

Gina shrugged. "So only three of you go on the show. Actually, it would probably be just fine if you were the only one—"

"Luna's much prettier—"

"Well, yeah, but she's so young. She doesn't have your authority."

Great. Now Jaine had "authority."

She tried to use some of that authority and infuse her tone with firmness. "I don't know. I don't like all this publicity, either. I'd rather the whole thing just faded away."

Gina looked at her in horror. "You can't mean that! Don't you want to be rich and famous?"

"Rich, I wouldn't mind. Famous, no. And I don't see how going on *Good Morning America* would make me rich."

"You could get a book deal out of this! One of those multimillion-dollar advances, you know, like those women who wrote the book about rules."

"Gina!" Jaine half-shouted. "Reality check here! How could the List be a book, unless the preferred size of a man's penis is discussed for three hundred pages?"

"Three hundred?" Gina looked dubious. "I think a hundred and fifty would be plenty."

Jaine looked around for something against which to bang her head.

"Please, please say you'll say yes to Pam," Gina pleaded, folding her hands together in the classic supplicant pose.

In a flash of inspiration, Jaine said, "I'll have to talk to the other three. It'll be a group deal, or nothing at all."

"But you said T.J.—"

"I'll talk to the other three," she repeated.

Gina looked unhappy, but evidently recognized some of that mysterious authority she thought Jaine possessed. "I thought you'd be thrilled," she mumbled.

"I'm not. I like my privacy."

"Then why did you put the List in the newsletter?"

"I didn't. Marci got drunk and let it slip to Dawna what's-her-name."

"Oh." Gina looked even more unhappy, as if she realized Jaine was even less thrilled about the whole situation than she had previously thought.

"My whole family is mad at me about this," Jaine grumbled.

Despite her disappointment, Gina was a nice woman. She sat down on the edge of Jaine's desk, her expression changing to one of sympathy. "Why? What does it have to do with them?"

"My opinion exactly. My sister says I've embarrassed her and she won't be able to hold her head up in church, and my fourteen-year-old niece got the entire transcript off the Web, so

Shelley's angry about that, too. My brother is angry because I've embarrassed him in front of the guys where he works—"

"I don't see how, unless they've been comparing themselves in the rest room and he came up short," Gina commented, then giggled.

Jaine said, "I don't want to think about that"; then she began giggling, too. She and Gina looked at each other and burst into gales of laughter, laughing until tears welled and ruined their mascara. Sniffing, they giggled their way to the ladies' room to repair the damage.

At nine o'clock, Jaine was called into her immediate supervisor's office.

His name was Ashford M. deWynter. Every time she heard the name, she thought she was dreaming of Manderley. She dearly wanted to ask if the *M* stood for "Max," but was afraid to find out. Maybe he was playing to the illusion, but he always dressed in a very European manner and had been known to say "*shed*ule" instead of "schedule."

He was also an asshole.

Some people come by it naturally. Others work very hard at it. Ashford deWynter did both.

He didn't ask Jaine to be seated. She sat anyway, earning a frown for her presumption. She suspected the reason for this little conference and wanted to be comfortable while he chewed her out.

"Ms. Bright," he began, looking as if he smelled something distasteful.

"Mr. deWynter," she replied.

Another frown, from which she deduced it hadn't been her turn to speak.

"The situation at the gate has become untenable."

"I agree. Perhaps if you tried a court order . . ." She let the suggestion trail off, knowing he didn't have the authority to obtain one even if there was a basis for it, which she doubted. The "situation" wasn't endangering anyone, nor were the newspeople hindering the employees.

The frown became a glare. "Your facetiousness is unappreciated. You know very well this situation is your doing. It's unseemly and distracting, and people are becoming unhappy."

For "people," she thought, read "his superiors."

"How is it *my* doing?" she asked mildly.

"That vulgar List of yours . . ."

Maybe he and Leah Street had been separated at birth, she mused. "The List isn't mine, any more than it's Marci Dean's. It was a collaborative effort." What *was* it with everyone, holding her solely responsible for the List? Was it that mysterious "authority" again? If she had that kind of power, maybe she should start wielding it more often. She could make shoppers let her go to the head of the line, or have her street plowed first when it snowed.

"Ms. Bright," Ashford deWynter said in quelling tones. "Please."

Meaning, please don't take him for an idiot. He was too late; she already did.

"Your brand of humor is very recognizable," he added. "Perhaps you weren't the only one involved, but you were undeniably the chief instigator. Therefore it falls to you to rectify the situation."

Jaine might gripe about Dawna to her friends, but she wasn't about to mention anyone else's name to deWynter. He already knew the other three names. If he chose to believe the majority of the fault was hers, nothing she could say would change his mind.

"Okay," she said. "I'll go to the gate at lunch and tell them you don't appreciate all this publicity and you want them to get off Hammerstead property or you'll have them arrested."

He looked as if he had swallowed a mackerel. "Ah . . . I don't think that would be the best way to handle things."

"What do you suggest?"

Now, there was a question. His expression went absolutely blank.

She hid her relief. It would have shredded her ego if deWynter had been able to think of a workable solution when she hadn't been able to come up with even an unworkable one.

"A staffer from *Good Morning America* has called," she continued. "I'll blow her off. *People* magazine is supposed to call, too, but I just won't take the call. All that free publicity can't be good for the company . . ."

"Television? National television?" he asked weakly. He stretched his neck like a turkey. "Ah . . . it *would* be a wonderful opportunity, wouldn't it?"

She shrugged. She didn't know if it was wonderful or not, but it was undeniably an opportunity. Of course, she had just talked herself into a corner; publicity was exactly what she didn't want. She undoubtedly had a serious character defect, since she couldn't bear to let Ashford deWynter get the best of her in anything.

"Maybe you should run the idea by the powers that be," she suggested, getting to her feet. If she was lucky, someone in the upper echelons would veto the idea.

He was torn between excitement and a reluctance to let her know that he had to ask anyone at all—as if she didn't know exactly what his position was and how much authority it entailed. He was in the middle of middle management, and that was as high as his cream was going to rise.

As soon as she got back to her desk, Jaine called a war council. Luna, Marci, and T.J. all agreed to meet for lunch in Marci's office.

She explained the current status to Gina and spent the rest of the morning, with Gina's aid, dodging calls.

At lunch the four of them, fortified with a selection of crackers and diet sodas, gathered in Marci's office.

"I think we can declare the situation officially out of control," Jaine said gloomily, and filled them in on Gina's sister and the calls that had come in that morning from NBC and *People* magazine, just as Gina had predicted.

They all looked at T.J.

T.J. shrugged. "I don't see any point in trying to put out the fire now. Galan knows. He didn't come home last night."

"Oh, honey," Marci said sympathetically, reaching out to touch T.J.'s arm. "I'm so sorry."

T.J.'s eyes looked bruised, as if she had spent the night crying, but she seemed calm. "I'm not," she said. "This just brought things out in the open. He either loves me or he doesn't. If he doesn't, then he should get the hell out of my life and quit wasting my time."

"Wow," Luna said, blinking her lovely eyes at T.J. "You go, girl."

"What about you?" Jaine asked Marci. "Any trouble with Brick?"

Marci gave her wry, seen-everything-tried-most-of-it grin. "There's always trouble with Brick. Let's just say he reacted in typical Brick fashion, with a lot of yelling and a lot of beer drinking. He was still asleep when I left this morning."

They all looked at Luna.

"I haven't heard from him," she said, and grinned at Jaine. "You were right about all the measurement offers and jokes. I'm just telling all the guys that my vote was for twelve inches, but the rest of you wanted to downsize. That generally stops them cold."

When they stopped laughing, Marci said, "Okay, my giving the local guys an interview didn't do the trick. What the hell—whaddaya say we stop trying to unring the bell and have fun with this thing?"

"DeWynter is running the idea of free national publicity by the suits upstairs," Jaine said.

"Like they won't fall on this like a starving woman on a chocolate bar?" T.J. scoffed. "I'm with Marci. Let's punch up the list and *really* have some fun with it; you know, add some items to it, expand on our discussions and explanations."

David and Shelley were going to have cows, Jaine thought. Well, they probably needed the milk.

"What the hell," she said.

"What the hell," Luna seconded.

They looked at each other, grinned, and Marci whipped out her pen and pad. "We might as well get started, give them a story worth printing."

T.J. gave a rueful shake of her head. "This will really bring the crazies out of the woodwork. Did any of you get any weird calls last night? Some guy—I think it was a guy, could have been a woman—whispered, 'Which one are you?' He wanted to know if I was Ms. A."

Luna looked startled. "Oh, I got one of those. And a couple of hang-ups that I thought might be him again. But you're right; the way he was whispering, you couldn't really tell if it was a man or a woman."

"I had about five hang-ups on my answering machine," Jaine said. "I had the phone turned off."

"I went out," Marci said. "And Brick threw the answering machine against the wall, so I'm temporarily messageless. I'll pick up a new one on the way home this afternoon."

"So probably all four of us got calls from the same guy," Jaine said, feeling a little uneasy and grateful that she had a cop living next door.

T.J. shrugged and grinned. "The price of fame," she said.

twelve

Jaine grumbled to herself all the way home, though she did remember to stop at the clinic and pick up a three-month supply of birth control pills. Upper management had decided that milking the situation for all the publicity they could was nothing but good, and things had happened fast after that. On behalf of the others she had accepted an interview on *Good Morning America*, though why a morning news show would be interested when it obviously couldn't get into the racier items on the list, she couldn't fathom. Maybe it was nothing more than network one-upmanship at work. She could understand the print organizations being interested—say, *Cosmopolitan*, or even one of the men's monthlies. But what could *People* print, other than a personal slant about the four of them and the impact the list had made on their lives?

Evidently sex sold even when it couldn't be discussed.

The four of them were supposed to go to the ABC affiliate there in Detroit at the supposedly reasonable hour of four A.M., and the interview would be taped. They were to be dressed, coifed, and mascaraed before they arrived. An ABC correspondent, not Diane or Charlie, was flying to Detroit to conduct the interview, rather than have them sit on an empty set with tiny plugs in their ears, talking to the air while someone back in New York asked the questions. Having an actual live person doing the interviewing was evidently a great honor. Jaine tried to feel honored, but merely felt tired in anticipation of having to get up at two A.M. in order to dress, coif, and mascara herself.

There was no brown Pontiac in the driveway next door, no sign of life in the house.

Bummer.

BooBoo had cushion stuffing clinging to his whiskers when he greeted her. Jaine didn't even bother to glance into the living room. The only thing she could do at this point to protect what was left of her sofa was close the door so he couldn't get into the living room, but then he would transfer his frustration to some other piece of furniture. The sofa already had to be repaired; let him have it.

A sudden suspicious feeling and a trip to the bathroom told her that her period had arrived, right on schedule. She heaved a sigh of relief. She was safe from her inexplicable weakness for Sam for a few days now. Maybe she should also give up shaving her legs; no way would she embark on an affair with bristly legs. She wanted to hold him off for at least a couple more weeks, just to frustrate him. She liked the idea of Sam being frustrated.

Going into the kitchen, she peered out the window. Still no brown Pontiac, though she supposed he could be driving his truck as he had yesterday. The curtains were closed on his kitchen window.

It was difficult to frustrate a man who wasn't there.

A car pulled into her driveway, parked behind the Viper. Two people got out, a man and a woman. The man had a camera slung around his neck and carried a variety of bags. The woman carried a tote bag and was wearing a blazer despite the heat.

There was no point in trying to evade any more reporters, but no way was she allowing anyone in her stuffing-strewn living room. Going to the kitchen door, she opened it and stepped onto the porch. "Come in," she said tiredly. "Would you like some coffee? I was just about to make a fresh pot."

Corin stared at the face in the mirror. Sometimes he disappeared for weeks, months, but there he was again in the reflection, as if he had never left. He hadn't been able to work today, afraid of what would happen if he saw them in the flesh. The four bitches. How dare they make fun of him, taunt him with their List? Who did they think they were? They didn't think he was perfect, but he knew better.

After all, his mother had trained him.

Galan was at home when T.J. arrived. For a moment her stomach knotted with nausea, but she didn't allow herself to hesitate. Her self-respect was on the line.

She lowered the garage door and entered the house through the mudroom, as always. The mudroom opened into the kitchen, her beautiful kitchen, with its white cabinets and appliances and gleaming copper pots hanging on the rack over the center island. Her kitchen was right out of a decorator's book, and it was her favorite room in the entire house—not because she liked cooking, but because she loved the ambience. There was a small alcove full of ferns and herbs and small blooming flowers, filling the air with freshness and perfume. She had snuggled two easy chairs and a table into the alcove, plus an over-stuffed footstool for weary feet and tired legs. The alcove was mostly glazed glass, letting in plenty of light but repelling the heat and cold. She loved to curl up there with a good book and a hot cup of tea, especially during the winter when outside the ground was blanketed in snow but inside she was all snug and comfortable, surrounded by her perpetual garden.

Galan wasn't in the kitchen. T.J. dropped her purse and keys in their usual place on the island, kicked off her shoes, and put on a pot of water to heat for tea.

She didn't call his name, didn't go looking for him. She supposed he was in his den, watching television and nursing his grudge. If he wanted to talk to her, he could come out of his cave.

She changed into shorts and a clingy tank top. Her body was still good, though more muscular than she liked, the result of years on a girls' soccer team. She would have preferred Luna's willowy build, or Jaine's more delicate curviness, but all in all was satisfied with herself. Like most married women, though, she had gotten out of the habit of wearing formfitting clothes, usually wearing sweats during the winter and baggy T-shirts during the summer. Maybe it was time she started making the most of her looks, the way she had when she and Galan were still dating.

She wasn't accustomed to having Galan home for supper. Her evening meal was usually either delivered or something she microwaved. Guessing that he wouldn't eat even if she cooked something—boy, that would show *her* if he went hungry, wouldn't it?—she went back to the kitchen and got out one of her frozen dinners. It was low in fat and calories, so she could indulge with an ice cream bar afterward.

Galan emerged from his den while she was licking the last of the ice cream from the stick. He stood watching her, as if waiting for her to jump in with an apology so he could proceed with his rehearsed rant.

T.J. didn't oblige. Instead she said, "You must be sick, since you aren't at work."

His lips thinned. He was still a good-looking man, she thought dispassionately. He was trim, tanned, his hair only a little thinner than when he was eighteen. He always dressed well, in stylish colors and silk blends, expensive leather loafers.

"We need to talk," he said grimly.

She lifted her brows in polite query, the way Jaine would have done. Jaine could accomplish more with the lift of a brow than most people could with a sledgehammer. "You didn't have to miss work just for that."

From his expression she could see that wasn't her scripted reply. She was supposed to attach more importance to their relationship—and his temper. Well, tough.

"I don't think you realize how seriously you've damaged me at work," he began. "I don't know if I'll ever be able to forgive you for making me a laughingstock. I'll tell you one thing, though: we don't have any chance of working this out as long as you're still hanging around with those three bitches you call friends. I don't want you seeing them again, do you hear me?"

"Ah, so that's it," T.J. said in dawning realization. "You think you can use this to tell me who I can have as friends and who I can't. Okay. Let's see . . . if I give up Marci, you can give up Jason. For Luna . . . oh, how about Curt? As for Jaine—well, if I give up Jaine, you're going to have to give up Steve, at least; though, personally, I've never cared for Steve, so I think you should throw in an extra just to keep things even."

He stared at her as if she had grown two heads. He and Steve Rankin had been best buds since junior high. They went to see the Tigers during the summer and the Lions during winter. They did major male-bonding stuff. "You're crazy!" he burst out.

"That I'd ask you to give up your friends? Fancy that. If I have to, you have to."

"I'm not the one tearing our marriage apart with stupid lists about who you think is the perfect man!" he yelled.

"Not 'who,' " she corrected. " 'What.' You know, things like consideration. And faithfulness." She watched him closely when she said the last, wondering suddenly if Galan's two-year suspension of affection had a more basic reason than simply growing apart.

His gaze flickered away from her.

T.J. braced herself against the crippling pain. She pushed it into a little box and tucked it away deep inside so she could function through the next few minutes, and days, and weeks.

"Who is she?" she asked in a tone so casual she might have been asking if he had picked up the laundry.

"Who is who? What she?"

"The famous other woman. The one you're always comparing me to in your head."

He flushed and stuffed his hands in his pockets. "I haven't been unfaithful to you," he muttered. "You're just trying to change the subject—"

"Even if you haven't been physically unfaithful, which I'm not certain I believe, there's still someone you're attracted to, isn't there?"

He turned even redder.

T.J. went to the cabinet and took out a cup and a tea bag. Placing the bag in the cup, she poured boiling water on it. After a minute she said, "I think you need to go to a motel."

"T.J.—"

She lifted a hand, not looking at him. "I'm not making any hasty decisions about divorce or even separation. I meant you need to go to a motel for tonight so I can think without you around trying to turn things around and blame everything on me."

"What about that goddamn list—"

She waved a hand. "The list isn't important."

"The hell it isn't! All of the guys at work are riding me about how you like monster cocks—"

"And all you had to do was say, yeah, you had me spoiled," she said impatiently. "So the list got a little risqué. So what? I think it was pretty funny, and evidently so do most people. We're going to be on *Good Morning America* tomorrow morning. *People* magazine wants to do an interview. We decided we're going to talk to whoever asks, so the thing will die a quicker death. Some other story will come along in a few days, but until then we're going to have fun."

He stared at her, shaking his head. "You're not the woman I married," he said in heavy accusation.

"That's okay, because you're not the man *I* married."

He turned and left the kitchen. T.J. looked down at the cup of tea in her hand, blinking back tears. Well, it was out in the open now. She should have seen what was going on a long time ago. After all, who knew better than she how Galan acted when he was in love?

Brick wasn't asleep on the sofa the way he usually was when Marci got home, though his old pickup was in the driveway. She went through into the bedroom and found him stuffing clothes in a duffel. "Going somewhere?" she asked.

"Yeah," he said sullenly.

She watched him pack. He was good-looking in a beer-drinking kind of way, with too-long dark hair, an unshaven jaw, slightly heavy features, and his usual costume of tight jeans, tight T-shirt, and scuffed boots. Ten years younger than her, never good at holding down a job, oblivious of anything that didn't involve sports—let's face it, he wasn't the catch of the century. She wasn't in love with him, thank God. She hadn't been in love with anyone in years. All she wanted was company and sex. Brick provided the sex, but he wasn't much company.

He zipped up the duffel, hefted it by the handles, and brushed past her.

"Are you coming back?" she asked. "Or should I forward the rest of your stuff to wherever you're going?"

He glared at her. "Why're you asking? Maybe you got somebody else all lined up to take my place, huh? Somebody with a ten-inch dick, just the way you like."

She rolled her eyes. "Oh, jeez," she muttered. "Lord save me from injured male egos."

"You wouldn't understand," he said, and to her surprise, she detected a note of hurt in his rough voice.

Marci stood blinking as Brick stormed out of the house and slammed into his truck. He slung gravel as he peeled out of the driveway.

She was astounded. Brick, hurt? Whoever would have thought?

Well, either he would be back or he wouldn't. She gave a mental shrug and opened the box containing her new answering machine, deftly hooking it up. As she recorded an outgoing message, she wondered how many calls she had missed because Brick had thrown the other answering machine against the wall. Even if he had bothered to answer the phone, he wouldn't have taken any messages for her, not in the mood he was in.

If there was anything important, she thought, they would call back.

She had barely completed the thought when the phone rang. She lifted the receiver. "Hello."

"*Which one are you?*" whispered a ghostly voice.

thirteen

Jaine cracked open one eye and glared at the clock, which was emitting an extremely annoying high-pitched beeping sound. Finally recognizing it as the alarm—after all, she'd never heard it at two A.M. before—she reached over and slapped it. She snuggled down in the renewed silence, wondering why in hell the alarm had gone off at that ungodly hour.

Because she had set it to go off at that ungodly hour, that was why.

"No," she moaned to the dark room. "I can't get up. I've only been in bed four hours!"

She got up anyway. She had had the presence of mind before going to bed to prepare the coffeemaker and set the timer for 1:50. The smell of coffee drew her, stumbling, to the kitchen.

She turned on the overhead light, then had to squint her eyes against the glaring brightness.

"Television people are aliens," she mumbled as she reached for a cup. "Real humans wouldn't do this on a regular basis."

With one cup of coffee in her, she managed to make it into the shower. As the water poured down on top of her head, she remembered that she hadn't intended to wash her hair. Since she hadn't factored in the time to wash and dry her hair when she calculated the time to get up, she was now officially behind schedule. She groaned and leaned against the wall. "I can't do this."

A minute later, she talked herself into trying. She rapidly shampooed and loofahed herself, and three minutes later jumped out of the shower. With another cup of coffee steaming close to hand, she blow-dried her hair, then used a dab of hair gloss to smooth down the flyaway tendrils. When one got up so early, makeup was necessary to cover the automatic look of horror and sheer disbelief; she applied it with a fast but lavish hand, going for the glamorous, just-left-a-party look. What she got was closer to a hangover look, but she wasn't wasting any more time on a hopeless cause.

Don't wear white or black, the television lady had said. Jaine put on a long, narrow black skirt, figuring the lady had meant to avoid black on her top half, which was what would be seen. She paired a scoop-neck, three-quarter-length-sleeved red sweater with the black skirt, cinched a black belt around her waist, and slipped her feet into black pumps at the same time as she was fastening classic gold hoops in her ears.

She glanced at the clock. Three A.M. Damn, she was good at this!

She would bite her tongue off before she ever admitted it.

Okay, what else? Food and water for BooBoo, who was staying out of sight. Smart kitty, she thought.

That little chore taken care of, she let herself out at five after three. The driveway next door was still empty. No brown Pontiac sat there, nor had she heard any other vehicle enter the driveway during the night. Sam hadn't come home.

He probably had a girlfriend, she thought, gritting her teeth. *Duh!* She felt like an idiot. Of course he had a girlfriend. Men like Sam always had a woman or two, or three, on their strings. He hadn't been able to get anywhere with her, thanks to her lack of birth control, so he had simply buzzed on over to the next flower in line.

"Jerk," she growled as she got into the Viper. She should have remembered her past experiences in the relationship wars and not let herself get so excited. Evidently her hormones had overruled her common sense and she had become drunk on ovarian wine, the most potent, sanity-destroying substance in the universe. In short, she had taken one look at his naked body and gone into heat.

"Forget about that," she muttered to herself as she drove the dark, quiet residential streets. "Don't think about it." Sure. Like she was going to forget the sight of that joystick of his waving proud and free.

She felt like crying at the thought of having to give up that awe-inspiring, mouthwatering erection when she hadn't even had a crack at it yet, but pride demanded. She refused to be one of a crowd in a man's head, much less his bed.

His only excuse, she thought, was if he was lying in a hospital somewhere, too badly injured to dial a telephone. She knew he hadn't been shot or anything; that would have been in the news, if a cop had been wounded. Mrs. Kulavich would have told her if he'd been in a traffic accident. No, he was alive and well, somewhere. It was the where that was the problem.

Just to cover all bases, she tried to work up a teeny bit of worry over him, but all she could manage was a heartfelt desire to maim him.

She knew better than to lose her head over a man. That was what was so humiliating: she *knew* better. Three broken engagements had taught her that a woman needed to keep her wits about her when dealing with the male species, or she could get seriously hurt. Sam hadn't hurt her—not much, anyway—but she had been on the verge of making a really stupid mistake and she hated to think she was so gullible.

Damn him, why couldn't he at least have called?

If she had a lock of his hair, she thought, she could put a curse on him, but she was willing to bet he wouldn't let her anywhere near him with a pair of scissors.

She entertained herself with thinking up imaginative curses just in case she did manage to get some of his hair. She particularly liked the one that gave him a bad case of wilt. Hah! Let him see how many women were impressed when his joystick became a joyless noodle.

On the other hand, maybe she was overreacting. One kiss did not a relationship make. She had no claim on him, his time, or his erections.

Like hell she didn't.

Okay, so much for logic. She had to go with her gut feeling here, because it wasn't allowing room for anything else. Her feelings for Sam were way out of the norm, composed of almost equal parts fury and passion. He could make her angrier, faster, than anyone else she had ever known. He also hadn't been far off the mark with his assertion that when he kissed her, they would both end up naked. If he had chosen his location better, if they hadn't been standing in her driveway, she wouldn't have regained her senses in time to stop him.

While she was being honest with herself, she might as well admit that she was exhilarated by their conflicts. With all three of her fiancés—in fact, with most people—she had held herself back, pulled her verbal punches. She knew she was a smart-ass;

Shelley and David had both gone out of their way to tell her so. Her mother had tried to get her to temper her responses and had partially succeeded. All through school she had struggled to keep her mouth shut, because the lightning-quick workings of her brain left her schoolmates bewildered, unable to keep up with her thought processes. Nor did she want to hurt anyone's feelings, which she had quickly learned she could do just by speaking her mind.

She treasured her friendships with Marci, T.J., and Luna because, as different as they all were, the other three accepted and weren't intimidated by her more caustic remarks. She felt the same sort of relief in her dealings with Sam, because he was as much of a smart-ass as she was, with the same verbal agility and speed.

She didn't want to give that up. Once she admitted that, she realized she had two choices: she could walk away, which had been her first inclination, or she could teach him a lesson about . . . about trifling with her affections, damn it! If there was one thing she didn't want anyone trifling with, it was her affections. Well, okay, there were two things—she didn't want anyone trifling with the Viper, either. But Sam . . . Sam was worth fighting for. If he had other women in his head and bed, then she would simply have to oust them, and make him pay for putting her to the trouble.

There. She felt better now. Her course of action was decided.

She arrived at the television station faster than she had anticipated, but then there wasn't much traffic on the freeways and streets that early in the morning. Luna was already there, climbing out of her white Camaro, looking as fresh and rested as if this were nine in the morning instead of not quite four. She was wearing a gold silk wrap dress that made her cream-and-coffee skin glow.

"This is spooky, isn't it?" she said when Jaine joined her and they walked to the back door of the station, as they had been instructed.

"Weird," Jaine agreed. "It's unnatural for anyone to be awake and functioning at this hour."

Luna laughed. "I'm certain everyone else on the road was up to no good, because why else would they be out?"

"Drug dealers and perverts, every one of them."

"Prostitutes."

"Bank robbers."

"Murderers and wife-beaters."

"Television personalities."

They were still laughing when Marci drove up. As soon as she joined them she said, "Did you see all the weirdos on the street? They must come out at midnight or something."

"We've already had that conversation," Jaine said, grinning. "I guess it's safe to say none of us is a party animal, crawling home in the wee hours of the morning."

"I've done my share of crawling," Marci said cheerfully. "Until I got tired of shoe prints on my hands." She looked around. "I can't believe I'm here before T.J.; she's always early, and I'm usually late."

"Maybe Galan had a tantrum and told her she couldn't come," Luna suggested.

"No, she would have called if she wasn't coming," Jaine replied. She checked her watch: five before four. "Let's go inside. They might have coffee, and I need a steady supply if I'm going to be coherent."

She had been in a television station before, so Jaine wasn't surprised by the cavernous space, the darkness, the snaking cables all over the floor. Cameras and lights stood like sentinels over the set, while monitors watched over everything. There were people around, jean-and-sneaker clad, plus one woman wearing a chic peach suit. She came toward them with a bright, professional smile on her face and her hand outstretched.

"Hello, I'm Julia Belotti, with *GMA*. I assume you're the

Ladies of the List?" She laughed at her own joke as she shook hands all around. "I'll be doing your interview. But aren't there four of you?"

Jaine refrained from making a show of counting noses and saying, "No, I think there are only three of us." That was smart-ass stuff, the sort she typically held back.

"T.J. is late," Marci explained.

"T.J. Yother, right?" Ms. Belotti wanted to show she had done her homework. "I know you're Marci Dean; I caught the local bit that was aired." She looked at Jaine, her gaze assessing. "You are . . .?"

"Jaine Bright."

"The camera is going to love your face," Ms. Belotti said, then turned with a smile to Luna. "You must be Luna Scissum. I must say, if Ms. Yother is as attractive as the rest of you, this will be a real hit. You do know the buzz your List is getting in New York, don't you?"

"Not really," Luna said. "We're surprised at all the attention it's been getting."

"Be sure and say something to that effect when we're taping," Ms. Belotti instructed, checking her watch. A tiny frown of annoyance began to pleat her brow; then the door opened and T.J. entered, her hair and makeup flawless, her dress a rich blue that flattered her warm coloring.

"Sorry I'm late," she said, joining the little group. She didn't offer any excuse, just the apology, and Jaine gave her a sharp look, seeing the fatigue under the makeup. They all had a good reason for looking fatigued, considering the hour, but T.J. had added stress.

"Where is the ladies' room?" Jaine asked. "I'd like to check my lipstick, if there's time, then find a cup of coffee if there is any."

Ms. Belotti laughed. "There's always coffee in a television

station. The ladies' room is this way." She directed them down a hallway.

As soon as its door swung shut behind them, everyone turned to T.J. "Are you all right?" Jaine asked.

"If you're asking about Galan, yeah, I'm all right. I sent him to a motel last night. Of course, he may have called his girlfriend to join him, but that's his choice."

"Girlfriend!" Luna echoed, her eyes widening in shock.

"Son of a bitch," Marci said, leaving it to T.J. to decide if she was calling Galan that or just using it as an expletive.

Jaine said, "He doesn't have much leverage now to use against you on this list thing, does he?"

T.J. laughed. "None, and he knows it." She looked at their concerned faces. "Hey, I'm okay. If he wants out of the marriage, I'd rather know now before I waste more time trying to keep things going. Once I decided that, I stopped worrying."

"How long has he been having an affair?" Marci asked.

"He swears he isn't, that he hasn't been physically unfaithful. Ask me if I believe that."

"Oh, sure," Jaine said. "I believe the sun rises in the west, too."

"He might be telling the truth," Luna put in.

"Possible, but not likely," Marci said with the voice of experience. "Whatever they admit to is only the tip of the iceberg. It's human nature."

T.J. checked her lipstick. "I don't think it makes much difference. If he's in love with someone else, then what does it matter whether or not he's slept with her? Anyway, forget about him. I am; if there's any making up to do, he'll have to be the one to do it. I'm going to play this list thing up as big as it'll get. And if there's any sort of book offer, I say we go for it. We might as well get some money for all the trouble we've been through."

"Amen to that," Marci said, and added, "Brick left. His feelings were hurt."

They gaped at that, trying to imagine Brick with feelings.

"If he doesn't come back," she complained, "I'll have to do the dating thing again. Man, I hate the thought of that. Going out dancing, letting men buy me drinks . . . it's awful."

They were laughing as they left the ladies' room. Ms. Belotti was waiting for them. She directed them to the coffee urn, where someone had procured four mugs for them. "We have a small set ready for taping whenever you get settled," she said, a subtle way of telling them to shut up and sit down. "The soundman needs to get you miked and sound-checked, and the lighting has to be adjusted. If you'll come this way . . ."

Their purses were stashed out of sight, and coffee mugs in hand, they settled on a set decorated to look like a cozy living room, with a sofa and two easy chairs, a couple of fake ferns, a discreet lamp that wasn't turned on. A guy who looked about twenty years old began attaching tiny microphones to them. Ms. Belotti clipped on her own microphone to the lapel of her jacket.

None of them had been intelligent enough to wear a jacket. Luna's gold wrap dress was okay, as was the collar-bone skimming neckline of T.J.'s dress. Marci wore a sleeveless, mockturtleneck sweater, which meant the only place the microphone could be attached was right on her throat. She would have to be very careful moving her head or the resulting noise would blot out everything else. Then the soundman looked at Jaine's red scoop-neck sweater, and said, "Uh-oh."

Jaine grinned and held out her hand. "I'll clip it on. Do you want it to the side or right in the middle?"

He grinned back at her. "I'd like it right in the middle, thanks."

"No flirting," she admonished as she slipped the mike under her sweater and clipped it to her neckline, between her breasts. "It's too early."

"I'll be good." With a wink, he taped the cord to her side,

then returned to his equipment. "Okay, I need all of you to talk, one at a time, so I can check the sound."

Ms. Belotti began an easy conversation, asking if they were all from the Detroit area. When the sound was duly checked and the cameras were set, Ms. Belotti looked at the producer, who then did the countdown, pointed to her, and she went smoothly into the lead-in comments about the famous—"or infamous, depending on your point of view"—List that had swept the country and was being discussed over breakfast tables in every state. Then she introduced them in turn, and said, "Do any of you have a Mr. Perfect in your lives?"

They all laughed. If only she knew!

Luna nudged Jaine's knee with her own. Taking the cue, Jaine said, "No one is perfect. We joked at the time that the list is really science fiction."

"Science fiction or not, people are taking it seriously."

"That's up to them," Marci put in. "The qualities we listed are *our* ideas of what would make the perfect man. A group of four other women would probably come up with different qualities, or list them in a different order."

"You do know that feminist groups are outraged at the physical and sexual requirements on the List. When women have struggled so long not to be judged by their looks or bust size, they feel you have damaged their position by judging men according to their physical attributes."

Luna raised one perfect eyebrow. "I thought part of the feminist movement was to give women the freedom to be honest about what they want. We listed what we want. We were honest." This line of questioning was her cup of tea; she thought political correctness was an abomination and never hesitated to say so.

"We also never thought the List would become public," T.J. put in. "Its release was accidental."

"You would have been less honest if you had known the List would be published?"

"No," Jaine cracked. "We would have upped the requirements." What the hell; why not have fun with it, as T.J. had suggested?

"You said you didn't have a Mr. Perfect in your life," Ms. Belotti said smoothly. "Do you have a man at all?"

Well, that little dig had been slipped in with the ease of an expert, Jaine thought, wondering if the slant of the interview was to paint them as women who couldn't keep a man. Grinning a little, she had to admit that, given all their circumstances, the slant was pretty damn accurate. But if Ms. Belotti wanted a little controversy, why not give it to her? "Not really," she said. "Not many men can measure up."

Marci and T.J. laughed. Luna restricted herself to a smile. From offstage came a quickly smothered snicker.

Ms. Belotti turned to T.J. "I understand you're the only one of the group who is married, Ms. Yother. What does your husband think about the List?"

"Not much," T.J. admitted cheerfully. "Any more than I liked it when he would turn around to ogle large breasts."

"So this is a bit of tit for tat?"

Too late she realized her choice of words wasn't the best in the world. "More tit than tat," Marci said gravely. Good thing the interview was taped instead of live.

"The thing is," Luna said, "most of the requirements are qualities all people should have. Number one was faithfulness, remember? If you're in a relationship, you should be faithful. Period."

"I've read the entire article about the List, and, if you're honest, you'll admit that most of your conversation wasn't about the qualities of faithfulness or dependability. The most intense discussion was about a man's physical characteristics."

"We were having fun," Jaine said calmly. "And we aren't crazy; of course we want men who look good to us."

Ms. Belotti checked her notes. "In the article, you aren't identified by name. You're listed as *A, B, C,* and *D.* Which of you is *A?*"

"We don't intend to divulge that," Jaine said. Beside her, she felt Marci straighten a little.

"People are very interested in who said what," Marci said. "I've had anonymous phone calls asking which one I am."

"So have I," T.J. put in. "But we aren't going to say. Our opinions weren't unanimous; one might have felt more strongly about a particular point than the other three did. We want to protect our privacy on that front."

Another poor choice of words. When their laughter died down, Ms. Belotti turned once more to the personal. "Are you dating anyone?" she asked Luna.

"No one exclusively." Take that, Shamal.

She looked at Marci. "And you?"

"Not at the moment." Take that, Brick.

"So only Ms. Yother is in a relationship. Do you think this means you might be too exacting in your requirements?"

"Why should we lower our standards?" Jaine asked, eyes flashing, and the interview went downhill from there.

"God, I'm sleepy," T.J. said, yawning, when they left the studio at six-thirty. Ms. Belotti had plenty of material to edit down for the short piece that would actually be aired. At one point she had abandoned her notes and passionately argued the feminist point of view. Jaine doubted any morning television show could use even a fraction of what had been said, but the studio crew had been fascinated.

Whatever was used, it was supposed to be aired next Monday. Maybe then all the interest would die down. After all, how long could the List be discussed? People had lives to lead, and the List had already long outlived its allotted fifteen minutes.

"Those phone calls worry me a little," Marci said, frowning at the bright, cloudless morning sky. "People are weird. You never know whose chain we're pulling."

Jaine knew one person whose chain she hoped to pull. If some of what she had said was aired, Sam would probably take it as a personal challenge. She certainly hoped he did—because that was exactly how she had meant it.

fourteen

O kay," Marci said when they had been served their coffee and given their orders at the diner where they had all stopped for breakfast, "tell us about Galan."

"Nothing much to tell," T.J. replied, shrugging. "He was at home yesterday when I got home. He began with a demand that I give up my friends—three in particular, and guess who *they* are. I countered with a demand that he give up one of his friends for each one of mine I had to give up. Then—I guess it was feminine intuition, because all of a sudden I wondered if he'd been so cold for the past two years because of another woman."

"What's wrong with him?" Luna demanded indignantly. "Doesn't he have any idea how lucky he is to have you?"

T.J. smiled. "Thanks for the vote. I'm not giving up, you

know. We might be able to work this out, but I'm not going to let it destroy me if we don't. I did some heavy thinking last night, and this isn't all Galan's fault. I'm not Mrs. Perfect any more than he's Mr. Perfect."

"*You* haven't been seeing another man," Jaine said pointedly.

"I didn't say we were *equally* at fault. If he's interested in keeping our marriage going, he has a lot of making up to do. But I have some things to make up to him, too."

"Like what?" Marci asked.

"Oh . . . I haven't exactly let myself go, but neither have I made any special effort to attract him. I've also been caving in to everything he says in an effort to please him, and let's face it, on the surface that sounds good for him, but if he wants an equal partner, then it must be maddening. I bounce ideas off you guys the way I used to do with him, but now it's as if I keep all the interesting parts of myself away from him. I give him the cook and housekeeper instead of the lover and partner, and that isn't good for a marriage. No wonder he got bored."

"Do you know how typical that is?" Jaine said, her tone shaded with indignation. "Whatever happens, women take the blame for it." She stirred her coffee, glaring into the cup. "I know, I know, sometimes we need to. I hate being wrong, damn it."

"That's a quarter," said three voices.

She dug in her purse for the change, but came up with only forty-six cents. She laid a dollar on the table instead. "One of you can make change for the other two. I need to stock up on change again. Sam wiped me out."

There was a long pause, with three pairs of eyes trained on her. Finally Luna said delicately, "Sam? Who's Sam?"

"You know. Sam. My neighbor."

Marci pursed her lips. "Would this be the same neighbor who turned out to be a cop but whom you've described at various times as a jerk, a drunk, a drug dealer, a bottom-feeding son of a bitch, a hulk who hasn't seen a razor or a shower in this millennium—"

"Okay, okay," Jaine said. "Yeah, it's the same guy."

"And you're now on a first-name basis with him?" T.J. asked, amazed.

Jaine's face heated. "Kind of."

"Oh my god." Luna's eyes were huge. "She's blushing."

"This is scary," Marci said, and the three pairs of eyes blinked in astonishment.

Jaine squirmed in the booth, feeling her face get even hotter. "It isn't my fault," she blurted defensively. "He has a red truck. A four-wheel drive."

"I can see where that would make a big difference," T.J. said, studying the ceiling.

"So he isn't *that* big a jerk," Jaine muttered. "So what? Actually, he is a jerk, but he has his good points."

"And the best one is in his pants, right?" quipped Marci, who, like a honey badger, always went straight for the groin.

Luna displayed a shocking lack of decorum by making a whooping sound and saying, *Dive! Dive! Dive!* just like in a submarine war movie.

"Stop it!" Jaine hissed. "I haven't done that!"

"Oh-ho!" T.J. leaned closer. "Just what *have* you done?"

"Exactly one kiss, smarty, and that's all."

"One kiss does not a blush make," Marci said, grinning. "Especially not on *your* face."

Jaine sniffed. "Obviously you've never been kissed by Sam, or you wouldn't make such an erroneous statement."

"That good, huh?"

She couldn't help the sigh that heaved out of her lungs, or the way her lips curved. "Yeah. That good."

"So how long did it last?"

"I told you, we haven't had sex! It was just a kiss." Like the Viper was just a car, and Mount Everest was just a hill.

"I meant the kiss," Marci said impatiently. "How long did it last?"

Jaine drew a blank on that. She hadn't exactly timed it, and besides, there had been a lot of other stuff going on, like an impending but ultimately denied climax, that had occupied most of her attention. "I don't know. Five minutes or so, I guess."

They all sat there blinking at her. "Five minutes?" T.J. asked weakly. "One kiss lasted five minutes?"

There went that damn blush again; she could feel it creeping up her face.

Luna slowly shook her head in disbelief. "I hope you're on birth control pills, because you're definitely in the red zone. He could score at any time."

"That's what *he* thinks, too," Jaine said, and scowled. "As it happens, I renewed my prescription yesterday."

"Evidently he isn't the only one who thinks it," T.J. cracked, and broke into a big grin. "Hey, this is something to celebrate!"

"You're all acting as if I was a lost cause."

"Let's just say that your social life sucked," Marci said.

"It did not."

"When was the last time you had a date?"

She had her there, because Jaine knew it had been a long time, so long she couldn't say exactly when. "So I don't date much. It's by choice, not necessity. My track record in picking men isn't exactly outstanding, remember."

"So what's different about this Sam cop person?"

"A lot," Jaine said vaguely, remembering him naked. After a moment of reverie she shook herself back to reality. "Half the time I want to strangle him."

"And the other half?"

She grinned. "I want to tear his clothes off."

"Sounds like the basis of a good relationship to me," Marci said. "That's certainly more than I had with Brick, and I kept him around for a year."

Jaine was relieved to have the topic shift away from Sam. How could she explain what she didn't understand herself? He was maddening, they rubbed sparks off each other, and he hadn't come home at all the night before. She should be running in the opposite direction instead of trying to plot ways to get him all for herself.

"What did he say?"

"Not much, which was surprising. When Brick's mad, he's about as reasonable as a two-year-old having a tantrum." Marci propped her chin on her folded hands. "I admit, he took me off guard. I was prepared for yelling and cussing, but not hurt feelings."

"Maybe he cares more than you thought," Luna said, but even she sounded dubious.

Marci snorted. "What we had was convenient for both of us, but not exactly the affair of the century. What about you? Have you heard from Shamal?" Marci's change of subject indicated she was as ready to abandon the subject of Brick as Jaine had been to talk about someone else other than Sam.

"As a matter of fact, I did." Luna looked thoughtful. "He was . . . I don't know . . . kind of impressed with all the publicity. As if I were suddenly a more valuable person, if you know what I mean. He asked me out for dinner, instead of saying he'd stop by the way he always has before."

A little pool of silence engulfed the booth. They all looked at each other, uneasy at Shamal's sudden change of attitude.

Luna's expression was still thoughtful. "I said no. If I wasn't interesting enough for him before, then I'm not interesting enough now."

"Way to go," Jaine said, immensely relieved. They exchanged

high fives all around the booth. "So what now? Is Shamal officially in the past, or are you in a holding pattern?"

"A holding pattern. But I'm not calling him again; if he wants to see me, he can do the dialing."

"But you turned him down," Marci pointed out.

"I didn't tell him to get lost; I just told him no, I had other plans." She shrugged. "If we're to have any kind of relationship, the ground rules are going to have to change, meaning I get to make some of them instead of playing everything his way."

"We're a mess," Jaine said, sighing, and sought refuge in her cup of coffee.

"We're normal," T.J. corrected.

"That's what I said."

They were giggling when the waitress brought their orders and plopped the plates in front of them. Their love lives were, collectively, a disaster, but so what? They had scrambled eggs and hash browns to make them feel better.

Because it was Friday, they kept to their tradition of eating at Ernie's after work. Jaine found it difficult to believe only a week had passed since they had so lightheartedly composed the List. In a week, a lot had changed. For one thing, the atmosphere at Ernie's: when they walked in, there was a round of applause and a chorus of boos. Some women, undoubtedly the outraged feminist contingent, joined in the booing.

"Can you believe this?" T.J. muttered as they were seated. "If we were prophets, I'd say we were about to be stoned."

"It was fallen women who were stoned," Luna said.

"That's us, too," Marci said, and laughed. "So we get a reaction from people. So what? If anyone wants to say something to our faces, I think we can hold our own."

Their usual waiter brought their usual drinks. "Hey, you guys are famous now," he said cheerfully. If he was upset by certain items on the List, he didn't show it. Of course, it was possible he had no idea what the items *were*.

Jaine said, "Just think, we came up with the idea last Friday night, sitting at that table right over there."

"You did? Wow." He looked at the table in question. "Just wait until I tell the boss."

"Yeah, maybe he can gild the table, or something."

The waiter slowly shook his head, looking doubtful. "I don't think so. Isn't that what you do to horses?"

She was tired, courtesy of getting up at the ungodly hour of two, so it took her a second to make the connection. "That's *geld*, not 'gild.' "

"Oh." Relief washed over his face. "I was wondering how you could do that to a table."

"Well, it takes four people," Jaine said. "One to hold each leg."

T.J. had her head down on the table, her shoulders shaking as she tried to stifle her mirth. Marci's eyes were looking a little wild, but she managed to give her order with only a mild shake to her voice. Luna, the most composed of them all, waited until all the orders had been taken and he had disappeared into the kitchen before she clapped her hands over her mouth and laughed until tears ran down her face.

"One for each leg," she repeated, gasping, and went off into more whoops.

Their dinner wasn't as relaxed as usual, because people kept coming up to their table and making comments, both snide and complimentary. When their orders arrived, their food was burned; evidently the cook was among the booers.

"Let's get out of here," Marci finally said in disgust. "Even if we could eat this charcoal stuff, we wouldn't have a chance to with all the interruptions."

"Do we pay for it?" Luna asked, examining the hockey puck that was supposed to have been a hamburger patty.

"Normally, I'd say no," Jaine replied. "But if we make a fuss tonight, it's likely to be in the paper tomorrow morning."

Sighing, they agreed. Leaving their plates largely untouched, they paid the tab and left. They usually lingered over their meal, but this time when they left, it was just after six; the summer sun still hung low in the sky, and the heat was scorching.

They all retreated to their respective cars. Jaine started the Viper's engine and sat for a moment listening to the rumbling purr of a powerful, well-tuned machine. She turned the fan on "high" and adjusted the air vents so the cold air blew on her face.

She didn't want to go home and see the news, in case the List was featured again. Deciding to buy groceries instead of waiting until tomorrow, she turned north on Van Dyke, zooming past the GM plant on the left and resisting the urge to turn right, which would have taken her to the Warren Police Department. She didn't want to see if a red pickup truck or a battered brown Pontiac was in the parking lot. All she wanted to do was stock up on food and get home to BooBoo; she had been gone so long he had probably started on another cushion.

Jaine wasn't one who lingered over grocery shopping. She hated doing it, so she attacked a grocery store as if it were a racecourse. Piloting a buggy at high speed, she zipped through the produce department, tossing cabbage and lettuce and an assortment of fruit into the basket, then raced up and down the other aisles. She didn't cook much, because it was too much trouble for just one person, but occasionally she would prepare a roast or something similar, then eat sandwiches made from it for a week. BooBoo's cat food was a necessity, though—

An arm wrapped around her waist and a deep voice said, "Miss me?"

She managed to strangle her shriek so it emerged as not much more than a squeak, but she jumped at least a foot straight up and almost crashed into a stack of Sheba cat food.

Whirling around, she quickly positioned the buggy between them and gave him a look of wide-eyed alarm. "I'm sorry," she said, "but I don't know you. You have me mixed up with someone else."

Sam scowled. Other shoppers were watching them with acute interest; at least one lady looked as if she intended to call the cops if he made one wrong move.

"Very funny," he growled, and deliberately removed his jacket, revealing the holster on his belt and the big black pistol that resided in it. Since his badge was also clipped to his belt, the wide-eyed tension on aisle seven melted away as murmurings of "He's a cop" reached them.

"Go away," Jaine said. "I'm busy."

"So I see. What is this, the Produce Five Hundred? I've been chasing you up and down the aisles for the last five minutes."

"No you haven't," she returned, checking her watch. "I haven't been here five minutes."

"Okay, three. I saw this red streak heading up Van Dyke and turned around to follow it, figuring it was you."

"Is your car equipped with radar?"

"I'm in my truck, not a city car."

"Then you can't prove how fast I was going."

"Damn it, I wasn't going to give you a ticket," he said, annoyed. "Though if you don't slow down, I'm going to call a patrolman to do the honors."

"So you came in here just to harass me?"

"No," he said with exaggerated patience, "I came in here because I've been gone and I wanted to check in."

"Gone?" she repeated, opening her eyes as wide as they would go. "I had no idea."

He ground his teeth together. She knew because she could see his jaw working. "All right, I should have called." The words sounded as if they had been ripped, painfully, from his gut.

"Really? Why is that?"

"Because we're . . ."

"Neighbors?" she supplied, when he couldn't seem to find the word he wanted. She was beginning to enjoy herself, at least as much as was possible when she was bleary-eyed from lack of sleep.

"Because we have this thing going." He scowled down at her, looking not at all happy about their "thing."

"*Thing?* I don't do *things.*"

"You'll do mine," he said under his breath, but she heard him anyway and had just opened her mouth to blast him when a kid, maybe eight years old, ran up and poked her in the ribs with a plastic laser weapon, making electric zinging noises as he repeatedly pulled the trigger.

"You're dead," he said victoriously.

His mother came hurrying up, looking harassed and helpless. "Damian, stop that!" She gave him a smile that was little more than a grimace. "Don't bother the nice people."

"Shut up," he said rudely. "Can't you see they're Terrons from Vaniot?"

"I'm sorry," the mother said, trying to drag her offspring away. "Damian, come on or you'll have to have a time-out when we get home."

Jaine barely refrained from rolling her eyes. The kid poked her in the ribs again. "Ouch!"

He made those zinging noises again, taking great pleasure in her discomfort.

She plastered a big smile on her face and leaned down closer to precious Damian, then cooed in her most alienlike voice, "Oh, look, a little earthling." She straightened and gave Sam a commanding look. "Kill it."

Damian's mouth fell open. His eyes went as round as quarters as he took in the big pistol on Sam's belt. From his open mouth began to issue a series of shrill noises that sounded like a fire alarm.

Sam cursed under his breath, grabbed Jaine by the arm, and began tugging her at a half-trot toward the front of the store. She managed to snag her purse from the buggy as she went past.

"Hey, my groceries!" she protested.

"You can spend another three minutes in here tomorrow and get them," he said with pent-up violence. "Right now I'm trying to keep you from getting arrested."

"For what?" she asked indignantly as he dragged her out of the automatic doors. People were turning to look at them, but most were following the sounds of Damian's shrieks to aisle seven.

"How about threatening to kill that brat and causing a riot?"

"I didn't threaten to kill him! I just ordered you to." She had trouble keeping up with him; her long skirt wasn't made for running.

He whirled her around the side of the building, out of sight, and plastered her against the wall. "I can't believe I missed this," he said in a goaded tone.

She glared up at him and didn't say anything.

"I was in Lansing," he snarled, bending down so close his nose nearly touched hers. "Interviewing for a state job."

"You don't owe me any explanations."

He straightened and looked skyward, as if seeking help from the Almighty. She decided to give an inch. "All right, so a phone call wouldn't have been *too* pushy."

He said something under his breath. She had a good idea what it was, but unfortunately, he wasn't paying out money for every cuss word. If he had been, she would have hit the jackpot.

She grabbed his ears, pulled his head down, and kissed him.

Just like that he had her pinned to the wall, his arms so tight around her she could barely breathe, but breathing wasn't number one on her list of priorities right then. Feeling him against her, tasting him—that was important. His pistol was on his belt, so she knew that wasn't what was prodding her in the stomach. She wiggled against it just to make certain. Nope, definitely not a pistol.

He was breathing hard when he lifted his head. "You pick the damnedest places," he said, looking around.

"*I* pick? I was in there minding my own business, doing a little grocery shopping, when I was attacked by not one but *two* maniacs—"

"Don't you like kids?"

She blinked. "What?"

"Don't you like kids? You wanted me to kill that one."

"I like most kids," she said impatiently, "but I didn't like that one. He poked me in the ribs."

"I'm poking you in the stomach."

She gave him a sweet smile, one that made him shudder. "Yeah, but you aren't using a plastic laser gun."

"Let's get out of here," he said, looking desperate, and hustled her to her car.

fifteen

"Do you want coffee?" Jaine asked as she unlocked the kitchen door and led him inside. "Or iced tea?" she added, thinking a tall, cool glass would be just the ticket right now, with the scorching heat outside.

"Tea," he said, ruining her image of cops living on coffee and doughnuts. He was looking around her kitchen. "How is it you've only lived here a couple of weeks and this place already looks more lived-in than mine?"

She pretended to consider the matter. "I believe it's called unpacking."

He looked up at the ceiling. "I missed this?" he muttered at the plaster, still seeking enlightenment.

Jaine sneaked several glances at him as she got two glasses from the cabinet and filled them with ice. Her blood was zinging through her veins, the way it always did when he was around, whether from anger or exhilaration or lust, or a combination of all three. Confined by her cozy kitchen, he seemed even bigger, his shoulders filling the doorway and his size dwarfing her small, made-for-four table with the inlaid ceramic tile top.

"What kind of state job were you interviewing for?"

"State police, field detective division."

Taking the pitcher of tea from the refrigerator, she poured the two glasses full. "Lemon?"

"No, just straight." He took the glass from her, his fingers brushing hers. That was enough to make her nipples pucker and stand at attention. His gaze zeroed in on her mouth. "Congratulations," he said.

She blinked at him. "Have I done something?" She hoped he wasn't referring to all the publicity over the List—oh, God, the List. She had forgotten about it. Had he read the entire thing? Of course he had.

"You haven't cussed once, and we've been together half an hour. You didn't even swear when I dragged you out of the supermarket."

"Really?" She smiled, pleased with herself. Maybe having to pay all those fines was working on her subconscious. She was still *thinking* a lot of swear words, but the fines didn't kick in unless she said them out loud. Progress was being made.

He tilted the glass up and drank. She watched, mesmerized, as his strong throat worked. She struggled with a violent urge to tear his clothes off. What was wrong with her? She had watched men drink all her life, and it had never before affected her like this, not even with any of her three ex-fiancés.

"More?" she asked when he drained the glass and set it down.

"No, thanks." That hot, dark gaze went over her, settled on

her breasts. "You look extra spiffy today. Anything special going on?"

She wasn't going to avoid the subject, no matter how touchy it was. "We had an interview for *Good Morning America* this morning—at four A.M. if you can believe it! I had to get up at two," she complained, "and I've been comatose most of the day."

"The List is getting that much publicity?" he asked, surprised.

"I'm afraid so," she said morosely, sitting down at the table.

He didn't sit down across from her, but took the chair beside her. "I tracked it down on the Web. It was funny stuff—*Ms. C.*"

She gaped at him. "How did you know?" she demanded.

He snorted. "Like I wouldn't recognize your smart-ass mouth even in print. 'Anything over eight is strictly for show-and-tell,' " he quoted at her.

"I might have known you'd remember only the sex stuff."

"Sex is much on my mind these days. And just for the record—I don't have anything for show-and-tell."

If he didn't, he hadn't missed it by much, Jaine thought, remembering with great fondness how he had looked in profile.

He continued, "I'm just happy I'm not in the point-and-laugh category."

Jaine shrieked with laughter and threw herself back in the chair so hard it tipped her out onto the floor. She sat there holding her ribs, which had pretty much stopped aching but now decided to resume at such rough treatment, but she couldn't stop laughing. BooBoo cautiously approached, but decided he didn't want to get within touching distance and instead sought refuge under Sam's chair.

Sam leaned down and scooped up the cat, settling him on his lap and stroking down the long, lean body. BooBoo closed his eyes and set up a buzz-saw purr. The cat purred, and Sam watched her, waiting until the gales of laughter had subsided to giggles and wheezing.

She sat on the floor with her arms wrapped around her ribs and her eyes wet with tears. If she had any mascara left, it had to be running down her cheeks, she thought. "Need any help getting up?" he asked. "I should warn you that if I get my hands on you, I may have trouble taking them off again."

"I can manage, thanks." Carefully, and not without some difficulty because of her long skirt, she got to her feet and wiped her eyes with a napkin.

"Good. I'd hate to disturb ... what's his name? BooBoo? What the hell kind of name for a cat is BooBoo?"

"Don't blame me; blame my mother."

"A cat should have a name it can live up to. Naming him BooBoo is like naming your son Alice. BooBoo shoulda been named Tiger, or Romeo—"

Jaine shook her head. "*Romeo*'s out."

"You mean he's—?"

She nodded.

"In that case, I guess BooBoo's a pretty good name for him, though BooHoo would be more appropriate."

She had to hold her ribs really, really tight to keep from bursting into more laughter. "You're such a *guy*."

"What the hell did you want me to be, a ballerina?"

No, she didn't want him to be anything except what he was. No one else had ever made excitement fizz along her veins like champagne, and that was quite an achievement, considering that a week ago they hadn't exchanged anything except insults. Only two days had passed since their first kiss, two days that had seemed like an eternity because there hadn't been any more kisses until she grabbed his ears at the supermarket and pulled him down to her level.

"How's your egg?" he asked, lids heavy over his dark eyes, and she knew his thoughts weren't far from hers.

"History," she replied.

"Then let's go to bed."

"You think all you have to do is say, 'Let's go to bed,' and I'll fall over on my back?" she asked indignantly.

"No, I hoped I'd have a chance to do a bit more than that before you fell over on your back."

"I'm not falling anywhere."

"Why not?"

"Because I'm having my period." Funny, she couldn't remember ever saying that to a man before, especially without even a twinge of self-consciousness.

His brows snapped down. "You're *what?*" he asked in growing anger.

"Having my period. Menstruating. Maybe you've heard about it. It's when—"

"I have two sisters; I think I know a little about periods. And one of the things I know is that the egg is fertile roughly in the middle of the cycle, not close to the end!"

Busted. Jaine pursed her lips. "Okay, so I lied. There's always a slight chance the timing is off, and I wasn't willing to take that chance, all right?"

It evidently wasn't all right. "You stopped me," he groaned, closing his eyes as if he were in acute pain. "I was damn near dying, and you *stopped* me."

"You make it sound on a level with treason."

He opened his eyes, glaring at her. "What about now?"

He was about as romantic as a rock, she thought, so why was she so turned on? "Your idea of foreplay is probably 'You awake?' " she grumbled.

He made an impatient gesture. *"What about now?"*

"No."

"Jeez!" He leaned back in the chair and closed his eyes again. "What's wrong with now?"

"I told you, I'm having my period."

"So?"

"So . . . no."

"Why not?"

"Because I don't want to!" she yelled. "Give me a break!"

He sighed. "I get it. PMS."

"PMS is *before,* you idiot."

"That's what you say. Ask any man and you'll hear a different story."

"Like they're experts," she scoffed.

"Honey, the *only* experts in PMS are men. That's why men are so good at fighting wars; they learned Escape and Evade at home."

She thought about throwing a frying pan at him, but Boo-Boo was in the line of fire, and anyway, she would have to find a frying pan first.

He grinned at the expression on her face. "Know why PMS is called PMS?"

"Don't you dare," she threatened. "Only women can tell PMS jokes."

"Because 'mad cow disease' was already taken."

Forget the frying pan. She looked around for a knife. "Get out of my house."

He put BooBoo on the floor and stood up, evidently ready to Escape and Evade. "Settle down," he said, putting the chair between them.

"Settle down, my ass! Damn it, where's my butcher knife?" She looked around in frustration. If she had only lived here longer, she would know where she had put everything!

He came out from behind the chair, around the table, and had a firm grip on both her wrists before she could remember which drawer held her cutting knives. "You owe me fifty cents," he said, grinning down at her as he pulled her against him.

"Don't hold your breath! I told you I wouldn't pay when it's your fault." She blew her bangs out of her eyes so she could glare at him more effectively.

He bent his head and kissed her.

Time stood still again. He must have released her wrists, because her arms slid around his neck. His mouth was hot and hungry, and he kissed the way no man should kiss and still be allowed to run free. His scent was as warm and musky as sex, filling her lungs, permeating her skin. He put one big hand on her bottom and lifted her off her feet, aligning their bodies more completely, groin to groin.

The long skirt hampered her, preventing her from wrapping her legs around him. Jaine arched in frustration, almost ready to cry. "We can't," she whispered when he raised his mouth a fraction of an inch.

"We can do other things," he murmured in reply, sitting down with her across his lap, tilted back across his supporting arm. Deftly he slipped his hand inside the scooped neckline of her sweater.

She closed her eyes in delight as his rough palm scraped over her nipple. He exhaled, a long, sighing sound; then it was as if they both held their breath as his hand shaped itself over her breast, learning her size and softness, the texture of her skin.

In silence he withdrew his hand and pulled the sweater off over her head, then deftly unclipped her bra and pushed it off her shoulders to fall to the floor.

She lay half-naked across his lap, her breath coming fast and shallow as she watched him looking at her. She knew her own breasts, but what were they like from a man's point of view? They weren't big, but were firm and upright. Her nipples were small and pinkish-brown, velvety soft and delicate compared to the rough fingertip he used to lightly circle one, making the aureole pucker even more tightly.

Pleasure speared through her, making her clench her legs tightly together to contain it.

He lifted her, arching her even more across his arm, and bent his head to her breasts.

He was gentle, totally without haste. She was stunned by his caution now, given his rapacious kisses. He nuzzled his face against the underside of her breasts, kissing the curves, licking gently at her nipples until they were reddened and so tight they couldn't possibly get any tighter. When he finally began sucking her with slow, firm pressure, she was so ready it was as if he had touched her with a live wire. She couldn't control her body, couldn't stop herself from arching wildly in his arms; her heart was thundering, her pulse racing so fast she was dizzy.

She was helpless; she would have done virtually anything he wanted. When he stopped, it was by his own willpower, not hers. She could feel him shaking, his strong, powerful body quaking against her as if he were chilled, though his skin was hot to the touch. He sat her upright and pressed his forehead to hers, his eyes squeezed shut and his hands roughly stroking her hips, her bare back.

"If I ever get inside you," he said in a strained tone, "I'll last, like, two seconds. Maybe."

She was crazy. She had to be, because two seconds of Sam sounded better than anything else she could bring to mind right now. She stared at him with glazed eyes and ripe, swollen mouth. She wanted those two seconds. She wanted them bad.

He looked down at her breasts and made a sound halfway between a whine and a groan. Muttering a curse, he leaned down and snagged her sweater from the floor, pressing it to her chest. "Maybe you'd better put this back on."

"Maybe I should," she said, and her voice sounded drugged even to herself. Her arms didn't seem to be working; they remained twined around Sam's neck.

"Either you put on the sweater, or we go to the bedroom."

That wasn't much of a threat, she thought, when every cell in her body was saying "Yes! Yes! Yes!" As long as she could keep her mouth from saying it, she was holding her own, but she was beginning to have serious doubts about holding him off for even a couple of days, much less a couple of weeks the way she had planned. Torturing him didn't sound like nearly as much fun as it had before, because now she knew just how much she would also be torturing herself.

He stuffed her arms inside the sweater and pulled it over her head, jerking the fabric into place. The sweater was inside out, she saw, but who cared? She didn't.

"You're trying to kill me," he accused. "I'm going to make you pay, too."

"How?" she asked with interest, leaning against him. The same thing that was wrong with her arms was also wrong with her spine; it wouldn't hold her upright.

"Instead of that half hour of thrusting time you claim you want, I'm going to stop at twenty-nine minutes."

She snickered. "I thought you were holding out for two seconds."

"That's just the first time. The second time we're going to set the sheets on fire."

It behooved her, she thought, to get off his lap. His erection was like an iron bar prodding her hip, and talking about sex wasn't helping any. If she really, really didn't want to go to bed with him now, she should get up. But she really, really *did* want to go to bed with him, and only a small portion of her brain was still cautious.

That small portion, however, was insistent. She had learned the hard way not to assume happily-ever-after would happen for her, and just because they were hot for each other didn't mean there was anything between them other than sex.

She cleared her throat. "I should get up, shouldn't I?"

"If you have to move at all, do it slowly."

"That close, huh?"

"Just call me Mount Etna."

"Who's Edna?"

He laughed, as she had intended, but the sound was strained. Gingerly she eased off his lap. He winced and awkwardly climbed to his feet. The front of his pants looked deformed, the way it was tented out. Jaine tried not to stare.

"Tell me about your family," she blurted.

"What?" He looked as if he was having trouble following the change of subject.

"Your family. Tell me about them."

"Why?"

"To get your mind off . . . you know." She indicated the "you know" in question. "You said you have two sisters."

"And four brothers."

She blinked. "Seven. Wow."

"Yeah. Unfortunately, my oldest sister, Dorothy, was the third child. My folks kept trying to have another girl so she wouldn't be the only one. They had three more boys trying to get Doro a sister."

"Where are you in the lineup?"

"Second."

"Are you a close family?"

"Fairly close. We all live here in the state except for Angie, the baby. She goes to college in Chicago."

The diversion had worked; he looked a little more relaxed than he had a moment before, though his gaze still had a tendency to settle on her braless breasts. To give him something to do, she poured another glass of iced tea and handed it to him.

"Have you ever been married?"

"Once, about ten years ago."

"What happened?"

"Nosy, aren't you?" he said. "She didn't like being a cop's wife; I didn't like being a bitch's husband. End of story. She split for the West Coast as soon as the papers were signed. What about you?"

"Nosy, aren't you?" she threw back at him, then hesitated. "Do you think I'm a bitch?" God knows she hadn't always been on her best behavior with him. Come to think of it, she'd *never* been on her best behavior with him.

"Nah. You're damn scary, but you aren't a bitch."

"Gee, thanks," she muttered; then, because fair was fair, she said, "No, I've never been married, but I've been engaged three times."

He paused with the glass halfway to his mouth and gave her a startled look. "*Three* times?"

She nodded. "I guess I'm not very good at the man-woman stuff."

His gaze went back to her breasts. "Oh, I don't know. You're doing pretty good at keeping me interested."

"So maybe you're a mutant." She shrugged helplessly. "My second fiancé decided he was still in love with an ex-girlfriend, who I guess wasn't all that ex, but I don't know what happened with the other two."

He snorted. "They were probably scared."

"*Scared!*" For some reason, that hurt, just a little. She felt her lower lip wobble. "I'm not that bad, am I?"

"Worse," he said cheerfully. "You're hell on wheels. You're just lucky I like hot rods. Now, if you'll put your clothes on right side out, I'll take you out to dinner. How does a burger sound?"

"I'd rather have Chinese," she said as she went down the short hall to her bedroom.

LINDA HOWARD

"Figures."

He muttered the reply, but she heard him anyway, and she was smiling as she closed her bedroom door and pulled off the red sweater. Since he liked hot rods, she was going to show him just how fast she could go. The problem was, he had to catch her.

178

sixteen

Corin couldn't sleep. He got out of bed and turned on the light in the bathroom, checking in the mirror to make certain he was still there. The face that stared back at him was that of a stranger, but the eyes were familiar. He had seen those eyes look back at him for most of his life, but sometimes he was gone and they didn't see him.

An array of yellow medicine bottles were lined up, according to size, on the vanity so he would see them every day when he got up and remember to take his medication. It had been several days now—he couldn't remember exactly how many—since he had taken the pills. He could see himself now, but when he took the pills, his thinking got clouded and he faded away in the mist.

It was better, they had told him, if he stayed in the mist, hidden away. The pills worked so well that sometimes he even forgot he was there. But there was always a sense of something wrong, as if the universe were askew, and now he knew what it was. The pills might hide him, but they couldn't make him go away.

He hadn't been able to sleep since he stopped taking the pills. Oh, he dozed, but real sleep eluded him. Sometimes he felt as if he were shaking apart inside, though when he held out his hands, they were steady. Was there something addictive in the pills? Had they lied to him? He didn't want to be a drug addict; addiction was a sign of weakness, his mother had always told him. He couldn't be addicted because he couldn't be weak. He had to be strong, he had to be perfect.

He heard an echo of her voice in his head. "My perfect little man," she had called him, stroking his cheek.

Whenever he failed her, whenever he was less than perfect, her wrath had been so overwhelming his world would threaten to come apart at the seams. He would do anything to keep from disappointing his mother, but he had kept an awful secret from her: sometimes he had deliberately transgressed, just a little, so she would punish him. Even now the thought of those punishments sent a thrill through him. She would have been so disappointed if she had guessed his secret delight, so he had always struggled to keep his pleasure hidden.

Sometimes he missed her so much. She always knew just what to do.

She would know, for instance, what to do about those four bitches who mocked him with their list for being perfect. As if they knew what perfection was! He knew. His mother had known. He had always tried so hard to be her perfect little man, her perfect son, but he had always fallen short, even on those times when he wasn't misbehaving just a little, on purpose, so she would punish him. He had always known there was an imperfection in *him* that he would never be able to correct, that he always disappointed his mother on a basic level just by being.

They thought they were so smart, the four bitches—he liked the way that sounded, the Four Bitches, like some perverted Roman deity. The Furies, the Graces, the Bitches. They tried to play it cute, hiding their identities by using *A, B, C,* and *D* instead of their names. There was one in particular he hated, the one who said, "If a man isn't perfect, he should try harder." What did they know? Had they ever tried to measure up to a standard so impossibly high only perfection could meet it, and fallen short every day of their lives? *Had they?*

Did they know what it was like for him to try and try, yet know deep inside he was going to fail, until finally he learned to enjoy the punishment because that was the only way he could live with it? *Did they know?*

Bitches like them didn't deserve to live.

He could feel that inner shaking again, and he wrapped his arms around himself, holding himself together. It was their fault he couldn't sleep. He couldn't stop thinking about them, about what they said.

Which one was it? Was it that bleached blonde, Marci Dean, who swished her ass in front of all the men like she was some goddess and they were nothing but dogs who would come running whenever she wanted? He had heard she would sleep with anyone who asked, but that most of the time she beat them to the punch. His mother would have been appalled at such trashy behavior.

"Some people don't deserve to live."

He could hear her whisper inside his head, the way she often did when he didn't take the pills. He wasn't the only one who disappeared when he took the medication the way they instructed; Mother disappeared, too. Maybe they went away together. He didn't know, but he hoped so. Maybe she punished him for taking the pills and making her disappear. Maybe that was why he took the pills, so he and Mother could go away and . . . No, that wasn't right. When he took the pills, it was as if he didn't exist.

He felt the thought slipping away from him. All he knew was that he didn't want to take the pills. He wanted to find out which bitch was which. That sounded funny so he repeated it to himself, and silently laughed. Which bitch was which. That was good.

He knew where they all lived. He had gotten their addresses from their files at work. It was so easy, for anyone who knew how, and of course no one had questioned him.

He would go to her house and find out if she was the one who had said that awful, stupid thing. He was pretty sure it was Marci. He wanted to teach that stupid, vicious bitch a lesson. Mother would be so pleased.

Marci was a night owl, even during the workweek. She didn't need much sleep, so even though she didn't party nearly as hearty as she had when she was younger—say, in her thirties—she seldom went to bed before one A.M. She watched old movies on television; she read three or four books a week; she had even developed a fondness for cross-stitching. She had to laugh at herself whenever she picked up her cross-stitch hoop, because this had to be proof the party girl was getting old. But she could empty out her mind when she was working cross-stitch. Who needed meditation to gain inner serenity when she could get the same effect by duplicating with needle and thread a small colored pattern of Xs? At least when she had completed a pattern, she had something to show for it.

In her time she had tried a lot of stuff that people probably wouldn't expect of her, she thought. Meditation. Yoga. Self-hypnotism. Finally she had decided a beer worked just as well and her insides were as serene as they were going to get. She was what she was. If anyone didn't like it, screw 'em.

Usually, on a Friday night, she and Brick would hit a couple of bars, do some dancing, drink a few beers. Brick was a fine dancer, which was surprising because he looked like someone who would rather die than get on a dance floor, kind of a cross between a truck driver and a biker. He wasn't much of a conversationalist, but he sure had some moves.

She had thought about going out without him, but the idea wasn't very exciting. With all the hoopla this week about that damn List, she was a little tired. She wanted to settle down with a book and rest. Maybe tomorrow night she'd go out.

She missed Brick. She missed his presence, anyway, if not him in particular. When he wasn't in the sack or on a dance floor, he was pretty boring. He slept; he drank beer; he watched television. That was it. He wasn't a great lover, either, but he sure was an eager one. He was never too tired and was always willing to try anything she wanted.

Still, Brick was just further proof she wasn't any good at picking men. At least she wasn't stupid enough any longer to marry them. Three times was enough, thank you. Jaine fretted because she'd been engaged three times, but at least she hadn't actually *married* three times. Besides, Jaine just hadn't met anyone yet who could hold his own with her. Maybe that cop . . .

Hell, probably not. Life had taught Marci that things seldom worked out just right. There was always a bump in the road, a glitch in the software.

It was after midnight when the doorbell rang. She placed a bookmark between the pages so she wouldn't lose her place and got up from the couch where she had been sprawled. Who on earth could that be? It wouldn't be Brick returning, because he had a key.

That reminded her: she needed to get her locks replaced. She was too cautious to simply get her key back and assume he hadn't made a duplicate. So far he hadn't displayed any thieving habits, but one never knew what a man might do when he was pissed at a woman.

Because she was cautious, she looked through the peephole. She frowned and stepped back to unlock the door and remove the chain. "Hey," she said, opening the door. "Is something wrong?"

"No," said Corin, and hit her in the head with the hammer he had been holding against his leg.

seventeen

On Monday, the elevator sign read: XEROX AND WURLITZER HAVE ANNOUNCED THEY WILL MERGE TO MARKET RE-PRODUCTIVE ORGANS.

Jaine was still chuckling when the elevator doors opened. She felt as if she were fizzing on the inside, a direct result of a weekend filled with Sam. *She* still hadn't been filled with Sam, but she had started on the birth control pills that morning. Not that she had told him she was going to, of course. Frustration was driving her crazy, but anticipation was lighting up her whole world. She couldn't remember ever feeling so alive, as if every cell in her body were awake and singing.

Derek Kellman stepped forward to exit the elevator as she was getting on. "Hi, Kellman," she said cheerfully. "How're things going?"

He turned bright red, and his Adam's apple bobbed in his throat. "Uh—okay," he mumbled as he ducked his head and hurried off the elevator.

Jaine smilingly shook her head and punched the button for the third floor. She couldn't imagine Kellman getting up enough nerve to grab Marci's ass; she and everyone else in the building would have paid good money to have seen it.

As usual, she was the first one in the office; she liked getting a jump on Monday mornings, with all the payroll to handle. If she could just keep her mind on the job, she was off to a good start.

The List thing was dying down, maybe. Everyone who wanted an interview had one, except for *People* magazine. She hadn't watched television that morning, so she had no idea what snippets of their Friday morning interview actually made it on air. Someone would be certain to tell her, though, and if she ever felt the urge to watch it, which wasn't likely, at least one of the other three would have taped the program.

Funny how she didn't much care. How could she worry about the List with Sam occupying so much of her time and thoughts? He was maddening, but he was funny and sexy and she wanted him.

After eating dinner together Friday night, he had awakened her at six-thirty Saturday morning by spraying her bedroom window with the water hose, then inviting her out to help him wash his truck. Figuring she owed him, since he had washed the Viper, she quickly pulled on some clothes, put on some coffee, and joined him outside. He hadn't wanted to just wash the truck; he wanted it waxed and buffed, all the chrome cleaned and polished, the interior vacuumed, all the windows washed. After two hours of intense labor, the truck had gleamed. He had then pulled it into his garage and asked what she was cooking him for breakfast.

They had spent the day together, arguing and laughing, watching a ball game on television, and were getting ready to go out for dinner when his beeper went off. He used her phone to call in, and before she knew it, he was out the door with a quick kiss and a "I don't know when I'll be back."

He was a cop, she reminded herself. As long as he remained a cop—and he seemed set on making a career of it, given his interview with the state police—his life would be a series of interruptions and urgent summons. Broken dates would come with the package. She had thought about it and decided what the hell, she was tough, she could handle it. But if he were in danger . . . she didn't know if she could handle that nearly as well. Was he still working on that task force? Was it something he was permanently assigned to, or were things like that temporary? She knew so little about law enforcement, but she would definitely be finding out more.

He had returned Sunday afternoon, tired, grumpy, and not inclined to talk about what he'd been doing. Instead of badgering him with questions, she let him nap in her big easy chair while she read, curled up on one of the two remaining cushions on the couch.

Being with him like that, not on a date or anything, just *being*, had felt somehow . . . right. Watching him sleep. Enjoying the sound of his breathing. And not daring, not yet, to put the L-word to what she was feeling. It was too soon, and she was still too wary from past experiences to blindly trust that this excitement when she was with him would last forever. Her wariness was also the real basis for her reluctance to sleep with him. Yeah, frustrating him was fun and she enjoyed the heat in his eyes when he looked at her, but deep down she was still afraid to let him get too close to her.

Maybe next week.

"Hey, Jaine!"

She looked up as Dominica Flores stuck her head in the door, her eyebrows raised in query.

"I just caught part of the thing on television this morning; I had to leave before it was finished, but I set the VCR. It was so cool! You looked hot, really hot. Everyone looked good, y'know, but, wow, you were great."

"I didn't see it," Jaine said.

"Really? Wow, if I were on national television, I'd stay out of work to watch myself."

Not if you were as sick of the whole thing as I am, Jaine thought. She managed a smile anyway.

At eight-thirty, Luna called. "Have you heard from Marci?" she asked. "She hasn't come to work yet, but when I called her at home, there wasn't an answer."

"No, I haven't talked to her since Friday."

"It isn't like her to miss work." Luna sounded worried. She and Marci were pretty tight, surprisingly so considering the gap between their ages. "And she didn't call in late or sick or anything."

That really wasn't like Marci. She hadn't reached her position as head of accounting by being unreliable. Jaine frowned; now *she* was worried. "Have you tried her cell phone?"

"It isn't on."

The first thought that sprang to Jaine's mind was that there had been a traffic accident. The Detroit traffic was horrendous during rush hour. "I'll call around and see if I can find her," she said, not voicing her sudden concern to Luna.

"Okay. Let me know."

As she hung up, Jaine tried to think of who to call to find out if there had been a traffic accident somewhere on the freeway between Sterling Heights and Hammerstead. And did Marci come down Van Dyke to hit I-696 or avoid Van Dyke and take one of the Mile roads over to Troy where she could pick up I-75?

Sam would know whom to call.

Quickly she looked up the number of the Warren Police Department, dialed it, and asked for Detective Donovan. Then she was put on hold. She waited impatiently, tapping a pen against the desktop, for several minutes. Finally the voice came back to say that Detective Donovan wasn't available, would she like to leave a message?

Jaine hesitated. She hated to bother him for something that could easily turn out to be nothing, but she didn't think anyone else at the department would take her concern seriously. So a friend was half an hour late to work; that wasn't generally cause enough to call out the troops. Sam might not take her seriously either, but he would at least make an effort to find out something.

"Do you have his pager number?" she finally asked. "It's important." It was important to her, though it might not be to them.

"What does this concern?"

Irritated, she wondered if women regularly called Sam at work. "I'm one of his snitches," she said, crossing her fingers at the lie.

"Then you should have his pager number."

"Oh, for God's sake! Someone could be hurt or dead—"She caught herself. "Okay, so I'm pregnant, and I thought he'd like to know."

The voice laughed. "Is this Jaine?"

Oh, my God, he'd been talking about her! Her face flamed. "Um—yes," she mumbled. "Sorry."

"Not a problem. He said if you ever called to make sure you got in touch with him."

Yeah, but how had he described her? She refrained from asking and jotted down his pager number. "Thanks," she said.

"You're welcome. Uh—about this pregnancy thing . . . "

"I lied," she said, and tried to work up a smidgen of shame in her tone. She didn't think she succeeded, because the woman laughed.

"You go, girl," said the woman, and hung up, leaving Jaine to wonder exactly what she meant.

She pressed the disconnect button on her desk phone, then dialed Sam's pager. It was one of the numerical pagers, so she left her number. Since it wasn't a number he would recognize, she wondered how long it would take him to return her call. In the meantime she called accounting. "Has Marci arrived yet?"

"No," was the worried reply. "We haven't heard from her."

"This is Jaine, extension three-six-two-one. If she comes in, tell her to call me immediately."

"Will do."

It was nine-thirty before her phone rang again. She snatched up the receiver, hoping Marci had finally shown up. "Jaine Bright."

"I hear we're going to be parents." Sam's deep voice purred over the telephone line.

Damn blabbermouth! she thought. "I had to say something. She didn't believe I was a snitch."

"Lucky I warned everyone about you," he said, then asked, "What's up?"

"Nothing, I hope. My friend Marci—"

"Marci Dean, one of the infamous List Ladies?"

She might have known he'd have the details on all of them. "She hasn't come in to work, hasn't called, isn't answering her home phone or cell phone. I'm afraid she might have been in an accident on the way to work, but I don't know who to contact to find out. Can you steer me in the right direction?"

"No problem. I'll get in touch with our traffic division and get them to check reports. Let's see, she lives in Sterling Heights, doesn't she?"

"Yes." Quickly Jaine gave him the address, then paused as another awful thought struck her. "Sam . . . her boyfriend was really upset about the List. He left Thursday night, but he might have come back."

There was a slight pause; then his tone turned brisk and businesslike. "I'll contact both the sheriff's department and the Sterling Heights P.D., have her place checked out. It's probably nothing, but it won't hurt to be certain."

"Thanks," she whispered.

Sam didn't like what he was thinking, but he'd been a cop too long to write off Jaine's concern as overreacting. An irate boyfriend—one with a wounded ego, at that, over that damn List—and a missing woman were ingredients in far too many incidents of violence. Maybe Ms. Dean's car had broken down, but maybe not. Jaine wasn't the type to panic over nothing, and she had definitely been afraid.

Maybe she had some feminine intuition going there, but he didn't discount that, either. Hell, his mom had eyes in the back of her head and had always, without fail, been waiting up for him and his brothers whenever they had been up to mischief. To this day he didn't know how she had known, but he accepted it nevertheless.

He placed two calls, the first to the Sterling Heights P.D., the next to a pal in traffic who could check for victims in any morning traffic accident. The Sterling Heights sergeant he spoke to said they would immediately send a car to check out Ms. Dean's residence, so he held off on calling the sheriff's department. He left his cell phone number with both contacts.

His pal in traffic checked in first. "No major accidents this morning," he said. "A few fender benders is all, and a guy dumped his motorcycle in the middle of Gratiot Avenue, but that's it."

"Thanks for checking," Sam said.

"Any time."

At ten-fifteen, his cell phone rang again. It was the Sterling Heights sergeant. "You called it, Detective," he said, sounding weary.

"She's dead?"

"Yeah. It's pretty brutal. You got a name for that boyfriend? None of the neighbors are at home for us to ask, and I think we need to have a little talk with him."

"I can get it. My lady friend is—was—Ms. Dean's best friend."

"Appreciate the help."

Sam knew he was treading on someone else's territory, but he figured since he had tipped them to the scene, the sergeant would cut him some slack. "Can you give me any details?"

The sergeant paused. "What kind of cell phone are you using?"

"Digital."

"Secure?"

"Until the hackers figure out a way to get the signal."

"Okay. He used a hammer on her. Left it at the scene. We might get some prints off it, might not."

Sam winced. A hammer did a god-awful amount of damage.

"Not much of her face is left, plus she was stabbed multiple times. And she was sexually attacked."

If the boyfriend had left his semen behind, he was nailed. "Any semen?"

"Don't know yet. The M.E. will have to do tests. He—ah— did her with the hammer."

Jesus. Sam took a deep breath. "Okay. Thanks, Sergeant."

"Appreciate the help. Your lady friend—is she who you intend to ask about the boyfriend?"

"Yeah. She called me because she was worried when Ms. Dean didn't show up for work this morning."

"Can you just ask her about the boyfriend, and stall her on the rest?"

Sam snorted. "I'd have a better chance of stalling sundown."

"One of those, huh? Can she keep it quiet? We're pretty sure this is Ms. Dean, but we haven't made a positive I.D. yet, and the family hasn't been contacted."

"I'll get her to leave work. She's going to be pretty upset." He wanted to be with her when he told her, anyway.

"Okay. And, Detective—if we can't locate any family locally, we may need your friend to identify the body."

"You have my number," Sam said quietly.

He sat for a minute after they hung up. He didn't have to imagine the gory details; he had seen too many murder scenes in all their bloody reality. He knew what a hammer or a baseball bat could do to the human head. He knew what multiple stab wounds looked like. And, like the sergeant, he knew that this murder had been perpetrated by someone who knew the victim because the attack had been personal; the face had been attacked. The multiple stab wounds were indicative of rage. And since most female murder victims were killed by someone they knew, usually the husband or boyfriend, or the ex-whatever, the odds were overwhelming that Ms. Dean's boyfriend was the killer.

He took a deep breath and dialed Jaine's number again. When she answered, he said, "Do you know Marci's boyfriend's name?"

She audibly inhaled. "Is she all right?"

"I don't know anything yet," he lied. "Her boyfriend—?"

"Oh. His name is Brick Geurin." She spelled the last name for him.

"Is 'Brick' his real name or a nickname?"

"I don't know. 'Brick' is all I ever heard her call him."

"Okay, that's enough. I'll get back with you when I hear something. Oh—want to meet me for lunch?"

"Sure. Where?"

She still sounded scared, but she was holding together the way he had known she would. "I'll pick you up, if you can get me through the gate."

"No problem. Twelve?"

He checked his watch. Ten-thirty-five. "Can you make it earlier, say eleven-fifteen or so?" That would just give him time to get to Hammerstead.

Maybe she knew, maybe she caught on then. "I'll meet you downstairs."

She was waiting for him at the front of the building when the guard let him through the gate. She was wearing another of those long, lean skirts that looked like a million bucks on her, which meant there was no way she could climb into his truck without help. He got out and walked around to open the door for her. Her eyes were anxious as she studied his expression. He knew he was wearing his cop face, as emotionless as a mask, but she went white.

He put his hands around her slender waist and lifted her into the truck, then walked back around to get behind the wheel.

A tear slid down Jaine's cheek. "Tell me," she said, her voice choked.

He sighed, then reached out and drew her into his arms. "I'm so sorry," he said against her hair.

She clutched his shirt. He could feel her shaking, and held her even tighter. "She's dead, isn't she," she said in a trembling whisper, and it wasn't a question.

She knew.

eighteen

Jaine had cried so much her eyes were swollen almost shut. Sam had simply held her through the initial storm of weeping, parked in front of Hammerstead; then when she regained a bit of control, he asked, "Can you eat anything?"

She shook her head. "No." Her voice was thick. "I need to tell Luna . . . and T.J.—"

"Not yet, honey. Once you tell them, it'll be all over the building; then someone will call the newspaper or a radio or television station, and it'll be all over the news. Her family hasn't been notified yet, and they don't need to hear it that way."

"She doesn't have much family." Jaine fished a tissue out of her purse, then wiped her eyes and blew her nose. "She has a sister in Saginaw, and I think an elderly aunt and uncle in Florida. That's all I ever heard her mention."

"Do you know her sister's name?"

"Cheryl. I don't know her last name."

"It's probably in an address book at her house. I'll tell them to look for a Cheryl in Saginaw." He dialed a number on his cell phone, and spoke quietly to whoever answered on the other end, imparting the information about Marci's sister.

"I need to go home," Jaine said, staring through the windshield. She reached for the door handle, but Sam stopped her, holding her in place with a firm hand on her arm.

"No way are you driving right now," he said. "If you want to go home, I'll take you."

"But my car—"

"Isn't going anywhere. It's in a secure place. If you need to go anywhere, I'll drive you."

"But you might have to leave."

"I'll handle it," he said. "You aren't driving."

If she hadn't been so shattered, she would have argued with him, but tears welled again and she knew she couldn't see to drive. Neither could she could go back inside; she couldn't handle facing anyone right now, couldn't handle the inevitable questions without breaking down. "I have to let the office know I'm going home," she said.

"Can you handle it, or do you want me to do it?"

"I can," she said, her voice trembling. "Just . . . not right now."

"Okay. Fasten your seat belt."

Obediently she buckled the belt around her and sat deathly still as Sam put the truck in gear and negotiated the freeway traffic. He drove silently, not intruding on her grief while she tried to accept that Marci was gone.

"You—you think Brick did it, don't you?"

"He'll be questioned," Sam said neutrally. At this point, Geurin would be the number one suspect, but the evidence would have to support it. Even while you played the odds, you had to always be aware that the truth could go against the percentages. Who knows? They might find out Ms. Dean had been seeing someone else, too.

Jaine began crying again. She put her hands over her face and sat hunched over, her shoulders shaking. "I can't believe this is happening," she managed to say, then wondered dully how many millions of other people said exactly the same thing during a crisis.

"I know, honey."

He did know, she realized. In his job, he probably saw way too many scenes of this sort.

"H-how did—? I mean, what happened?"

Sam hesitated, reluctant to tell her Marci had been both bludgeoned and stabbed. He didn't know the exact cause of death, hadn't seen the crime scene, so he didn't know if she had died from head trauma or if she had died from the stab wounds.

"I don't know all the details," he finally said. "I know she was stabbed. I don't know the time of death or anything." Those three statements were true, without being anywhere close to the whole truth.

"Stabbed," Jaine repeated, and closed her eyes as if trying to visualize the crime.

"Don't," he said.

She opened her eyes and looked questioningly at him.

"You were trying to imagine what happened, how she looked, if it hurt," he said, more harshly than he intended. "Don't."

She took a deep breath, and he expected her to lash out at him, transferring the focus of her grief and anger to him, but instead she nodded, trusting that he knew best. "I'll try, but—how do I not think about it?"

"Think about her instead," he said, because he knew she would anyway. It was part of the grieving process.

She tried to say something, her throat working, but tears

welled up again, and she settled for a jerky nod. She didn't say anything else all the way home to Warren.

She felt old as she walked across their driveways to her house. Sam went with her, his arm around her, and she was grateful for his support as she ponderously climbed the steps to the kitchen door. BooBoo came meowing, tail twitching, as if asking why she was home so early. She leaned down to scratch behind his ears, taking comfort in the warmth of the sinuous body and the softness of his fur.

She put her purse on the table and sank down in one of the kitchen chairs, holding BooBoo on her lap and stroking him while Sam called his sergeant and carried on a quiet conversation. She tried not to think about Marci, not yet. She did think about Luna and T.J., and the anxiety they must feel because they hadn't yet heard from Marci. She hoped Marci's sister was contacted soon, because when she reported off for the rest of the day, her friends would know something was dreadfully wrong. If they called here to check on her, she didn't know what she would say or if she could even manage to talk to them.

Sam set a glass of tea in front of her. "Drink it," he said. "You've leaked enough to be dehydrated."

Impossibly, that earned a shaky smile. He kissed the top of her head, then sat down beside her with his own glass of tea.

She put BooBoo down, sniffed, and blotted her eyes. "Exactly what did you tell everyone at the department about me?" she asked, just for something to talk about.

He tried for an innocent look. On that rough-hewn face, it didn't work very well.

"Nothing much. Just that if you called, to tell you how to get in touch with me. I should have thought to give you my pager number anyway."

"Nice try," she commented.

"Did it work?"

"Nope."

"Okay, I told them you cuss like a sailor—"

"I do not!"

"—have the sweetest ass this side of the Rocky Mountains, and if you called, to get in touch with me pronto because I've been trying to get you into bed and you might be calling to say yes."

He was trying to cheer her up, she thought. She felt her chin wobble. "That's so sweet," she managed to say, and burst into tears again. She hugged herself, rocking back and forth. This outburst was violent but short, as if mentally she couldn't sustain such anguish for a long period of time.

Sam scooped her onto his lap and held her head against his shoulder. "I told them you were special," he murmured, "and that if you called, I wanted to talk to you no matter where I was or what I was doing."

That was probably a lie, too, she thought, but it was as sweet as the other one. She gulped and managed to say, "Even if you're doing your task force stuff?"

He paused. "Maybe not then."

Her head was aching from crying so much, and her face felt hot. She wanted very much to ask him to make love to her now, but she swallowed the words. As much as she needed the comfort and closeness, the affirmation of life, she wouldn't feel right; their first time shouldn't be under such circumstances. Instead she snuggled her face against his neck and inhaled his warm male scent, taking what comfort she could from his closeness.

"What exactly does a task force do?"

"Depends. Task forces are formed for different reasons."

"What does *your* task force do?"

"It's a multidepartment violent crimes task force. We apprehend violent criminals."

She didn't like the sound of that. She was more comfortable thinking of him asking questions, writing stuff down in a little notebook; in short, detecting. Apprehending violent criminals sounded as if he was breaking down doors and stuff like that, and facing mean people who were likely to shoot at him.

"I want to ask you some questions about that," she said, lifting her head to frown at him. "But not right now. Later."

He blew out a relieved breath.

He held her on his lap for quite a while. He held her close while she called the office and reported off for the rest of the day. She managed to keep her voice even, but Mr. deWynter wasn't in and she had to talk to Gina, who was full of questions and also reported that both Luna and T.J. had called several times.

"I'll call them back," Jaine said, and hung up. Miserably she buried her face against Sam's shoulder again. "How long do I have to dodge them?"

"At least until they aren't at work. I'll check with the sergeant at Sterling Heights to see if her sister has been contacted yet. And just don't answer your phone; anyone who needs me will either page me or call on my cell phone."

Eventually she left the comfort of his lap and went to the bathroom to wash her face with cold water. She peered at herself in the mirror. Her eyes were red, and her entire face was puffy from crying; she looked like hell, and didn't care. Wearily she changed into jeans and a T-shirt, and took two aspirin for her pounding head.

She was sitting on the side of the bed when Sam came looking for her. He loomed in the doorway, big and masculine and utterly comfortable even in the feminine environs of her bedroom. He sat down beside her. "You look tired. Why don't you take a nap?"

She *was* tired, almost overwhelmingly so, but at the same time she didn't think she could sleep. "At least lie down," he said, seeing the doubt on her face. "And don't worry; if you do go to sleep and I learn something, I'll wake you up immediately."

"Scout's honor?"

"Scout's honor."

"Were you ever a scout?"

"Hell, no. I was too busy getting into trouble."

He was being so sweet she wanted to hug him to pieces. Instead she kissed him and said, "Thanks, Sam. I don't know what I'd have done today without you."

"You'd have managed anyway," he said, and returned the kiss with interest, but drew back before it could heat into anything serious. "Sleep if you can," he said, and quietly left the room, closing the door behind him.

She lay down and closed her burning eyes. Eventually the aspirin began to work on her headache, and when she opened her eyes, she realized that the afternoon had grown late. She looked at the clock in some astonishment; three hours had passed. She had slept after all.

She had some treated eye pads for soothing tired and puffy eyes, so she placed two of them over her lids and rested for a little while longer, trying to muster some energy for the next few draining days. When she sat up and removed the eye pads, the puffiness was noticeably less. She brushed her hair and teeth, then wandered out to find Sam watching television with Boo-Boo asleep in his lap.

"Any news?"

He had considerably more details now than he had earlier, but none he wanted her to know. "The sister has been notified, and the press knows Marci's identity now. It'll probably be on the evening news."

Her face tightened with sorrow. "Luna? T. J.?"

"I turned off your phones after you went to sleep. There are a couple of messages from them on your machine, though."

She checked the time again. "They're on their way home

from work now. I'll try their numbers in a few minutes. I'd hate for them to hear it on television."

She had barely gotten the words out of her mouth when two cars pulled into her driveway: Luna's Camaro and T.J.'s Buick. Jaine briefly closed her eyes, trying to brace herself for the next few minutes, and walked barefoot out onto the front porch to meet her friends. Sam came out behind her.

"What's going on?" T.J. half-yelled, her pretty face haggard with tension. "We can't find Marci, you left work and won't answer your telephone—damn it, Jaine . . ."

Jaine felt her face start to crumple. She clamped a hand over her mouth, trying to hold back the sobs that convulsed her chest.

Luna stopped in her tracks, tears welling. "Jaine?" she asked in a shaky voice. "What's happened?"

Jaine took several deep breaths, fighting for control. "It—it's Marci," she managed to say.

T.J. paused with one foot on the first step. She clenched her hands, already beginning to cry even as she asked, "What is it? Is she hurt?"

Jaine shook her head. "No. She—she's dead. Someone killed her."

Luna and T.J. came to her in a rush, and they clung together, weeping for the friend they loved and had lost forever.

Corin sat in front of the television, rocking back and forth as he waited, waited. For three days he had caught every newscast, but so far no one knew what he had done and he thought he would burst. He wanted the world to know the first of the four bitches was dead.

But he didn't know if she was the right one. He didn't know if she was *A*, *B*, *C*, or *D*. He hoped she was *C*. *C* was the one who had said that awful thing about trying harder to be perfect. *C* was the one who really, really needed to die.

But how could he make sure? He had called them, but one never answered her phone, and the other three wouldn't tell him anything.

But there was one he didn't have to worry about now. One down and three to go.

There! The newscaster, looking oh-so-serious, said, "A shocking murder in Sterling Heights takes the life of one of the Detroit area's latest celebrities. Details when we return."

At last! Relief filled him. Now everyone would know they shouldn't say such things about Mother's perfect little man.

He rocked back and forth, singing softly to himself. "One down and three to go. One down and three to go . . ."

nineteen

inding Meldon Geurin, nickname "Brick," didn't take very long. A few questions led to his favorite bar, which led to the names of some of his friends, which led to the statement that, "Yeah, Brick, uh, he and his old lady, uh, had a fight or something, and I heard he's crashing with Victor."

"What's this Victor's last name?" Detective Roger Bernsen asked very nicely, but even when he asked nicely, it came out sounding somehow like a threat, because Detective Bernsen was about two hundred and fifty pounds tightly packed on a five-eleven frame, with a twenty-inch neck, a bullfrog voice, and an expression that said he was about an inch away from a 'roid rage. He couldn't help his voice, didn't care about his weight, and practiced the expression. The total package was very intimidating.

"Uh—Ables. Victor Ables."

"Any idea where Victor lives?"

"In the city, man."

So the Sterling Heights detective contacted the Detroit P.D., and Meldon "Brick" Geurin was picked up and held for questioning.

Mr. Geurin was in a surly mood when Detective Bernsen sat down to talk with him. His eyes were bloodshot and he stank of stale booze, so his surliness could perhaps be attributed to the wrath of grapes.

"Mr. Geurin," said the detective in a polite tone that nevertheless made Mr. Geurin flinch, "when did you last see Ms. Marci Dean?"

Mr. Geurin's head snapped up, a movement he seemed to regret. When he could speak, he said sullenly, "Thursday night."

"Thursday? Are you certain of that?"

"Yeah, why? Did she say I stole something? She was there when I left, and if she says I took something of hers, she's lyin'."

Detective Bernsen didn't respond to that. Instead he said, "Where have you been since Thursday night?"

"In jail," Mr. Geurin said, even more sullenly than before.

Detective Bernsen sat back, the only outward evidence of his astonishment. "Where were you in jail?"

"Detroit."

"When were you picked up?"

"Thursday night sometime."

"And you were released when?"

"Yesterday afternoon."

"So you spent three days as a guest of the city of Detroit?"

Mr. Geurin smirked. "Guest. Yeah."

"What were the charges?"

"Drunk driving, and they said I resisted."

All of that could easily be checked out. Detective Bernsen offered a cup of coffee to Mr. Geurin but wasn't surprised when it was refused. Leaving Mr. Geurin alone, the detective stepped out to make a call to the Detroit P.D.

The facts were as Mr. Geurin had stated them. From 11:34 P.M. Thursday night until 3:41 P.M. Sunday afternoon, Mr. Geurin had been in jail.

As an alibi, it was tough to beat.

Ms. Dean had last been seen alive when she and her three friends left Ernie's on Friday night. Given the condition of the body and the progression of rigor mortis, factored in with the temperature in the climate-controlled house, Ms. Dean had been killed some time Friday night or Saturday morning.

Mr. Geurin, however, was not the killer.

That simple fact presented the detective with a more difficult puzzle than he had first assumed. If Mr. Geurin hadn't done it, who had? So far they hadn't turned up any other romantic relationships, no frustrated lover enraged by her refusal to leave Mr. Geurin. Since she and Mr. Geurin had, in effect, broken off their relationship on Thursday night, that theory didn't fly anyway.

But the attack had been a very personal one, characterized by rage, overkill, and the attempt to blot out the victim's identity. The stab wounds were postmortem; the hammer blows had killed her, but the killer had still been in a rage and had resorted to the knife. The wounds had bled very little, indicating that her heart was no longer beating when she received them. The sexual attack had also been postmortem.

Marci Dean had known her killer, had probably let him into the house, since there were no signs of forced entry. With Mr. Geurin out of the picture, the detective was back to square one.

He would have to retrace her steps Friday night, he thought. Start at Ernie's. Where had she gone from there? Had she hit a bar or two, maybe picked up some guy and taken him home with her?

His brow creased in thought, he returned to Mr. Geurin, who was slumped in the chair with his eyes closed. He sat up when Detective Bernsen entered the room.

"Thank you for your cooperation," Detective Bernsen said politely. "I'll arrange a ride for you if you need it."

"That's it? That's all you wanted to ask me? What's this about?"

Detective Bernsen hesitated. If there was one thing he hated doing, it was bearing the news of death. He could remember an army chaplain coming to the door in 1968 and advising the detective's mother that her husband wouldn't be returning alive from Vietnam. The memory of grief was seared on his brain.

But Mr. Geurin had been put to some trouble in this matter and deserved an explanation. "Ms. Dean was attacked in her home—"

"Marci?" Mr. Geurin sat upright, suddenly alert, his entire manner changed. "Is she hurt? Is she all right?"

Detective Bernsen hesitated again, caught by one of those uncomfortable insights into human emotion. "I'm sorry," he said as gently as possible, knowing the news would be more upsetting than he had previously supposed. "Ms. Dean didn't survive the attack."

"Didn't survive? You mean she . . . she's dead?"

"I'm sorry," the detective said again.

Brick Geurin sat stunned for a moment, then slowly began to collapse. He buried his unshaven face in his hands and sobbed.

Her sister, Shelley, arrived on Jaine's doorstep before seven the next morning. "I wanted to catch you before you went to work," she said briskly when Jaine opened the kitchen door.

"I'm not going to work today." Jaine automatically took another cup from the cabinet and filled it with coffee, then passed

it to Shelley. What now? She didn't feel up to dealing with sisterly outrage.

Shelley set the cup on the table and put her arms around
Jaine, holding her close. "I didn't hear about Marci until I
caught the morning news, and I came right over. Are you okay?"

Tears stung Jaine's eyes again, when she had thought she
couldn't possibly cry any more. She should have been all cried
out. "I'm okay," she said. She hadn't slept much, hadn't eaten
much, and felt as if only half her cylinders were firing, but she
was dealing. As much as Marci's death hurt now, she knew she'd
get through this. The old saw about time marching on was an
old saw precisely because it was so true.

Shelley held her at arm's length, studying her colorless face
and raw, swollen eyes. "I brought a cucumber," she said. "Sit
down."

A cucumber? "Why?" Jaine asked warily. "What are you
going to do with it?"

"Put slices on your eyes, silly," Shelley said in exasperation.
She often sounded exasperated when dealing with Jaine. "It'll
make the swelling to down."

"I have some eye pads for that."

"Cucumbers are better. Sit down."

Because she was so tired, Jaine sat. She watched as
Shelley took an enormous cucumber out of her shoulder
bag and washed it, then looked around. "Where are your knives?"

"I don't know. One of the drawers."

"You don't know where your knives are?"

"Please. I haven't lived here even a month yet. How long did
it take you to get unpacked when you and Al moved?"

"Well, let's see, we moved eight years ago, so . . . eight
years." Humor sparkled in Shelley's eyes as she began methodically opening and closing cabinet drawers.

There was one hard rap on the kitchen door; then it opened

before she could get up. Sam stepped into the kitchen. "I saw a strange car and came over to make sure no reporters were bothering you," he said to Jaine. Legions of reporters had called the night before, including representatives from all four major television networks.

Shelley turned around with the huge cucumber in her hand. "Who are you?" she asked bluntly.

"Her neighbor the cop," Sam said. He eyed the cucumber. "Have I interrupted something?"

Jaine wanted to hit him, but she didn't have the energy. Still, something in her lightened at his presence. "She's going to put it on my eyes."

He gave her a sideways, you-gotta-be-kidding look. "It'll roll off."

She decided she would definitely hit him. Later. "Cucumber *slices.*"

His expression changed to skeptical, I-wanna-see-this. He went to the cabinet and took down another cup and poured himself some coffee. Lounging against the cabinets with his long legs crossed, he waited.

Shelley turned to Jaine, more than a little bemused. "Who *is* this?" she demanded.

"My neighbor," Jaine said. "Shelley, this is Sam Donovan. Sam, my sister, Shelley."

He held out his hand. "Pleased to meet you."

Shelley shook hands, but she looked as if she didn't want to. She resumed looking for a knife. "You live here three weeks, and you already have a neighbor who just walks in and knows where your coffee cups are?"

"I'm a detective," Sam told her, grinning. "It's my job to find out stuff."

Shelley gave him her Queen Victoria look, the one that said she was not amused.

Jaine thought about getting up and hugging him, just because he made her feel better. She didn't know what she would have done without him yesterday. He had been a rock, standing like a wall between her and all the phone calls, and when Sam told someone to stop calling, there was a note in his voice that made people pay attention.

But he wouldn't be there today, she realized. He was dressed for work, in light tan slacks and a crisp white shirt. His pager was clipped to his belt, and his pistol rode on his right kidney. Shelley kept eyeing him as if he were some exotic species, only half her attention on finding a knife.

She finally opened the correct drawer, though, and pulled out a paring knife.

"Oh," Jaine said with mild interest. "So that's where they are."

Shelley turned to face Sam, knife in one hand and cucumber in the other. "Are you sleeping together?" she asked in a hostile tone.

"Shelley!" Jaine said sharply.

"Not yet," Sam said with utter confidence.

Silence fell in the kitchen. Shelley began peeling the cucumber with short, vicious strokes of the knife.

"You don't look much like sisters," Sam observed, as if he hadn't just stopped the conversation cold.

They had heard that comment, or a version of it, their entire lives. "Shelley looks like Dad but has Mom's coloring, and I look like Mom but have Dad's coloring," Jaine said automatically. Shelley was tall, almost five inches taller than Jaine, and lanky and blond. The blond hair was purchased, but looked good with Shelley's hazel brown eyes.

"Are you staying with her today?" Sam asked Shelley.

"I don't need anyone to stay with me," Jaine said.

"Yes," said Shelley.

"Run interference and keep the reporters away from her, okay?"

"I don't need anyone to stay with me," Jaine repeated.

"Okay," Shelley said to Sam.

"Fine," Jaine said. "This is just my house. No one pay any attention to me."

Shelley whacked off two slices of cucumber. "Tilt your head back and close your eyes."

Jaine tilted and closed. "I thought I was supposed to lie down for this."

"Too late." Shelley plopped the cold green slices on Jaine's sore eyelids.

Oh, that felt good, cold and moist and incredibly soothing. She would probably need an entire grocery bag full of cucumbers before Marci's funeral was over, Jaine thought, and just like that the sadness was back. Sam and Shelley had pushed it away for a few moments, and she was grateful to them for the respite.

"I got a call from the investigating detective," Sam said. "Marci's boyfriend, Brick, was in jail in Detroit from Thursday night until late Sunday afternoon. He's in the clear."

"A stranger broke in and killed her?" Jaine asked, removing the cucumber slices and raising her head to look at him.

"Whoever it was, there was no sign of forced entry."

She had read that much in the morning paper. "You know more than you're telling, don't you?"

He shrugged. "Cops always know more than they tell."

And he wasn't going to divulge any details; she could tell by the way his expression slipped into his cop mask. She tried not to imagine what those details might be.

He drained his coffee and rinsed out the cup, turning it upside down on the drainboard. Then he bent down and kissed her, the pressure on her mouth warm and brief. "You have both my pager and cell phone numbers, so if you need me, call."

"I'm okay," she told him, and meant it. "Oh—Do you know if Marci's sister is here?"

He shook his head. "She's gone back to Saginaw. There's nothing she can do here, yet. The house is still cordoned off, and an autopsy is required in murder cases. How long that will take depends on the M.E.'s workload. The funeral may not be until this weekend."

That was another detail she didn't want to think about, Marci's body lying on a refrigerated slab for several days.

"I'll go to work tomorrow, then. I'd like to help her sister with the arrangements, if she wants, but I don't guess there's anything to do yet."

"Not yet." He kissed her again, then lifted her hands, still holding the cucumber slices, and replaced them on her eyelids. "Keep them there. You look like hell."

"Gee, thanks," she said dryly, and heard him chuckle as he left.

There was that silence again. Then Shelley said, "He's different."

Different from Jaine's three ex-fiancés, she meant. No joke. "Yeah," she agreed.

"This looks pretty serious. You haven't known him for long."

If Shelley only knew! She was probably counting the entire three weeks Jaine had lived here. There was no telling what she would say if she knew that for the first two of those weeks Jaine had thought Sam was either a drunk or a drug dealer.

"I don't know how serious it is," she said, knowing she was lying. "I'm not rushing into anything." For her part, she couldn't get much more serious. She was in love with the big jerk. Exactly how or what he felt was still open for discussion.

"That's good," Shelley said. "The last thing you want is another broken engagement."

She could have gone all day without mentioning Jaine's miserable track record, but then Shelley had never been noted for her tact. On the other hand, Jaine had never doubted that her sister loved her, which made up for a lot of tactlessness.

The phone rang. Jaine removed the cucumber slices and reached for the cordless at the same time Shelley did. "Sam said for me to answer the phone," Shelley hissed, as if whoever was calling could hear her.

Ring.

"Since when do you take orders from someone you just warned me against?" Jaine asked dryly.

Ring.

"I didn't exactly *warn*—"

Ring.

Knowing the mini-argument could go on for half an hour, Jaine punched the "talk" button before the answering machine could pick up. "Hello."

"Which one are you?"

"What?" she asked in astonishment.

"Which one are you?"

She disconnected and set the phone down, frowning.

"Who was it?" Shelley asked.

"A crank call. Marci, T.J., and Luna have been getting them since the List came out." Her voice caught a little when she mentioned Marci. "It's the same guy, he always says the same thing."

"Have you reported to the phone company that you're getting obscene calls?"

"They aren't obscene. He says, 'Which one are you?' in this weird whisper. I guess it's a guy, because it's hard to tell when someone's whispering."

Shelley rolled her eyes. "A crank call about the List? You can bet it's a guy. Al says all the guys at work have been really ticked off about parts of it. I'll let you guess which parts they don't like."

"The parts having to do with their parts?" As if she had to guess.

"Men are so predictable, aren't they?" Shelley moved around the kitchen, opening drawers and doors.

"What are you doing?"

"Finding out where everything is so I won't have to look for anything when I start cooking."

"You're cooking? What?" For a slightly disjointed moment, Jaine wondered if Shelley had brought over the ingredients of whatever she planned to cook for her family's supper that night. After all, she had pulled a gigantic cucumber out of her purse; God only knew what else was in there. A roast, maybe?

"Breakfast," Shelley said. "For us. And you're going to eat it, too."

Actually, Jaine was hungry this morning, having skipped supper the night before. Did Shelley think she was crazy? No way was she going to argue with food. "I'll try," she said meekly, and replaced the cucumber slices on her eyes while her sister bustled around preparing made-from-scratch pancakes.

Corin sat staring at the phone, feeling his disappointment wash through him in waves. She hadn't told, either. At least she hadn't snapped at him the way the others had. He had thought she would, had prepared himself for whatever she might say. She had a big mouth on her, as his mother would have said. He often disapproved of the way she talked at work, with all that cursing. His mother wouldn't have liked her at all.

He didn't know what to do now. Killing the first bitch had been . . . so overwhelming. He hadn't expected that wild, hot rush of joy, almost of ecstasy. He had gloried in it, but afterward he had been frightened. What would Mother do if she knew he enjoyed it? He had always been so afraid she would find out his secret pleasure at her punishments.

But the killing . . . oh, the killing. He closed his eyes, swaying back and forth a little as he relived every moment of it in his mind. The shock in the bitch's eyes that split second before the hammer hit her, the sodden thudding sounds, then the joy that leapt through his veins and the feeling of being all-powerful, of knowing she was helpless to stop him because he was so strong— Tears welled into his eyes, because he had enjoyed it so much and now it was over.

He hadn't enjoyed anything so much since the day he had killed Mother.

No—don't think about that. They said he shouldn't think about that. But they said he should take the pills, and they were wrong about that, weren't they? The pills made him go away. So maybe he *should* think about Mother.

He went into the bathroom and checked in the mirror. Yes, he was still there.

He had brought a tube of lipstick from the bitch's house. He didn't know why. After she was dead, he had walked around, looking at her things, and when he was in her bathroom checking himself in the mirror, he had noticed the ungodly amount of makeup strewn about the bathroom, covering every flat surface. The bitch had certainly believed in beautifying herself, hadn't she? Well, she wouldn't be needing this anymore, he had thought, and slipped the lipstick into his pocket. Since that night it had been sitting on the vanity in his bathroom.

He uncapped the tube and twisted the bottom. The obscenely shaped crimson length poked out, like a dog's penis. He knew what a dog's penis looked like because he had—no, don't think of that.

Leaning forward, he carefully outlined his lips in bright red. He straightened and stared at himself in the mirror. He smiled, his red lips stretching over his teeth, and he said, "Hello, Mother."

twenty

It was amazing, Jaine thought the next morning when she stepped onto the elevator at work, how her world could be so altered while most of the people who worked at Hammerstead were unaffected by Marci's death. Of course Luna and T.J. were as grief-stricken as she, and the people in Marci's department were sad and shocked, but most of the people she met on the way in had either not mentioned it at all or said something along the lines of, "Yeah, I heard about that. Awful, isn't it?"

The computer nerds, of course, were unaffected by anything that didn't involve gigabytes. The elevator sign this morning read: NEW PRESS RELEASE BY THE FDA: RED MEAT IS NOT BAD FOR YOU. RESULTS OF TESTS SHOW IT IS FUZZY GREEN MEAT THAT IS BAD FOR YOU.

Since fuzzy green meat sounded like the ordinary contents of the average computer nerd's refrigerator, that notice probably had deep personal meaning for most of them, Jaine thought. On any other day, she would have laughed. Today she couldn't summon up even a smile.

Neither T.J. nor Luna had worked the day before, either. They had arrived on her doorstep a little after eight A.M., their eyes in the same condition hers had been. Shelley had whacked off more slices from her cucumber, then set about making more pancakes, which were as comforting to her friends as they had been to Jaine.

Shelley had never met Marci, but she was willing to listen to them talk about her, which they had done all day long. They had cried a lot, laughed some, and wasted a lot of time hazarding theories about what had happened, since Brick was undeniably in the clear. They knew they weren't going to stumble on The Truth, but talking about it helped. Marci's death was so unbelievable that only by endlessly rehashing it could they gradually come to terms with losing her.

For once, she wasn't early. Mr. deWynter was already there, and he immediately asked her to step into his office.

Jaine sighed. She might be head of payroll, but unfortunately the position carried no power, only responsibility. By leaving work early on Monday and not working at all on Tuesday, she had left them shorthanded. DeWynter must have been sweating, wondering if they would get everything finished in time; people tended to get unreasonable when their paychecks didn't arrive on schedule.

She was prepared to accept his criticism, so she was taken aback when he said, "I want to tell you how sorry I am about your friend. That's an awful thing to happen."

She had sworn she wouldn't cry at work today, but deWynter's unexpected sympathy almost did her in. She blinked to hold back the tears. "Thank you," she said. "It *is* awful. And I want to apologize for leaving the department in the lurch on Monday—"

He shook his head. "I understand. We put in some extra hours, but no one complained. When is the funeral service scheduled?"

"It hasn't been, yet. The autopsy—"

"Oh, of course, of course. Please let me know when it will be; a lot of people here at Hammerstead would like to attend."

Jaine nodded her promise, and escaped back to her own desk and a pile of work.

She had known the day would be tough, but she hadn't anticipated quite how tough. Gina and all the others in her department had to extend their sympathies, of course, which almost had her weeping again. Since she didn't have a cucumber with her, she had to fight the tears all day long.

Without it being planned, both T.J. and Luna showed up at lunchtime. "Railroad Pizza?" T.J. asked, and they all got in T.J.'s car for the short drive.

They had just received their vegetarian pizzas when Jaine remembered she hadn't told them about the crank phone call she had received just before they arrived they day before. "I finally got one of those 'Which one are you?' calls," she said.

"Aren't they creepy?" Luna took an unenthusiastic bite of pizza. Her lovely face looked as if she had aged ten years in the last two days. "Since the rest of us have had at least two of them, I'm surprised it took him so long to get to you."

"Well, I have had a lot of hang-ups on my answering machine, but I just assumed they were from reporters."

"Probably. God knows we've all had plenty of those." T.J. rubbed her forehead. "My head is pounding. I think it finally really hit me last night when I got home, and I cried until I was sick. Galan—"

Jaine looked up. "Yes, how *is* the Galan situation? Is he still bunking down in a motel?"

"No. He was at work Monday when we heard, of course, but he had called several times and left messages for me, and he came home that night. I guess the situation is still up in the air. What with Marci, I haven't felt like hashing things out with him. He's been pretty quiet, but . . . considerate, too. Maybe he's hoping I'll forget." She took an almost vicious bite of pizza.

"Guess there's not much chance of that," Jaine said dryly, and Luna smiled.

"Not in this lifetime," T.J. said. "But let's talk about something interesting, like Sam." She got a mischievous sparkle in her eyes. "I can't believe you thought that sexy hunk was a drug-dealing drunk."

Jaine found that she, too, could smile today. "What can I say? He cleans up well. You should see him when he's wearing old, torn clothes, hasn't shaved, and is in a really bad mood."

"Those dark eyes . . . Wow." Luna fanned herself with her hand. "Plus he has a really nice set of shoulders, in case you haven't noticed."

Jaine refrained from saying that she had noticed everything about Sam. They didn't need to know about the kitchen-window episode. Funny, she thought, she had regaled them almost every day with tales about her fractious encounters with him when she still thought he was a drunken jerk, but once things started getting more personal between them, she had stopped talking about him.

"He's hot for you, too," T.J. added. "That man wants to jump your bones. Take my word for it."

"Maybe," Jaine said vaguely. She didn't want to discuss how badly her bones wanted to be jumped by him, or how close they had already been to making love.

"You don't have to be psychic to know that," Luna told T.J., her tone wry. "He came right out and said so."

T.J. laughed. "So he did. He isn't shy, is he?"

No, shy was one thing Sam Donovan definitely wasn't.

Brash, cocky, arrogant, smart, sexy, sweet—those words described him down to his bones. She doubted he had a single shy gene in his body, thank God.

T.J.'s cell phone rang. "It's probably Galan," she said, sighing as she fished it out of her purse. She flipped it open and punched the receive button. "Hello?"

Jaine watched as her face turned red. "How did you get this number?" she snapped, and punched the off button. "Bastard," she muttered as she returned the phone to her purse.

"I take it that wasn't Galan," Jaine said.

"It was that creep." T.J.'s voice quivered with anger. "I'd like to know how he got my cell number, because I don't give it out a lot."

"Is there an information for cell numbers, maybe?" Luna asked.

"The account's in Galan's name, not mine, so how would he know I'm the one who carries the phone?"

"What did he say?" asked Jaine.

"The usual 'Which one are you?' crap. Then he said, 'Marci.' Just her name. Damn him, that's a sick thing to do."

Jaine put down her slice of pizza. She was suddenly cold all over, the fine hairs at the nape of her neck standing up. My God, what if those phone calls had something to do with Marci's murder? Maybe it was a stretch, but maybe it wasn't. Maybe it was some weirdo who really, really hated them because of the List, and now he was coming after them one by one—

She was hyperventilating. T.J. and Luna were both staring at her. "What's wrong?" Luna asked in alarm.

"I just had the most horrible thought," Jaine whispered. "What if he's the one who killed Marci? What if he's after us all?"

Twin expressions of pure shock crossed their faces. "No way," Luna said in instant rejection.

"Why not?"

"Because! That's so crazy. Things like that don't happen. Well, maybe to celebrities, but not to normal people."

"Marci was murdered," Jaine said, still unable to get much volume to her voice. "Was that normal?" She shivered. "The phone calls at home I didn't think much about, but you're right, T.J., how did he get your cell phone number? I'm sure there are ways, but most people wouldn't know how. Are we being stalked?"

Both of them stared at her again.

"Now *I'm* scared," Luna said after a moment. "You live alone, I live alone, Galan doesn't get home until almost midnight, and Marci was alone."

"But how would he know that? I mean, Brick was living with her until just the day before," T.J. protested.

Her intuition gave Jaine another kick in the gut. She thought she was going to be ill. "It was in the newspaper—'no sign of forced entry.' I heard Sam talking on the phone. They thought it was Brick because he was her boyfriend and he had a key, but it wasn't Brick, so they think it was someone else Marci knew. She let him in and he killed her." She swallowed. "It's someone we *all* know."

"Oh, my God." Luna clapped both hands over her mouth, her eyes wide with horror.

T.J. dropped her slice of pizza. She looked sick, too, and suddenly afraid. She tried for a shaky laugh. "We're scaring ourselves, like little kids telling ghost stories around a campfire."

"Good. If we're scared, we'll be more careful. I'm going to call Sam as soon as I get back to the office—"

T.J. took her cell phone out of her purse and turned it on. "Here," she said, extending it across the table to Jaine. "Call him now."

Jaine dug in her purse for the scrap of paper on which he had written both of his numbers. Her hands were shaking as she tried his cell phone first. The connection was made and a ring sounded in her ear. Twice. Three times—

"Donovan."

She gripped the little phone hard with both hands. "This is Jaine. Sam—we're scared. We've all been getting crank calls since the List came out, but I haven't mentioned it because they weren't threatening or anything, he just asks which one we are— you know, *A, B, C,* or *D*—but he just called T.J. on her cell phone and said Marci's name. How did he get T.J.'s number? The phone's in her husband's name, so how would he know T.J. is the one with the phone instead of Galan? I heard you say Marci probably knew her killer and let him in the house, and whoever called T.J. knows her because otherwise how would he have her number, and I know I sound hysterical, but I'm scared and I wish you would tell me I'm letting my imagination run away with me—"

"Where are you?" he asked quietly.

"Railroad Pizza. Please tell me I'm letting my imagination run away with me."

"I think you need to get Caller ID," he said, his tone still too even. "If T.J. and Luna don't have it, tell them to get it. Today. Call the phone company from work to get it started, and stop on the way home to buy the units."

She took a deep breath. "Okay. Caller ID."

"Do you have a cell phone? Or Luna?"

"No, just T.J."

"Both of you need to get one, and keep it with you, so you'll have a way to call for help if you can't get to a land line. And I mean *with* you, in a pocket, not in your purse or car."

"Cell phones. *Check.*" They were going to have several stops on the way home, she thought.

"Did anything about his voice sound familiar?"

"No, he whispers, but it's kind of a loud whisper. It sounds funny."

"Any background noise that you can identify?"

She relayed the question to T.J. and Luna. They shook their heads. "No, nothing."

"Okay. Where do T.J. and Luna live?"

She gave him their addresses. T.J. lived in Mount Clemens, Luna in Royal Oak, all towns on the north side of Detroit.

Sam swore. "Royal Oak is in Oakland County. That's four different departments in two different counties who need to get a heads-up on this."

"You were supposed to tell me I'm crazy," she said in a shaky voice, though somehow she had known he wouldn't.

"Marci's dead," he said bluntly. "All four of you have gotten the same crank call. Do you want to trust your life to coincidence?"

Put in those terms, maybe she wasn't crazy after all. She took a deep breath. "What should we do?"

"Tell T.J. and Luna that, until we find out who's making these calls, not to let anyone in their houses except family, don't get in a car with anyone except family, not even if they have a breakdown and someone offers a ride. Keep their doors and windows locked, and if either of them has an automatic garage door, make sure no one gets inside when the door raises."

"How long will it take to find this creep?"

"Depends. If he's just a dumb fuck making phone calls, the Caller ID may nab him, or the call return number. If not, we'll put a trace on your lines."

"But if he's a dumb f—" She caught herself before she said the word. "If he's a dumb you-know-what, how did he get T.J.'s cell phone number?"

"Like you said. He knows her."

As T.J. parked in front of Hammerstead, they all looked out at the big brick building. "It's probably someone who works here," Jaine said.

"It would almost have to be," Luna said. "Some jerk who thinks it's funny to scare us."

"Sam said we shouldn't trust our lives to coincidence. Until we know better, we should assume that the guy who's making the phone calls is the same guy who killed Marci."

"I can't believe we work with a murderer," T.J. said faintly. "I just can't. It's too unbelievable. Jerks, yes. Just look at Bennett Trotter. Marci hated his guts."

"So do we all." Bennett Trotter was the resident slimeball. A twinge of memory made Jaine frown as she tried to nail it down. "The night we came up with the List . . . remember, Marci was telling us about Kellman grabbing her ass? Wasn't it Bennett who had something to say about it?"

"I think so," T.J. said, but doubtfully. "I don't really remember."

"I do," said Luna. "Bennett said something about taking Kellman's place if Marci was that hard up."

"He's a bottom feeder, but I can't see him killing anyone," T.J. said, shaking her head.

"The point is, we don't *know*, so we have to assume everyone is guilty. When Sam finds out who has been making the calls, if whoever it is has an alibi, then we can relax. Until then, we're on guard against everyone." Jaine wanted to shake T.J.; she just couldn't seem to grasp that they might be in danger, too. They probably weren't; she hoped they weren't. But the whole thing with the telephone call today took the crank calls to another level, and she was deeply uneasy. Part of her agreed with T.J.; the whole supposition was too fantastic, too unbelievable. She was simply letting her imagination run away with her. Another, more primal, part of her brain said that Marci was dead, murdered, and whoever killed her was still out there. That seemed even more unbelievable than the other, yet it was true.

She tried another tactic. "If Sam thinks we should be extra

careful, that's good enough for me. He knows a lot more about these things than we do."

"That's true," T.J. said. "If he's worried, we should do what he said."

Jaine mentally rolled her eyes. After their first exposure to Sam, T.J., Luna, and even Shelley had all begun acting as if he were the Grand Pooh-Bah. Well, whatever worked; what mattered was that they were cautious.

They walked together into the building, then parted to go to their different departments. Mindful of Sam's instructions, she called the phone company to arrange for Caller ID and all the other bells and whistles, including call forwarding. It occurred to her that it might come in handy to be able to transfer her incoming calls to, say, Sam's house.

Sam called Detective Bernsen. "Roger, my gut tells me we have a bigger problem than we thought."

"How's that?"

"You know that Ms. Dean was one of the List Ladies, right?"

"Yeah, what about it, other than giving the reporters something to howl about?"

"Turns out all four of the ladies have been getting crank calls from the same guy. He asks them which one they are."

"Which one?"

"Yeah. Have you read the List?"

"I haven't had the pleasure. My wife has quoted parts of it to me, unfortunately."

"The four women are identified only as *A, B, C,* and *D.* So this guy asks them which one they are, like it's important to him. Today while they were at lunch, he called on T.J.'s cell phone and asked the usual question, then said Ms. Dean's name. No threats or anything like that, just her name."

"Huh," said Roger, which meant he was thinking.

"T.J.'s cell phone is in her husband's name, so most people would think he's the one who carries it. This guy not only knew the number, he knew T.J. is the one with the phone."

"So he's either familiar with the ladies or he knows the husband."

"Why would a husband give his wife's cell phone number to another man?"

"Good point. Okay, the caller knows the ladies. Huh."

"The odds are Marci Dean knew the killer. She opened her door and let him in, right?"

"Right. She had a peephole in the door. She could see whoever came knocking."

"The crank caller disguises his voice, speaks only in a whisper."

"Meaning they might recognize his voice if he spoke normally. You think the killer and the crank caller are the same guy?"

"Either that or it's a big coincidence."

"Son of a bitch." Like most cops, Roger wasn't big on coincidence. "Where does this guy know all of them from? They work together or something?"

"Yeah, at Hammerstead Technology, just off I-696 at Southfield. He probably works there, too."

"He's someone with access to their personal information. That should narrow it down."

"Hammerstead develops computer technology. A lot of people there would know how to access the personnel files."

"It couldn't be easy, could it?" Roger asked wearily.

"My gut tells me something about the List set him off, and he's going to be coming after the other three."

"Jesus. You may be right. You got their names and addresses?"

"T.J. Yother, Mount Clemens, husband's name is Galan. Luna Scissum, Royal Oak, unmarried and lives alone." He gave Roger the street addresses. "Jaine Bright, the third one, is my next-door neighbor. She's single, too."

"Huh. Is she your lady friend?"

"Yeah."

"So you're dating one of the List Ladies? Man, that takes balls." Roger caught his own joke and laughed.

"You have no idea." Sam grinned, thinking of Jaine and her stubborn chin with that cute little dent in it, and her almost-dimples and sparkling blue eyes. She attacked life, rather than simply letting it happen; he'd never before met anyone so annoying and funny and sharp. He had major plans for her, the most immediate of which was getting her under him. No way would he let anything happen to her, even if he had to quit his job and become her twenty-four-hour-a-day bodyguard.

"Okay, if you're right, at least we have a place to start," Roger said, briskly returning to the subject. "Hammerstead Technology. I'll get the ball rolling on getting access to their personnel files, see what shakes out of the tree, but if you're right about the computer geeks, this could take a while. Officially, I don't know what we can do to keep the ladies safe. You're talking four different towns—"

"And two counties. I know." The administrative hassle would be a bitch. Sam got a headache just thinking about it.

"Unofficially, we'll work out something. We'll call in favors, maybe get some guys to volunteer for watchdog duty. The ladies do know to be cautious, right?

"They're all supposed to get Caller ID and cell phones today. We might get lucky if he calls one of them again. I also told them not to let anyone in except family, not to accept rides from anyone. I don't want this son of a bitch to be able to get anywhere near them."

twenty-one

Jaine found herself studying every man she saw at work that day, wondering if he was the one. That one of them could be a killer was almost beyond belief. They all seemed so normal, or at least as normal as any other large group of men who worked in the computer industry. Some of them she knew and liked, some of them she knew and didn't like, but she couldn't see any of them as killers. A lot of guys, particularly the ones on the first two floors, she knew by sight but not by name. Had Marci known one of them well enough that she had let him into her house?

Jaine tried to think what she would do if someone she recognized knocked on her door at night, maybe claiming to have had car trouble. Until today, she probably would have opened her door without hesitation, wanting only to be helpful. The killer, even if he turned out to be some stranger, had forever robbed her of that trust, that inner sense of security. She had liked to think she was smart and aware, that she didn't take chances, but how often had she opened her door at a knock without asking who was on the other side? She shuddered now to think of it.

Her front door didn't even have a peephole in it. She could see who was at the door only if she climbed on her sofa and pulled back the curtain, then leaned far to the right. And the upper half of her kitchen door was nothing but nine small panes of glass, easily smashed; then all any intruder would have to do was reach in and unlock it. She had no alarm system, no means of protecting herself—nothing! The best she could hope to do if anyone broke into her house while she was there was escape out the window, assuming she could get it open.

She had a lot of work to do, she thought, before she would feel safe in her house again.

She worked half an hour later than usual, doing a little catch-up on the pile of paperwork that had accumulated during her absence. As she was crossing the parking lot, she noticed there were only a handful of cars remaining and, for the first time, realized how vulnerable she was leaving work late like this, alone. All three of them, she and Luna and T.J., should time their arrivals and departures with the crowd, to take advantage of the safety in numbers. She hadn't even told them she intended to work late.

There was so much she had to think about now, so much inherent danger in things she had never before had to consider.

"Jaine!"

As she crossed the parking lot, the sound of her name broke into her consciousness, leaving her aware that someone had called her at least twice, maybe more. She turned around, mildly surprised to see Leah Street hurrying after her.

"I'm sorry," she apologized, though she wondered what Leah

wanted. "I was thinking and didn't hear you at first. Is something wrong?"

Leah stopped, her graceful hands fluttering, an uncomfortable expression on her face. "I just—I wanted to say I'm sorry about Marci. When is the funeral?"

"I don't know yet." She didn't feel up to explaining again about the autopsy. "Marci's sister is making the arrangements."

Leah nodded jerkily. "Let me know, please. I'd like to attend."

"Yes, of course."

Leah seemed to want to say something else or maybe didn't know what else to say; either condition was awkward. Finally she bobbed her head and turned to hurry to her own car. Her full skirt flew around her legs. Today's dress was particularly hopeless, a lavender print that did nothing for her coloring and with a small ruffle around the neckline. It looked like a yard-sale reject, though Leah pulled down a good salary—Jaine knew exactly how much—and probably shopped at nice department stores. She simply had no fashion sense.

"On the other hand," Jaine muttered to herself as she unlocked the Viper, "I have no people sense." Her judgment must be seriously off, because the two people from whom she would never have expected sympathy and sensitivity—Mr. deWynter and Leah Street—were the two who had gone out of their way to tell her they were sorry about Marci.

Mindful of Sam's instructions, she drove to an electronics store and bought a Caller ID unit, signed up for cellular service, went through all the paperwork for that, then had to choose a phone. The selection engrossed her; did she want one of the little flip-tops or one that didn't flip? She decided on the non-flipper, figuring that if she were running for her life from a crazed murderer, she didn't want to have to deal with flipping up before dialing.

Next she had to decide on a color. She immediately dismissed black as too basic. Neon yellow? It would be difficult to misplace. The blue one was cute; she didn't see many blue ones. On the other hand, there was nothing like red.

Once she selected the red phone, she had to wait for it to be programmed. By the time she left the electronics store, the late summer sun was almost down, clouds were sweeping in from the southwest, and she was starving.

Because a cool wind was blowing in off those clouds, promising rain, and she still had two more stops to make before she went home, she got a fast-food burger and a soft drink and gulped them down as she drove. The burger wasn't very good, but it was food, and that was all her stomach required.

Her next stop was a firm that installed security systems, where she answered questions, selected the system she wanted, and wrote a large check. The system would be installed a week from the upcoming Saturday.

"But that's ten days!" Jaine said, frowning.

The beefy man consulted an appointment book. "Sorry, but that's the earliest we can get to you."

Deftly she reached over the desk and plucked her check from where it lay in front of him. "I'll call around and see if someone else can get to me sooner than that. Sorry I wasted your time."

"Hold on, hold on," he said hastily. "Is this some kind of emergency? If someone is having trouble, we move them to the top of the list. You shoulda said so."

"It's an emergency," she said firmly.

"Okay, let me see what I can do." He studied the appointment book again, scratched his head, tapped his pencil on the book, and said, "I can work you in this Saturday, since it's an emergency."

Careful not to let any triumph show in her expression, she returned the check to him. "Thank you," she said, and meant it.

Her next stop was a building materials store. It was a huge place, with everything one would need to build a house, except the money. She bought a peephole for the front door—the instructions said "Easy to install"—and a new kitchen door that wasn't half glass and two new deadbolts. After making arrangements for the door to be delivered on Saturday, and paying extra for the privilege, she heaved a sigh of relief and started home.

Rain began splattering on the windshield just as she turned onto her street. Darkness had fallen, deepened by the cloud cover. Lightning flashed briefly in the west, lighting up the belly of the storm system, and thunder rumbled.

Her house was dark. She usually got home well before dark, so she didn't leave any lights on. Normally she wouldn't worry about stepping into a dark house, but tonight she felt a chill creep up her spine. She was edgy, more aware of her vulnerability.

She sat for a moment in the car, reluctant to turn off the motor and go inside. No vehicle was parked in Sam's driveway, but there was a light on in his kitchen; maybe he was at home. She wished he would leave his truck in the driveway instead of parking it in the garage, so she could tell when he was there and when he wasn't.

Just as she turned off the headlights and ignition, she saw movement to her left. Her heart jumped into her throat, then she realized it was Sam, coming down his front steps.

Relief flooded through her. She gathered her purse and plastic shopping bags and got out of the car.

"Where the hell have you been?" he shouted, looming behind her as she locked the car door.

She hadn't expected him to start yelling; startled, she dropped one of the bags. "Damn it!" she said as she leaned down to pick it up. "Do you have to make a career out of scaring me?"

"Someone needs to scare you." He grabbed her upper arms and hauled her up to face him. He was shirtless, and she found herself nose-to-pectoral-muscle with him. "It's eight o'clock, you may have a killer stalking you, and you don't bother to call and let anyone know where you are? You deserve more than just being scared!"

She was tired, nervous, the rain was getting heavier by the minute, and she was in no mood to be yelled at. She lifted her head to glare at him, and water trickled down her face. "*You* told me to get Caller ID and a cell phone, so if I'm late, it was your idea!"

"It took you three goddamn hours to accomplish what a normal person can do in half an hour?"

Was he saying she wasn't normal? Incensed, she put both hands on his bare chest and shoved him as hard as she could. "Since when did I start answering to you?"

He staggered back maybe an inch.

"Since about a week ago!" he said furiously, and kissed her.

His mouth was hard and angry, and his heart pounded like a sledgehammer beneath her hands. As always when he kissed her, it was as if time spun away, leaving only the here and now. The taste of him filled her; his bare skin was hot to the touch, despite the rain beating down on them. He locked her against him, his arms so tight she couldn't draw a deep breath, and against her belly she felt the thrust of his erection.

He was shaking, and suddenly she realized just how scared he had been on her behalf. He was big and rough-looking, and strong enough to hold his own with an ox; every day he probably saw, without flinching, things that would make the average person cringe in horror. But tonight he had been afraid—afraid for her.

Her chest ached suddenly, as if her heart squeezed. Her knees wobbled and she sank against him, melting into him, rising on tiptoe to meet his kiss with equal force, equal passion. He groaned, deep in his throat; the kiss changed, the anger fading, to be replaced by violent hunger. She had surrendered totally, but that didn't seem to be enough for him because he sank his hand in her hair and pulled her head back, arching her neck and exposing her throat to his mouth. Rain spattered in her face, and she closed her eyes, helpless in his iron grip and not wanting to be anywhere else.

After the emotional upheaval of the past three days she needed to lose herself in the physical, to push all the grief and fear away and feel only Sam, think only of Sam. He lifted her off her feet and began walking with her, and she didn't protest except when he stopped kissing her, didn't struggle except to get closer.

"Damn it, would you stop wiggling?" he growled in a strained tone, shifting her to one side as he climbed his front steps.

"Why?" Her voice sounded smoky, sexy. She hadn't known her throat would do that.

"Because I'm going to come in my jeans if you don't," he half-shouted in raw frustration.

Jaine thought about his problem for maybe half a heartbeat. Since the only way she could be certain not to overexcite him was to tear herself out of his grip and not touch him at all, that meant she would be depriving herself.

"Suffer," she told him.

"*Suffer?*" He sounded outraged. He wrenched open his front door and carried her inside. It was dark in the living room, the only light filtering through from the kitchen. He smelled of heat and rain and wet hair. She tried to run her hands over those broad shoulders and found herself still encumbered by purse and shopping bags. Impatiently she dropped them to the floor, then attached herself to him like a limpet.

Cursing, he staggered a few steps and pinned her to the wall. He tugged at her slacks with rough hands, attacking the button and zipper until the button flew off and the zipper yielded. Her slacks slid down her legs and pooled around her feet. She kicked off her shoes, and he lifted her out of the circle of fabric. Immediately she wound her legs around his hips, feverishly trying to get closer, to meld their bodies and ease this wildfire of need that was burning her up on the inside.

"Not yet!" Panting, he leaned his weight against her to keep her in place against the wall and unwrapped her legs from his waist. Her ribcage depressed by his weight, Jaine could manage only the first protesting moan before he hooked his fingers in the waistband of her panties and tugged them down her thighs.

Oh.

She tried to think why she had been going to make him wait another couple of weeks, at least, maybe even a whole menstrual cycle. Nothing reasonable came to mind, not when making him wait also meant making herself wait—not when she was so scared that the same person who had killed Marci might also be targeting the rest of them and she would kick herself if she died without knowing what it was like to make love with him. Right here, right now, there was nothing more important than trying this man on for size.

She kicked her panties away, he lifted her high once again, and she coiled her legs around him. His knuckles brushed between her legs as he unfastened his jeans and let them drop. She caught her breath as the last barrier fell from between them and his penis pressed against her, naked and hot, searching. Pleasure zinged through her, making her nerve endings sizzle. She arched helplessly, seeking more, needing more.

He swore softly, under his breath, and hitched her just a little higher to adjust her position. She felt the head of his penis probing at her, smooth and hard and hot, then an almost incredible sense of pressure as he eased his support and let her weight sink down on it. Her body resisted at first, then began to stretch and admit him, inch by searing inch. She felt everything in her begin to tighten as sensation roared through her—

He stopped, breathing hard, his hot face buried against her neck. His voice muffled, he said rawly, "Did you go on the pill?"

Jaine dug her nails into his bare shoulders, almost sobbing with need. How could he stop *now?* Only the thick head of his penis was inside her, and it wasn't enough, wasn't nearly enough. Her inner muscles clenched around him, trying to draw him deeper, and an explosive curse tore from his throat.

"Damn it, Jaine, did you go on the pill?"

"Yes," she finally managed to say, and her tone was just as raw as his.

He braced her against the wall and with one rough thrust pushed his entire length inside her.

She heard herself cry out, but the sound was distant. Every cell in her body focused on the thick shaft pounding back and forth inside her, his rhythm hard and fast, and she climaxed the same way. Sensation exploded in her, and she bucked against him, screaming, her hips jerking and her entire body shuddering. The rest of the world spun completely away.

He came a second later, driving into her with almost brutal force. She thudded against the wall with each deep thrust, her weight sliding down and forcing him even deeper, so deep that she stiffened convulsively and climaxed again.

Afterward, he rested heavily against her, his skin damp with sweat and rain. He was breathing hard, his chest heaving as he sucked in air. The house was dark and silent except for the rain drumming on the roof and the gasping sounds of their overtaxed lungs. The wall was cool against her back, but uncomfortably hard.

Jaine tried to think of something clever to say, but her mind refused to work. This was too serious, too damn important, for quips. So she closed her eyes and rested her cheek on his shoulder while her galloping heartbeat slowly began to calm and her loins relaxed around his shaft.

He muttered something unintelligible and tightened his grip on her, holding her with one arm around her back and the other under her bottom as he stepped out of his jeans and unsteadily walked to the bedroom. He was still inside her, her body anchored to his, as he lowered them to the bed and settled on top of her.

The room was dark and cool, the bed wide. He stripped off her silk shirt and unclipped her bra, tossing both garments to the floor. Now they were both totally naked, his chest hair rasping her nipples as he began to move again. His rhythm this time was slower but no less powerful as each thrust took him in to the hilt.

To her surprise, the fever began to build again. She had thought she was too exhausted to be aroused again, but she found out differently. She hooked her legs around his and ground her pelvis up to meet each thrust, clinging to him, pulling him even deeper into her, and when she came, the paroxysm was even stronger than the others. He made a guttural sound, climaxing while she still shuddered beneath him.

A long time later, when pulses had slowed, sweat had dried, and muscles had become halfway responsive again, he levered himself off her and rolled onto his back, one arm draped over his eyes. "Shit," he said under his breath.

Because the room was so quiet, she heard him. A tiny flare of temper made her eyes narrow. She still felt like a limp, overcooked noodle, so a tiny flare was all she could manage. "Gee, that's romantic," she said sarcastically. The man hadn't been able to keep his hands off her for a week, and now that they had finally made love, "shit" was the best comment he could make, as if the whole experience had been a mistake?

He lifted the arm covering his eyes and turned his head to glare at her. "I knew you were trouble the first time I saw you."

"What do you mean, trouble?" She sat up, glaring back at him. "I am not trouble! I'm a very nice person except when I have to deal with jerks!"

"You're the worst kind of trouble," he snapped. "You're *marrying* trouble."

Considering three men had already found better things to do than marry her, that wasn't the most tactful comment he could have made. It was especially hurtful coming from a man who had just given her three explosive orgasms. She snatched up the pillow and whacked him on the head with it, then bolted out of bed.

"I can take care of that problem for you," she said, fuming as she searched the dark bedroom for her bra and shirt. Damn it, where was the light switch? "Since I'm so much *trouble*, I'll stay on my side of the driveway and you can stay the hell on your side of the driveway!" She was shouting by the time she was finished. There—that white blur might be her bra. She swooped down on it and picked it up, but it was a sock. A smelly sock. She threw it at him. He swatted it aside and lunged out of bed, reaching for her.

"What did you do with my damn clothes!" she bellowed at him, evading his outstretched hand and storming around the room in the dark. "And where's the damn light switch?"

"Would you settle down!" he said, sounding suspiciously as if he were snorting with laughter.

He was *laughing* at her. Tears stung her eyes. "Hell, no, I won't settle down!" she shouted, and swung toward the door. "You can keep the damn clothes, I'll walk home *naked* before I stay here with you another minute, you insensitive jerk—"

A hard-muscled arm locked around her waist and sent her airborne. She shrieked, arms flailing; then she bounced on the bed and the air left her lungs with a "whoof."

She had time to suck in just a little air before Sam landed on her, his heavy weight flattening her and forcing another exhalation. He was laughing as he subdued her with ridiculous ease; in five seconds flat she couldn't wiggle anything.

To her astonishment and rage, she discovered he had another erection; it throbbed against her closed thighs. If he thought she would open her legs for him again after—

He shifted, expertly pressed with his knee, and her legs

opened anyway. Another shift and he slid smoothly inside her, and she wanted to scream because he felt so good and she loved him and he was a *jerk*. Her lousy luck with men was still holding.

She burst into tears.

"Ah, babe, don't cry," he said soothingly, moving gently inside her.

"I will if I want to," she sobbed as she clung to him.

"I love you, Jaine Bright. Will you marry me?"

"No way in hell!"

"You have to. You owe me your next paycheck for all the cussing you've done tonight. You won't have to pay up if we get married."

"There's no rule like that."

"I just made one." He framed her head with his big hands and stroked her cheeks with his thumbs, wiping away the tears.

"You said *shit.*"

"What else is a man supposed to say when he sees his glorious bachelor days coming to a swift and ignominious end?"

"You've been married before."

"Yeah, but that didn't count. I was too young to know what I was doing. I thought fucking was the same as loving."

She wished he would be still. How could he carry on a conversation while doing what he was doing to her? No—she wished he would shut up, and keep doing exactly what he was doing, except maybe a little faster. And a little harder.

He kissed her temple, her jaw, the almost-dent in her chin. "I always heard that sex was different with a woman you loved, but I didn't believe it. Sex was sex. Then I got inside you and it was like sticking my cock in an electrical outlet."

"Oh. Was that what all that shaking and yelling was about?" She sniffled, but she was paying attention.

"Smart-ass. Yeah, that's what it was about, not that I was

the only one doing some shaking and yelling. It was *different.* Hotter. Stronger. And when it was over, I wanted to do it all over again."

"You did do it all over again."

"That proves it, then. For God's sake, I've already come twice and here I am hard again. That's either a fucking miracle, no pun intended, or it's love." He kissed her mouth, slowly and deeply, using his tongue. "Watching you throw a temper tantrum always gets me hard."

"I don't throw tantrums. Why is it when a man gets mad, he's *aaangry,* but when a woman gets mad, it's just a tantrum?" She paused, struck by what he'd said. "Always?"

"Always. Like when you knocked over my trash can, then yelled at me and poked me in the chest."

"You were hard?" she asked in astonishment.

"As a rock."

She said wonderingly, "Well, son of a b—gun."

"So answer my question."

She opened her mouth to say "yes," but caution made her remind him, "I don't do really well with engagements. Gives the guy too much time to think."

"I'm skipping the engagement part. We're not getting engaged; we'll just get married."

"In that case, yes, I'll marry you." She turned her face into his throat and inhaled the heat and scent of his body, thinking that if the perfumers of the world could bottle whatever it was Sam had, the female population would be in perpetual heat.

He growled in frustration. "Because you love me?" he prompted.

She smiled, her lips moving against his skin. "Crazy, wild, absolutely, insanely in love with you," she affirmed.

"We'll get married next week."

"I can't do that!" she said in horror, drawing back to stare up at him as he loomed over her, slowly moving back and forth, back and forth, like seaweed floating on the tide.

"Why the hell not?"

"Because my parents won't be back from vacation for . . . I've lost count of the days. About three weeks, I think."

"Can't they come home early? Where are they, anyway?"

"Touring Europe. And this is Mom's dream vacation, because Dad has Parkinson's, and even though the medication really helps, he's gotten a little worse lately and she was afraid this would be their last chance. He was always too busy before he retired to get away for that length of time, so this is special to both of them, you know?"

"Okay, okay. We'll do it the day after they get home."

"Mom won't even be unpacked!"

"Tough. Since we aren't getting engaged, we can't do the big church wedding thing—"

"Thank God," she said feelingly. She had gone through that experience with number two, the bastard, with all the expense and planning and trouble, only to have him back out at the last minute.

He heaved a sigh of relief, as if he had been afraid she would say she *wanted* a big wedding. "We'll have everything ready to go. All your parents will have to do is show up."

Jaine had been doing a really good job concentrating on the conversation while he was doing what he was doing, and she was impressed out of her skull that he could keep up *his* side of the conversation under these circumstances, but her body suddenly reached the point of no return. She gasped, her hips rising convulsively against him.

"We'll talk later!" she said hoarsely, grabbed his butt, and pulled him hard into her.

They didn't talk at all for quite a while.

* * *

Jaine stirred, yawning. She would have been content to lie in his arms all night long, but a sudden thought made her bolt upright. "BooBoo!"

Sam made a noise halfway between a grunt and a groan. "What?"

"BooBoo. He must be starving! I can't believe I forgot about him." She scrambled out of bed. "Where's the light switch? And why don't you have any bedside lamps?"

"Beside the door, right side. Why would I need bedside lamps?"

"For reading." She swept her hand along the wall, found the switch, and flipped it up. Bright light flooded the room.

Sam shielded his eyes, blinking, then flopped over on his stomach. "I read in the living room."

Her own eyes took a minute to adjust. When they did, her pupils widened at the wreck they had made of the bed. The covers were twisted and hanging off, the pillows were—where *were* the pillows?—and the bottom sheet was pulled free at one corner and wadded in the middle of the bed. "Holy cow," she said in astonishment, then shook herself and looked around for her clothes.

Sam opened his eyes and propped up on one elbow, his dark eyes both sleepy and intent as he watched her search the room. She found her shirt tangled in the bedcovers. She got down on her knees to peer under the bed for her bra; he scooted closer so he'd have a better view of her backside waving in the air.

"How on earth did it get under the bed?" she fussed, dragging the bra out of its hiding place.

"Crawled," he suggested.

She gave him a quick grin and looked around. "And my pants are . . .?"

"In the living room."

She went into the living room, turned on a lamp, and was in the process of untangling her pants when Sam wandered in, stark naked and carrying a pair of sneakers. Jaine didn't bother with her bra, but slipped into her panties, then pulled on her shirt and pants. Sam stepped into his jeans and pulled them up, then sat down and put on the sneakers.

"Where are you going?" she asked.

"Walking you to your door."

She opened her mouth to say that wasn't necessary; then she remembered it *was* necessary, at least for now. She put on her shoes, stuffed her bra in her purse, then gathered up her shopping bags. Sam slid his pistol out of its holster, holding it in his right hand. "Give me your key and stay behind me," he said.

She dug her key chain out of her purse, selected the house key for him, and handed it over.

The rain had stopped, leaving the night warm and humid. Crickets chirped, and at the end of the street the corner light wore a misty halo. They crossed both driveways and went up the steps to the kitchen door. Sam tucked the pistol in his waistband while he unlocked the door; then he returned the keys to her and drew the pistol once more. He opened the door, reached inside, and flipped on the light switch.

He uttered a vicious curse. Jaine blinked at the destruction illuminated by the overhead light, then she screamed, "Boo-Boo!" and tried to lunge past Sam. He blocked her with an outthrust arm, turning so that his big body barred the entrance. "Go to my house and call nine-one-one," he barked. "Now!"

"But BooBoo—"

"Go!" he yelled, giving her a shove that almost sent her flying off the stoop. Then he wheeled and stepped into the house.

He was a cop; she had to trust him in this. Her teeth chattering, she ran back to his house and into the kitchen, where she knew he had a cordless. Grabbing it up, she punched the talk button, then 911.

"Where are you calling from?" The voice was impersonal and almost uninterested.

"Uh—next door." Jaine closed her eyes. "I mean, I'm calling from my next door neighbor's. My house has been ransacked." She gave her own address. "My neighbor is a cop, and he's going through the house right now." Carrying the phone, she walked out on the front porch, staring across the driveways at her little house, where lights now blazed from two of the windows. As she watched, the light in her bedroom came on. "He's armed—"

"Who is?" The dispatcher sounded suddenly alarmed.

"My neighbor is! Tell the police if they see a half-naked man with a gun, don't shoot, he's one of them!" She took a deep breath, her heart pounding so hard she thought she would be sick. "I'm going over there."

"No! Ma'am, don't go over there. If your neighbor is a policeman, stay out of his way. Ma'am, are you listening?"

"I'm here." She didn't say she was listening. Her hand was shaking, clattering the phone against her teeth.

"Stay on the phone, ma'am, so I can keep the responding officers up-to-date on the status. Units have already been dispatched to your address; they'll be there in a few minutes. Just be patient, please."

She couldn't be patient, but she could be sensible. She waited on the porch, tears tracking down her face as she stared unblinkingly at her own house, where Sam was methodically searching it and putting his life in danger every time he entered a room. She didn't dare think about BooBoo. The dispatcher said something else but she had stopped listening, though she did make a noise to let the woman know she was still there. In the distance she could hear the shrill of sirens.

Sam stepped out on the kitchen stoop, BooBoo cradled in his left arm.

"BooBoo!" Jaine threw down the phone and ran across to them. Sam let her take the cat from him, then he tucked the pistol in his waistband.

"Whoever did it didn't hang around," he said, putting his arm around her and urging her back toward his house.

With BooBoo safe and disgruntled in her arms, she dug in her heels. "I want to see—"

"Not yet. Let the techs do their job first, maybe find something that will give us a clue who this bastard is."

"*You* went in—"

"And I was careful not to disturb anything," he said, exasperated. "Come on, let's sit down. The guys will be here in a minute."

She remembered that she had thrown the phone aside. She picked it up and handed it to him. "Nine-one-one is still on the line."

He put it to his ear, but kept a firm grip on her while he succinctly outlined the situation and said the house was clear, then disconnected. He put both arms around Jaine—and BooBoo—and held her close.

"Where did you find BooBoo?"

"He was hiding under that shelf thing in the hallway."

She stroked the cat's head, so grateful he was all right that she almost cried again. Her mom would never forgive her if anything happened to BooBoo.

"Do you think it was him?" she asked Sam, her voice low.

He was silent for a moment. The sirens were much closer now, the sound growing louder and louder in the still night air. As two cars turned the corner onto their street, Sam said, "I can't afford not to think it."

twenty-two

Lights were coming on up and down the street, heads poking out of doors, as Sam and Jaine went to meet the patrolmen. "Detective Donovan," said one of the patrolmen, grinning. "So you're the half-naked man we were told not to shoot."

Sam scowled down at Jaine. She cuddled BooBoo closer. "You're carrying a pistol," she explained. "I didn't want them to shoot you by mistake."

Sadie and George Kulavich came down their sidewalk and stood peering at the flashing lights. They were both wearing robes over their nightclothes; Mr. Kulavich wore bedroom slippers, but Mrs. Kulavich had put on rain boots. Mrs. Kulavich craned her neck, then came closer. Across the street, Jaine could see Mrs. Holland come out her front door.

Sam heaved a sigh. "I checked the house," he said to the patrolmen. "It's been trashed, but no one is in there. You guys take over while I go put on a shirt."

Mrs. Kulavich had edged close enough to hear him. She beamed at him. "Don't bother on my account," she said.

"Sadie!" Mr. Kulavich said in rebuke.

"Oh, hush, George! I'm old, not dead!"

"I'll remind you of that the next time I want to watch the Playboy Channel," he growled.

Sam coughed and strode into his house, keeping his pistol held low against his leg so their bright-eyed old neighbors wouldn't spot it and get too excited.

Jaine became aware of the speculation in the neighbors' eyes as they studied her. She remembered that she hadn't put on her bra, and her silk shirt probably made that fairly obvious. She didn't look down to check, just kept BooBoo cradled to her chest. She didn't reach up to check her hair, either, because she knew it was a mess. The rain had wet it, then she had wallowed in bed with Sam for a couple of hours; it was probably sticking out in spikes. Given Sam's state of undress . . . well. She imagined the conclusion they were jumping to was pretty damn accurate.

Thinking about the neighbors was easier than thinking about her house.

After her first horrifying glimpse of the kitchen, she didn't know if she wanted to see the rest of the house. This, coming so soon after the trauma of Marci's death, was almost more than she could bear, so she concentrated on other things, such as the way Mrs. Kulavich winked at her when Sam came out of the house wearing a neat oxford shirt with the tails tucked into his jeans and his badge clipped to his belt. She wondered if he had put on underwear.

"Are you official?" she asked, eyeing the badge.

"Might as well be. I'm on the scene, and we're all on call after eleven."

She gaped at him. "After elev—what time is it, anyway?"

"Almost midnight."

"Poor BooBoo," she said in horror. "Could you try to find some of his food and let me have a can, so I can feed him?"

Sam looked down at her, the expression in his dark eyes telling her he knew she was avoiding facing the reality about her house, but also saying that he understood. "Okay, I'll find something for him." He glanced over at Mrs. Kulavich. "Sadie, why don't you and Eleanor take Jaine in my house and put on a pot of coffee, okay?"

"Of course, dear."

With Mrs. Kulavich and Mrs. Holland flanking her, Jaine went back inside Sam's house and into the kitchen. She put Boo-Boo down and looked around with interest, since this was the first time she had seen much of the house. Before, they hadn't bothered to turn on a light until she was getting dressed, so she had seen the bedroom and the living room, both of which were furnished with only the essentials. The kitchen, like hers, had a small table and four chairs occupying one end of it, and the stove was about twenty years old. The refrigerator, though, looked brand new, and so did the coffeemaker. Sam had his priorities.

Mrs. Kulavich efficiently prepared the coffee and turned on the machine. Jaine became aware of a pressing need. "Um . . . do you know where the bathroom is?"

"Of course, dear," said Mrs. Holland. "The big bathroom is the second door on the left in the hallway, and there's a small bathroom opening off Sam's bedroom."

Funny that they knew that when she hadn't, but then it was difficult to explore much when one was flat of her back with a two-hundred-pound man on top of her.

She chose the big bathroom, because it was closer, and carried her purse with her. Hurriedly she stripped off her clothes, used the facilities, then found a washcloth and washed away the evidence of four hours of sex. She used his deodorant, combed her hair—which was indeed sticking out in spikes all over her head—and this time when she dressed she put on her bra.

Feeling more in control, she returned to the kitchen for a much-needed cup of coffee.

"It's terrible about your house, dear," said Mrs. Holland, "but wonderful about Sam. I take it congratulations are in order?"

"Eleanor," admonished Mrs. Kulavich. "Times are different now. Young people don't get married just because they've been jumping each other's bones."

"That doesn't mean they shouldn't," said Mrs. Holland severely.

Jaine cleared her throat. So much had happened that she could barely comprehend it all, but the hours in bed with Sam stood out clearly in her mind. "He did ask me to marry him," she confided. "And I said yes." She didn't use the cursed word "engaged."

"Oh, my!" Mrs. Kulavich beamed at her.

"That's wonderful! When's the wedding?"

"In about three weeks, when my parents get back from vacation." She made a rash decision. "And everyone on the street is invited." So their small wedding just got a little bigger; so what?

"You'll have to have a bridal shower," said Mrs. Holland. "Where's a pen and notepad? We have to make plans."

"But I don't need—" Jaine began, then saw the expressions on their faces and stopped in mid-sentence. Belatedly she realized that she did indeed need a bridal shower, to help replace what had just been destroyed.

Her chin wobbled. She quickly firmed it as one of the patrolmen stepped into the kitchen carrying two cans of cat food. "Detective Donovan sent these over," he said.

Grateful for the distraction, Jaine looked around for Boo-Boo. He wasn't anywhere in sight. Upset at being plopped down in a strange environment, he was probably hiding. She knew all his favorite hiding places in her house, but she had no idea where he would hide in Sam's.

As bait, she opened one of the cans of food, then crawled through the house softly calling BooBoo's name, pushing the open can in front of her. She finally found him behind the couch, but even with the lure of food, it took her fifteen minutes to coax him out of his hiding place. He crept out and daintily began eating, while she stroked him and took comfort in his warm, sinuous body.

He would have to go to Shelley's house, she thought. She couldn't risk letting him stay with her now.

Tears seared her eyes, and she bent her head to hide them, concentrating on the cat. When she hadn't been at home, the maniac had taken out his rage on her possessions. While she was grateful beyond telling that she had been in Sam's bed rather than her own, she couldn't risk BooBoo and her dad's car again—

The car. Oh, my God, the car.

She sprang to her feet, startling BooBoo so much he darted back behind the couch. "I'll be right back," she called to Mrs. Kulavich and Mrs. Holland, then ran outside.

"Sam!" she yelled. "The car! Did you check the car?"

Her yard and Sam's were full of neighbors. Since the Viper was sitting right there in her driveway, startled faces turned toward her. She hadn't thought to check the Viper, but as much as she loved it, her dad's car was at least five times more valuable, and totally irreplaceable.

Sam came out on the kitchen stoop. He glanced at the garage and jumped from the stoop. Together they ran to the garage.

The door was still padlocked. "He couldn't have gotten in, could he?" Jaine asked in an agonized whisper.

"Maybe he wouldn't have tried, since your car was sitting in the driveway. He probably thought the garage was empty. Is there another way in?"

"No, not without knocking a hole in the wall."

"Then the car is okay." He put his arm around her and walked her back toward the house. "You don't want to open the door with all these people watching, do you?"

She gave an emphatic shake of her head. "I'll have to move the car," she said, planning ahead. "David will have to take it. And Shelley will have to take BooBoo. Mom and Dad will understand, under the circumstances."

"We can put the car in my garage, if you want."

She thought about it. At least it would be close to hand, and whoever was doing this didn't know about the car in the first place, so it should be safe. "Okay. We'll move it when everyone leaves."

She didn't look at the Viper as she walked by it, but she stopped. Staring hard at the blue lights on top of the patrol cars, she asked Sam, "Is my car okay? I can't look."

"It looks okay. I don't see any scratches or anything, and nothing's broken."

She heaved a sigh of relief and sort of sagged against him. He hugged her, then sent her back to his kitchen and the care of Sadie and Eleanor.

It was dawn before she was allowed to enter her house. She was surprised at the amount of attention given to what was essentially vandalism, but she supposed Sam was responsible for that. Of course, he didn't think it was just vandalism.

Neither did she.

She couldn't. Walking through her house, looking at the destruction, she noticed immediately how *personal* it all was. Her television hadn't been touched—strange, since it was an expensive item—but all her dresses and underwear had been shredded. Her jeans and pants, however, hadn't been touched.

In the bedroom, her sheets and pillows and mattress had been hacked to pieces, her perfume bottles broken. In the kitchen, everything made of glass had been broken, all her plates and bowls, glasses, cups, even the heavy lead-crystal serving trays she had never used. And in the bathroom, her bath linen was untouched, but all her makeup was destroyed. Tubes were smashed, powder dumped, and all the compacts of eyeshadow and blush looked as if they had been stomped, then ground to pieces.

"He destroyed everything feminine," she whispered, looking around. The bed was kind of generic, but her bed linen was feminine, in soft pastels with lace-trimmed edges.

"He hates women," Sam agreed, coming to stand beside her. His face was grim. "A psychiatrist would have a field day with this."

She sighed, exhausted from lack of sleep and the sheer size of the task before her. She glanced at him; he hadn't had any more sleep than she had, which amounted to nothing more than a couple of short naps. "Are you going to work today?"

He gave her a startled look. "Sure. I have to get with the detective working Marci's case and bring him up to speed on this."

"I'm not even going to try to work. It'll take a week to get this mess cleaned up."

"No, it won't. Call a cleaning service." He put a thumb under her chin and tilted up her face, looking at the bruises of fatigue that shadowed her eyes. "Then go to sleep—in *my* bed—and let Mrs. Kulavich oversee the cleaning. She'll be thrilled."

"If she is, then she's in dire need of therapy," Jaine said, once more surveying the wreckage of what had been her home. She yawned. "I also need to go shopping, to replace my clothes and makeup."

He grinned. "The kitchen stuff can wait, huh?"

"Hey, I know what's important." She leaned against him and looped her arms around his waist, reveling in the freedom to do so, reveling also in the way his arms automatically went around her.

She suddenly stiffened. She couldn't believe she hadn't once thought about Luna and T.J. tonight. Her brain must be misfiring, that was the only explanation.

"I forgot about Luna and T.J.! My God, I should have called them immediately, warned them—"

"I did," said Sam, folding her back in his arms. "I called them last night, on my cell phone. They're okay, just worried about you."

She yawned and relaxed against him once more, letting her head nestle on his chest. His heart thump-*thumped* in her ear. She was exhausted but couldn't stop her thoughts from circling like buzzards around a fresh kill. If she couldn't wind down, she would never be able to sleep.

"How do you feel about medicinal sex?" she asked him.

Interest lit his dark eyes. "Does it involve swallowing?"

She chuckled against his shirt. "Not yet. Maybe tonight. What this involves now is relaxing me enough so I can sleep. Are you interested?"

For answer, he took her hand and placed it over the fly of his jeans. He had a long, thick growth under his zipper. She hummed with pleasure as she ran her fingers up and down the length of it, feeling the tiny, spasmodic movements of his body that he couldn't control.

"God, you're easy," she said.

"Thinking about swallowing always gets me hard."

Hand in hand, they walked back to his house, where he relaxed her.

"The evidence techs didn't find a usable fingerprint," Sam told Roger Bernsen a couple of hours later. "But they did find a partial shoe print. Looks like a running shoe; I'm trying to get a make on the brand by the tread pattern."

Detective Bernsen said what Sam already knew: "He broke in intending to kill her, and trashed her place instead when she wasn't there. You got a fix on the time?"

"Between eight P.M. and midnight, roughly." Mrs. Holland kept a close watch on the street, and she said she hadn't seen a strange car or anyone unknown to her before Sam himself had arrived home. After dark, everyone was inside.

"Lucky she wasn't at home."

"Yeah." Sam didn't want to think about the alternative.

"We gotta start running down those personnel files at Hammerstead."

"The C.E.O. is my next call. I don't want anyone else knowing that we're checking the files. He can have them pulled without anyone questioning him. Maybe they can be copied to our computers so we don't have to risk going there."

Roger grunted. "By the way, the M.E. has released Ms. Dean's body. I've contacted her sister."

"Thanks. We need to have someone videotaping the funeral."

"You think he'll be there?"

"I'm betting on it," Sam said.

twenty-three

Corin hadn't been able to sleep, but he didn't feel tired. Frustration gnawed at him. *Where had she been?*

She would have told him, he thought. Sometimes, most of the time, he didn't like her at all, but sometimes she could be nice. If she had been feeling nice, she would have told him.

He didn't know what to think about her. She didn't dress like a whore the way Marci Dean had, but men always looked at her anyway, even when she was wearing pants. And when she was being nice, he liked her, but when she cut people to shreds with her tongue, he wanted to hit her and hit her, and just keep hitting her until her head was all soft and she couldn't do those things to him anymore . . . . But was that her, or Mother? He frowned, trying to remember. Sometimes things got so confused. Those pills must still be affecting him.

Men looked at Luna, too. She was always sweet to him, but she wore a lot of makeup and Mother thought her skirts were always too short. Short skirts made men think nasty thoughts, Mother said. No good woman ever wore short skirts.

Maybe Luna just acted sweet. Maybe she was really bad. Maybe she was the one who had said those things, and made fun of him, and caused Mother to hurt him.

He closed his eyes and thought of how Mother had hurt him, and a tingle of excitement went through him. He ran his hand down his front, the way he wasn't supposed to, but it felt so good that sometimes he did it anyway.

No. That was bad. And when Mother had hurt him, she had just been showing him how bad that thing was. He shouldn't enjoy it.

But the night hadn't been a total waste. He had a new lipstick. He took off the top and twisted the base so the vulgar thing slid out. It wasn't bright red like Marci's, it was more of a pinkish color, and he didn't like it nearly as well. He painted his lips, scowled at his reflection in the mirror, then wiped off the color in disgust.

Maybe one of the others would have a lipstick that suited him better.

Laurence Strawn, C.E.O. of Hammerstead Technology, was a man with a boisterous laugh and a knack for seeing the big picture. He wasn't good with details, but then, he didn't need to be.

That morning he had received a call from a Warren detective named Donovan. Detective Donovan had been very persuasive. No, they didn't have a warrant to search Hammerstead's personnel records, and they preferred to keep this as quiet as possible. What he was asking for was cooperation in catching a murderer before he could kill again, and they had a hunch he worked at Hammerstead.

Why was that? Mr. Strawn had asked, and was told about the

phone call to T.J. Yother's cell phone, whose number he wouldn't have known was hers unless he had access to certain information about her. Since they were fairly certain Marci Dean had known her killer and that the same man was the one who had called T.J.'s cell phone, then it followed that they *both* knew him, that, in fact, all four of the friends knew him. That made it highly probable that he worked at Hammerstead with them.

Mr. Strawn's immediate reaction was that he didn't want this leaking to the press. He was, after all, a C.E.O. His second, more thought-out reaction, was that he would do whatever possible to stop this maniac from killing more of his employees.

"What do you want me to do?" he asked.

"If we have to, we'll come to Hammerstead to go over the files, but we'd prefer not to alert anyone that we're looking. Can you access the files and attach them to an E-mail to me?"

"The files are on a separate system that isn't on-line. I'll have them copied to a CD for my files, then send it to you. What's your E-mail address?" Unlike a lot of chief executive officers and corporate presidents, Laurence Strawn knew his way around computers. He'd had to become proficient just to understand what the loonies on the first two floors were doing.

"T.J. Yother works in human resources," he added as he copied down Detective Donovan's E-mail address, another talent he had, that of doing two things at once. "I'll have her do it. That way we know there won't be a leak."

"Good idea," said Sam. With that accomplished with surprising ease—he thought he'd like Laurence Strawn—he turned his attention to the partial shoe print the techs had lifted from Jaine's bathroom floor, where the bastard had stepped in the ruins of her makeup and left a pretty good imprint behind. He just hoped it was enough to identify the style. O. J. Simpson aside, when they caught this guy, it would help if they could prove he owned the type of shoe that had made the print, and in the same size. It would be even better if there were still little clumps of makeup caught in the treads.

He spent most of the morning on the phone. Who said detective work wasn't dangerous and exciting?

Last night had been a little more dangerous and exciting than he liked, he thought grimly. He didn't like playing "what if," but in this case he couldn't help it. What if he had been called away? What if Jaine hadn't been late, he hadn't been worried, and they hadn't argued? They might have parted with a good-night kiss, Jaine going to her house alone. Considering the destruction of her house, he shuddered to think what would have happened if she had been there. Marci Dean had been both taller and heavier than Jaine, and she hadn't been able to fight off her attacker, so the chances of Jaine doing so were practically nil.

He sat back in his chair and laced his fingers behind his head, staring at the ceiling and thinking. Something was getting by him here, but he couldn't put his finger on it. Not yet, anyway; sooner or later, it would come to him, because he wouldn't be able to stop worrying it until he found the answer. His sister Doro said he was a cross between a snapping turtle and a rat terrier: once he had his teeth in something, he never let go. Of course, Doro hadn't meant it as a compliment.

Thinking of his Doro reminded him of the rest of his family, and the news he had to break. He scribbled on his notepad: *Tell Mom about Jaine.* This was going to come as a big surprise to them, because the last they'd heard he wasn't even dating anyone regularly. He grinned; hell, he still wasn't. He was skipping that part, as well as the engagement, and just going straight to marriage, which was probably the best way to get Jaine there.

But the family stuff would have to wait. Right now he had

dual priorities: catch a killer, and keep Jaine safe. Those two tasks didn't leave time for anything else.

Jaine woke up in Sam's bed a little after one P.M., not really rested but with her batteries recharged enough that she felt ready to take on the next crisis. After dressing in jeans and a T-shirt, she went next door to check on the cleaning progress. Mrs. Kulavich was there, walking from room to room to make certain no shortcuts were taken. The two women who were doing the cleaning seemed to take her supervision in stride.

They certainly were efficient, Jaine thought. The bedroom and bathroom were already clean; the savaged mattress and box spring were gone, the shreds of cloth swept up and put in trash bags that sat bulging beside the stoop. Before going to sleep, she had called her insurance agent and found that her homeowners' insurance, so recently converted from renters' insurance, would cover part of the replacement cost of the household goods. Her clothes weren't covered at all.

"Your insurance agent was here not an hour ago," Mrs. Kulavich said. "He looked around and took pictures, and was going to the police department to get a copy of the report. He said he didn't think there would be any problem."

Thank goodness for that. She had been out a lot of money lately, and her bank account was seriously shriveled.

The telephone rang. It was one of the nonfeminine things that hadn't been damaged, so Jaine picked it up. She never had gotten around to hooking up the Caller ID unit, she remembered, and the bottom dropped out of her stomach at the thought of answering without knowing in advance who was calling.

It could be Sam, though, so she hit the talk button and put the phone to her ear. "Hello?"

"Is this Jaine? Jaine Bright?"

It was a woman's voice, vaguely familiar.

Relieved, she said, "Yes, it is."

"This is Cheryl . . . Cheryl Lobello, Marci's sister."

Pain shot through her. That was why the voice sounded familiar; it reminded her of Marci's. Cheryl's voice lacked the smoker's rasp, but the underlying tone was the same. Jaine gripped the phone tighter. "Marci talked about you a lot," she said, blinking back the tears that hadn't been very far away since Monday when Sam had told her about Marci's death.

"I was going to say the same thing to you," Cheryl said, managing a sad little laugh. "She was always calling to tell me some remark you had made that cracked her up. She talked about Luna a lot, too. God, this doesn't seem real, does it?"

"No," Jaine whispered.

After a choked silence, Cheryl marshaled her control and said, "Anyway, the medical examiner has released her b-body to me, and I'm making the funeral arrangements. Our parents are buried in Taylor, and I think she would want to be close to them, don't you?"

"Yes, of course." Her voice didn't sound like Marci's, Jaine thought; it was too thick with tears.

"I've arranged for a graveside service Saturday at eleven." Cheryl gave her the name of the funeral home and instructions on how to get to the cemetery. Taylor was south of Detroit and just east of Detroit Metro airport. Jaine wasn't familiar with the area, but she was really good at following instructions and stopping for directions.

She tried to think of something to say that would lessen Cheryl's pain, but how could she when she couldn't even lessen her own?

Then it hit her, what she and Luna and T.J. should do. Marci would love it.

"We're going to hold a wake for her," she blurted. "Would you like to come?"

"A wake?" Cheryl sounded taken aback. "An Irish wake type of thing?"

"Kind of, though we aren't Irish. We're going to sit around and lift a beer or two in her honor, and tell all sorts of stories about her."

Cheryl laughed, this time a real laugh. "She would get a kick out of that. I'd love to come. When is it?"

Since she hadn't talked to Luna and T.J. about it yet, she wasn't certain exactly when this wake would begin, but it would have to be Friday night. "Tomorrow night," she said. "Let me get back to you with the time and place—unless you think the funeral home would let us sit up with her and have it there?"

"I kind of don't think so," Cheryl said, and sounded so much like Marci that Jaine got a lump in her throat all over again.

After writing down Cheryl's number, Jaine went over to Sam's and got the bag containing her Caller ID unit and new cell phone, which she hadn't even turned on yet.

She sat at the table and carefully read the instructions, frowned, then wadded them into a ball and threw them in the trash. "It can't be that complicated," she muttered. "Just hook this thing between the line and the phone. How else would it work?"

Looked at logically, it was simple enough. She unplugged the phone from the wall jack, took the phone wire provided with the unit, and hooked the unit to the jack, then connected the phone to the unit. Presto bingo. Then she went over to Sam's house and dialed her number to see if the thing worked.

It did. When she pressed the display button, Sam's name popped up in the little window, with his number under it. Man, technology rocked.

She had a list of calls to make, and the first one was to Shelley. "I need you to take BooBoo for the rest of Mom and Dad's vacation," she said.

"Why?" asked Shelley belligerently, her hurt feelings evident.

"Because my house was vandalized last night and I'm afraid BooBoo will be hurt."

"What?" Shelley fairly shrieked. "Someone broke into your house? Where were you? What happened?"

"I was with Sam," Jaine said, and left it at that. "And the house was pretty well trashed."

"Thank God you weren't at home!" Then she paused, and Jaine could hear her sister's thoughts churning. Shelley wasn't slow. "Wait a minute. The house has already been trashed and BooBoo *wasn't* hurt, was he?"

"No, but I'm afraid he might be."

"You expect them to come back and trash your house again?" Shelley was shrieking again. "It's that List, isn't it? You have a bunch of crazies after you!"

"Just one, I think," Jaine said, and her voice caught.

"Oh, my God. You think the man who killed Marci broke into your house? That's what you think, isn't it? Jaine, my God, what are we going to do? You have to get out of there. Come stay with me. Stay in a hotel. Something!"

"Thanks for the offer, but Sam beat you to it, and I feel safe with him. He has a gun. A big one."

"I know; I saw it." Shelley was silent a moment. "I'm scared."

"So am I," Jaine admitted. "Sam's working on it, though, and he has a couple of leads. Oh, by the way, we're getting married."

Shelley began shrieking again. Jaine took the phone away from her ear. When there was silence again, she put the phone back and said, "The tentative date is the day after Mom and Dad get back."

"But that's only three weeks! We can't get everything done! What about the church? What about the reception? *What about your gown?*"

"No church, no reception," Jaine said firmly. "And I'll find a gown. I don't have to have one made for me; one off the rack will do fine. I have to go shopping anyway, because the creep cut up most of my clothes."

More shrieking. She waited until Shelley's outrage died down. "Hey, let me give you my new cell phone number," she said. "You're the first one."

"I am, huh?" Shelley sounded fatigued from all her shrieking. "What about Sam?"

"Even he doesn't have it."

"Wow, I'm honored. You forgot to give it to him, didn't you?"

"Yeah."

"Okay, let me get a pen." There were rustling noises. "I can't find one." More noises. "Okay, shoot."

"You found a pen?"

"No, but I have a can of Cheez Whiz. I'll write your number on the counter with it, then find a pen and copy it."

Jaine recited her number and listened to the spewing noise as Shelley Cheez-Whizzed it on her countertop.

"Are you at home, or at work?"

"At home."

"I'll come pick up BooBoo now."

"Thanks," Jaine said, relieved that worry was taken off her hands.

Next she called Luna and T.J. at work, and did the three-way calling thing. They fussed over her, too, and she could hear the underlying knowledge in their voices that it could have happened to them. As Jaine had expected, they loved the idea of a wake for Marci. Luna immediately volunteered her apartment, and the time was set. She gave them her cell phone number, too.

"I have something to tell both of you," T.J. said, keeping her voice low. "But not while I'm here."

"Come by when you get off work," Jaine said. "Luna, can you make it?"

"Sure. Shamal called again, but I'm not in the mood to go out with him, not with Marci—" She stopped, and audibly swallowed.

"You shouldn't go out with him anyway," Jaine said. "Remember what Sam said: family only. That means no dates."

"But Shamal isn't—" Luna stopped herself again. "This is awful. I can't be certain, can I? I can't take the chance."

"No, you can't," T.J. said. "None of us can."

No sooner had Jaine hung up from talking with her friends than the phone rang. Al's name and number popped up in the little window. She picked up the phone and said, "Hi, Shelley."

"You finally got Caller ID," Shelley said. "Listen, I think we should call Mom and Dad."

"If you want to tell them I'm getting married, fine, though I'd rather do it myself. But don't even *think* about telling them to come home because of this crazy guy."

"This crazy guy is a killer, and he's after you! You don't think they would want to be here?"

"What could they do? And I don't intend to let him get me. I'm having an alarm system installed, and I'm staying with Sam. Mom and Dad would just be worried, and you know how Mom has looked forward to this vacation."

"They should be here," Shelley insisted.

"No, they shouldn't. Let them enjoy this. You think I'd let a crazy guy stand between me and my wedding? This one is going to go through if I have to hog-tie him and drag him to the altar. Or whatever," she added, remembering that it wasn't going to be a church wedding.

"You're trying to distract me, and it isn't working. I want to call Mom and Dad."

"I don't, and it's my situation, so what I say goes."

"I'm going to tell David."

"You may tell David, but no one, absolutely no one, is to tell Mom and Dad. Promise me, Shel. No one in your family, no one in David's family, neither friend nor foe, is to tell Mom and Dad about this. Or send them an express letter. Or a telegram, E-mail, or any other form of communication, including skywriting. Have I covered all the bases?"

"I'm afraid so," Shelley said.

"Good. Let them enjoy their vacation. I promise I'll be careful."

Sam got a call from Laurence Strawn early in the afternoon. "I'm leaving myself wide open for a lawsuit for invasion of privacy," he said. "But a court order would take time and might alert the guy, so to hell with it. If this gives you an edge, then it's worth a hundred lawsuits."

Sam definitely liked this guy.

"Check your E-mail," Strawn continued. "It's a hell of an attachment, it will probably take quite a while to download."

"That was fast."

"Ms. Yother has incentive," said Strawn, and hung up.

Sam turned to his computer and downloaded his E-mail. When he saw how many Ks of RAM the attached file took, he winced. "I hope I have the memory," he muttered, then clicked on the attachment and opened the file.

Thirty minutes later, it was still downloading. He drank some coffee, did some paperwork, called Bernsen and told him he had the personnel files, drank some more coffee. Bernsen was on his way over to get a copy, and Sam hoped the damn thing finished downloading before he arrived.

Finally the screen cleared. He loaded the paper tray in the printer and set it to printing. When the tray was empty, he loaded it again. Damn it, going through this many files would take forever, even if he and Bernsen didn't have other cases to work and could concentrate on this. It looked as if he would be doing a lot of night reading.

The printer ran out of toner. Cursing, Sam stopped the task, hunted down a toner cartridge, and was doing battle with it when one of the clerks took pity on him and popped it in place. The printer resumed spitting out pages.

Bernsen arrived, and they sat together watching the printer. "I'm tired just looking at this," Bernsen said, eyeing the enormous stack of paper.

"You take half and I'll take half. We'll run the names, see what the computer spits out."

"Thank God we only have to do the men."

"Yeah, but the computer industry is heavily male. Most of these files are on men; it's not a fifty-fifty split."

Bernsen sighed. "I wanted to watch the ball game tonight." He paused. "I got the M.E.'s report on Ms. Dean. No sperm."

Sam wasn't really surprised. In a lot of sexual abuse cases there weren't any sperm present, either because the perpetrator used a condom—some actually did—or because he didn't ejaculate. It would have been nice to have the DNA for positive identification, just in case they needed it.

"He did find a hair, though, that wasn't Ms. Dean's. I'm impressed he spotted it, because Ms. Dean was blond, and so is this guy."

A wolfish smile spread across Sam's face. A hair. Just a single hair, but it gave them the DNA they needed. The case was slowly coming together. A partial shoe print, a single hair; it wasn't much to go on, but they were making progress.

twenty-four

When Sam got home that afternoon, both T.J. and Luna were just going in his front door. That meant Jaine was in his house, rather than hers. He liked that. He hoped she was making herself comfortable, because he didn't intend to let her sleep in her own house until after he had caught Marci's killer, and maybe not even then. Having her around was way too much fun to give up, even temporarily.

The day was miserably hot, and sweat crawled down his spine as he went inside. He put the heavy stack of paper, half of the printed-out personnel files from Hammerstead, on the coffee table, then stood for a minute inhaling the blessedly cool air. With his lungs rescued from heat damage, he shrugged out of his jacket and followed the noise into the kitchen.

Jaine was pouring four glasses of iced tea, which meant she had seen him drive up.

"You're just in time," she said.

He removed his pistol and badge and laid them on the counter next to the coffeemaker. "For what?" He took one of the glasses of tea and drank deeply, his throat working.

"We're planning a wake for Marci. Her sister, Cheryl, is going to come."

"Where and when?" he asked briefly.

"Tomorrow night, at my apartment," said Luna.

"Okay. I can be there."

Looking startled, Jaine said, "But if we're all together, aren't we safe?"

"Not necessarily. You could just be providing him with a golden opportunity to get all of you at once. I won't intrude, but I'll be there."

Jaine snorted. If Sam was anywhere around, he intruded. He was one of those people you couldn't ignore.

T.J. slanted a meaningful look at him. "Before we get started, I have news."

"I have news," said Jaine.

"So do I," said Sam.

They all waited. No one said anything. Luna finally spoke up. "Since I'm the only one who *doesn't* have news, I'll direct this." She pointed at T.J. "You go first. You've had my curiosity up since we talked on the phone."

T.J. raised her eyebrows at Sam, and he knew she was asking if it was all right to tell the other two what she had been doing. Since she would have told them anyway if he hadn't shown up, he said, "Go ahead."

"I made copies of all the personnel files for Mr. Strawn," she said. "He said a certain detective had asked to see them, and he was granting permission."

Three sets of eyes turned in his direction.

He made a face. "I brought a lot of paperwork home with me. We're running all the names for prior convictions or outstanding warrants, too."

"How long will that take?" Jaine asked.

"If nothing pops up on the computer to point us in the right direction, we'll have to go through all the files and see if something sticks out, maybe dig deeper."

"A day? Two days?" she prodded.

"You're an optimistic little cuss, aren't you?" He took a long swallow of the cold tea.

Luna made a T with her hands, signaling a time-out, then pointed at Sam. "Your turn."

"The M.E. found a blond hair on Marci that wasn't hers."

The three women went very still, and he knew their minds were racing, trying to think of all the blond men at Hammerstead. "Does anyone spring to mind?" he asked.

"Not really," Jaine said. "And what you call blond, we might call light brown." She looked at the others, who shrugged. "There are a lot of guys at work who qualify."

"Don't drop your guard," he warned. "She might have picked up the hair somewhere else. It's a lead, and when we catch him, if the DNA matches, then we have him nailed. Just be extra careful around the blond guys."

"That's a cheerful thought," Luna said glumly. "I think I'm the only brunette in sales."

"I'm going to go through the files by department, starting with accounting, since Marci was the first target. By the way," he said to T.J., "thanks for giving them to me broken down into the separate departments."

She gave him a wry look. "Anything I can do to help."

Luna directed the conversation again, pointing at Jaine. "It's your turn."

Jaine took a deep breath. After three broken engagements, she had to brace herself to announce that she intended . . . again . . . to get married. She glanced at Sam, and he winked at her.

"SamandIaregettingmarried," she said in a rush, running the words together as if they would attract less attention that way. What the gods didn't notice, they couldn't squash.

Sam put his fingers in his ears to block out the squeals that erupted. T.J. hugged Jaine. Luna hugged Sam. Then they somehow all ended up hugging each other. The circle was too small without Marci, Jaine thought, but she refused to let tears ruin this little celebration. Life went on. It was sadder without Marci, emptier, but it went on nevertheless.

"How? I mean, when?" T.J. asked.

"In three weeks, when her folks get home," Sam replied. "I was thinking maybe in a judge's chambers, but my family would never fit, and they'll all want to be there."

"Maybe a park," Jaine said.

"Why a park? Someone's house should be large enough. My folks have a big place; they had to have, with seven kids."

She cleared her throat. "Well, there's my family, your family, T.J. and Luna, your cop friends, and I kind of . . . um . . . invited everyone on the street."

"Well, yeah," he said. "George and Sadie would have to come, and Eleanor, and . . . and, goddamn it, our small wedding is already up to about a hundred people, isn't it?" he finished in a frustrated tone.

"Afraid so, kemo sabe."

"That means food, and stuff like that."

"You got it."

"Who the hell is going to handle all this?" His expression clearly said *he* wasn't.

"Shelley will. She loves this kind of sh— stuff. Nothing fancy, though. I'm on a tight budget, with the house payment and new security system, the cell phone, and now I have to buy new clothes and a new mattress and box spring—"

"You don't need the mattress and box spring," he pointed out, and T.J. and Luna began hooting with laughter. T.J. got five bucks from her purse and slapped it in Luna's hand.

"Told you," Luna crowed.

Jaine narrowed her eyes at them. "You've been betting on my love life," she accused.

"Yes, and I have to say, I'm disappointed in you," T.J. said, trying for a severe tone. She was still laughing, so the attempt didn't quite come off. "I thought you'd hold him off for at least another couple of weeks."

"She couldn't resist me," Sam said smugly, pouring himself another glass of tea.

"I felt sorry for him," Jaine corrected. "All that whining and begging. It was pitiful."

His grin promised retribution. She felt a thrill of anticipation. She might have to make love with him, oh, three or four times to soothe his hurt feelings. What a sacrifice!

She loved the way he was so comfortable with her friends. He sat down at the table and helped them plan the wake, though his contribution was, "Beer and popcorn. What more do you need at a wake?" Which proved he had no understanding of women and food.

After T.J. and Luna left, they went out to move her dad's car from her garage to his. As he helped her fold the tarp back and uncover the little silver bullet of a car, he said, "Do you have the keys with you?"

She fished them out of her jeans pocket and dangled them in front of his eyes. "Wanna drive?"

"Are you trying to suck up to me, to make up for that crack about whining and begging?"

"No, I planned on making that up to you later."

He grinned and swiped the keys out of her hand. "Oh, man," he sighed as he toed off his shoes and swung one long leg over the door, then the other, and slid down into the driver's seat. The little car fit him like a glove. He ran his hands over the steering wheel. "How did you say your dad got it?"

"He bought it, back in 1964, but he had an 'in.' You know: 'Built by Shelby, Powered by Ford.' Dad was on the production team that developed the motor. He fell in love with the car. Mom was furious with him for spending so much money on a car when they had a baby—Shelley—and needed to buy a house with more space. Only a thousand of them were built. One thousand and eleven, to be exact. So now Dad has one of the original Cobras, and it's worth more than they paid for their house."

He glanced over his shoulder at the Viper sitting in her driveway. "Your dad isn't the only one who spends a fortune on cars."

"I'm a chip off the old block. Besides, I bought the Viper used, so it isn't like I shelled out the full sixty-nine grand for it. I lived off Hamburger Helper and tuna casserole for three years to pay for it."

He shuddered. "But it's paid for, right?"

"Free and clear. I couldn't have afforded the house if I still had to make those car payments. It's Dad's fault I bought it, anyway."

"How's that?"

She nodded at the Cobra. "What do you think he used to teach me to drive?"

Sam looked aghast. "He let a *beginner* drive it?"

"That's how he taught us all how to drive. He said if we could handle the Cobra, we could handle anything. But Shelley and David didn't really have the knack for it, they were more comfortable in Mom's Lincoln. Some people like comfort over speed, I guess." Her expression said she didn't understand it, but accepted it anyway.

"Jesus." He was actually pale at the thought of three untutored teenagers behind the wheel of this car.

"Dad hates my Viper," she confided, then grinned. "Part of it is because it isn't a Ford, but he really, really hates that the Viper has him beat at top-end speed. The Cobra has faster acceleration, but over any distance I can catch him."

"You've been racing?" he bellowed, looking as if he would jump out of the car.

"Just to see what the horses could do," she assured him. "And it wasn't street racing. We went to a test track."

He closed his eyes. "You and your dad are a lot alike, aren't you?" he asked, his tone as filled with horror as if he had just discovered they were typhoid carriers.

"Yeah, you'll like him."

"I can't wait."

When Luna arrived at her apartment, she was startled to see Shamal King sitting on the floor beside the door. He stood up when he saw her, and she stopped in her tracks, irrational fear flooding her. Shamal was big and well-muscled. For a terrified instant she thought he—but that was impossible. The killer was a blond, a white man. She swallowed, weak from panic and relief, one following so closely on the heels of the other.

"What are you doing here?" she asked, reaction making her blunt, and saw surprise in his eyes at her lack of welcome.

"I haven't seen you lately," he purred in the velvety voice that had women flocking to him, though the millions he made carrying a football didn't hurt. He usually had a small entourage of hangers-on around him; he loved his fame and the limelight, and made the most of it.

"The last two weeks have been crazy," she said. "First there was the List, then Marci—" She stopped, her throat seizing. She still couldn't believe Marci was gone. No; she did believe it. She just hadn't accepted it.

"Yeah, I'm sorry about that. The two of you were tight, weren't you?"

He really didn't know much about her, she thought. Their relationship, such as it was, had always been about him.

"She was my best friend," she said, and tears blurred her eyes. "Look, Shamal, I'm not in the mood for—"

"Hey, I didn't come here for that," he said, frowning as he stuffed his hands in the pockets of his tailored silk pants. "If it was just sex I wanted, I could get that from—" He stopped, evidently realizing that wasn't the wisest thing to say. "I've missed *you*," he said helplessly, ill at ease. That wasn't the type of thing Shamal King said to women.

Luna stepped past him and unlocked her door. "Really," she said in a dry tone. It was funny; for almost a year, since the moment she met Shamal, she had dreamed about him saying something like that, indicating that she was, in any way, special to him. Now that he had, she wasn't inclined to give an inch. Maybe she had already given all she could, gone as far as possible.

He shifted from one foot to the other. He didn't know what to say, she realized. He had always been too handsome, too gifted, and now he was too rich; girls had always chased him. He had been sought after and idolized and pandered to since junior high, when his running ability became obvious. This was new territory for Shamal King.

"Would you like to come in?" she finally asked.

"Yeah, sure."

He looked around her small apartment, as if he was seeing it for the first time. Going over to the bookcase to examine the books she had there, and the family photographs. "Your dad?" he asked, picking up a photo of a stern, handsome Marine major.

"Yes, right before he retired."

"So you're an army brat?"

"A *Marine* brat," she corrected, concealing her wince at his failure to recognize the uniform.

He looked uncomfortable again. "I don't know anything about the military. All I've ever done is play football. I guess you've traveled all over the world, huh?"

"Parts of it."

"I could tell you're sophisticated." He returned the photograph to its place, precisely lined it up as she'd had it. "You know wines, and things like that."

Luna felt a twinge of surprise. He sounded a little insecure, an emotion she would never have associated with him. He was always so cocky and brash, as if he thought it only natural to receive as much attention as he did. He lived in a mansion, she thought, and he was intimidated because she had traveled some and been exposed to a lot of formal dinners.

"Would you like something to drink?" she offered. "I don't have anything stronger than beer. There's also fruit juice and milk."

"A beer," he said, relieved. Maybe he'd been afraid she would offer him a selection of white wines.

She got two beers out of the refrigerator and twisted the tops off, then handed him one. He watched, fascinated, as she took a long swallow.

"I've never seen you drink beer."

She shrugged. "It's kind of endemic to a military base. I like it."

He sat down and rolled the frosty bottle between his hands. After a moment of gathering his courage, he said, "Luna—the reason I'm here—" He stopped, and did some more bottle rolling.

She sat down across from him and crossed her long legs. He eyed the elegant length of exposed skin, as she had meant for him to do. "Yes?"

He cleared his throat. "When you stopped coming around, I . . . well, it kind of surprised me. I thought we . . . that is—"

"We had sex," she said gently, deciding to help him along. At the rate he was going, he would still be trying at midnight to spit out whatever it was he wanted to say.

"That's all it ever was to you, and all you seemed to want. I wanted more, but I guess you get that a lot from all your other girlfriends."

More discomfort. "It—uh . . . it was more than just sex."

"Um-hmm. That's why you have something like three girls for every day of the week, a party in every city you go to. Shamal, I'm not an idiot. I woke up and smelled the coffee. I wanted to be special to you, but I'm not."

"Yes, you are," he insisted. He examined the beer bottle again, a flush darkening his face. "More special than you know," he mumbled. "I don't want to lose you. What do I have to do?"

"Lose all the other girls," she said promptly. "If you can't be faithful, I'm not interested."

"Yeah, I know." He managed a faint grin. "I read the List. Parts of it I can't manage."

She smiled. "Parts of it were a joke. The first five items weren't."

"So if I . . . lose the other girlfriends, you'll come back?"

She thought about it, thought about it for so long that he began to sweat, even in the air-conditioned apartment. She had already written him off in her mind, she realized, even if her heart hadn't quite been convinced. Turning things back around would take some effort.

"I'll give it a try," she finally said, and he collapsed back on the couch with a "whoosh" of relief. She held up a slender hand. "*But*—if you're unfaithful at all, that means even just groping a girl at a party the way I've seen you do, then I'm history. No second chances, because you've already used them all up."

"I swear," he said, holding up his right hand. "No more fucking around."

"Screwing," she said.

"What?"

"Screwing around."

"That's what I said. Same thing."

"No, your language could use a little cleaning up. That's what I meant."

"Babe, I'm a football player. We swear."

"That's fine, when you're on a field, but you aren't on a field now."

"Man," he complained, but good-naturedly. "Already you're trying to change me."

She shrugged in a take-it-or-leave-it manner. "My dad can peel your skin off when he's swearing, but he watches his language around Mom because she doesn't like it. I don't care for it either. My friend Jaine is trying to stop swearing and has done a really good job. If she can do it, anyone can."

"Okay, okay. I'll try." Suddenly he grinned. "Hey, this is kind of homey, isn't it? Domesticated. You ragging on me, and me promising to do better. Like a couple."

Luna laughed, and went into his arms. "Yes," she said. "Just like a couple."

twenty-five

Bleary-eyed at dawn on Saturday morning, Sam yawned and sat up on Luna's couch. Around midnight the women had decided he could watch the apartment just as well from inside as he could outside, and insisted he come in. He was tired, so he did. He hadn't had much sleep for two days and nights—he would have gotten more if there hadn't been a certain smart-ass lying under him, insisting on wiggling her pretty butt—and was disgusted after a day chasing leads that turned out to be nothing on another case he was working, plus not getting anywhere on the files from Hammerstead. The computers hadn't turned up anything so far on the names they had run, except for the odd unpaid ticket and a few domestic disturbances.

By midnight, fueled by beer and chocolate, the four women were still going strong. Cheryl turned out to be a toned-down version of Marci, similar in looks and voice and with the same boisterous sense of humor. They had talked until they were hoarse, laughed and cried, drunk beer and eaten everything they could get their hands on. It had been an amazing sight.

They moved the wake into the kitchen, and he stretched out on the couch. He had slept, but with one ear attuned to the noise from the kitchen. Nothing alarming had happened, except he discovered that Jaine sang a lot when she was tipsy.

When he woke, he noticed immediately that the noise had died down. In fact, it was downright quiet. Quietly he opened the kitchen door and peeked in. They were all asleep, breathing with the heaviness of fatigue and alcohol. T.J. was snoring slightly, a delicate sound that didn't qualify as a full-fledged snore. Having grown up in a house with four brothers and his dad, he knew exactly how a full-fledged snore sounded.

Jaine was under the table. Literally. She was curled up with her head pillowed on her folded hands, looking like an angel. He snorted; that was a real con. She had probably practiced sleeping like that since she was a little kid.

Luna rested her head on her folded arms, like a child in grammar school. She was a sweet kid, he thought, though she had to have some grit to her to hold her own with the others. Cheryl's head was on the table, too, but she was using a pot holder as a pillow—a flat one. With enough beer inside you, a lot of things made sense that normally wouldn't.

He searched for and found the coffee and filters and put on a pot of coffee, not making any attempt to be quiet. They continued to sleep. When the coffee was ready, he hunted through the cabinets for the coffee cups, and got down five of them. He poured four of them only half full, in case there were some shaky hands, but his he filled to the rim. Then he said, "Okay, ladies, time to wake up."

He might as well have been talking to the wall for all the effect his announcement had.

"Ladies!" he sounded, more loudly.

Nothing.

"Jaine! Luna! T.J.! Cheryl!"

Luna lifted her head an inch and looked blearily at him, then let her head drop back down on her arms. The other three didn't stir.

A grin spread over his face. He could shake them awake, he supposed, but that wouldn't be much fun. What was fun was finding a pot and a metal spoon and banging them together, then watching the four women bolt upright, wild-eyed. Jaine hit her head on the table and yelled, "Son of a bitch!"

His mission accomplished, Sam distributed the coffee cups, bending over to give Jaine hers; she was sitting under the table, rubbing her head and glaring. God, he loved that woman.

"C'mon, get it in gear," he said to the group at large. "The funeral is in roughly five hours."

"Five hours?" Luna groaned. "Are you sure?"

"I'm sure. That means you have to be at the funeral home in four hours."

"No way," T.J. pronounced, but she managed a sip of coffee.

"You have to sober up—"

"We aren't drunk," came a growl from beneath the table.

"—eat something, if you can, shower, wash your hair, whatever it is you have to do. You don't have time to sit under the table growling."

"I'm not growling."

No, that was more like a snarl. Maybe some medicinal sex would sweeten her mood—if he lived through it. At the moment, he kinda knew how the male praying mantis felt when he was approaching Ms. Mantis, knowing the sex was going to be great but he was going to get his head bitten off.

Ah, well. Some things were worth losing your head.

Cheryl stood up, very creakily. She had the imprint of the pot-holder loop on her cheek. She drank some coffee, cleared her throat, and said, "He's right. We have to get moving, or we'll be late."

A slender arm thrust out from under the table, holding an empty coffee cup. Sam got the carafe and refilled the cup. The arm was retracted.

God willing, he could look forward to forty or fifty years with her. It was scary. What was even scarier was that he liked the idea.

T.J. finished her coffee and got up for a refill, so she was functional. She said, "Okay. I can do this. Let me pee and wash my face, and I'm good to drive home." She stumbled down the short hall, and a sudden wail floated back: "*God,* I can't believe I told Sam I have to pee!"

Fifteen minutes later he had them all lined up, even Jaine, and they were all scowling at him. "I can't believe you're making us do this!" she snapped, but obediently blew into the Breathalyzer.

"I'm a cop. No way am I letting any of you drive until I've checked that you're okay." He looked at the reading and grinned, shaking his head. "It's a good thing I'm here, babe, because you aren't driving anywhere. You're slightly over the limit."

"I am not!"

"Yes, you are. Now drink some more coffee and be quiet while I check the others."

Cheryl was okay. T.J. was okay. Luna was okay, barely.

"You cheated!" Jaine accused, her expression thunderous.

"How in hell can I cheat? You're the one who blew into it!"

"Then it's wrong! It's defective. We all drank the same amount, so how can I be over the limit when no one else is?"

"They outweigh you," he said patiently. "Luna's pushing the edge, but she's legal. You aren't. I'll drive you home."

Now she looked like a sulky kid. "Which vehicle are we going to leave here, yours or mine?"

"Yours. Let it look as if Luna has company, if anyone checks the parking lot."

That argument got to her. She was still pouting, but after a minute she said, "Okay." With only a little more trouble he got her bundled into his truck, where she promptly went back to sleep.

She woke up enough to get into his house under her own power, but she stood glowering as he turned on the shower and began stripping himself, then her.

"Did you intend to wash your hair?" he asked.

"Yes."

"Good. Then it won't matter when I do this." He picked her up and swung her into the shower, directly under the stream of water. She sputtered and coughed, but didn't fight him. Instead she heaved a big sigh, as if the water felt good.

After her hair was shampooed and rinsed, she said, "I'm not in a good mood."

"I noticed."

"I'm always cranky when I haven't had enough sleep."

"Oh, is that the problem?" he asked dryly.

"The biggest part. I'm usually very happy when I've had a few beers."

"You were happy last night. This morning is a different story."

"You think I have a hangover. I don't. Well, a little headache, but not much. Just let this be a warning to you if you keep me from sleeping again tonight."

"I kept you from sleeping? *I* kept *you* from sleeping?" he repeated incredulously. "You *are* the same woman who shook me out of a sound sleep at two A.M. yesterday morning, aren't you?"

"I didn't shake you. I kind of bounced on you, but I didn't shake you."

"Bounced," he repeated.

"You had a hard-on. I couldn't let it go to waste, could I?"

"You could have woke me up *before* you started not letting it go to waste."

"Look," she said, exasperated, "if you don't want it used, don't lie on your back with it sticking up like that. If that isn't an invitation, I don't know what is."

"I was asleep. It does that on its own." It was doing it on its own right now, as a matter of fact. It poked her in the stomach.

She looked down . . . and smiled. It was a smile that made his testicles draw up in fear.

With a sniff, she turned her back on him and ignored him as she finished showering.

"Hey!" he said, to get her attention. Alarm was in his tone. "You aren't going to let this one go to waste, are you?"

They made it to the funeral home on time, but it was close. He drove her back to Luna's to pick up her car, so if the killer was at the funeral, he wouldn't see her getting out of Sam's truck and figure out where she was staying. With the Cobra in his garage, he had to park the truck either in the driveway or in Jaine's garage, which was a pain in the ass, since she didn't have an automatic garage door opener.

He was relaxed, and Jaine was in an infinitely more mellow mood, too. Medicinal sex was great stuff. She had managed to resist him for a full five minutes, but just when he was beginning to really sweat, she cuddled up to him with a sparkle in those blue eyes and whispered, "I'm feeling tense. I think I need relaxing."

She looked great, he thought, watching her from across the room. She wore a neat little navy suit that hit right at her knees, and sexy pumps. She had let him watch while she put on what she called her "funeral face." Evidently women had a makeup strategy for every occasion. The eyeliner and mascara were waterproof, to head off smudges. No blush or foundation, just powder, because she would be hugging people and didn't want to leave smears on their clothing. And kiss-proof lipstick in what she called a "discreet mauve," though he had no idea what in hell mauve was. Her lipstick looked pinkish, but women couldn't just say "pink."

Women were a different species. Aliens. That was the only explanation.

Cheryl wore black and looked very dignified. Her husband had joined her, and stood beside her, holding her hand. T.J. wore a dark green suit, and her husband also attended with her. Mr. Yother was a trim, all-American type, with neat brown hair and regular features. He didn't hold T.J.'s hand, and Sam noticed that T.J. didn't look at him very often. There was trouble there, he thought.

Luna wore a form-fitting column of red that hit her at midcalf. She was, simply, beautiful. She walked over to join Jaine, and Sam moved closer, to hear what they were saying.

"Marci loved red," Jaine said, smiling at Luna and reaching for her hand. "I wish I had thought of it."

Luna's lips trembled. "I wanted to send her off in style. This isn't in bad taste, is it?"

"Are you kidding? It's great. Everyone who knew Marci will understand, and if they didn't know Marci, then they don't matter."

Roger Bernsen was there, trying to blend in. He didn't do it very well, but he was trying. He didn't come over to speak, but then, they weren't here to socialize. They moved around, studying the crowd, listening to conversations.

There were several blond men in attendance, but Sam carefully studied each one of them and none seemed to be paying any special attention to Jaine or the others. Most of them were with their wives. The killer could be married, he knew, and live a very normal life on the surface, but unless he was a stone-cold serial killer he would show some kind of emotion when faced with his handiwork, and his other targets.

Sam didn't think they were dealing with that kind of killer; the attacks were too personal, and too emotional, like someone out of control.

He continued to watch all during the graveside service, which was mercifully brief. The heat was already stifling, though Cheryl had scheduled the service as early as possible to avoid the worst part of the day.

He caught Bernsen's eye, and Roger slowly shook his head. He hadn't spotted anything either. Everything was being taped, and they would watch the film later, to see if there was anything they had missed, but Sam didn't think there was. Damn it, he'd been certain the killer would attend.

Cheryl was weeping a little, but mostly keeping it under control. Sam saw Jaine blot her eyes with the edge of a folded tissue: more female strategy to preserve the makeup. He didn't think his sisters knew all these tricks.

A pretty, slender woman in a black dress approached Cheryl and was extending her condolences when she suddenly broke down and collapsed in Cheryl's startled arms, sobbing. "I just can't believe it," she wept. "The office isn't the same without her."

T.J. and Luna moved closer to Jaine, both of them eyeing the woman with "what's going on?" expressions. Sam walked over, too. People were grouping in clusters, politely ignoring the emotional storm, so he wouldn't be conspicuous doing the same thing.

"I might have known Leah would play this for all she's worth," T.J. muttered in disgust. "She's a drama queen," she added, for Sam's benefit. "She's in my department, and she does this on a regular basis. Give her something the least bit upsetting and she turns it into a tragedy."

Jaine was watching the display in disbelief, her eyes wide.

She shook her head and said mournfully, "The wheel's still going around, but her hamster's dead."

T.J. choked on a bark of laughter and tried to turn it into a cough. She quickly turned her back, her face red as she tried to control herself. Luna was biting her lower lip, but a snicker broke through and she, too, had to turn her back to the scene. Sam covered his mouth with his hand, but his shoulders were shaking. Maybe people would think he was crying.

A red dress! The bitch wore a red dress. Corin couldn't believe his eyes. That was so shameful, so cheap. He wouldn't have believed it of her, and he was so shocked it was all he could do to keep his hands off her. Mother would be horrified.

Women like that didn't deserve to live. None of them did. They were dirty, filthy whores, and he would be doing the world a favor by getting rid of them.

Luna sighed with relief when she finally stepped into her apartment and could kick off her high heels. Her feet were killing her, but looking good for Marci was worth the pain. She would do it all again if she had to, but she was glad she didn't.

Now that the funeral was over, she felt numb, exhausted. The wake had helped immensely; talking about Marci, laughing, crying, had been a catharsis that had allowed her to get through the day. The funeral itself, the ritual, was its own comfort. Her dad had told her that military funerals, with all the pomp and protocol and the precisely orchestrated movements, were a comfort to the families. The rituals said: This person counted. This person was respected. And the services were sort of an emotional marker, a point at which the grieving could honor the dead and yet have a starting place for the rest of their lives.

It was funny how they had all connected to Cheryl. It was

like having Marci, but different, because Cheryl was definitely her own person. It would be nice to stay in touch with her.

Luna twisted her arms to reach the back zipper of her dress, and had it half unzipped when someone rang her doorbell.

She froze, sudden panic freezing her veins. Oh, my God. *He* was out there, she knew it. He had followed her home. He knew she was here alone.

She edged toward the phone, as if he could see through the door and know what she was doing. Would he break it down? He had broken into Jaine's house, by knocking out a pane of glass, but was he strong enough to break down a door? She had never even thought to find out if her door was reinforced, or a simple wooden door.

"Luna?" The voice was puzzled, low. "It's Leah. Leah Street. Are you okay?"

"Leah?" she said weakly, relief making her dizzy. She bent over at the waist, breathing deeply to fight off the shakes.

"I tried to catch up with you, but you were in too much of a hurry," Leah called.

Yes, she had been. She had been desperate to get home and out of those shoes.

"Just a minute, I was about to change clothes." Why on earth was Leah here? she wondered as she crossed to the door and unchained it. Before she unlocked it, however, she put her eye to the peephole to make certain it was Leah, though she knew she had recognized the voice.

It was Leah, looking sad and tired, and suddenly Luna felt guilty about the way they had laughed at her at the funeral. She couldn't imagine why Leah wanted to talk to her, they had never exchanged more than a few words in passing, but she unlocked the door. "Come in," she invited. "It was miserably hot at the service, wasn't it? Would you like something cold to drink?"

"Yes, please," Leah said. She was carrying a large shoulder

bag, and she eased its weight off her shoulder, clutching it in her arms like it was a baby.

As Luna turned to go to the kitchen, she noticed how Leah's blond hair glistened in the light. She checked, a tiny frown knitting her brow, and started to turn back.

She was too late.

twenty-six

Jaine woke up at ten-thirty Sunday morning. She woke up then only because the phone was ringing. She started to fumble for the receiver, remembered this was Sam's house, and snuggled back into the pillow. So what if it was on her side of the bed? His phone, his responsibility.

He stirred beside her, all heat and hardness and musky male scent.

"Get the phone, will you?" he said sleepily.

"It's for you," she mumbled.

"How d'you know?"

"It's your phone." She hated having to point out the obvious.

Muttering something under his breath, he heaved himself up on one elbow and leaned over her to reach the phone, squashing her into the mattress. "Yeah," he said. "Donovan."

"Yeah," he said again, after a short pause. "She's here." He dropped the phone onto the pillow in front of her and smirked. "It's Shelley."

She thought a few swear words, but didn't say them. Sam still hadn't made her pay for the "son of a bitch" she'd yelled when she hit her head on the table, and she didn't want to remind him. Cradling the phone to her ear, she said, "Hello," as Sam lay down beside her again.

"Long night?" Shelley asked sarcastically.

"About twelve, thirteen hours. The usual for this time of year."

A hard, warm body pressed against her back, and a hard, warm hand smoothed over her belly on a slow sweep up to her breasts. Something else that was hard and warm prodded her bottom.

"Ha, ha," said Shelley. "You have to come get this cat." She didn't sound like the point was negotiable.

"BooBoo? Why?" Like she didn't know. Sam was rubbing her nipples, and she put her hand over his to still his fingers. She needed to concentrate, or she might get stuck with BooBoo again.

"He's destroying my furniture! He's always seemed like such a sweet cat, but he's a destructive demon!"

"He's just upset at being in a strange place." Deprived of her nipples, Sam moved his hand down to another interesting spot. She clamped her legs together to halt the slide of his fingers.

"He isn't nearly as upset as I am!" Shelley sounded more than upset; she sounded outraged. "Look, I can't take care of planning your wedding when I have to watch this demon cat every second of the day."

"Do you want to risk him getting killed? Do you want to tell Mom that you let a psycho nutcase killer mutilate her cat because you care more about your furniture than you do her feelings?" Boy, that was good, if she did say so herself. Masterful.

Shelley was breathing hard. "You fight dirty," she complained.

Sam tugged his hand free from the clamp of her thighs and

chose another angle of attack: her rear guard. That thought-destroying hand stroked her bottom, then slid on down and around, finding just what he wanted and working two long fingers into her. She gasped and almost dropped the phone.

Shelley also chose another angle of attack. "You aren't even staying at your house, you're staying with Sam. BooBoo will be all right there."

Oh, no. She couldn't concentrate. His fingers were big and rough, and they were driving her out of her mind. It was his revenge for making him answer the phone, but if he didn't stop it he was going to have an outraged cat shredding everything in his house.

"Just pet him a lot," she managed to gasp. "He'll settle down." Yeah, in a couple of weeks. "He especially likes to have his ears scratched."

"Come get him."

"Shel, I can't just bring a cat into someone else's house!"

"Sure you can. Sam would put up with a herd of maniac demon cats just to get in your pants. Use your power now, while it lasts! In a few months he won't even bother to shave before crawling into bed with you."

Great. Shelley was trying to turn this into a male-female power issue. Sam's knuckle rubbed over her clitoris, and she almost mewed. She managed to say, "I can't," though she wasn't certain to whom she was saying it, Sam or Shelley.

Sam said, "Yes, you can," in a low, smoky voice, and Shelley shrieked in her ear, "Oh, my God, you're doing it right now, aren't you? I heard him! You're talking to me on the phone while Sam is boinking you!"

"No, no," Jaine babbled, and Sam promptly made a liar out of her by sliding out his fingers and replacing them with a hard thrust of his full-grown morning erection. She bit her lip, but a strangled sound escaped anyway.

LINDA HOWARD

"I can see I'm wasting my time talking to you now," Shelley said. "I'll call again when you aren't *occupied.* How long does it usually take him? Five minutes? Ten?"

Now she wanted an appointment. Since biting her lip hadn't worked, Jaine tried biting the pillow. Desperately reaching for a moment of control, just a moment, she managed to say, "A couple of hours."

"Two hours!" Shelley was shrieking again. She paused. "Does he have any brothers?"

"F-four."

"Man!" There was another pause as Shelley evidently weighed the advantages and disadvantages of dumping Al in favor of a Donovan. She finally sighed. "I'm going to have to rethink my strategy. You'd probably let BooBoo tear my house down, brick by brick, before you'd do anything to upset that particular applecart, wouldn't you?"

"You got it," Jaine agreed, her eyes closing. Sam shifted position, getting to his knees and straddling her right leg, with her left one hooked over his arm. Forking her that way, his penetration was deep and straight in, and his left thigh rubbed right where it did the most good. She had to bite the pillow again.

"Okay, I'll let you go." Shelley sounded defeated. "I tried."

"Bye," Jaine said thickly, and fumbled to return the phone to its hook, but couldn't quite reach it. Sam leaned forward to do the honors, and the movement pushed him so deeply inside her that she shrieked and climaxed.

When she could speak, she pushed her hair out of her face and said, "You're evil." She was panting and weak, unable to do anything except lie there.

"No, babe, I'm good," he countered, and proved it.

When he was lying beside her, sweaty and limp, he said sleepily, "I gather we almost got BooBoo back."

"Yeah, and you weren't helping matters," she grumbled. "She knew what you were doing, too. I'll probably never live this down."

The phone rang again. Jaine said, "If it's Shelley, I'm not here."

"Like she'll believe that," he said as he groped for the receiver.

"I don't care what she believes, as long as I don't have to talk to her right now."

"Hello," he said. "Yeah, she's here."

He extended the phone, and she took it, glaring at him. He mouthed, "Cheryl," and she sighed with relief.

"Hi, Cheryl."

"Hi. Listen, I've been trying to call Luna. I have some photos of Marci that she wanted to have copied, and I wanted her address to mail them to her. I was just there yesterday, but who pays attention to street signs and numbers? Anyway, she isn't answering her phone, so do you have the address?"

Jaine sat upright, a chill roughening her bare skin. "She isn't answering? How long have you been trying to call?"

"Since eight, I guess. About three hours." Cheryl suddenly got it, and said, "Oh, God."

Sam was out of bed, pulling on his pants. "Who?" he asked sharply, and turned on his cell phone.

"Luna," Jaine answered, her throat tight. "Listen, Cheryl, maybe it's nothing. Maybe she went to church, or out to breakfast with Shamal. Maybe she's with him. I'll check and have her call you when I find her. Okay?"

Sam punched out numbers on the cell phone as he pulled a clean shirt out of the closet and shrugged into it. Carrying his socks and shoes, he left the bedroom, talking so quietly into the little phone she couldn't hear what he was saying.

To Cheryl she said, "Sam's calling some people. He'll find her." She hung up without saying good-bye, then vaulted out of bed and began fumbling for her own clothes. She was shaking, the tremors growing worse by the second. Just a few minutes ago she had been so blissed out, and now this awful terror was making her sick; the contrast was almost paralyzing.

She stumbled into the living room, fastening her jeans, as Sam was going out the door. He was wearing his pistol and his badge. "Wait!" she cried, panicked.

"No." He stopped with his hand on the doorknob. "You can't go."

"Yes I can." Wildly she looked around for her shoes. They were in the bedroom, damn it. "Wait for me!"

"Jaine." It was his cop voice. "No. If anything has happened, you'll only be in the way. You wouldn't be allowed inside, and it's too damn hot to sit out in the truck. Go over to T.J.'s and wait there. I'll call you as soon as I know something."

She was still shaking, and now she was crying, too. No wonder he didn't want her along. She swiped her hand over her face. "P-promise?"

"I promise." His expression softened. "Be careful on the way to T.J.'s. And, babe—don't let anyone in the door, okay?"

She nodded, feeling worse than useless. "Okay."

"I'll call," he said again, and was gone.

Jaine slumped down on the sofa and cried in raw, ragged gulps. She couldn't do this again; she just couldn't. Not Luna. She was so young and beautiful, that bastard couldn't have hurt her. Luna had to be with Shamal; she had been so luminously happy at his sudden turnaround that they were probably spending every spare moment together. Sam would find her. Shamal's number was unlisted, but cops had ways of getting unlisted numbers. Luna would be with Shamal, and then Jaine would feel silly for panicking this way.

Finally she stopped crying and mopped her face. She had to get to T.J.'s, to wait for Sam's call. She started to the bedroom, then abruptly turned back and locked the front door.

She arrived at T.J.'s twenty minutes later, having done nothing more than brush her teeth and hair and finish dressing. She leaned on the doorbell. "T.J., it's Jaine! Hurry!"

She heard running footsteps, the cocker spaniel barking; then the door was wrenched open and T.J.'s worried face swam before her. "What's wrong?" T.J. asked, jerking her inside the door, but Jaine couldn't tell her; she couldn't get the words out. Still barking hysterically, the cocker spaniel, Trilby, jumped up on their legs.

"Trilby, hush!" T.J. said. Her chin trembled, and she swallowed. "Luna?"

Jaine nodded, still unable to talk. T.J. put her hand over her mouth as awful, gut-wrenching cries tore from her throat, and she fell back against the wall.

"No, no!" Jaine managed to say, putting her arms around T.J. "I'm sorry, I'm sorry, I didn't mean—" She took a deep breath. "We don't know yet. Sam's on his way over there, and he's going to call here when he knows—"

"What's going on?" Galan asked in alarm, stepping into the foyer. A section of the Sunday paper was in his hand. Trilby ran over to him, her little stump of a tail wagging ferociously.

That damn shaking had started again. Jaine tried to control it. "Luna's missing. Cheryl hasn't been able to get her on the phone."

"So she's gone grocery shopping," Galan said, shrugging.

T.J. gave him a look of such fury it should have scorched his skin. "He thinks we're hysterical and Marci was killed by some doper."

"That makes a lot more sense than the bunch of you being stalked by a maniac," he shot back. "Stop dramatizing everything."

"If we're dramatizing it," Jaine said, "so are the police." Then she bit her lip. She didn't want to get in the middle of a domestic dispute. T.J. and Galan had enough trouble without her adding to it.

Galan shrugged again. "T.J. said you're marrying a cop, so he's probably humoring you. Come on, pooch." He turned and walked back to his den and his newspaper, Trilby scampering around his feet.

"Forget him," T.J. said. "Tell me what happened."

Jaine related what Cheryl had said and the time frame. T.J. glanced at the clock; it was now just after noon. "Four hours, at least. She isn't grocery shopping. Has anyone called Shamal?"

"His number's unlisted, but Sam will take care of it."

They went into the kitchen, where T.J. had been reading. Her open book lay in the alcove. T.J. put on a pot of coffee. They were each on their second cup, the cordless phone at T.J.'s elbow, when it finally rang. She snatched it up. "Sam?"

She listened for a moment, and watching her face, Jaine felt the hope die out of her. T.J. looked stunned, all color draining from her. Her lips moved, but no sound emerged.

Jaine grabbed the phone. "Sam? Tell me."

His voice was heavy. "Baby, I'm sorry. It looks like it happened last night, maybe as soon as she got home from the funeral."

T.J. laid her head on the table, weeping. Jaine reached to touch her shoulder, trying to offer comfort, but she could feel herself folding in, giving in to the grief, and she didn't know if she had any comfort to offer.

"Stay there," Sam said. "Don't go anywhere. I'll be there when I can get free. This isn't my jurisdiction, but we're all putting our heads together. It may be several hours, but don't go anywhere," he repeated.

"Okay," Jaine whispered, and hung up.

Galan came to the door and stood hovering, staring at T.J. as if he hoped she was still overreacting, but something in his face said that this time he knew better. He was pale. "What?" he croaked.

"That was Sam," Jaine said. "Luna's dead." Then her fragile

control broke, and it was a long time before she could do anything except weep and hold on to T.J.

It was sunset before Sam arrived. He looked tired and angry. He introduced himself to Galan, because neither Jaine nor T.J. thought to.

"You were at the funeral," Galan said suddenly, his gaze sharpening.

Sam nodded. "A Sterling Heights detective was, too. We hoped we could spot him, but he's either too slick or he wasn't there."

Galan glanced at his wife. T.J. was sitting quietly, absently stroking the black-and-white cocker spaniel. Yesterday Galan's gaze had been remote, but there was nothing remote about the way he was watching her now. "Someone's really after them. It's so damn hard to believe."

"Believe it," Sam said briefly, his guts twisting with fury as he remembered what had been done to Luna. She had suffered the same vicious, personal attack, her face battered beyond recognition, the multiple stab wounds, the sexual abuse. Unlike Marci, she had still been alive when he stabbed her; the apartment floor was awash in blood. Her clothes had also been shredded, just like Jaine's. When he thought how close Jaine had come to dying, what she would have suffered if she had been at home on Wednesday night, he could barely contain his rage.

"Did you get in touch with her parents?" Jaine asked hoarsely. They lived in Toledo, so they weren't far away.

"Yes, they're already here," Sam said. He sat down and put his arms around her, cradling her head on his shoulder.

His pager beeped. He reached for his belt and silenced it, then glanced at the number and cursed, rubbing his face. "I have to go."

"Jaine can stay here," T.J. said, before he could ask.

"I don't have any clothes," Jaine said, but she wasn't protesting, just stating a problem.

"I'll drive you home," Galan said. "T.J. will go, too. You can pack whatever you need, stay as long as you want."

Sam nodded in approval. "I'll call," he said as he went out the door.

Corin rocked back and forth. He couldn't sleep, couldn't sleep, couldn't sleep. He hummed to himself, the way he had done when he was little, but the magic song didn't work. He wondered when it had stopped working. He didn't remember.

The bitch in red was dead. Mother was so pleased. Two down and two to go.

He felt good. For the first time in his life, he was pleasing Mother. Nothing he had ever done before had been good enough for her because he had always been flawed, no matter how hard she tried to make him perfect. He was doing this right, though; she was very pleased. He was ridding the world of the whoring bitches, one by one by one. No. Too many "ones." He hadn't done three yet. He had tried, but one hadn't been at home.

He remembered seeing her at the funeral, though. She had laughed. Or was it the other one? He felt confused, because the faces kept swimming in his memory.

One shouldn't laugh at funerals. It was very hurtful to the bereaved.

But which one had laughed? Why couldn't he remember?

It didn't matter, he thought to himself, and felt better. They both had to die, and then it wouldn't matter which one had laughed, or which one was "Ms. C." It wouldn't matter, because finally—finally—Mother would be happy and she would never, never hurt him again.

twenty-seven

On Monday morning, Sam sat in the Warren P. D. with his head propped on his hands, wading through the Hammerstead files again and again. The NCIC computers hadn't given them a hit on any of the names, so he and Bernsen were simply reading and rereading, looking for something that would click in their heads and give them the clue they needed.

It was there; Sam knew it was. They just hadn't found it yet. He suspected he already knew what it was, because of that nagging gut feeling he had missed something. He couldn't put his finger on it, but it was there, and sooner or later the bell would chime. He just hoped it was sooner, like in the next minute.

This guy hated women. He wouldn't get along with them,

wouldn't like working with them. There might be a note in his file about a complaint lodged by someone, maybe even a harassment charge. Something like that should have jumped out at them on the first once-over, but maybe the complaint had been worded in such a way that the charge wasn't actually spelled out.

Neither Jaine nor T.J. was working today. They were still together, though they had moved from T.J.'s house to Shelley's, along with that yappy little cocker spaniel that sounded the alarm at any kind of intrusion, whether it was a bird on the patio or someone coming up the walk. He had been afraid Jaine would want to spend the day at home, since her new alarm system had been installed—under the eagle eye of Mrs. Kulavich, who was taking her guardian duties seriously—on Saturday while they were attending Marci's funeral. An alarm system was fine, but it wouldn't stop a determined killer.

But Jaine hadn't wanted to be alone. She and T.J. were clinging together, shocked and dazed at what had happened to their tight little circle of friends. There was no doubt in anyone's mind now that the List was what had triggered the violence, and the area police departments were putting together a task force to coordinate and work the cases, since no two of the friends lived in the same jurisdiction.

The national news organizations had been all over the story. "Who is killing the Ladies of the List?" one newscaster had intoned. "The Detroit area has been shocked by the violent murders of two of the women who authored the humorous and controversial Mr. Perfect List that took the nation by storm a couple of weeks ago."

Reporters were camped outside Hammerstead again, wanting to interview anyone who was acquainted with the two victims. The task force had arranged to get copies of any interview tapes the reporters might make, in case their guy gave in to his ego and wanted to see himself on national television, mourning his two "friends."

Reporters had also been at Jaine's house, but left when they discovered no one was at home. He imagined they had checked out T.J.'s, too, which was why he had called Shelley and told her to ask Jaine and T.J. to spend the day with her. Shelley had been more than glad to comply. He figured that the snoops would talk to people who knew people and eventually find Shelley, but for today at least Jaine and T.J. weren't being bothered.

Sam rubbed his eyes. He had gotten maybe two hours sleep. The page last night had been to the scene of another homicide, a teenage boy. That had quickly wrapped up with the arrest of the kid's new girlfriend's ex, who had taken it personally that the kid had told him to eat shit and die. The paperwork, however, was always a bitch.

Where was the report on the shoe tread they had found in Jaine's house? Getting an answer usually didn't take this long. He searched his desk, but no one had laid it there in his absence. Maybe it had gone to Bernsen, since they had cross-referenced each other on all the paperwork. Before Luna's death, not everyone had been convinced the break-in at Jaine's house had anything to do with Marci's murder, but he and Bernsen had been. Now, of course, there was no doubt in anyone's mind.

He called Roger. "Did the report on that shoe tread come to you?"

"Haven't seen it. You mean you don't have it yet?"

"Not yet. The lab must have lost it. I'll shoot them another request." Damn it, he thought as he hung up. The one thing they didn't need was a delay. Maybe the shoe print wasn't important, but maybe the shoe was a rare one, so unusual that someone at Hammerstead would say, "Oh, yeah, so-and-so has a pair. Paid a fortune for them."

He went back to the files, frustrated almost to the point of breaking something. It was right here under his nose; he knew it. All he had to do was figure it out.

Galan left work early. Yesterday's events had left him so shaken he couldn't concentrate. All he wanted was to pick up T.J. at Jaine's sister's house and take her home where *he* could watch over her.

He didn't know how they had lost touch with each other. No—he knew, all right. The innocent flirting at work with Xandrea Conaway had started to seem important, and maybe it had never been so innocent. When had he started comparing everything T.J., and everything she said and did, to Xandrea, who was always dressed up and never nagged?

Of course T.J. wasn't dressed up at home, he realized. Neither was he. That was what homes were for, relaxing and being comfortable. So what if she complained when he didn't take out the garbage? He complained if she left her makeup scattered all over the vanity. People who lived together inevitably got on each other's nerves sometimes. That was part of being married.

He had loved T.J. since he was fourteen years old. How had he lost sight of that, and of what they had together? Why had it taken the terror of realizing a killer actually was stalking T.J. and her friends for him to realize it would kill him to lose her?

He didn't know how he could make it up to her. He didn't know if she would even let him. For the past week or so, since she had guessed he was infatuated with Xandrea, she had pulled away from him. Maybe she believed he'd actually been unfaithful to her, though he had never let the situation between him and Xandrea get so far out of hand. They had kissed, yes, but nothing more.

He tried to imagine how he would feel if another man kissed T.J., and felt sick to his stomach. Maybe kisses weren't so forgivable.

He would crawl on his belly to her if she would smile at him again like he mattered to her.

Jaine's sister lived in a big, two-story Colonial in St. Clair Shores. The doors were down on the triple-bay garage, but Sam Donovan's red muscle-truck was parked in the driveway. He parked beside it and went up the curving walk to the double front doors, where he rang the bell and waited.

Donovan answered the door. Galan noticed Sam was still wearing his pistol. If he had one, he thought, he would probably wear it too, legal or not.

"How are they?" he asked softly, stepping inside.

"Tired. Still in shock. Shelley said they slept off and on all day, so I guess they didn't get much sleep last night."

Galan shook his head. "They sat up talking most of the night. Funny; they didn't talk much about the bastard who did this, or how close Jaine came the other night when he broke into her house. They just talked about Luna and Marci."

"It's like losing two family members so close together. It'll take them a while to recover from this." Sam dealt with grief on a regular basis; he knew Jaine *would* recover, because that kick-ass spirit of hers just wouldn't stay down, but he also knew it could take weeks, maybe even months, before the shadow of pain left her eyes.

In part of the house, things were normal. Shelley's husband, Al, watched television. Their teenage daughter, Stefanie, was upstairs on the phone, while eleven-year-old Nicholas played video games on the computer. The women had gathered in the kitchen—why was it always the kitchen?—to talk and drink diet sodas and eat whatever comfort food Shelley had on hand.

The ravages of grief had left both Jaine and T.J. pale, but they were dry-eyed. T.J. looked startled to see her husband.

"What are you doing here?" She didn't sound particularly glad to see him.

"I wanted to be with you," he replied. "I know you're tired, so I didn't want you to have to wait until midnight to go home. Not to mention Shelley and her family probably go to bed a lot earlier than that."

Shelley waved her hand dismissively. "Don't worry about that. We usually stay up late while the kids are out of school."

"What about the reporters?" T.J. asked. "We won't have any peace if they're still swarming the place."

"I doubt they would hang around forever," Sam said. "They'd like an interview, yeah, but they can get statements from other people. More than likely, since you weren't at home today, they'll call instead of camping out in your yard."

"Then I would like to go home," T.J. said, standing. She hugged Shelley. "Thanks a million. You were a lifesaver today."

Shelley returned the hug. "Any time. Come back tomorrow, if you don't go to work. Whatever you do, don't stay home alone!"

"Thanks. I may take you up on it, but . . . I think I'll go to work tomorrow. Getting back into the routine will help take my mind off things."

Jaine said, "I think Sam and I will go home, too. He looks as exhausted as I feel."

"Are you going to work tomorrow?" T.J. asked.

"I don't know. Maybe. I'll call and let you know."

"Trilby," T.J. called, and the dog jumped up, bright eyes sparkling and her entire body wagging in enthusiasm. "C'mon, girl, let's go home."

Trilby barked and scampered around T.J.'s legs. Galan leaned down to pet her, and she licked his hand. "Where's your leash?" he asked, and she dashed off to find it. Usually the dog's antics could make T.J. laugh, but tonight she couldn't manage even a smile.

On the drive home, T.J. sat staring out the window. "You didn't have to leave work early," she said. "I'm fine."

"I wanted to be with you," he repeated, and drew a deep breath. He would prefer to have this talk once they were home, where he could put his arms around her, but maybe now was the best time. At least she couldn't walk away. "I'm sorry," he said softly.

She didn't glance at him. "For what?"

"For being an asshole; for being a stupid asshole. I love you more than anything or anyone else on earth, and I can't stand the thought of losing you."

"What about your girlfriend?" She made the word sound so immature, as if he were a horny teenager who couldn't see past the moment.

He winced. "I know you don't believe me, but I swear I haven't been *that* stupid."

"Exactly how stupid *have* you been?"

She had never let him get away with anything, he remembered. Even in high school, T.J. would pin him to the wall if he tried to evade telling her whatever she wanted to know.

Keeping his eyes on the road, because he was afraid to look at her, he said, "Flirting stupid. And kissing stupid. But no more than that. Not ever."

"Not even groping?" Her tone said she didn't believe him.

"Not ever," he repeated firmly. "I . . . Damn it, T.J., it didn't feel right, and I don't mean anything physical. She wasn't you. I don't know; maybe I let my ego get the best of me, because I kind of liked the thrill, but it was wrong and I knew it."

"Who exactly is 'she'?" T.J. asked.

Saying her name took every ounce of courage he had, because putting an actual name to the woman personalized it, made it real. "Xandrea Conaway."

"Have I met her?"

Galan shook his head, then realized she still wasn't looking at him. "No, I don't think so."

"Xandrea," she repeated. "She sounds like a mixed drink."

He knew better than to say anything the least bit nice about Xandrea. Instead he said, "I do love you. Yesterday when you found out about Luna and I realized—" His voice cracked. He had to swallow before he could continue. "When I realized you're in danger, it was like a slap in the face."

"Being hunted by a psycho killer is kind of an attention getter," she said dryly.

"Yeah." He decided to go for broke and asked, "Will you give me another chance?"

"I don't know," she said, and his heart sank. "I told you I wouldn't be hasty or do anything drastic, and I won't. My attention is a little splintered right now, so I think we should just shelve this discussion for a while."

Okay, he thought. That was a swing and a miss, but he hadn't struck out yet.

"May I sleep with you?"

"You mean have sex?"

"No. I mean sleep with you. In our bed. I'd like to make love with you, too, but if you won't do that, will you at least let me sleep with you?"

She thought about it for so long that he began to think he'd swung at and missed another ball. Finally she said, "Okay."

He heaved a sigh of relief. She wasn't brimming over with enthusiasm, but she wasn't kicking him out, either. It was a chance. They had a lot of years together, and that was holding them together when couples without much of a history might already have called it quits. He couldn't expect to undo in one night the accumulated damage he had wrought over the past two years.

But she had hung in there with him, so he wasn't going to

quit now, no matter how surly she got, or how long it took him to make her believe he loved her. The most important thing was keeping her alive, even if she walked out on him afterward. He didn't know if he could stand losing her, but he knew he sure as hell couldn't stand burying her.

"I'm so tired," Jaine said. "You must be exhausted."

"I've been running on coffee all day long," Sam replied. "The jolt is wearing off, though. Want to make it an early night?"

She yawned. "I don't think I have a choice. I doubt I could stay awake if I tried." She rubbed her forehead. "I've had a splitting headache all day, and nothing I've taken has been able to touch it."

"Damn," he said mildly. "We aren't even married yet, and already you're having headaches."

That earned a faint smile.

"Did Shelley whip out a giant cucumber today?"

The smile grew a little, though it was tinged with sadness. "Yeah. Every time we closed our eyes, she plastered us with cucumber slices. I don't know if they work, but they feel good." She paused. "Did you make any progress today?"

He grunted in disgust. "All I've done is tread water. The computer didn't turn up anything, so Bernsen and I have been going over the files to see if we missed something. Do you remember any harassment complaints, or any trouble between two employees?"

"I remember when Sada Whited caught her husband fooling around with Emily Hearst and they had a brawl in the parking lot, but I doubt that's what you're looking for." She yawned again. "Harassment complaints, huh? I can't remember any. Bennett Trotter probably should have a sexual harassment complaint filed against him every day, but I don't think anyone has. And he has dark hair."

"We haven't ruled out brunettes. We haven't ruled out anyone. Marci could have picked up that blond hair from someone she brushed against in the grocery store. Tell me more about Bennett Trotter."

"He's a jerk, always making comments that he thinks are sexy, but he's the only one who thinks they are. You know the type."

He did. He wondered if Bennett Trotter could provide proof of his whereabouts on the two days in question.

"There are several people whom no one likes," Jaine continued. "My boss, Ashford deWynter, is one. He was in a real snit over the List, until the company decided to go with the free publicity, then he mellowed out."

Sam added Ashford deWynter to his mental list. "Anyone else?"

"I don't know everyone. Let's see. No one likes Leah Street, but I don't guess she counts."

The name was familiar. It took him only a second to place it. "She's the drama queen."

"And a pain in the rear. I'm glad she's not in my department. T.J. has to put up with her every day."

"Anyone else besides Trotter and deWynter?"

"No one that sticks out. I remember a guy named Cary or something like that who was really bent out of shape when the List first came out, because some of the women were ragging him about it, but he wasn't violent about it, just sulky."

"Can you find out his name for certain?"

"Sure. Dominica Flores was one of the women needling him. I'll call her in the morning."

It was strange how altered everything was, T.J. thought the next morning as she entered Hammerstead. Marci and Luna weren't here. They would never be here again. As difficult to accept as Marci's death was, Luna's was impossible. T.J. still couldn't get her mind around it. Luna had been so damn bright and sweet, how could anyone want to kill her over a stupid list?

The killer was here in this building, she thought. She might walk past him in the hallway. Maybe coming to work wasn't the smartest thing to do, but in a weird way she had wanted to be here *because* he was here. Maybe he would say something, though she knew that possibility was remote. Maybe she would catch an expression on his face—something, anything, that would help them figure out who he was. She wasn't any kind of Sherlock Holmes, but she wasn't stupid, either.

Jaine had always been the most intrepid of their group, but T.J. figured she could be a little daring, too. Coming to work today felt daring. Jaine wasn't coming in; the headache she'd had yesterday hadn't let up, and she was spending another day with Shelley, being pampered.

T.J. had to admit she also liked the idea of Galan worrying about her. It was silly, maybe even stupid, to come to work when she knew he was alarmed about it, but he had taken her for granted for so long that his present intense concern was like balm to her hurt feelings. He had surprised her last night with what he said. Maybe they *could* make it together. She wasn't going to rush into accepting his apology any more than she had rushed into a divorce when their marriage first started crumbling, but she did love him, and for the first time in a long while, she thought he might love her, too.

Luna and Shamal had finally worked out their differences, too, right before she had been killed. She had had two days of happiness with him. Two days, when she should have had a lifetime.

T.J. felt a sudden chill. Did she herself have only two days with Galan, to work on their fragile truce?

No. The killer was *not* going to get to her, the way he had to Marci and Luna. She couldn't imagine how Luna could have let him into her apartment the way the police thought. Maybe he had already been inside, waiting for her. Sam said they hadn't found any sign of forced entry, but maybe he could pick locks or something. Maybe he had somehow gotten his hands on a key. She didn't know how he could have, but he had to have gotten in somehow.

If Galan was at work when she got home this afternoon, she thought, she wasn't going inside the house alone. She would get a neighbor to walk through the house with her. And she had Trilby for added security; nothing got past the little dog. Cockers were very protective of their families. Sometimes her barking was a nuisance, but now T.J. was thankful she was so alert.

Leah Street looked up in surprise when T.J. entered the office. "I didn't expect you today," she said.

T.J. hid her own surprise. Leah's clothing was never flattering, but she was at least neat. Today she looked as if she had grabbed something off the floor. She wore a skirt and blouse, but the skirt sagged on one side and the hem of her slip showed. T.J. hadn't realized anyone still wore slips when they didn't have to, especially in the late-summer heat. Leah's blouse was wrinkled, and there was a stain on the front. Even her hair, which was usually so immaculate, looked as if she hadn't combed it before coming to work.

Realizing Leah was watching her expectantly, T.J. pulled her mind back to what had been said.

"I thought working would help. You know, the routine of it."

"Routine." Leah nodded, as if the word was somehow profound.

Weird. But then, Leah had always been a couple of french fries short of a Happy Meal. Nothing drastic, just a little . . . off.

From what T.J. could tell, Leah was really off today, occupying her own little world. She hummed, she filed her nails, she answered a few calls. She *sounded* rational, at least, if not very effective. "I don't know, I'll get back to you," seemed to be her phrase of the day.

A little after nine she disappeared, and came back ten minutes later with dirt stains on her blouse. Coming over to T.J., she leaned down and whispered, "I'm having a problem getting to some files. Will you help me move some boxes?"

What files? What boxes? Almost all their files were on computer. T.J. started to ask what she was talking about, but Leah gave a quick, embarrassed look around the office as if she was in some difficulty that had nothing to do with files, and didn't want the others to know.

Why me? T.J. thought, but sighed and said, "Sure."

She followed Leah to the elevator. "Where are these files?" she asked.

"Downstairs. In the Storage room."

"I didn't know anything was actually stored in 'Storage,' " T.J. joked, but Leah didn't seem to get it.

"Of course there is," she said, sounding bewildered.

The elevator was empty, and they didn't meet anyone in the first floor hallway, which wasn't surprising considering the time of morning. Everyone was in his or her office, the computer nerds were probably having a spitball war, and it wasn't time yet for the morning coffee break, when people started moving around more.

They went down the narrow, puke green hallway, and Leah opened the door marked "Storage," stepping aside for T.J. to enter ahead of her. T.J. wrinkled her nose at the smell, dank and sour, as if no one had been in there for quite a while. It was also dark.

"Where's the light switch?" she asked, not stepping inside.

Something hard hit her in the back, shoving her forward into the dark, smelly room. T.J. sprawled on the rough concrete floor, scraping skin off her hands and knees. Sudden horrified realization exploded in her mind, and she managed to roll to the side and scramble to her feet as a long metal pipe came whistling down.

She screamed, or she thought she did. She wasn't certain, because her heartbeat was thunderous in her ears and she couldn't hear anything else. She tried to grab the pipe, and wrestled briefly for possession of it. But Leah was strong, very strong, and with a hard shove knocked T.J. off her feet again.

T.J. heard that whistling noise again; then lights exploded in her head and she didn't hear anything else.

twenty-eight

A door opened out in the hallway. Corin froze, listening to the heavy footsteps as they crossed the hall; then there was the sound of another door opening and closing. It was someone in maintenance, he realized. If the man had looked in this direction and seen the open door of the storage room, he would certainly have come to investigate.

Corin was agonized. Why hadn't he thought of the possibility that one of the maintenance workers could be nearby? He should have; he hadn't been careful enough, and Mother would be angry.

He looked at the woman lying on the dirty concrete floor, barely visible in the light coming through the open door of the storage room. Was she breathing? He couldn't tell, and he was afraid to make any noise now.

He hadn't done this right at all. He hadn't planned well, and that frightened him, because when he didn't do something perfectly, Mother was enraged. He had to please her, had to think of something he could do, some way he could make up for his mistakes.

The other one. The one with the smart mouth. He had made a mistake with her, too, but it wasn't his fault she hadn't been at home, was it? Would Mother understand?

No. Mother never accepted excuses.

He would have to go back and *get it right.*

But what would he do if she wasn't at home, again? She wasn't here; he knew, because he had checked. Where could she be?

He would find her. He knew who her parents were and where they lived, he knew the names of her brother and sister, and their addresses. He knew a lot of things about her. He knew a lot of things about everyone who worked here, because he loved reading their private files. He could write down their social security numbers and dates of birth and find out all sorts of things about them on his computer at home.

She was the last one. He couldn't wait. He needed to find her now, needed to finish the task Mother had given him.

Very quietly he laid down the pipe beside the unmoving woman, and crept out of the storage room. He closed the door as silently as possible, then tiptoed away.

Detective Wayne Satran stopped by Sam's desk with a fax. "Here's the report on the shoe print you've been waiting for." He dropped the fax on top of a pile of reports and continued to his own desk.

Sam picked up the report and read the first line: "The tread does not match—"

What the hell? All crime labs had books or databases on sneaker tread patterns, updated on a regular basis. Sometimes a manufacturer wouldn't get around to sending in an update whenever they changed their styles or refused to do so for reasons of their own. When that happened, usually a lab would simply buy a pair of the shoes in question to get the pattern.

Maybe the shoes had been bought in another country. Maybe they were an obscure off-brand, or maybe the guy was slick enough to have used a knife to change the tread pattern. He didn't think so, though. This was no organized killer; this guy operated on emotion and opportunity.

He started to toss the report, but realized it was rather wordy for a simple "does not match." He couldn't afford to overlook a single detail, couldn't let his sense of urgency distract him. He began reading again. "The tread does not match that of any athletic shoe for men. The pattern does, however, match an exclusive style that is manufactured only for women. The section of tread pattern available is insufficient for determining exact size, but indicates probable size between eight and ten."

A woman's shoe? The guy was wearing women's shoes?

Or . . . the guy was a woman.

"Son of a *bitch!*" Sam said between his teeth, lunging for the phone and punching in Bernsen's number. When Roger answered, he said, "I got the report back on the shoe. It's a woman's."

There was dead silence for a moment; then Roger said, "You're shitting me." He sounded as appalled as Sam felt.

"We excluded the female employees from the NCIC search. We hog-tied ourselves. We have to go through their files, too."

"You're telling me a *woman*—" Roger fell silent, and Sam knew he was thinking of the things that had been done to Marci's body, and Luna's. "Jesus."

"Now we know why Luna opened her door. It didn't make sense that she would. But she was on guard against a man, not a woman." That feeling of having missed something was growing stronger.

A woman. Think of a blond *woman.* Immediately he flashed to Marci's funeral, and the tall blond woman who had broken down and wept in Cheryl's arms. A drama queen, T.J. had said, but Jaine had a different take on it: *The wheel's still going around, but her hamster's dead.* She thought the woman had a loose screw, that there was something wrong there. Damn it! She had even mentioned her when he asked about employees who had experienced difficulty getting along with others at work.

T.J. had said something else, something that hadn't clicked at the time: the woman was in her department, human resources. The woman had access to everything, all the information in all the files, including private phone numbers and the names and addresses of relatives to call in case of an emergency.

That was it. That was what had been nagging at him. Laurence Strawn had specifically told him the personnel files weren't on computers with Internet connections; it was impossible to hack into them. Whoever had called T.J.'s cell phone number had gotten it from her file, but that file, without specific authorization, was accessible only to those in H.R.

What was her name? *What was her damn name?*

He reached for the phone to call Jaine, but the name popped into his head before he could dial Shelley's number: Street. Leah Street.

He dialed Bernsen instead. "Leah Street," he rasped when Roger answered. "She's the one who was crying all over Marci's sister at the funeral."

"The blonde," Roger said. "Shit! She fit the profile, too."

Right down to the ground, Sam thought. The nervousness, the excessive emotion, the inability to stay in the background.

"I've got the file here," Roger said. "There are several complaints about her attitude. She didn't get along with people. God, this is classic. We'll bring her in for questioning, see what we can shake loose."

"She'll be at work," Sam said, and alarm clawed his gut. "T.J. went to work today. They're in the same department, Human Resources."

"Get on the phone to T.J.," Roger said. "I'm on my way."

Sam quickly looked up the number at Hammerstead. An automated answering message picked up on the first ring, and he ground his teeth. He had to listen until the recording gave the appropriate extension for Human Resources, which took valuable time. Damn it! Why didn't companies use real people to answer the phone? Messages were cheaper, but in an emergency the delay could cause real trouble.

Finally the recorded message gave the extension he wanted, and he punched it in. A harried voice picked up on the fourth ring. "Human Resources, Fallon speaking."

"T.J. Yother, please."

"I'm sorry, Ms. Yother has stepped out of the office."

"How long has she been gone?" he asked sharply.

Fallon wasn't a pushover. "Who is this?" she asked just as sharply.

"Detective Donovan. It's important I find her. Listen to me: is Leah Street there?"

"Why, no." Fallon's tone had changed. She was a lot more cooperative now. "She and T.J. left together about half an hour ago, I guess. The phones have been ringing like crazy and with both of them gone we've been short-handed. They—"

Sam interrupted, "If T.J. returns, tell her to call me immediately, Detective Sam Donovan." He gave the number. He thought about alerting Fallon to the situation but quickly decided against it; if Leah hadn't bolted, he didn't want to alarm her. "Can you switch me to Mr. Strawn's office?" Only Laurence Strawn had the authority to do what he wanted.

"Yes—sure. Of course." She paused. "Do you want me to?"

Sam closed his eyes and bit back a raw curse. "Yes, please."

"Okay. Hold on."

A series of electronic tones sounded in his ear, then the smooth voice of Mr. Strawn's executive secretary. Sam cut into her practiced welcoming spiel. "This is Detective Donovan. Is Mr. Strawn available? It's an emergency."

The two words "detective" and "emergency" got him put through immediately to Strawn. Quickly Sam outlined the situation. "Call the gate and don't let anyone leave, and start searching for T.J. Check every broom closet and bathroom stall. Don't confront Ms. Street, but don't let her leave. Detective Bernsen is on the way."

"Hold on," Strawn said. "I'll call the gate right now."

He was back on the line in about thirty seconds. "Ms. Street left the premises about twenty minutes ago."

"Was T.J. with her?"

"No. The guard said she was alone."

"Then find T.J.," Sam said urgently. He simultaneously wrote a note and signaled Wayne Satran. Wayne took the note, read it, and jumped into action. "She's somewhere in the building, and maybe she's still alive." Maybe. Marci had been dead from the first hammer blow. Luna hadn't died immediately, but she had also suffered head trauma so severe she died before she could completely bleed out from the stab wounds. The M.E. estimated, based purely on his personal experience, that she had lived, maybe, a couple of minutes after the initial attack. The attacks were vicious and overwhelming.

"Should I be discreet about it?" Strawn asked.

"At this point, finding her fast is what's most important. Leah Street has already escaped. Alert everyone in the building to assist in the search. When you find her, if she's alive, do whatever you can to help her. If she's dead, try to preserve the scene. Emergency personnel are on the way." That was what Wayne had been doing, getting the wheels rolling. Law enforcement officers from several different jurisdictions were converging on Hammerstead, as well as medics and evidence techs.

"We'll find her," Laurence Strawn said quietly.

Sam's instinct, as a cop, was to go to the scene. He stayed where he was, knowing he could do more good right there.

Leah Street's file was on Roger's desk. Sam called the Sterling Heights P.D. and got the detective who answered to look in the file and give him Leah's home address and phone number, plus her social security number.

After a minute the detective picked up the phone and said, "I don't find a Leah Street. 'There's a 'Corin Lee Street,' but no 'Leah.' "

Corin Lee? Jesus. Sam rubbed his forehead, trying not to wonder what in hell that meant. Was Leah a man or a woman? The names were too similar for coincidence.

"Is Corin Street a man or a woman?" he asked.

"Let me see." A pause. "Here it is. Female."

Maybe, Sam thought. "Okay, thanks. That's the one I want." The detective read off the information Sam had requested. He copied it down, accessed the motor vehicle department and got her license plate number and description of the car.

He then had a BOLO—"be on the lookout"—issued for the car. He didn't know if she was armed; so far, she hadn't used a firearm, but that didn't mean she didn't have one, and she might well have a knife with her. She was unstable as hell, like nitroglycerin; she had to be approached with caution.

Where had she gone? Home? Only a real looney-tunes would—but Leah Street was a real looney-tunes. He got officers en route to her house.

While he was getting everything in motion, he tried not to think about T.J. Had they found her yet? Were they too late?

How much time had lapsed? He checked his watch; ten minutes since he had talked to Strawn, so that was thirty minutes since Leah had left Hammerstead. She could hit the interstate highway system and in half an hour could be anywhere in the Detroit area, or have crossed over into Windsor, Canada. That would be great; they already had four or five jurisdictions involved, so why not bring in another nation?

He thought about calling Jaine, but decided to wait. He didn't know anything definite about T.J. and couldn't put her through the ordeal of waiting to hear, not so soon after Luna.

Thank God Jaine was at Shelley's house. She wasn't alone, and she was safe, because Leah didn't know who Shelley was or where she lived—

Unless Jaine had listed Shelley as her "contact in case of emergency."

Because he and Roger had divided the personnel files alphabetically, with Sam taking the top half of the stack of printed sheets and Roger the bottom half, Roger had Leah Street's file—and he had Jaine's. There were more Bs than any other letter of the alphabet, and he hurriedly riffled through the stack. When he found Jaine's file, he jerked the pages out and quickly scanned them.

Shelley was listed.

The bottom dropped out of his stomach. He didn't bother with a land line; he dialed Shelley's number on his cell phone and was running when he went out the door.

The reporters had done some investigating and tracked down Shelley, looking for Jaine. The constantly ringing phone got on their nerves so much that Shelley had finally turned it off, and they went out on the patio in back to sit by the pool. Sam had been so insistent that Jaine keep her cell phone with her that she took it outside with her and laid it beside her hip on the cushion of the teak chaise.

A large umbrella was angled overhead to block the sun,

and Jaine dozed a little while Shelley read. The house was blessedly quiet; knowing Jaine's nerves were raw, Shelley had sent Nicholas to a friend's house to play, and Stefanie had gone to the mall with her friends. A CD of classical piano pieces was playing softly in the background, and Jaine felt her headache finally begin to recede, like a wave pulling back from the shore.

She couldn't think any more about Marci and Luna, not right now. Her mind and emotions were exhausted. In her lightly dozing state, she thought about Sam, and what a rock he was. Was it only three weeks ago she had thought he was the blight of the neighborhood? So much had happened that she had lost her perspective of time; it seemed as if she had known him for months.

They had been lovers for almost a week, and in another few weeks they would be married. She couldn't believe she was making such an important move so hastily, but it felt right. *Sam* felt right, as if they were interlocking pieces of a jigsaw puzzle. She hadn't rushed into anything with her other three fiancés, and look how well those engagements had turned out. This time she was just going to do it. To hell with caution; she was going to marry Sam Donovan.

There was so much to do, so many details to handle. Thank God for Shelley, because she was in charge of all the tactical problems, such as location and food, music, flowers, invitations, large awnings for shade and shelter. Never shy, Shelley had already talked to Sam's mother and oldest sister, Doro, and involved them in the preparations. Jaine was a little chagrined to realize she hadn't yet met any of Sam's family, but with Marci's death and funeral, and now Luna, she hadn't had the opportunity. She was just happy Sam had thought to tell his folks before Shelley called, or it would have been an even bigger shock.

The doorbell chimed softly in the background, pulling her from her drifting thoughts. She sighed as she glanced over at

Shelley, who wasn't moving. "Aren't you going to see who's at the door?"

"No way. It's probably just a reporter."

"It might be Sam."

"Sam would have called—Oh, right. I turned off the phones. Damn it," Shelley griped, putting her book facedown on the table between the two chaises. "I'm getting into a really good part. Just once I'd like to read a book without being interrupted. If it isn't the kids, it's the telephone. If it isn't the telephone, it's the doorbell. Wait until you and Sam have kids," she warned as she opened the glass patio door and stepped inside.

Sam alternated between cussing and praying as he wove between cars, his dash light flashing. There was no answer at Shelley's. He had left a message on the answering machine, but where could they be? Jaine wouldn't have gone anywhere without calling him, not under the current circumstances. He had never before in his life been so terrified. He had patrol cars on the way to Shelley's house, but, God, what if it was already too late?

He remembered Jaine's cell phone. Driving with one hand, the gas pedal pressed to the floorboard, he glanced at his phone and pressed Jaine's speed-dial number. Then he waited for the connection to be made, and he prayed some more.

The patio gate rattled. The privacy fence around the pool was eight feet high, constructed of wooden slats in a solid lattice weave, but the gate was made of wrought-iron bars. Startled, Jaine sat up and glanced over.

"Jaine!"

It was Leah Street, of all people. She looked frantic, and with one hand she rattled the gate again as if she could shake it open.

"Leah! What's wrong? Is it T.J.?" Jaine bolted from the

chaise and ran toward the gate. Her heart almost leaped from her chest, so strong was the panic that seized her.

Leah blinked, as if Jaine's question surprised her. Her strangely intent gaze locked on Jaine. "Yes, it's T.J.," she said, and shook the gate one more time. "Open the gate."

"What's happened? Is she all right?" Jaine skidded to a halt in front of the gate and reached to open it, then realized she didn't have a key to the lock.

"Open the gate," Leah repeated.

"I can't, I don't have the key! I'll get Shelley—" Jaine was almost weeping in terror as she turned away, but Leah reached through the gate and grabbed her arm.

"Hey!" Startled out of her panic, Jaine jerked free and whirled to stare at Leah. "What the hell—"

The words died in her throat. Leah's outstretched hand had blood on it, and two of her fingernails were broken. The woman pressed closer to the gate, and Jaine saw more red splotches on the baggy skirt.

Instinct had Jaine backing up a step.

"Open the goddamn gate!" Leah shrieked, shaking the gate with her left hand as if she were a crazed chimpanzee on the inside of a cage. Her feathery blond hair flew around her face.

Jaine stared at the blood, and the blond hair. She saw the weird glitter in Leah's eyes, the twisted expression on her face, and everything inside her went cold. "You murdering bitch," she half-whispered.

Leah was as quick as a striking snake. She whipped her right arm away from her side and thrust it through the bars of the gate, swinging something at Jaine's head. Jaine lurched backward and lost her balance, stumbling several more steps before falling. She twisted to the side as she fell, landing on her hip. Driven by adrenaline, she bounced to her feet before she felt any pain from the jarring impact.

Leah swung again. It was a tire tool, Jaine saw. She backed farther away from the gate and screamed, "Shelley! Call the police! Hurry!"

On the chaise, her cell phone began to ring. Involuntarily she glanced toward it, just as Leah, on a surge of insane strength, began beating the gate with the tire tool. The metal rang under the force of the blows, and the lock gave way.

Leah shoved the gate open, an unholy expression twisting her face as she stepped inside. "You're a whore," she rasped, raising the tire tool. "You're a lewd, vulgar whore, and you don't deserve to live."

Not daring to take her gaze off Leah, even for a second, Jaine inched to the side, trying to get at least a chair between them. She knew what the blood on Leah's hands and clothing meant, knew that T.J. was dead, too. All of them were gone, now. All of her friends. This insane bitch had killed them.

She had backed up too much. She was almost on the edge of the pool. Quickly she adjusted her direction, angling away from the pool.

Shelley stepped out of the house, her face white and her eyes wide. She carried one of Nicholas's hockey sticks. "I called the police," she said, her voice shaking as she stared at Leah like a mongoose watching a cobra.

And like a cobra, Leah's attention swung to Shelley.

No, Jaine thought, the word like a faint whisper in her mind. Not Shelley, too.

"No!" The roar burst out of her throat, and she literally felt herself expanding as a wildfire of rage burst through her, as if her skin couldn't contain it. A red mist swam in front of her eyes, and her vision narrowed, focused until she saw only Leah. She wasn't aware of lunging forward, but Leah wheeled back to face her, tire tool raised.

Shelley swung the hockey stick, momentarily distracting

Jaine. The thick wood hit Leah on the shoulder, and she screamed in rage, but didn't drop the tire tool. Instead she swung it in a broad, sideways arc that caught Shelley across the rib cage. Shelley screamed in pain and folded forward. Leah raised the heavy iron to hit Shelley on the back of the head, and Jaine crashed into her, all the force of her fury lending her strength.

Leah was taller, heavier. She gave way under Jaine's assault, banging Jane's back with the tire tool, but Jaine was too close for her to get in an effective blow. Leah stiffened and recovered her balance, and thrust Jaine away. She raised her weapon again and took two quick steps toward Jaine.

Shelley straightened, holding her ribs, her face suffused with rage. She lunged forward, too, and the three of them staggered back under her momentum.

Jaine's left foot slipped off the edge of the pool, and like dominoes, all three of them plunged into the water.

Tangled together, struggling, they went to the bottom. Leah still gripped the tire tool, but the water impeded her swings and she couldn't get any force behind them. She twisted wildly, try-ing to break free.

Jaine hadn't had time to gulp in air before she went under. Her lungs burned, her chest convulsing, as she fought not to in-hale water. She wrenched away and lunged for the surface, drag-ging in huge breaths of air as soon as her face was clear. She choked and sputtered, and looked wildly around.

Neither Shelley nor Leah had surfaced.

Jaine took a deep breath and ducked back underwater.

Their struggle had taken them farther into the deep end of the pool. She saw the froth of bubbles, their twisting forms and floating hair, and Leah's full skirt billowing around them like a jellyfish. Jaine scissored her legs, kicking herself toward them.

Leah had one arm around Shelley's neck. Wildly, Jaine latched her hand in Leah's hair and pulled back as hard as she could, and Leah couldn't maintain her hold. Shelley shot upward like a balloon.

Leah twisted and got one hand on Jaine's throat, her fingers digging in. The incredible pressure made Jaine gag, and water rushed into her mouth.

She brought her legs up and braced them on Leah's stomach, and pushed. Nails clawed her neck as she tore free, and red stained the water in front of her face.

Then Shelley was there again, pushing Leah down on the bottom of the pool. Jaine clawed her way through the water to add her strength to Shelley's, pushing and fighting and not daring to let go, needing air again, unable to breathe, unwilling to release Leah and surface. Leah's clawing hands fastened on her blouse and locked tight.

Leah's struggles grew weaker. Her bulging eyes glared at them through the crystal clear water, then slowly glazed over.

The water exploded behind them. Weakly Jaine turned her head and saw a dark shape, then another, surging toward them in a stream of bubbles. Strong hands wrenched her out of Leah's death grip, while another pair pulled Shelley away and shoved her upward. Jaine saw her sister's bare legs kicking, and she tried to follow her, but she had been longer without air than Shelley and she no longer had the strength to kick. She felt herself sort of sink to the bottom, then one of the uniformed cops grabbed her and kicked strongly toward the surface, carrying them both up into life-giving air.

She was only half-aware of being dragged out of the pool, of being stretched out on the concrete. She gagged, coughing convulsively and curling in on herself as she fought to get air past her swollen throat. She heard Shelley's hoarse cries, and the cops were talking simultaneously, the words jumbling in her head. People were rushing around, and someone else jumped into the water, droplets arcing upward in the bright sunshine and splashing in her face.

Then Sam was there, his face utterly white as he lifted her to a sitting position and braced her in his arms. "Don't panic," he said reassuringly, his voice steady though his arms trembled. "You can breathe. Don't fight so hard. Just take slow breaths. Easy, babe. That's the way. Breathe in nice and easy."

She concentrated on his voice, on doing what he said. When she stopped gulping so frantically, her throat relaxed and oxygen rushed past the swollen membranes. Weakly she let her head rest against his chest, but she managed to put a reassuring hand on his arm to let him know she was conscious.

"I couldn't get here in time," he said rawly. "My God, I couldn't get here in time. I tried to call, but you didn't answer. *Why didn't you answer the goddamn phone?*"

"Reporters kept calling," Shelley gasped. "I turned the phones off." She winced and clutched her ribs, her face colorless.

There seemed to be a thousand sirens piercing the air, the sound reverberating in Jaine's ears. Just when it became unbearably loud, the sound cut off in mid-shriek, and a moment later, or maybe it was several minutes later, white-shirted medics were surrounding her and Shelley, and she was taken from Sam's supporting arms.

"No—wait!" She twisted frantically, screaming Sam's name, except the scream was a barely audible croak. He motioned for the medics to back off a minute, and put his arms around her again.

"T.J.?" she managed to ask, scalding tears burning her eyes.

"She's alive," Sam said, his own voice still raw with emotion. "I got the word on the way over. They found her in a storage room at work."

Jaine's eyes asked what had to be asked.

Sam hesitated. "She's hurt, honey. I don't know how bad it is, but the important thing is, she's alive."

Sam didn't stay to watch Leah's—Corin Lee's—body being removed from the pool. There were enough officers present to handle everything, and this wasn't his jurisdiction anyway. He had more important things to do, such as be with Jaine. When she and Shelley were transported to a local hospital, he followed in his truck.

They were whisked away to treatment cubicles. After making certain the hospital notified Al right away, Sam leaned against the wall. He was sick to his stomach; he had sworn to serve and protect, but he hadn't been able to protect the woman he loved more than anyone else in the world. Until the day he died, he would never forget the feeling of helpless terror as he raced through the streets, knowing he was already too late and couldn't get to Jaine in time to save her.

He had put the pieces of the puzzle together, but too late to save her and T.J. from harm.

T.J. was in critical condition. According to Bernsen, the only thing that saved her was that when she fell, she somehow rolled so that her head was partially protected by the base of an old office chair. Something must have frightened Leah away before she could finish the job, and she had gone in search of Jaine.

Sam was slumped in one of the uncomfortable plastic chairs in the waiting area when Bernsen came in.

"Jesus, what a nightmare," Roger said, dropping into the chair beside Sam's. "I heard their injuries are minor. What's taking so long?"

"I guess no one's in a hurry. Shelley—Jaine's sister—is being x-rayed for a broken rib. They're checking Jaine's throat. That's all I know." He rubbed his face. "I damn near fucked up, Roger.

I didn't put it together until it was almost too late, then I couldn't get to Jaine in time."

"Hey, you put it together in time to get other people to them. T.J.'s alive, which she wouldn't be if they hadn't found her when they did. The uniforms who dragged the women out of the pool said they all came close to drowning. If you hadn't alerted them, got the officers there ahead of you—" Roger broke off and shrugged. "Personally, I think you did a helluva job, but I'm just a detective, what the fuck do I know?"

The E.R. doctor finally came out of Jaine's cubicle. "We're going to admit her, keep her overnight for observation," he said. "Her throat is bruised and swollen, but the larynx isn't ruptured and the hyoid bone is intact, so she'll make a full recovery. We're admitting her just as a precaution."

"May I see her now?" Sam asked, standing.

"Sure. Oh—her sister has two cracked ribs, but she'll be all right, too." He paused. "Looks like it was one hell of a fight."

"It was," said Sam, and stepped into the treatment cubicle, where Jaine was sitting on a vinyl examination table. Her eyes brightened when she saw him, and though she didn't say a word, her expression was enough as she reached out her hand to him. Gently he took it in his, then used it to pull her closer and fold her in his arms.

Twenty-two hours later, T.J. managed to open one swollen eye a tiny slit, and move her fingers just enough to squeeze Galan's hand.

twenty-nine

"I can't believe you haven't told your parents," T.J. said. Her voice was still weak and slightly slurred, but the scolding tone was clear. "No, wait—I can believe *you* didn't tell them, but I can't believe neither Shelley nor David did. How can you not tell your parents someone tried to kill both you and Shelley and almost succeeded?"

Jaine rubbed her nose. "Remember when you were a kid and you'd do almost anything to keep your parents from finding out you were in trouble? It was kind of like that, but it . . ." She shrugged. "It was over. You were alive, and Shelley and I were both okay, and I didn't want to talk about it. There was all the media coverage driving me crazy, Luna's funeral to get through, and I couldn't handle anything else."

T.J. carefully turned her head, which was still swathed in bandages, to look out her hospital window. She had been out of I.C.U. for a week and change now, but much of the preceding week was forever lost to her. She remembered nothing about the day of the attack, so exactly what had happened was unknown. Sam and Detective Bernsen had put forth a logical theory, but no one would ever know for certain.

"I wish I had been able to go to her funeral," she said, her expression sad and distant.

Jaine didn't say anything, but inwardly she shuddered. *No, you don't,* she thought. She wished she didn't have that memory.

Two weeks had passed, and every night she had jerked awake from a sound sleep, drenched in sweat, her heart pounding in terror from a nightmare she couldn't remember. Of course, considering Sam's prescription for disturbed sleep, the experience hadn't been all bad. She might wake up in terror, but she went back to sleep with every muscle limp from an overdose of pleasure.

Sam had had a few bad nights himself, especially at first. Hero that he was, it bothered him that he hadn't been able to reach her first. That lasted until she climbed into the shower one night, stuck her head under the water, and started yelling, "Help, help, I'm drowning!" Well, she had tried to yell, anyway, but her throat had still been bruised and swollen, and Sam said she sounded more like a bullfrog's mating croak. He had jerked the shower curtain back and stood there glaring at her while water splattered all over the floor.

"Are you making fun of my hero complex?"

"Yeah," she said, and stuck her head back under the stream of water for another drowning imitation.

He turned the water off with a snap of his wrist, slapped her on the bare butt sharply enough to make her say, "Hey!" in indignation, then wrapped his arms around her and lifted her bodily from the tub.

"You have to pay for that," he growled, striding toward the bed and tossing her onto it, then stepping back to strip off his damp clothes.

"Oh, yeah?" Naked and wet, she stretched sinuously, arching her back. "What do you have in mind?" With one hand she reached out to stroke his bobbing erection, then rolled onto her stomach and captured him in her grip. He went very still.

Delicately, like a cat, she licked. He shuddered.

She tasted the entire length. He groaned.

She licked again and ran her tongue along the underside. "I think I should really, really have to pay," she murmured. "And I think it should involve . . . swallowing." She took him in her mouth and suited actions to words.

Since then, at least once a day, Sam would put on a pitiful face and say, "I feel so guilty."

Hah.

His attitude, more than anything, had helped her through the trauma. He hadn't babied her. He had loved her, comforted her, made love to her so often she was sore, but that was it, and it was more than enough. She had been able to laugh again.

She had visited T.J. every day. Already T.J. was taking physical therapy daily to help her overcome the resultant disabilities from her head injuries. Her speech was slurred, but better every day; and her control over her right leg and arm was iffy at best, but that too, with work, would improve greatly. Galan had been constantly by T.J.'s side, and if the naked devotion in his eyes was any indication, their marital difficulties were behind them.

"Back to your parents," T.J. said now. "Are you going to tell them when you meet them at the airport today?"

"Not right away," Jaine said. "I have to introduce them to

Sam first. And we have the wedding to talk about. Besides, I thought Shelley and I should tell them together."

"You'd better do it before they go home, because their neighbors are bound to rush straight over when they see your folks are back."

"Okay, okay. I'll tell them."

T.J. grinned. "And tell them they can thank me for delaying your wedding a week, which will give them time to rest."

Jaine snorted. True, delaying the wedding a week would allow T.J. to attend, albeit in a wheelchair, but she doubted her dad, at least, would thank anyone. Having the wedding the next day would have suited him just fine, because there would be less hoopla for him to endure.

She checked her watch. "I gotta go. I'm meeting Sam in an hour." She leaned over the bed and kissed T.J.'s cheek. "I'll see you tomorrow."

Galan entered the room bearing a huge bouquet of lilies, filling the room with their perfume. "Just in time," Jaine said, winking at him as she sailed past.

"Yes," said J. Clarence Cosgrove, his voice reedy with age, "I remember Corin Street very well. The situation was very strange, but there was nothing we could do. We didn't even know Corin was a girl until she reached puberty. Oh, her sex was on her birth certificate, of course, but who checks that? Her mother said Corin was her son, so . . . we accepted it."

"She was raised as a boy?" Sam asked. He was at his desk, his long legs propped on an open drawer, the phone glued to his ear.

"To my knowledge, the mother never admitted or even acted as if she knew Corin was female. Corin was a badly disturbed child. Badly disturbed," Mr. Cosgrove repeated. "She was a constant discipline problem. She killed a classroom pet, but Mrs. Street wouldn't accept that Corin could ever do anything like that. She made the statement, often and to anyone who would listen, that she had the perfect little boy."

Bingo, thought Sam. *Mr. Perfect.* That was the trigger that had set Corin Lee Street off like a bomb that had been slowly ticking down over the years. It wasn't the content of the List itself, but rather the title that she had found so unbearable.

"She took Corin out of my school," Mr. Cosgrove continued. "But I made a point of finding out what I could about the child. The behavioral problems worsened over the years, of course. When Corin was fifteen, she killed her mother. I remember it was a particularly brutal murder, though I can't recall the specific details. Corin spent several years in a mental institution and was never charged with the murder."

"Did the murder take place there in Denver?"

"Yes, it did."

"Thank you, Mr. Cosgrove. You've helped fill in a lot of the blanks."

After he hung up, Sam tapped his pen on his desk as he pondered what he had learned so far about Corin Lee Street. She had entered the mental institution as Corin, but she was Leah—evidently chosen because of the name's similarity to "Lee"—when she came out. The picture that had emerged was that of an extremely unstable and dangerous woman who had been abused both mentally and physically by her mother until the violence that had been leaking out all of her life finally burst out of control. The psychiatrists could argue all day about which came first, the abuse or the violent personality, but Sam didn't care. He just wanted a clear picture of the woman who had wreaked so much destruction.

After he talked to Mr. Cosgrove, Corin's middle-school principal, he called the Denver P.D. and eventually got to talk with the detective who had investigated Mrs. Street's gruesome murder. Corin had beaten her mother to death with a floor lamp, then poured rubbing alcohol on the woman's face and set it on fire. When the body was discovered, Corin was incoherent and obviously mentally unsound. She had been confined in a mental institution for seven years.

More digging turned up the psychiatrist who had treated Corin. On being informed of Corin's death and the circumstances, the woman sighed. "She was released against my better judgment," she said. "But she functioned better than I expected, if she went that many years before she began deteriorating. When she was on her medication, she was functional, but she was still—I hate to use labels, even when they're accurate—psychotic. In my opinion, it was only a matter of time before she began killing. She had all the classic symptoms."

"How did she change from Corin into Leah?"

"Corin was her maternal grandfather's name. Her mother simply refused to accept that her child was female. Females were . . . 'Unworthy' and 'dirty' were the terms Corin used. Mrs. Street gave Corin a male name, she raised her as a boy, dressed her as a boy, told everyone Corin was her son. If Corin ever made any sort of mistake, even as a very small child, she was punished in a variety of ways: beaten, jabbed with pins, locked in dark closets. Then she reached puberty, and all hell figuratively broke out. Mrs. Street couldn't bear the changes in Corin's body. Menstruation particularly upset her."

"I bet," Sam said, feeling almost nauseated at this litany of abuse.

"After puberty, whenever Corin made a mistake, she was punished in a sexual manner. I leave the details to your imagination."

"Thanks," Sam said dryly.

"She hated her own body, hated female sexuality. With therapy and medication, she did finally develop a rather rudimentary female personality, and she named herself Leah. She worked hard at being a woman. I never had any hopes, though, of her having a normal sexual relationship, or a normal relationship of any kind. She learned some female mannerisms, and the medication controlled her violent tendencies, but her grasp of reality was tenuous at best. I'm really surprised she was able to work at the same job for a number of years. Is there anything else you'd like to know?"

"No, Doctor, I think you've answered all my questions," Sam replied. He had needed to know. If Jaine ever wanted to know, he would have the answers for her, but so far she hadn't asked a single question about Leah Street.

Maybe that was good. He had known Jaine was a fighter, but he had been surprised by how fiercely she tackled recovery, as if it were an adversary to be whipped into shape. She wasn't going to let Leah Street defeat her in anything.

He checked the time and saw he was running late. "Damn it," he muttered. She would never let him hear the end of it if they were late meeting her folks at the airport. He had some important news for her, news that couldn't wait, and he didn't want her to be angry when he told her.

He drove like a maniac to meet her at her parents' house on time. Since all four of them and six weeks' worth of luggage couldn't fit in either her Viper or his truck, they were driving her mom's Lincoln to the airport. She was already in the driver's seat, motor running, when he skidded to a stop in the driveway and leaped out of the truck.

"You're late," she said, chirping the tires as soon as his butt hit the seat. He reached for his seat belt.

"We'll make it," he said confidently. With Jaine at the wheel, he had no doubt. Maybe he should warn her about speeding, he thought, then thought better of it.

"Remember that interview I had with the state a few weeks back?"

"You got the job," she said.

"How did you know?"

"Why else would you mention it?"

"I trained at the state police academy, so I won't have to do that again. I can go straight into detective work. The problem is, I'll have to relocate."

"So?" She rolled her eyes.

"Don't do that! Watch the road."

"I am watching!"

"It doesn't bother you that we'd have to move? You just bought your house."

"What would bother me," she said succinctly, "is if you lived in one city and I lived in another. That would suck."

Oh, man, his favorite word.

She reached the airport in record time and parked the car. As they were hurrying to the arrival gate, she said, "Remember, Dad has Parkinson's, so if his arm is shaking, that's why."

"I remember," he said, his long legs easily keeping stride with her.

They had just reached the gate when passengers began pouring out. Her parents appeared almost immediately. Jaine squealed and ran to her mother, throwing her arms around her and hugging fiercely, then repeating the procedure with her dad.

"This is Sam!" she said, dragging him forward. Her folks already knew about the impending marriage, so her mother threw her arms around him and he got hugged, too.

Jaine's dad extended a wildly trembling right hand. "Here," he said. "You hold my hand while I take care of the shaking."

Sam burst into a roar of laughter. Jaine's mother said, "Lyle! Really!"

"What?" he asked, looking affronted at her rebuke. "If I can't have a little fun with it, what's the point in having it?" In those bright blue eyes, Sam saw a gleam that told him Jaine was a chip off the old engine block.

"We have a lot of news," Jaine said, linking arms with her mother and walking down the concourse. "You have to promise not to get mad."

That was guaranteed to keep them calm, Sam thought.

Lyle Bright said, "Just as long as you haven't wrecked my car."